WATER IN THE WINE

WATER
IN THE
WINE

April Oursler Armstrong

McGraw-Hill Book Company, Inc.
NEW YORK   TORONTO   LONDON

To the memory of my mother,
Grace Perkins Oursler,
who wrote her novels as if she lived them,
and who lived as if life rushed on
in chapters, suspenseful to the end.

ONE

He stood on his porch, Christopher McNamara: textbook editor, speaker on the Communion Breakfast circuit, free-lance contributor to Catholic magazines, commuter, father of six, a man other men called a nice guy.

He was wondering what it would be like to have to live without his wife, yet with her. He did not want to think about it at all.

Chris sniffed the air, read the thermometer, and considered the weather. It was one of those days on which approaching winter pouts. Sulky grey clouds hung over the dark hemlocks, refusing either to snow or rain.

A city man moving to the suburbs seems to need to pose as a weather expert, as he needs a red and black flannel shirt, and Army & Navy-store workboots. Weather, irrelevant in the city, is a commuter's second wife, nagging him with a hundred chores, planning and unplanning his free time. Four years ago, when Chris moved his family into the new white colonial on Sweetfern Road in St. Rose's parish in Rockhill, Connecticut, he found himself compelled

1

to make some things grow and others not grow, to keep water out of the cellar and cold out of the house, to deal with snow shovels and tire chains, mildew, attic fans, candles and firewood.

His acre had once been farmland but years ago the topsoil had been scraped and sold to beautify the Merritt Parkway. He had to buy peatmoss and grass seed for his hardpan and clay, but he did still have the farmer's stone wall with its hundred-year patina of green and grey. And it made him feel close to American heritage and grass roots to stand with his boots on his own land. He bought the *Old Farmer's Almanac* at a Grand Central Station newsstand, collected clippings on the habits of woolly-bear caterpillars, and togged himself out as a man in touch with raw nature. His pose as an outdoor man was his only indulgence in the intoxicating sport of façade. Considering all he read of the elaborate poseurs of status and wealth in his corner of suburbia, it was surprising that he did not personally know any who qualified as organization men or status-seekers. He knew they existed, rode the same train, lived in the same town, but their lives never touched his.

He sat down now on a wooden rocker. He let the cloak of Sunday afternoon drift over his shoulders, wrapped himself in it and vanished into his own thoughts. It was a secret he had learned as a child to get away from grownups. Now that he was a grownup he was escaping his own children. It was silent on the porch. There would be little silence at home now with the new baby. New little Teresa, just born.

He sighed. He had come out to the porch because he knew he should think about Jane and Dr. Polla, and himself. He had done his best to postpone thinking about it. Now he must.

He was glad she did not want to tell anyone else. He ran his hand over the flat back of his head where a few hairs usually stood up from the cowlick. To tell Jane's mother or his own would complicate things. Jane said her mother would not understand because she was not a Catholic. But his parents would not understand because they were.

Annie and James McNamara were Catholics of a different generation and world, old New York Irish Catholics. On his one trip abroad Chris had been to Mass in Mexico, where people talked and wandered around the church as if it were a marketplace. Bewildered by color and smell and confusion, shocked by what seemed to him irreverence, he understood that this gaudy mob was part of a different culture, a different way among the Catholic ways, not to be condemned by him. But he had not liked it.

Almost as drastic a gulf separated his faith from the faith of his father and mother. Annie and James were good Catholics, but their definition of a good Catholic was not his. Annie went to all the card parties, made her novenas, loved St. Anthony, said a rosary during Mass and read tea leaves regularly. James gave memorials in churches and went to wakes, grumbled about greedy priests, and thought the Pope had no business changing the fast laws. And Annie and James had had only one child.

Annie had not yet recovered from the shock of finding her son headlined on the cover of *Holy Family* magazine as an authority on "The Christian Meaning of Sex." Voluble on the subject of childbirth pain, Annie was always silent on the ghastly direct causes of pregnancy. As for James McNamara, he would have rewritten the Hail Mary rather than face answering a child who asks what a "womb" is.

Other families Chris knew as a boy in those proud brownstones in the West Forties, or in the modest apartments in the East Eighties to which they moved when the old neighborhood declined, were equally limited. He had concluded that the cause of the notorious drunkenness of immigrant Irish men lay in the bedrooms of their wives, who feared for health and budget, and thought men beasts.

Jane and he would keep their problem to themselves. And with God's help he would not have to take the Pledge, nor take to sleeping in the parlor. A wry smile touched the left cheek of his thin bony face. He nodded in sudden appreciation of an irony.

He had always secretly hungered to defend his religion with shining courage. But his boyhood dreams of braving jungles and pythons were translated now into the sacrifice of cigarette money for real missionaries like his uncle, Father Tom McNamara. Young Chris had read avidly tales of St. Isaac Jogues among the Indians, of St. Thomas More jesting with his executioner. But martyrdom today came to men in China, in Hungary, in the land of the Mau Mau, not in New York, not in the suburbs. Never had anything heroic been demanded of Christopher McNamara.

Until now.

And now? The sacrifice heaven asked of Christopher McNamara was one the world would not know. And if the world did know, it would deem it useless, unnecessary. Just as Chris thought Jehovah's

Witnesses mad to let a child die rather than permit blood transfusion, so he would be thought mad by a world that knew the value and ease of preventing the consequences of married love. He was aware of what men of the world would say.

He remembered the words from his own speech: "Where some cultures approved harems, mistresses, or prostitutes, the modern American, insistent on morality and cleanliness, rejects these modalities in favor of contraception. He considers himself wise, prudent and godly in practicing birth prevention. We must not condemn him. He does not understand the mystery of sex as we do. He has not seen the world of grace. And if he considers us souls to be rescued from stork-worship and the hardship of large families, let us respect his motives, honor his altruism, accept as genuine his sense of civic responsibility. And wish he would do the same for us.

"Living our faith in a world of men who consider sex apart from the Christian mystery, in a world convinced of the *virtue* of birth prevention, can be true heroic unsung martyrdom."

Those were the words he had used in the statement, quoted and requoted in so many Catholic columns, that so embarrassed his mother. He stood retesting those words now. Here he was, in corduroy pants and windbreaker, lanky, dark, a bit short on muscle, long on brain, a nice enough guy. But not the type to wear a hero's halo. He supposed some people would think Dr. Polla's lab findings presented a chance to prove heroic virtue. He was sure Jane did. He himself felt totally unheroic.

He had been presented with a fact, a disturbing one. There was no question in his mind what had to be done.

TWO

Jane McNamara had had the baby with no trouble. An old hand, the nurses called her. After all, Teresa was her sixth.

Later, in her bed in the private corner room, the luxury Chris delighted in providing for her, she held his hand and sipped water through a bent tube.

"Chris, I like having babies. I mean, do you know having a baby is being awfully like God? Do you know what I mean?"

He smiled. "No. And neither do you. You're still a little groggy. Tell me tomorrow."

Jane nodded.

"And remember that I love you," he said.

"You sound like you're going home. You can't go yet. We haven't had our wine. We can't break our tradition now."

"You're not supposed to have anything yet."

"I'm hungry. Healthy hungry as a peasant. And I'm waking up, really."

So Mr. and Mrs. McNamara dined on chicken sandwiches and red wine sipped from a hospital bathroom glass.

It had been on chicken sandwiches and wine that they feasted their first night together, an unplanned picnic in a moonlit frozen field in the middle of nowhere, miles from their hotel. They had sat then feeling frightened and adventurous, strangely newborn. The star-shimmered air was piercing cold, but for them it seemed suspended in mysteriously temperatureless color. The stubble of the field they saw was rough and prickered and chilling. Yet they sat as on soft grass. In that stranger's field all creation became for a moment only a setting for them, obedient so a dream could be lived. The love which spun around them in the stillness created them anew. They were beautiful not only to each other, but to themselves.

The air and the stirring of the branches and the shadows and the wine made them giddy. Like children they laughed under the stars. Later Chris said gravely he believed that in that field God had given them a glimpse of Eden, and of that Cana wedding when he changed water into wine. In their new state as man and wife, unabashed and praying as they lay in bed, they thanked him for letting them peer into the intended, spurned glory.

Now, eleven years and six children later Jane, her hair disheveled, her face pale, grinned up at Chris over her glass of wine. The memory of their first *agape* was still stronger than the wine now in the glass.

The next morning Jane lay awake in the dark, face washed, hair combed. Down the corridor the little bell ringing in the sister's hand heralded the Lord. Starched rustle of white skirt, the whisper of the priest's purple vestment.

"Corpus Domini nostri Jesu Christi . . ."

She received the Lord Jesus Christ. She closed her eyes and asked him for more children.

An hour later the pain was in her back, blinding pain radiating to both sides. Her obstetrician, Dr. Polla, was speaking to her. Faces and voices came and went. A strange doctor's mustache leaned over her face. The voices faded. The pain dimmed. She slept.

That afternoon Dr. Polla, rereading the report of the consulting urologist, sighed, lit a cigarette, and asked his nurse to call Mr. McNamara and set up an appointment at the hospital for early that evening.

Jane was wide awake, conscious of a ghost of pain not fully exorcised, when the conference took place.

"Here's the pitch," Dr. Polla said. His brown suit jacket hung open to reveal one of the wardrobe of vests that was his trademark. This one, Chris noted with impatience, was a gold and green Paisley print with tiny brass buttons.

"Jane had a pain, and the pain was from the kidney area. Her blood pressure was up. She's always had normal pressure. This morning it was one-sixty over one-ten. Urinalysis showed the urine loaded with white blood cells, or pus, and many many casts. I called in the urologist. This girl needed more than an OB."

Chris nodded.

"He ran an IVP which showed a bilateral hydronephrosis with dilated ureters on both sides. Cystoscopy confirmed it. She has a BUN of thirty-four which is not, repeat not, good. So there you are."

The doctor smoothed a cigarette between his fingers, tapped it on his watch crystal. "Now, what does that mean? It means that for some reason—we do not know why—a sudden destructive action has set in, a degeneration, in the calyces of the kidneys. What brought it on? Who knows? However, it is not dangerous. Not fatal by any means. Painful this morning, but the pain will soon be all gone. Medication. Salt-free diet. High-protein. No cocktails. And she'll never know she has it." He smiled triumphantly, as if he had completed a pretty trick of sleight-of-hand.

Jane, propped up in bed, smiled back. Her toes, mountains under snowy sheets, seemed far away.

Chris looked at her uncertainly, and asked the doctor, "You're sure she'll be all right?"

"Positive, Chris. Nothing to worry about. She'll be her old self."

"How long will she be in the hospital?"

"Maybe a few days longer than last time. Two weeks, at the most three. She'll be home before Thanksgiving."

6

Chris stood up, lean, looming over the doctor. He let out his breath and scratched the back of his neck. "It was a scare, I don't mind telling you."

"Scared me more," said Jane.

"Oh, your kind isn't easily killed off," Dr. Polla said. "You can live forever with this little trouble. But." He put his thumb into his vest pocket. "But. And there is a big but. I would not want to see Jane becoming pregnant with this situation. Pregnancy is the one thing that could turn this hydronephrosis into a nasty situation."

"Oh, I see," said Chris.

"I would most strongly urge no pregnancies until the hydronephrosis diminishes. Then perhaps. If it does not, I must be firm in advising you not to get her pregnant."

Jane's face flushed. The voice seemed to be apart from her, something overheard, irrelevant, with the manufactured intensity of a sound track.

"We'll accept your advice. You know that." Chris's voice was calm, clear, official. "God knows we would never risk anything like that."

"I'm not saying now—and get the pitch straight on this because I'm giving it straight—I'm not saying she'd absolutely die if she had another baby. I'm saying just this: I cannot urge too strongly that you kids skip having another baby while this other thing's going on. Just stay away from each other for a while. By the time of her six-week checkup we'll have begun working this thing out. In two months or so we'll have the urologist check her." He stood up. "I know it seems rhythm doesn't work for Jane, but there are things far more reliable than calendars. And don't look at me like that. If you don't know by now how I stand—well, I'm a Catholic too."

"I'm sorry," said Chris, the words sounding vaguely wrong to him.

"If you think for one minute I'm going to advise you to choose between hell and complete eternal continence you're not the intelligent guy I know you to be. Rhythm is still a new thing. We've only known about it since the thirties. Science is working on it still. There are new pills to help regulate cycles. It may not be forever for you and Jane. Wait and see. I'd hope to have her stabilized and a fairly secure cycle established within a year or so." Dr. Polla buttoned his jacket over his vest. "No use saying there won't be a problem. If there weren't, you'd be a peculiar married couple. But it may not be forever."

He headed for the door. "And now, if some gal doesn't decide to have a few pains ahead of schedule, I'll get on home to dinner on time for once and make my wife happy." He waved at Jane. "So long, doll. Be good."

THREE

Augusta Peabody always came down from Massachusetts when her older daughter was having a baby. She sat now in Jane's chair with Jane's mending, waiting for Chris, listening to the children upstairs. Jane's friend, Victoria Burke, was giving them their bath.

"Hi, Mrs. Peabody! Haven't seen you since the last baby. Came to clean the monsters up for you." Just like that, Tory walked in and took over. "It's too much for you, Mrs. Peabody," she said.

"That's a very kind thing for you to do, Tory," Mrs. Peabody answered. "You're a real friend to Jane." But it did not seem proper that someone else should run things with a perfectly capable grandmother here.

Gussie frowned over the mending. To tell the truth, she had never understood why Jane bothered with this Tory person. Such a noisy young woman, and that dark red hair not very ladylike even if the white stripe in it was natural, as Jane claimed. But Jane said Tory Burke was her best friend.

Then there was that Clare Sullivan person, so girlishly sweet she looked like a child herself. Clare came and took Peter and Mary off to her house. Certainly that was kind. Christian neighborliness. I thanked her. But I could have taken care of Peter and Mary myself. They aren't orphans to be shunted to the Sullivans or anywhere. It's not proper.

And when Clare Sullivan left what had she said? "My, aren't you proud of your daughter, Mrs. Peabody? Six babies now."

"Six babies in ten years."

Clare had cocked her head, smiling. "It's not as bad as it sounds. And God must be taking special care of her. Look how well and happy she is."

8

Might as well say God wants my daughter wearing herself out with childbearing, Mrs. Peabody thought. "How many do you have, Mrs. Sullivan?"

"Seven. And another coming."

"Seven! And you're taking Peter and Mary to your house?"

"That's no trouble. We're looking forward to it." Clare still had a neat figure under her skirt and sweater, Mrs. Peabody noticed. She did not look like the mother of seven. "And they'll be happy."

"They're certainly in a hurry to go," said Mrs. Peabody. Perhaps even that Tory was a better friend for Jane than Clare, Gussie thought. At least Tory didn't have an indecently large family—only four children, three of them nearly grown now and one a toddler. But Jane had been quick to assure her mother that the size of Tory's family was a result of God's plan, not Tory's, and much as she would have liked to suggest otherwise, Gussie knew in her heart it was so.

She looked up from the sewing now and sighed. She felt so out of things. And she was worried. When Chris told her about the kidney business he called it a flare-up. An incident. The doctor says she's fine now. Nothing to worry about. Gussie didn't believe him.

The phone rang again. She added another name to the neatly penned list of friends who called to congratulate Jane and offer help. These people act as if Jane just won some kind of sweepstakes, and they're celebrating. Among our people birth has dignity. One does not rush in asking questions. One waits till one is told. But these people Jane has chosen are different. Nothing about these Catholics is proper, and that's not bigotry, it's just the way things are. They like being different.

Gussie Peabody had believed her children should be allowed to choose their own religions. When Jane became a Catholic, when her other daughter Gloria became nothing, Gussie triumphantly minded her own business. If Jane wanted to worship with Papist candles and incense, that was all right with Gussie. But this church did more than affect Jane's worship. It reached into her life and controlled it. Even here, in a nice place like Rockhill, where goodness knows there were some fine educated people, outmoded ways and laws held firm. Shaking her head she went into the kitchen to heat supper for Chris's return.

Waiting, she sat at the table and put her face in her hands.

"Lord in heaven, don't let anything happen to Jane. Thou know-

9

est she thinks she follows Thee. She chose this church and she has remained faithful to what she thinks is Thy service. Protect her. She is intelligent and has so much in her background, and she is my daughter, and Thou must rescue her."

Though her beloved Lawrence was dead these many years, though she had only Gloria and Jane, though tonight she was quite alone in this peculiar world Jane had chosen, Augusta Peabody would stand strong. No one here knows how I feel, she thought, what it means to know your daughter's life is being wasted and she is suffering when she need not be. "How many more will you have?" I asked her. . . . Everyone here seems to think that having children is something holy.

"I've never mentioned it to her, Lord, except that once. But Lord, Thou knowest these outmoded laws are wrong for her. Let her understand somehow. If I cannot help her, send someone who can tell her what to do. She's living in the dark ages, and she's my daughter."

Tory's footsteps sounded on the stair. Gussie sniffled, found her hankie, her her head up again.

"They're all in bed, Mrs. Peabody. Oh—you've been crying! Are you worried because Jane was sick?"

"No, dear." Mrs. Peabody smiled. "No. You just don't know what it's like till your own child has a child. I'll be all right."

"I'm sure you will." The white forelock against Tory's red hair shone in the kitchen light. Jane said she had gotten it from a childhood blow to the head. "I'm sure Jane's going to be all right too," Tory was saying. "I ought to hurry home now to get Al's dinner, but I'll stay if it would make you feel better."

"My grandmother watched on a widow's walk at the harbor house. My mother worked as a suffragette. We are made of strong stuff, we Peabodys."

"Jane is too," said Tory. "She's like you. That's why I don't worry about her. I lean on her. She's my rock."

"There is a tradition of strength in New England. My mother used to call it a fabric of courage woven through the years," said Mrs. Peabody.

"Doctor says Jane's fine now," Chris reported when he came in. "You can go visit her tomorrow, see for yourself. She looks great."

She watched him eat. She suspected that neither he nor Jane

would tell her if something was wrong, not something as personal and controversial as she had a hunch this was.

"I'm going to stay a little longer than usual," Gussie said. "Jane and I can have nice long visits in the hospital."

FOUR

Pete and Mary McNamara were glad to be at the Sullivans'. In their opinion, Luke and Kilian and the babies, left home with Grandma Peabody, would have a rough time.

The McNamara children were not cut to the sentimental pattern of the big happy family. Chris and Jane had been startled and disappointed at times to find their young ones devoid of brotherly love. Peter, who was ten, seemed to have no use for Mary, who was nine, and seldom bothered with Kilian and Luke, who were five and six. When Mary was not fighting with Peter she was bossing the little boys around, or crying that they had injured her, hoping to get them punished. Luke and Kilian, so close in age, reacted on each other like baking soda and vinegar. Only toward baby Meg did all four seem able to express love without embarrassment. Even Peter considered her kisses an honor, and reported her accomplishments as marks of genius.

But in times of crisis, which meant mostly the times their mother was in the hospital, the four talking McNamara children rallied close together.

"I wish Luke and Kilian were here," Mary said to Mrs. Sullivan. "They'd like it."

"But your grandma would miss them. She loves fussing over them."

"Aw, she's forgotten about kids," Pete said. "She makes good brownies and all that. But she's always getting insulted." What made it hard, both Pete and Mary knew, was that Luke and Kilian were still so young. Pete and Mary remembered how it was to be young, when you just couldn't make sense out of how you felt.

Luke always did very bad things whenever he was unhappy. He would wreck furniture, or go out in the snow with just his socks on and no shoes, or throw a tantrum and lie down on the kitchen linoleum because it felt cool on his face. And he worried about doing these bad things unless Mother was there, because she understood. Grandma didn't.

And Kilian. He was always sort of half asleep when he was unhappy. Because he had to cry, he would start about something ridiculous—a teddy bear he lost two years ago, or he'd say the lady down the street was mad at him. People who lived with Kilian, *family,* understood he had to pick something to say he was crying about. But Grandma Peabody and Grandma McNamara and babysitters were awfully logical with him.

None of this could Peter and Mary have put into words. Words, as far as Pete was concerned, were like pieces of a game he did not yet understand. Often, when he tried to use them, he would find what he said meant to grownups something quite different from what he had in mind.

Peter liked the noise and confusion of the Sullivan house and he knew precisely how to be alone in it without seeming to withdraw from the gang. He would sit by the TV and cup his chin in his hands. No one thought that odd. Then he moved into a world where there were only dramatic darting colors, and feelings in his throat and belly. He had learned that these things were not what other people called thoughts.

What are you thinking? someone would ask. You could not say you were not thinking. That was against the rules. It made you sound stupid. But you couldn't say the truth: that you were feeling a darkness in your stomach and a green-gray-gold color. That sounded stupider. So Peter learned to translate these feelings so they sounded like thoughts. He sometimes wondered if other people actually did think in neat words and paragraphs. There seemed no way to find out.

At the moment he was feeling an intense about-to-be-ness inside him. Under where he breathed was that old familiar diamond-shaped rock that burned. That meant fear. There was a sort of Christmas-ball red and goldness about the baby, and a blue for his mother like the so-far-away blueness of outdoor Christmas lights on big mansion trees at night.

Last year someone's mother died having a baby. Her children went to the funeral and saw the bodies and they did not come back to school right away. People did die having babies. That was an oil-green shadow within Peter. But beside it was the big laughter of his own mother, all sunlight, and the softness of her where he put his head under her heart. She will be thin when she comes home, he understood. And she did not die having a baby.

He hitched up his blue jeans, turned off the television, and went searching for the bowl of apples. His teeth needed to bite on an apple, to catch in something. He wondered what his mother was doing. She was, he guessed, feeding the baby and thinking about her Pete and wishing she could come home and be with him. He hoped she was happy anyway.

If he had asked her, she would have said she was happy as a clam. Her time in the hospital made her feel strangely as if she had escaped back to her college or boarding school days. A bit of visiting from room to room, avoiding the supervision of nurses, a few late-night snacks. The hours when she could close her door, read in bed. Daydream. Do nothing. Let other, newer mothers fret to go home. Let other, newer mothers complain of stitches and nurses and thermometers and plain food. Pity those with baby-blues. Pity those with real pain and trouble. She put her hands behind her head under the pillow, and wondered if she'd ever be on the maternity floor again.

Long ago, in a camel's-hair coat and knee socks she had perched on a wicker-seated ladder-back chair while a priest whose face she could not remember said:

"I suppose that the Church's attitude toward birth control will be the hardest thing for you to accept. It usually is for girls coming in."

Even then, in the midst of conversion, she had not been what she called emotional about religion. The stark, clean intellectual pillars of the Church appealed to her more than anything else.

Bryn Mawr College made her aware for the first time of other modes of life than her own. She tasted beer and spaghetti and lox and chow mein, read books her mother did not own, like D. H. Lawrence and Dostoevski and Kahlil Gibran. She attended a Friends Meeting, took a course in Oriental religions, dated an atheistic medical student, and in her sophomore year became a Roman Catholic. The priest, who was kind enough to make it difficult for her to enter the Church, repeatedly posed the problems of marriage to her.

"Someday you may marry. God's law is not easy to accept. It can be very hard."

"Where's the problem, Father? It's beautiful, really." Her an-

13

swer, so glib then, had remained unchanged except that as time went on she could see where the problem did exist for some. At times it seemed that for the busy tongues and earnest worried eyes around her, there was no other problem in the world. After each baby's birth she got letters from Planned Parenthood. Magazine articles, speeches, forums all busied themselves helping her understand the "population explosion" and why she ought not to have so many children. Even her own mother.

The constant controversy over babies by choice or by fiat actually had not bothered her deeply. She was, she liked to say, a logical woman who knew what she believed and why.

Oddly, what bothered her most was what her mother would say if she knew.

"Jane, you're a martyr, my dear, an absolute martyr."

"Nonsense," she would argue back mentally, "you're over-dramatizing the whole thing, Ma."

Nevertheless, Jane admitted to herself now, it was a basically dramatic situation. Three things were important in any life: the avoidance of death, faith in God, and love. When the three worked against each other and collided, it was no fun to be in the middle.

She remembered, one day before her baptism, trying to explain to her mother about grace: "We become more than we are. I will have God living in me, and I will live with the life of God. Outside everything will seem the same. But Ma, every breath, every thing I do has a new and beautiful and terrible meaning."

Gussie had liked that. But she would say this business now was rank nonsense. She would not understand. Jane herself did not quite understand. The challenge was so sudden.

There are two things I can do, she thought. I can give up love— not that it would be giving up love, only a part of it—but still it is giving up something important, God knows. Or I can keep love and give up life—not that it would be giving up life, only being willing to risk my life, and trusting God to take care of us, and that would mean being rash or being supremely holy, I don't know which. And either way, there's Chris, getting a raw deal.

Two choices. But, to be fair, she added, there are three. I could do what I know some Catholic women do, and ignore the Church on this one point. That's the choice my mother would say to take. If I did—all I would give up then is my God.

"You always were a bit intense, my dear, even as a little girl." That's what her mother would answer to that. "You don't have to be so hard on yourself. It's done all the time, even by your kind of people. I've heard Catholics say, and their arguments make sense really, that the Church will change its mind someday."

Intense? Jane smiled. She knew the Church would not change its mind. This was God's law, a forever law. To break it was to commit mortal sin. Catechism called mortal sin an act that killed the life of grace in the soul. But for Jane it meant personally, deliberately, knowingly, give a new death-wound to Jesus Christ.

She did not, could not, understand the Catholic who committed mortal sin once, let alone again and again, being forgiven, letting God live in his soul again only to destroy him again. Christ told her she was wrong to judge them. But her heart had no patience with halfway love. All or nothing. I'd as soon quit the Church and be damned as commit a mortal sin. There were not three choices for Jane McNamara.

"Only one," she said. She got out of bed, walked barefoot to the window. The lights of Rockhill shone in the night. Leaning on the sill between the roses from the Burkes and the yellow gladioli from Chris's office, she considered the thoughts and feelings within her.

It had not occurred to her that she could be glad. She thought she knew herself well. But the prospect of living as brother and sister did not depress her now at all. I am glad because there will be an end, and it is an end without reproach or guilt. An end to giving. An end to wondering what the cost of the gift will be. No one can blame me now if I refuse. I am glad. A few days ago I prayed for more children. Well, the prayer was answered. God's will: no more children. The decision was not in my hands. Chris made the decision. Absolute self-denial rather than any risk. Poor Chris.

She wanted to cry. For the first time since Teresa's birth she wanted desperately to break down and cry, for Chris.

She opened the door to the darkened hallway, and tiptoed to the pantry to get a drink of ginger ale. She thought she heard the nurse coming. Her heart beat as hard as when she had sneaked into the dormitory after lights out in college.

You haven't grown up yet, Jane Peabody, she said to herself, for all that you're Mrs. McNamara now.

15

FIVE

Father John Temple was a great truster in Divine Providence. If he had not been he could not have endured being pastor of St. Rose's in Rockhill.

He was seventy-two and he had been pastor of St. Rose's for twenty-five years. He had come to Rockhill filled with zeal, built a neat small stone church, and later a school, and paid off his debts. Ten years ago he had reached the point where, in the words of young Father Macy, he had it made. He'd pictured himself growing old and serene in the small stone church, perhaps indulging in some little eccentricities to fit the popular notion of nicely aging priests.

In those more gentle days ten years ago, Father Temple's only real worry was his secret unconquered horror of visiting the sick and the dying. This revulsion he surmounted physically but he could not rid himself of it emotionally no matter how much he prayed and read. He considered this phobia a grave fault against charity and a healthy reminder of his own unworthiness for the priesthood. . . .

This night in January, sitting among his parakeets, he looked back at those pre-explosion days and sighed. What ten years had done to him and to St. Rose's! He was growing old, but not serene. When he was new in Rockhill, he had the care of six hundred souls. He had now, by the last yearly census, which was of course already out of date, four thousand seven hundred and two. The church he built during the depression had seated two hundred and fifty and was then comfortably filled for the three Masses on Sunday. The new St. Rose's, completed last year, seated a thousand at each of the five Masses on Sunday. A while back the parish had been debt-free. Now Father Temple owed the bank three quarters of a million dollars. And that debt would, God willing, be increased this spring when construction began on the new convent.

The village of Rockhill was village no more. It was a suburb. The word sat on Father Temple's tongue like sour phlegm.

The suburb, in his opinion, was mostly his fault. He, Father Temple, had built a school. In the innocence of his heart he built that nice little school right after the war. There were few parochial schools in Connecticut in those days. The bishop had not encouraged them. When that bishop died and Father Temple built his school, he was celebrated as a man of initiative and vision. Pastors from all over the state were brought to Rockhill to see what marvels could be wrought in a small but loyal parish.

Father Temple grunted in his semidark bedroom. If he had been guilty of vanity and pride in those first days of the school, he was doing ample penance now. By mysterious instinct, like seals migrating to hidden islands to breed, families swarmed to his parish. In the meadows and brookpaths where he had been wont to walk and meditate and gather watercress for his housekeeper's salad bowl, now suddenly were barbecues and playpens and houses, houses, houses. On every house was a mortgage, a TV aerial, and a challenge: the demand that Rockhill remain "country" in the face of invasion from the city, and still provide schools, shopping facilities, sewers, and a place to put down roots and grow in godliness, peace, and comfort.

There were all kinds of people in these new houses, but mostly, in Rockhill, there were Catholics. Father Temple's school had been the magnet. The fact that his school could hold only three hundred children did not deter any one of these new families. They knew kindly old Father Temple, that apostle of parochial education, would not turn a child away.

He built for the school a new wing three times the size of the main body. He built the new church. Now fifteen sisters were huddled in the same old firetrap which once housed four. They had been patient, bless them, but they must have a decent convent. When a woman handles a class of sixty children singlehanded all day for the love of God, then for the love of God the least you can do is give her a tiny cell to call her own. And a chapel big enough for all the nuns to say their prayers together.

It would cost a quarter of a million.

Father Temple leaned out the window to look at his church and felt a little dizzy. To make an act of faith in Divine Providence now sometimes took hours on his knees. God would provide, he knew. But there was no denying that it would have been easier if God had provided Father Temple with training in business school.

In the sleet and rain of this winter night the doors of his mortgaged house of God swung open and shut like theater doors. People streamed in and out for confession. Father Mongiano and Father Macy were in the boxes now. When they came back for the supper break, Father Macy would say they were doing a good business tonight. Father Temple could just hear him. A twinge of disgust twisted his lips. He apologized quickly to the Blessed

Mother. "I should be praising God that the people come to the sacraments," he said aloud. "They're good people. And I'm sure Father Macy is good for them."

They were good people. But puzzling. And there was so little time now for the pastor to get to know them.

"I can't be bookkeeper and executive and a good pastor, Mary," the priest said. "And I don't think these people like me anyway. I'm not much use to them. I don't even speak their language. All this business of laity and lay participation and lay action. Chris McNamara's a great one for talking about that. And his chum, Al Burke. And their wives make me nervous. And they know it."

His voice startled the parakeets in the huge scrolled green wire cage. He closed the window and opened the cage. Pepe, the blue bird with the yellow beak, whose temper matched his master's, ran up the sleeve of his cassock and perched on his head. Father winced. He never got used to the ugly feeling of claws on his bare scalp. But he loved Pepe, and Pepe loved him, and the bird liked to play with the few whisps of hair still available. You pay a price for everything, thought Father, for building a school or for the friendship of a bird.

Father Temple switched on the light and looked at himself, a skimpy candle of a man with a parakeet on his pate.

"If the people could see me now they'd call me daft. At least that's the word they would have used in the old days. Now, if it were young Walter Burke, he'd say I've gone off my rocker, I suppose. And his father Al, he'd say: 'That's the way the cookie crumbles.' Or something. I believe I have the idiom confused. But no matter."

He checked the buttons of his cassock, found two had slipped out of frayed buttonholes, and prayed for a moment for the Burkes and the McNamaras and all those like them who deserved, so he thought, a pastor who spoke their language.

He put Pepe carefully back in his cage, and went down to supper.

Father Macy, with a handsome smile, rubbed his large freckled hands.

"Well, we're doing a good business tonight," said Father Macy.

Father Temple nodded. "Good evening, Father," he said.

He always called both curates Father. He did not complain when they called each other by first names, any more than he complained about Father Macy's zippered cassocks. If a curate was too lazy for the discipline of buttoning buttons, that was his own affair.

Father Temple kept his opinions entirely to himself, so he thought.

Father Temple looked at the young men tenderly, growled away the mucus in his throat, watched the smiles fade from their faces, and shouted the prayer.

They were an odd family, these three fathers. Father Augustine Macy, senior curate, a redheaded lad who would never look old, was a man born to informality. He walked the spiritual aisles of the Church with an outward nonchalance that delighted the young men of the CYO and appalled Father Temple. Across from Father Gus was Father Joseph Mongiano, junior curate, a movie producer's dream of a priest, tall, with diffidently curly hair and smudgy black eyes. The oils of ordination were scarcely dry on his hands and he was, so old ladies and Sisters agreed, a beautiful sight at the altar.

When Father Mongiano offered Mass on weekdays it took at least thirty-five minutes. When Father Macy said Mass it took never longer than twenty-three. These were the two men who with Father Temple shepherded the flock of Rockhill. Father Macy ran the inquiry classes, the CYO, the Newman Club, Holy Name, all fund-raising, census and choirs. Father Mongiano took care of Cana, Christian Family, study groups, nocturnal adoration, altar boys and the library.

"I was down at the hospital today and the new McNamara baby is here," Father Mongiano said. "Chris seems worried about Jane. She was very sick for a while."

"I'm glad it's not serious," said Father Macy cheerfully. "We'd miss his voice in the choir."

"I didn't know you got along with him so well, Father," shouted the pastor. "I thought I heard him out-intellectualizing you about the unliturgical rosaries you were selling. The ones with Lourdes water in the beads?"

Father Macy grinned. "Oh, Chris is always reading things, you know. But he's the kind that knocks himself out for a good cause. A nice guy. He's the one I think ought to head up this convent drive."

Father Mongiano wiped his mouth. He was, Father Temple observed, about to disagree. The pastor found the differences of opinion between his two curates reassuring but preferred not to get involved in them. Instead he withdrew into his own thoughts.

"Don't you think Chris McNamara has enough troubles?" Father Mongiano said. "He's too busy to be burdened with a fund drive, I think, Father."

"Everyone has troubles, and everyone is busy, Joe. That's the way it is in this day and age." Father Macy's face grew solemn. "Yet the Church is growing by leaps and bounds, and it's those with troubles, those who are busy, who are helping it grow. If you want something done, go to a busy man. The parish is alive with thought and action and we must swim with the tide or be lost. You have to get with it and make hay now."

Father Mongiano bent his head. He asked the Lord daily now for the actual grace to love Father Macy and his clichés. He asked again now, this instant, for the grace to smile and be still. The two hours of confession had taken their toll of him.

He longed to be able to go and sit in solitude and silence somewhere until he could find himself again. He had a letter from his parents and would have liked to reread it. But he believed in the sacrament of the present moment, and what God asked him to do at this present moment was to find something affable to say to Father Macy.

"It's good we have you, Father," he said. "If it weren't for you I sometimes think St. Rose's would be half dead, and in a very bad way."

Father Macy winced at the sincerity of that tone. He chewed some heavy rye bread so that he could not speak out in irritation. The sincerity with which Joe always managed to utter corn bothered him intensely. He knew what Joe thought of him, knew what the pastor thought of him, too. They just didn't understand one another at all. Heaven knew, only God's grace could make them live together in peace. Or mostly in peace. He still remembered clearly the day Father Temple had shouted at him that just because his name was Macy he didn't have the right to turn the Church into a bargain basement for souls. He had forgiven the pastor, naturally, but he could not forget. He tried to be patient with Joe, too.

The trouble was, Joe didn't recognize that the modern American suburb demanded a new kind of piety. It demanded quick Masses, else the parking lot became a most unholy traffic jam. It demanded modern techniques in setting up shop. Take confession. Joe handled only fifteen people an hour on the average, which meant his line backed up and looked unwieldy. Father Macy took care of thirty or forty an hour. In this parish, to meet the needs of hundreds and hundreds, could you take time to give a special sermon to each person? Joe did. Father Macy regarded him as a traffic-control man might regard a beautiful antique auto in rush-hour traffic.

"I've been trying to get that young Michael O'Shea to take some interest in this schoolbus matter," said Father Temple unexpectedly. "Politically. I knew his father well. Of course, Mike's not as successful at politics as his father."

The curates' eyes met. On one subject they agreed: the pastor, and his monologues.

"He can't be as successful as his father, and I've tried to tell him that, you know," Father Temple continued. "He's trying to follow the grand old tradition of Irish politicians. Can't see the town's gone beyond that." He nodded sadly. "But Michael O'Shea doesn't want a priest telling him anything."

"I don't know if that's exactly the trouble," Father Macy interrupted, in a tone that said perfectly clearly he did know it wasn't. "It seems to me Mike is trying too hard to go Ivy League. There's nothing wrong with those conservative Brooks Brothers suits he wears, except that he always looks as if he's borrowed them for the occasion. That thick Irish neck? That hearty Irish voice? He can't shake them. He'll always look and sound like an old-time Irish politician no matter what he does. That's *his* handicap."

Father Temple never felt more annoyed with Father Macy than when he was right.

"Nonsense!" he boomed fiercely. "All he lacks is his father's courage. He'd be a lot more successful if he had some of his father's fire." Father Temple knew he'd shifted his ground, knew too that Father Macy wouldn't dare say so. "Just take this schoolbus issue as an example," he went on. "With the Catholic population of Rockhill as high as it is, even the Protestants and the Jews would probably agree that our people are entitled to use the buses our taxes help pay for, if Mike would put it squarely before them. And they'd respect him for it. But when I try telling him that—" he shrugged and glared at Father Macy triumphantly.

"Try talking to his wife," Father Macy suggested.

The pastor looked alarmed, and Father Macy smiled. "There are no flies on Lidwina, you'll have to admit. A more stylish-looking woman would be hard to find. It's enough to make you wonder what she sees in him. And Lidwina's a good gal, too. She can sell more raffle tickets in a day than anyone else in a week. You ought to try talking to her."

Father Mongiano smiled to himself. He knew as well as Father

Macy did that Father Temple wouldn't talk to Lidwina or any other of the young wives. Of them all, only Jane McNamara seemed to make the old man feel at ease.

"Mrs. McNamara was asking about you, Father Temple. She'll be in the hospital quite a while. She hopes you might come see her," Father Mongiano said.

"I think I may just do that," Father Temple boomed gratefully at him, and before either of them could answer, he plunged into the prayer that ended the meal.

As the priests returned to duty, the church parking lots were already filling with the evening crowd. Chris McNamara, arriving from the hospital, ran through the sleet, passing Al and Tory Burke as they hurried their children toward the church. There was hardly time for the friends to wave.

Near the confessionals people waited, praying, coughing, nudging children to silence, glaring at the bold few who sidled ahead in line.

The priests knelt briefly, and then took their posts. The lights clicked on, the tiny red and green traffic lights signaling which sides of the confessionals were occupied—an efficient touch which delighted Father Macy and annoyed the more nervous parishioners whose shifting knees clicked the lights conspicuously on and off.

Once again the power of the sacrament was summoned.

Kneeling at the altar rail, Chris McNamara found himself beside Al. Al nodded to him and smiled. Chris smiled back and then bent his head in prayer. His penance said, he lingered, grateful for the comfort of this moment. Everything is normal here, he thought. His awareness of the danger that had threatened Jane receded a little under the impact of familiarity—the church, the sacrament, and his friend at his side.

Chris had known Al Burke only four years, yet he felt closer to Al than to any other man friend of his life. They had been thrown together by Jane's friendship for Tory. With the husbands of most of Jane's friends, Chris maintained only pleasant, casual acquaintance. But the Burkes and the McNamaras had meshed into a special foursome. Chris and Al had suffered together through their wives' antique-store sprees, and the indignities of being Cub Scout Fathers. They had fished together on the Sound, talked of Al's dream of owning a boat, gone on retreat together at the Holy Ghost Fathers, and shared a rare taste in anticlerical jokes. They insulted each other's expanding waist lines. But Chris, alone of all Al's friends, never teased Al about his rapidly thinning hair, because he knew Al was more sensitive about that pink scalp than he liked to admit.

On a night like this, when your wife is in the hospital, Chris thought, if you have any sense you thank God for a friend. He doesn't have to do anything. Just to know you have one is enough.

For his part, Al too felt a sudden warmth.

There was, he decided, something manly and splendid about sharing the moment after sacrament with one's friend. He felt suddenly that he would be glad to die to defend St. Rose's. Hell, he'd even take a pledge to build the convent, that's the way he felt about it.

He got up to leave. Tory was still waiting to go to Father Mongiano, so Al took baby Cyril from her and went out to the vestibule. He stood by the pamphlet rack nodding to the people he knew tramping in and out. That was one wonderful thing about the Church. It was a home and a community that could be carried with you anywhere in the world.

He thought of all the places he and Tory had lived, of Cincinnati and Portland and New Orleans and Atchison. They had been shunted about in the Army and in the corporation as if they were equipment, not human beings. But at least wherever they were sent, there was always the Church, one place they could feel at home. And of all the parishes they had belonged to, St. Rose's had given them the most—close friends like the McNamaras, and active laymen's societies where a man could be a Catholic among other Catholic men. Al liked it.

Chris came out and stood beside him.

"How's Jane now?" Al asked.

"The doctor says she'll be okay. But she gave us a scare."

"Tory told me. You know, anything we can do, just ask. We're all in this messy life together!" He smiled. "Good things, bad things, no one is alone. Couldn't be if we wanted to. And who wants to!"

SIX

Chris liked commuting, though he had acquired the prudence not to say so. Self-respecting commuters complained about the surly inefficiency of the railroad, its chronic physical breakdowns, its rising rates.

Only to Jane could he explain: "That time on the train keeps my sanity. The train's a sort of decompression chamber to keep me from getting the bends. There are two climates, two lives, one here with you and the brood, one there with the city. When I go to New York I have to be geared up, convinced that what I'm doing is important, that I'm a big deal. There I need to know what's going on in the world, who's saying what. Even an editor of textbooks has to sound important. I don't want to be like that here with you. It takes time to make the transition every day. Besides, that's where I get my peace and quiet. I can get articles and talks half written while I'm riding."

This morning he glanced over the paper, with an eye out for topics good for a paragraph of comment in his column. In New York people argued over a movie made by a maverick producer defying Hollywood's own code of ethics, cashing in on shock appeal. Ads capitalized on the ballooning breasts of a movie star. The copy read: BOLD! MATURE! FOR ADULTS WHO DARE TO THINK FOR THEMSELVES!

He folded the paper.

It was getting harder all the time to think about things other than sex. In the subway he stood with his nose almost hitting a bra ad. Last night with Mary and Pete he'd been watching an old children's movie on TV and the commercials had shown in detail the gentle crotch of a girdle. This is the marvel of electronics in my living room! And I am supposed to sell my kids the idea of a soul and heaven and hell, or even of the value of thinking? The thinking man smokes X. And thinks about—what?

He was thinking, later that morning, in his office. He leaned back in his chair, looked out the window and thought about women and offices. There were always women in offices. Even in celibate offices. His uncle, Father Tom, was always sounding off about the secretaries in the staid office of Our Lady of Mercy Society for Foreign Missions.

24

"In the seminary they told us we must stay away from women, not think about them, avoid long conversations with them," Father Tom said. "Fine. Then they dump me in an office and give me a secretary. Chris, women are impossible. We've had five secretaries and they think every man needs a woman to take care of him. They put flowers on my desk and sulk if I don't notice them. They cry because I don't do what they think is for my good. They can't leave a man alone."

He doesn't begin to know, thought Chris, thinking back over the women in his office life. At his first job there had been one who had trouble with legs and skirts. And one who kept asking him earnest questions a girl should maybe not even ask her mother.

And now it was Millie. Millie was miserable, and Millie wasn't even important in his life, being just a typist in the pool, but Millie had come to him with her problem. The IBM man had insulted her. He had suggested her trouble with the electric typewriter was because her chair was so low that her chest kept pressing on the keys inadvertently. How much more tactfully could a man put it? But Millie thought that was just awful.

"See what I mean?" the IBM man asked Chris in desperation.

Anyone could see what he meant, just looking at Millie.

Chris tried to convince her that the repair man was not getting fresh. He helped the man escape. Now, safely alone, he looked out the window grinning.

He stretched his legs up to the windowsill, put his feet next to the philodendron Millie nurtured there, and wondered what she and all the others thought of him.

He was a curiosity in the office, he knew. Part of the reason for this, though no one admitted it, was that he was Catholic. People here went out of their way to convince him that his being Catholic meant nothing to them. "You're too self-conscious," he was told the one time he tried to mention it. "You have a ghetto complex. We never even think of you as a Catholic, for God's sake." It wasn't true. They consulted him on certain matters of publishing policy as if he were an official Church spokesman. Give us the Catholic reaction, they'd say, as if there could be one representative Catholic reaction. And unofficially, just talking, they'd often cast a canny eye to see if some remark ruffled him, or if he could take a dirty joke. He remained as self-conscious as if he were a Hasidim with beard and long curls among the crewcuts.

And, though no one admitted it, he was a marked man because

had fed Luke and Kilian and Margaret and put them to bed, which was exhausting and especially hard in her clothes, designed for committee meetings and shopping. Annie's corset and her new shoes hurt her. She had finally removed them. And then Gussie felt she could take the tortoise-shell combs out of her hair and slip into a housecoat. In relief, they could not be formal with each other.

"She doesn't get enough rest," said Gussie. "Even in the hospital. She's not well."

"Visitors. She has too many friends. They talk too much and stay too long."

"You know," said Gussie, "I don't understand the way they talk. The way they gossip. Sometimes I feel it clinging to me."

"Gossip? Your daughter's no gossip," said Annie with a belligerent cock of her head.

"No. She's not. And it's not gossip. It's not about other people. It's about themselves. Talk about babies and marriage. Or else about prayer." Gussie turned warily to see if she was offending Annie's faith, but apparently not. "And I don't pretend to understand that, because after all it is a different church, and a different language, even when they talk about it in English."

Annie put down her teacup without even peeking at the leaves. "Well, I'll tell you something, Augusta. You may not believe this, but it's true. I don't understand what they're talking about either, and Lord knows I've been a good Catholic all my life." She nodded emphatically and caught her breath. "But you should be proud that Jane has so many close friends. And Chris, too, he was always well-liked. . . ." Her voice drifted off. She suspected Gussie disapproved of Chris for fathering so many children.

"Yes," said Gussie. "Yes. But Jane was always part of a—well, I was about to say a bigger world. But when I said that to Jane today she was insulted. I suppose it sounds wrong. What I mean is, she was able to talk about current events, art, literature, so many things that matter. Now she's all wrapped up in Clare Somebody-or-other's seventh Caesarean coming up."

"Seventh Caesarean!" Annie's eyes rolled. "Well!"

"Exactly. She's a sweet pale little girl. Good breeding in her face. Clare Sullivan, that's the name. And she's proud of the Caesareans. But Jane? What did she say to me? She said, if I remember right, that this was what she loved about living here. She felt she was part of some great web of life, something called the Mystical Body. Well, I did not understand it."

28

Annie looked into the teacup. "I don't know," she said, with that rising inflection which betokens not lack of knowledge but lack of interest. "I don't know."

Then she said, "I hope they don't have any more children. They should stop."

Gussie's eyes flickered with interest. "I'm worried for Jane's health."

"I told Chris she shouldn't have any more children," Annie said nervously. "It's not right."

"You can't blame Chris," said Gussie.

"You don't blame him?"

"Oh, a man is a man."

"There's nothing I can do," said Annie.

"Of course not." Gussie nodded. "But perhaps I can. She is my daughter. And I may know a way, without seeming to meddle."

That night, after Annie had gone home to New York, Gussie faced Chris over the kitchen table in her pink flannel monogrammed robe. "I don't want to be a meddler, Chris. But I am a mother. I can't help worrying about Jane. I know you give her the best of care, and your doctors here in Connecticut are fine men. But I would feel safer if we had her gone over by Dr. Perkins. A complete checkup. He's one of the most famous men in the country, you know, when it comes to females. I know him, and I'll talk to him."

As she stood there with her wrinkled face unpowdered and her eyelashes short and bare, he saw her for the first time as old and sad.

"After all," she said, "she's the mother of six now and we have to take extra good care of her. Those six deserve a mother who is strong and healthy and happy and well."

"Of course, Gussie."

"Chris, I don't want her to have another child."

"Nor do I, Gussie. Nor do I."

EIGHT

Toys were everywhere, plastic cars cracking under her unwary feet, tiny men and tiny trucks and tiny essential screws and bolts hid among crumbs and grit under the sofa pillows. As her strength slowly returned, and the baby began sleeping through the night, Jane tackled the housecleaning.

Almost more than anything Jane wished she had a playroom. Even the O'Sheas next door were having a playroom built now, and judging from the time that private contractor was spending there it would be pretty fancy. Lidwina O'Shea, in Jane's opinion, did not need a playroom. Her two children were both in their early teens. Besides, Lidwina had everything anyway. Lidwina had once won the *Vogue* Prix de Paris, and never let anyone forget it. Usually Jane consciously tried to overcome her catty thoughts about Lidwina by considering how difficult it must be to be married to Mike O'Shea. Today she deliberately did not make the effort. She wished the man were building the McNamaras a playroom instead.

The door of his panel truck slammed, the wheels grated on the icy gravel of Lidwina's driveway. He always left just before two, and the return of the youngsters. His going had come to serve as a signal reminding Jane to fetch her own children from St. Rose's School.

Kilian was eating an apple in the living room.

"You're in charge, boy. Be right back," Jane called.

"Yup." Kilian was proud of his dignity as babysitter for Meg, still napping upstairs, and Teresa in her bassinet.

"I don't know how you dare leave those babies alone," Annie McNamara had said. No use answering that Kilian was a big boy now. At five he was still a baby in grandmotherly eyes. "What could he do in a fire?" Annie asked.

Jane went over that conversation in her mind as she drove to school. I have to pick them up, she thought. There's no parochial bus and they can't ride the public schoolbus, so there's nothing else to do, unless or until someday somebody like Michael O'Shea'll stick his neck out and get something done politically. Mike never will. Peter could walk home, but it's three miles, and no sidewalks, and Luke and Mary are too small. I have to pick them up. So, God knows about it, and the guardian angels will help Kilian babysit, and I'm gone only about fifteen minutes.

But Annie worried. She often mailed Jane clippings of tragedies that happened while the mother was gone ten minutes.

The first time Jane met her, Annie had sat on her velvet and gilt chair and said:

"My sister Nora's husband went to sea and drowned. And my sister Kathleen had four children and a husband who died young.

And my sister Clara's husband went off and left her. They've all had terrible hard lives." She said it jealously.

Poor Annie, Jane thought. A fine son, a successful husband, and it's not enough for her. All that mummery-flummery of tea leaves and tabloid newspapers. She knows she's missing something. If you ask me, she's been looking for a good juicy tragedy to liven things up for years. And she's never had one yet. She thinks death is terrible. She's afraid of it. You can talk to her forever and she's still scared of death. Jane shrugged. Some people are like that. I'm not.

If Annie wants a tragedy, Lord, let her have one. Only don't let it happen at my house, please.

She jockeyed into her accustomed place in the parking lot as the school doors opened. She watched Peter emerge from the group, striding through the slush, bookbag swinging, cap low on his forehead. He saw her and smiled, and his face lost its tough look.

Mary frisked daintily from one dry patch to another in the parking lot. My pretty one, my little girl, Jane thought, and then remembered that she had noticed that Mary was not so pretty any more. Her new second teeth seemed enormous. The little turned-up nose no longer fitted her face. The gawky homely age was coming. Mary stopped to scold Luke, who was running behind her, splashing her red tights. Luke, with the face of a bulldog, let his red plaid schoolbag rest in a puddle while he argued with Mary.

After the strict silence of school they were all in full voice as Jane drove them home. Sister says. Teacher says. Guess what. We have only two subs to write. A boy threw up in school.

"I saw Pete talking to Cathy Gillis today. Pete has a girl friend. Ha, ha."

Suddenly all three were singing:

"Mine eyes have seen the glory of the burning of the school. . . .

Glory, glory hallelujah,
Sister hit me with a ruler . . ."

For a moment Jane wondered how it happened that she, the quiet little Peabody girl, had become mother and nursemaid of those voices. And she had suddenly a feeling of suffocation, of being locked into a life she did not understand or want.

NINE

"It's not enough that the kids have chicken pox and the sink is leaking, we have to have Gloria here too? I've had a hard day. Don't ask me to be nice to her." Chris frowned in irritation as Jane closed the icebox.

"Who's asking you? You were wonderful during dinner."

"The least your sister could do is help you with the dishes," he said.

"Gloria?" Jane laughed. "It wouldn't occur to her."

"I know it. I liked it better in the old days when she didn't come visit us at all."

"You just don't understand her, Chris," Jane said earnestly.

He smiled and raised his eyebrows. "I'm going to fix the sink."

"Good. Gives us girls a chance to talk."

"Don't talk too much. Every time she comes she makes you unhappy."

"Oh, that's not true," she said.

Chris noticed that Jane was using her better coffee cups and silver on the teakwood tray, as if to impress Gloria.

"I'll carry it in for you," he said, by way of apology.

Gloria was in the rocker in the corner, her legs in black tights tucked under an orange and pink felt skirt.

"You wear the craziest things, old girl." Chris put the tray near her.

She smiled up at him. "You get cuter every day, Chris. Too bad Jane saw you first. Hey—am I keeping you?"

"I have an important engagement with leaky plumbing. I have to tear myself away and fix it."

"Don't you just call a plumber?"

"Plumbers come high. They make more than editors."

"Chris can fix almost anything now," Jane said.

"Clever man."

Chris went upstairs to change into work clothes.

"I should think," said Gloria, "it must be awful for a man like Chris to have to fix sinks. Isn't it wiser to pay the plumber and use his own time for something more satisfying?"

"Forget it, Gloria," said Jane. "You don't understand our life, or Chris, so forget it."

"You understand him so well?" With swift grace Gloria crossed the room to sit by her sister. "Sorry. Didn't mean to sound that way. You are really happy with him, aren't you?" The way she said it, it wasn't a question. "Funny. I never pictured you growing up to have this: Chris, an army of kids. Much less being happy about it."

"I'm happy," Jane said quietly. So often now she felt as if she and Gloria were strangers, travelers from different worlds meeting by chance where two opposite routes cross. And she had never gotten over being lonesome for the old days when they had been so close after their father's death. That one day, that unforgettable day, stood like a milestone in her memory.

It was Gloria's birthday. And their father had been driving her to the toyshop to get a dollhouse, when a drunk crossed the road. Their father had swerved to avoid hitting him, crashed into a telephone pole, and died. Gloria, lying in a hospital bed, missed the funeral. When she came home she bore no visible scars. But there were scars that could not be seen, scars of shock and bitter bewilderment.

Their mother had not wept. Even then Gussie always took pride in not showing emotion. And little Gloria had hated her for it. Jane remembered, still not without pain, how well she had understood both Gloria's feelings and her mother's. She herself had been only a child, but she had been torn between them, trying with her own love to soothe them both. And for a time she and Gloria had been closer than close. For a time. Until Jane loved Chris, and married him. Then it had been Jane's turn to be bewildered. Then suddenly Gloria had seemed driven to assert her individuality, to be different from Jane and to sound superior to her. For years after their marriage Chris and Jane had scarcely seen her at all. Then recently she'd begun spending weekends with them. Yet she could not, or would not, get along with Chris and disapproved elegantly of everything about Jane's life.

"Gloria's not a bit like you," Chris had said. "But what she is makes no sense. She wants to be an intellectual, no emotions, all stern rationalism. So how come she's a glamorpuss? All the intellectual gals I ever knew were sloppy and had uncombed hair and wore flat shoes. It's crazy," Chris had said, "but I think all she's doing is trying to insist she's different from you, and she doesn't dare find out what she really is herself. Did you ever think of that?" he had asked.

Privately, Jane admitted, she had thought just that. It's as if she

33

hates me for having been drawn into another life. As if she's afraid of having the same thing happen to her. As if she's afraid of love. And she won't even let herself like me any more. Why? Jane wondered. Was I that overwhelming? she asked herself guiltily.

She could not explain it to Chris, but feeling obscurely responsible, she kept waiting and praying, hoping to find again the Gloria she once knew, the little sister of other simpler days.

"I'm glad you're happy," Gloria said now, quietly.

Jane looked at her with shy fondness. "And you?"

"You know me. Always happy."

"It's nice having you visit us so often all of a sudden. But you don't expect me to believe it's a sudden affection for all your nephews and nieces. I must say I've been wondering. Could you be in love, Gloria?"

Gloria laughed. "Never."

"I've been watching you," Jane said. "Something's going on behind all that eyeshadow."

"Jane dear, please. Hands off. Don't go looking for wedding bells for me. I don't want them."

"What about this guy Hack you keep talking about? He is the reason you've been coming up here, isn't he? So you can see him in New York?"

"Hack and I are friends. More than friends. Perhaps we love each other. But—no marriage."

"Okay." Jane, finishing her coffee, reached for a sweater she was knitting for Mary. "When do you finish school?"

"You think it's silly, don't you, my still going after degrees?"

"No. Of course not." Jane smiled, watching Gloria yawn and stretch on the couch. She always was beautiful, Jane thought, and she still is, and I wish I could put on makeup the way she does, but she doesn't need it, and she'd look better without it.

"I'm taking courses now on the impact of different cultures on mental health," Gloria said. "I have me a fellowship for next year. I want to get abroad to do some first-hand research."

"Paris?"

"Research, I said. Field work. I want to go to Africa."

"Oh. And Hack?"

"He's getting his Ph.D. too. But Hack and I, well, it's fine for now . . ."

"But not six kids and a kitchen."

"Exactly." Gloria smiled, the slightly oblique smile that had been her trademark ever since their father died. She decided not to tell Jane that Hack was a born Catholic, reacting violently against Catholic family life.

Chris was working in the downstairs bathroom. They could hear him grunting and banging and muttering.

"Did I tell you we're going to have a party?" Jane asked. "Nice big party. We didn't get to have our usual Christmas one because it took so long for me to get my strength back after this baby."

"You need more parties. Remember the times we used to have at the Cape? You were great at those parties, Jane. A long time ago."

"It was a long time ago. And, this won't be any dancing party, you know. Just a lot of friends. Want to come? And bring Hack? You said he's in New York most of the time?"

Gloria pouted her stylishly pale lips. "Wish I could. But this'll be my last weekend for a while."

Chris emerged with his tools and a gleam of satisfaction in his eye. "Your pipes, my love, are as good as new. So. Talking about the party? Wish you would bring Hack. Like to see what the guy looks like."

"You'll have to live in suspense," said Gloria.

"By the way, Jane," Chris said, filling his hands with peanuts from a bowl. "Why don't we invite Krena McDowell?"

"With her husband?" asked Jane.

"I don't think so. He's out on the Coast somewhere."

"Okay, if you want."

"Look, Jane, you sound as if you don't like her. I think Krena likes you. She wants to be friends." The questioning inflection of his voice was meant to be coaxing yet gay.

"With me?" Jane stood up. "It's time for Teresa's bottle."

Gloria stretched. "Jane, who's Krena?"

"A lady editor in Chris's office. Very rich. Very fancy. She's nice, rather unhappy, with no children," Jane said.

"That's why she's unhappy?"

"Believe it or not, it could be," said Chris stiffly, as Jane went upstairs for the baby. "She has almost everything else. Big house over in Jordan, which is, you know, swankier than Rockhill. But mostly she's lonely. Her husband is away too much."

"I see." Gloria studied Chris's face. "You work together?"

"Some. I'm giving her a hand with something new."

Jane came back with a warm bottle and Teresa. "Krena can come, of course," she said. "You ask her."

"This Krena gal sounds dangerous to me," Gloria crossed her black-stockinged legs.

"Oh, hell," Chris said. "Get off it."

"My, you're touchy. That's a bad sign."

Jane inspected a white pearl spot on the baby's cheek.

"And what is it a sign of?" Chris asked quietly.

"I mean, no one gets mad about something that isn't true. You got mad when I said Krena might be more than a mere co-worker. Simple as that."

"I get mad when you start trying to analyze people. You like to think you can stand off and watch and know everything. Every time you come here I have a feeling you look at me as if I were some quaint native."

"The native is restless tonight." Gloria laughed. "Oh, Chris, don't be mad at me. Hey, could I have a drink maybe?"

"Scotch?"

"I feel exotic tonight. Liqueur? B and B? Whatcha got?"

"You may feel exotic, but this isn't an exotic spot," snapped Jane. "We're fresh out of everything exotic. You know. We're the plebeian type. Bourgeois."

"Scotch, then. Gee, Jane, I'm sorry. I'm not being bitchy really. Forgive me?" She knelt beside the baby. "Beautiful. She is, Jane. And what more could anyone want?"

The short black waves of her hair fell forward as she traced the line of Teresa's cheek. Chris handed her a Scotch on the rocks.

"I'm drinking alone?" She winked. "Then a toast to Chris"— she gulped half of it quickly and easily—"who gets mad at me, and whom I love anyway." She finished the drink slowly. "He's getting more handsome with the years, you know, Jane. Offbeat. Lincolnesque." Chris made a face, but Gloria apparently did not notice. "I meant it as a compliment when I warned you about this office beauty, Jane. A guy like Chris needs watching. A smart cookie might just come along and snap him up. Couldn't blame her."

"Gloria, you're crazy," said Jane. "You're in over your head."

They went to bed after the baby's burping, stowing Gloria on the folding cot in Chris's den. Often before they had found themselves angry after a visit from Gloria. Tonight they kept silence, because as long as it was not put into words Jane could afford to agree sadly

36

with Chris's opinion of her sister. They were grateful to each other for the silence.

A loneliness filled them and they turned to each other, to the comfort of warm hands and nearness. Then they turned away again. Chris slept. In the darkness Jane lay apart, awake, content to know that none of Gloria's insinuations alarmed her, or made her mistrust Chris. Ours is a good marriage, she thought.

And then, from nowhere, came fear. Unbidden, it slithered from its lurking place and hovered over her bed. The fear of death. The idea of what it would be like to die compelled her and she could not take her eyes away.

Her hand would not move, though she ached to lift it. She heard nothing, saw nothing. She wanted to speak, but no sound came. Her lips could not move. Her lungs labored and ached and shuddered and no breath came. It was as if she needed to cling to her own skin to keep warmth within her. Nothingness. There is only nothingness. I shall be nowhere. And I am not ready, I am not through, I have not yet—

She flung herself upright in the bed, a hand pressed to her mouth. In the next room the children stirred in their beds. She listened. The house creaked, as if the specter of her fear were moving back into hiding. She had not known she feared death.

She hid her face in the pillow and forced herself to forget. It was hours before she dared to sleep.

TEN

"Jane, this time you can't say no," said Clare sweetly. "This time you've got to come and meet Father Juniper."

"Clare dear, you know I've been working very hard at not meeting him. I just don't like holy men." Jane smiled. She liked and admired Clare, in spite of her pious enthusiasms. But she mistrusted Father Juniper precisely because Clare considered him a living saint.

"I'm bringing Christine Newman over to meet him because she wants him to pray for her husband. And she says she'd feel better if you came too, less self-conscious. This is the day your cleaning woman is here, isn't it?"

"You trapped me."

"It'll do you good. You haven't been yourself ever since you came home from the hospital. And you'll love Father Juniper."

Privately, Jane felt it might have been kinder of Clare to refrain from busying herself with Christine's problems. Not that Clare was any ordinary busybody. She meddled with holy intention, sweetly, and for the love of God, which made it exasperatingly hard to stop her. And after all, Clare had nothing more to offer than a visit to a supposed saint, who might well be just a crackpot. That hardly seemed a solution to Christine's worries.

Christine's problem was real and subtle. Her Julian was not a Catholic. He was kind and wonderful, and contributed generously to the church, and worked at the bazaars, and even went to Mass. Christine was happily married, and the very happiness of her marriage had in recent years become an unexpected cross. Hers was a mixed marriage that worked. And that meant, Christine realized with dismay, that every bright-eyed youngster in the parish who wanted to marry a non-Catholic, or even date one, used Christine Newman's success as an example to quell all warnings.

Jane smiled. She was fond of Christine, and sympathized whole-heartedly. Even Tory's son Walter, when he had the crush on the Rosenberg girl, had triumphantly thrown Christine's marriage in his father's face, and Al had been furious. It was an uncomfortable position for a woman as earnest as Christine, who knew perfectly well that most mixed marriages don't work. She was weary of explaining to her would-be imitators that she and Julian were exceptions. She had decided the best answer would be for heaven to give Julian the gift of faith as quickly as possible.

At the altar in the small oratory at the Franciscan friary Father Juniper stood motionless, stiff golden vestment over brown habit and white linen, arms spread in prayer. On the altar's wooden step Brother Ernest shifted his knees, looked at his watch and folded his arms. His stomach growled.

It was a privilege, and a stiff penance, to serve Father Juniper's Mass. If the old man got lost in prayer his Mass could take as long as two hours. That was why the Superior obliged him to say Mass in the oratory instead of the big chapel, because no one knew when Juniper would go off into an ecstasy and forget all about everything.

The first time Ernest served for Juniper he wrote his mother in Detroit and told her he had assisted a saint. Secretly, Ernest had hoped he himself might glimpse a vision. But as the years went on with no miracles, Ernest's devotion was tempered with bursitis and an increasing hunger for breakfast in the mornings. He loved Father Juniper and was proud of him. But it was difficult coping with him.

The priest lowered his arms. The head rose. The words of the Mass sounded again over the calls of the bluejays outside the oratory.

Father Juniper, a farm boy, sixteenth child of a pair of Irish immigrants to the Midwest, had always wanted to be a priest.

"My old mother and all the brothers and sisters who were within walking distance and I, we made a novena to know what order Our Lady wanted me in. And there we were, at the altar on her feast day, and she told me herself, the Blessed Mother, quite clearly, to go to the Franciscans. And so I did," he would explain gravely.

Young Juniper had such difficulty with Latin and theology that he almost failed to be ordained. But those superiors who knew he was not schooled enough for the priesthood happened to fall ill with flu and be interred in a hospital. Their replacements happened to ask of Juniper only the questions he knew in the examination. And in 1904 Juniper, ordained a priest forever, was sent to New York City.

No one in the Franciscan beehive on Thirty-first Street knew what to do with Juniper. He was a poor preacher, and too weak in theology and canon law to be let loose on people seeking convert instruction or advice on how to rectify a bad marriage. They put him in charge of enrollments in the Franciscan Missionary Union. He inscribed names on scrolls, assigned the names to other priests to pray for, and kept records of donations received. Eventually the bookkeeping was entrusted to more capable hands, and Juniper was limited to handwriting.

In the early thirties, when the line for St. Anthony's bread stretched two blocks from the friary door, Father Juniper's hidden talent came to light. He was the best beggar the Order had. The needy of that depression era came for soup and bread at the front door and Juniper scooted out the back door to beg for food to give them. No one knew his source of supply. He blinked behind his steel-rimmed glasses and said he could not remember where he had been on his foraging expeditions.

He looked now at Brother Ernest as if again he could not remember where he had been. Slowly, he made the sign of the cross in the air, then raised the Host in his fingers.

"Ecce Agnus Dei. Ecce. qui tollis peccata mundi!"

Brother Ernest lifted his eyes and beheld the Lamb of God who takes away the world's sins. Once, ever so gently, Father Juniper had rebuked him for not following the meaning of the Latin: ",I am saying *Ecce,* Behold! Then, my son, behold!"

In the car Clare was saying sweetly, "When you talk with him you can just hear the sound of heaven in his voice. Yes. I know you'll love him. Yes. At least, I hope you will."

"You said once you thought he works miracles. Do you really think so?" asked Christine.

"I've heard that he does. Yes. But, somehow it's more what he does to your soul. You'll see what I mean."

"I'm going to ask him to pray for Julian," sighed Christine. "Poor Julian, he gets so cross about little things, you know, like bills and charge accounts. He'd be so much more peaceful if he could get all the way into the Church. I just know it."

In spite of her reluctance to join this expedition Jane would have had to admit, if she had been asked, that she was enjoying herself. Christine Newman always struck her as a breath of fresh air. A tall, large-boned woman, Christine had thick, curly hair that could never, no matter how she tried, be persuaded to conform to any fashionable style. And no matter how she tried, she could never manage to look quite neat. Fate seemed to have decreed that buttons would come off Christine's coat or lifts off her shoes every time she left the house, and these mishaps always embarrassed her. She was as incapable of affectation as a ten-year-old boy, and as appealing.

Jane was always amused when Christine spoke of Julian's crossness. He might be formidable at the bank during working hours, but on his own time he was easygoing in a strong-silent fisherman style. Precise himself, he seemed to cherish Christine's buoyant disorder.

The friary was an old estate. A manor house set on wide lawns with an apple orchard, a swimming pool and tennis courts. The outdoor stations of the cross were nestled in woodland with a view of the Sound. By the stone wall hung the sign Brother Ernest had painted: "Our Lady Queen of Heaven Friary, Franciscan Fathers, *Pax et Bonum!*" In the garden was a statue of St. Anthony holding the Child Jesus in his arms, looking as startled and nervous as a new father.

They found Juniper inside cautiously lettering a scroll of membership in the Franciscan Missionary Union.

"Clare! Good morning!" He peered over his glasses at her with squirrel-bright eyes.

Jane and Christine stood back, inspecting this man who was either a saint or a fool, depending on who was describing him. His beard, still full and brown, fell like a second cowl over the front of his habit. He came to meet them and Jane saw that he had ugly toes, flat, thick-nailed, with gnarled blue veins running down to them over his instep. His sandal straps seemed part of his skin, so closely did they follow his movements.

"Pax et bonum!" He held out his hand.

"Jane McNamara, Father. She has a new baby girl, a Teresa," Clare said, fluttering.

"Yes," the priest said, peering into Jane's face.

"And this is Christine Newman. She has a wonderful family too."

"Ah-hah!"

Then the four of them stood looking at the floor, wondering what to say.

Clare smiled expectantly but Father Juniper was obviously in no mood to be demonstrated. He scratched his left ear methodically. "Well, unless there's something I can do for you, ladies, I must get back to work."

"I'm glad to have met you, Father," said Christine helpfully. She had been toying with her purse catch and it sprang open now. She grabbed to catch the tissues which popped out.

"Didn't you want to enroll your Julian?" asked Clare. "Father will give you a scroll."

"Oh. Well, yes. If you please. I mean, will you, Father?" Christine said awkwardly.

"Julian is your husband?"

"Yes. I've been praying for him to come into the Church."

"Yes. Well, have you been patient?"

"Years."

"Good. Good." Suddenly he scuttled closer to her, looking up into her face, and his smile was very gentle indeed. "We have to be always asking, like little children, and always patient. Patient. The word I am told comes from passion, suffering. A bit of suffering while we wait. And always, always, always, love."

When the scroll was inscribed he took Christine's donation, held her hand clasped in the two of his and said good-bye. She looks, thought Jane pursing her lips, as if she had been honored by a king.

Jane herself turned to leave with no effort at politeness. Obviously, Father Juniper wasn't interested in her, and she wasn't hurt, mind you, but she wasn't going to fall over herself being nice to him, either. She was almost to the door when she heard the sandals creaking behind her.

The tears in the old priest's eyes startled her.

"Good-bye, Jane." He blinked, but his eyes still were wet. "I wanted to talk to you."

"I just came with the others," she said. "There is nothing to talk about."

"Good-bye. It means God-be-with-ye, you know. Good-bye Jane. I—" his voice broke as if something he had seen saddened him beyond speech.

Jane smiled. "Good-bye to you, Father."

Outside she avoided Clare's rueful eyes.

"He's something!" said Christine, holding the certificate as if it were a check drawn on heaven.

Jane smiled politely and said nothing. He was something, all right, she thought. He looked at me as if I were a freak. Or as if he were a soothsayer seeing omens.

ELEVEN

Chris drove her to Dr. Perkins' office.

"I'm not scared. It's just that I don't like going to the doctor. No one does," said Jane. "Especially a doctor you don't know."

"That's all?"

She turned in the front seat to inspect his profile. "Are you afraid of what he'll say? That maybe I'm sicker than Polla said?"

"No." Chris smiled. "No. Know what I really keep thinking? Maybe the great man'll prove all the local guys are wrong. That there's no danger at all. You seem healthy enough, God knows."

"I'm fine. The checkup from the urologist showed that. Still trouble, still deterioration, but fine." She opened her pocketbook, closed it again, sighed.

"What's the matter?"

"Well, you don't seem very worried about me."

"Do you want me to be?" He laughed.

"No. Yes, I think so." She looked out the window at the snow lying on the parkway laurels.

"Then I will worry," he said. "Starting now."

"Maybe I should be like women used to be, all silent and wan and martyred. I don't think wives used to tell their husbands personal things like this. It wasn't considered nice. Maybe they had a point. A little mystery keeps a man intrigued. You said last night you weren't happy at home any more."

"I said last night you were getting edgy. Stop twisting my words."

"You think it's easy for me?"

"Jane—" He took a hand off the steering wheel to hold hers. "Why is it we can't ever talk about anything any more without your getting upset?"

"I don't know."

"I said I was worried for you. I am. But it's almost three months now since the baby and you're fine. You'll be all right if you don't have another. And you're not going to."

"But you're the one who's edgy," said Jane. "And I know why. And how do you think that makes me feel?"

He drew his hand away, pulled the car up to the toll booth, paid, and raced on toward New York.

"You're always thinking about how you wish we could make love," she said.

"Terrible of me," Chris agreed.

She laughed in spite of her mood.

"This Dr. Perkins is a friend of your mother's. He isn't a Catholic, is he?" asked Chris.

"No."

There was a pensive silence. Then Chris said casually, "I'll pick you up when you call me. Any idea when?"

"He said to come and spend the day."

She spent the day. She was shuttled from room to room, amid bulging velvet sofas with rose-chintzed pillows, mirrors, dressing tables, all contrived to disguise the fact that this was a day of intensive medical examination.

She saw Dr. Perkins himself first at nine in the morning, a genteel interview which made her feel as if she were considering the purchase of a diamond necklace rather than asking for diagnostic reports. His office was done in Wedgwood blue and white. A small fountain played delicately among a collection of home-grown orchids.

She was conducted through the tests with one pause for lunch brought in from the French restaurant next door, and another for tea and *petits fours*. She felt out of place, awkward, too long-legged, too apt to suffocate under the velvet and roses. Her slip, which was new, was too plain. She sweated, and her nose itched, and by four-thirty she was a complete stranger to herself.

Dr. Perkins received her then with a compassionate smile. On his desk, within reach of his hand, was a winsomely carved alabaster bust of a small boy. It looked like Luke.

"You are a wonderful person, Mrs. McNamara. Wonderful. Seven perfect children to whom you have given life. You can be very proud. You have done a fine job."

Jane smiled. "Six. They are wonderful children."

"You know that you have a kidney condition."

"Yes. That's why I came."

"Of course. And I am glad to tell you you have no cause for alarm. I have seen the reports of your urologist and your obstetrician. They are excellent men. I confirm everything they told you."

"Then there's nothing to worry about? I'm fine?" She felt again in command of her body, at home in it.

"You could live to be ninety with those kidneys. You can live a full and normal life. Except, of course, as you are aware, you cannot afford to have more children. You have done a great job of bringing these into the world. You must now do the job of staying with them."

"Dr. Polla warned me."

"I cannot stress too strongly the intense danger of running any risk."

"Yes."

"The question then is, what will you do about it? There are several courses open to you and you must choose which is best for you." The doctor's hands cradled the alabaster boy's head. "You are young. You have no trace of any disease save this. I would not recommend sterilization for you."

"Sterilization?" The room seemed to fade away till all she heard was the fountain and the blood coursing in her head.

"I said I would not recommend it." Dr. Perkins smiled. "From a purely physical point of view it would be the best prevention and the best care I could offer your health. But you are not a purely physical being. You are a woman with a mind and emotions. For you it would be wrong."

"Dr. Perkins, I—"

"You are a Catholic. I know. And I am a physician. I speak to you from the point of view of a physician, not to seduce you to what you may call sin but to give you facts, in a spirit of honesty and service. What you decide is up to you."

He stood up, resting his hands on the polished desk top and she smiled at him because he was doing what he believed was his duty and he was expecting her to permit him to say what he saw as holy and right. It occurred to her that her mother had hoped he would suggest this.

"The formula we use at our hospital is to offer sterilization for multiparity after the sixth living child. Earlier if the mother is at the less impulsive age and is, say, nearing thirty-five when she has her fourth and fifth."

Jane said nothing.

"But for you, I recommend instead a well-planned method of birth prevention. You are not in that group of the lower class that will not or cannot follow directions. For them the operation is the only sensible thing. You have what they lack, a strong motivation because of your health, and the education and prudence to cooperate with your doctor."

He stood by the fountain, put his hands behind his back, and bowed his head as men do at prayer in a civic meeting.

"I know this comes as a shock to you. To have your deep beliefs challenged, to have your whole way of thinking set aside in open discussion as if it did not exist." He paused. "I suggest though that you think deeply, and pray, about this. You are evidently not one of those for whom the rhythm method works?"

"No."

"Certainly rhythm, by its naturalness, its freedom from all that is mechanical, is the ideal method of birth limitation from the point of view of the spirit, the soul, of love and marriage. But it does not rate high on the efficiency scale."

She smiled in spite of herself. She wondered if what he was doing was against the state law. It would be in Connecticut. But she knew she would not do anything about it if it were.

"Each night," he said, lighting a cigarette with a small butane lighter, "each night perhaps five million people in this country practice one of the most ancient and common of human decisions. In spite of argument and taboo and ignorance and laws, this decision has been implemented by billions of people of all lands and all times in history. And thoughtful men today are working with all the sincerity—"

Sincerity. Yes. She marveled that this man should be so full of good will, so earnest, and she thought of Saul who became Paul. His voice went on ticking off the various devices now in use, and some of the names were familiar to her and some were not, and she sensed that he spoke as he did in order to take away false modesty and the fear of the unknown.

"Learning to use this is not too difficult. A doctor's supervision. Used with the material I just spoke of it is as safe as possible, no trouble, no barrier to normal life."

Jane stood up, her pocketbook straps clutched tightly in joined hands. A spasm of laughter threatened her throat as she wondered what would have happened if Eve had gathered her things together and thanked the serpent for his time and flounced away. She could not think of a single appropriate thing for Jane McNamara to say, nothing that would sound right in this elegant room. She knew only that she wanted desperately to get away from the Wedgwood blue and the suave voice.

"Did my mother ask you to tell me this?"

He looked at her gravely. "Your mother wanted me to give you advice. The advice is mine. Forgive me. I did not mean to upset you. I know the beliefs of your Church, and honor them as beliefs. I know too that not all Catholics heed those laws of the Church. Half my clinic patients are Catholic. Most, of course, are Puerto Ricans. But I have found that often my patient needs help in facing her own inner convictions. The Catholic who wishes my help may be too painfully inhibited to ask for it. The Catholic who, like yourself, cleaves firmly and open-eyed to her faith is strengthened by having had the opportunity to test her conviction." He moved toward her with a disarming seriousness. "You've had that opportunity, and you found, Mrs. McNamara, that you were certain. And you must understand that that certainty may be invaluable to you in the years ahead."

A frown of surprise crossed her forehead.

"I recommend that you follow stringently the advice Dr. Polla gives you. There is much fine new work being done now to predict the natural times. Properly used, the rhythm method has only fourteen per cent failure compared to six or seven per cent failure in contraceptives. I shall forward to Dr. Polla the report of our examination. And now, may I say it has been a pleasure to meet you."

Bowing slightly, smiling under a heavily grey-feathered brow, Dr. Perkins showed her to the door.

TWELVE

It was a week later that Chris's uncle, Father Tom, dragged a crate the size of a small icebox out of his car into Jane's laundry room. "Peace be to all!"

The thunder of his voice and the stamping of his feet as he scraped the mud off them shook the house. Father Tom was built like one of those monster papier-mâché soldiers which are carried on human legs in a Mardi Gras parade. Taller than a man had a right to be, he floated in sedately ridiculous splendor through life and its upper environs. He appeared physically incapable of any feat more difficult than lifting a fork or a beer stein. He was actually a veteran of twenty-one years' service in African missions, a man who had built by hand dams and cathedrals, a hunter, electrical worker, dentist and roadmaker, and the best roughhouser the McNamara children had yet met. Peter, the eldest, was inordinately proud of this grand-uncle, and found it difficult to believe his prosaic father related to such a fabulous person.

"Jane!" The priest strode into the living room, removing coat, jacket and rabat in a trail through the kitchen. "I'm here!"

She leaned over the stairs. "Shh!"

Chastened, Father Tom looked up. "Sorry."

"Chicken pox," she said, coming down. "All of them except Mary, who's out. If you wake them up I'll run away from home. Come on, let's sneak a cup of coffee."

She picked up his clothes and hung them in the bathroom. The coat buttons hung by threads. The suit jacket had a hole under the left sleeve.

He stood by the laundry room waiting for her to notice the crate.

"What in the world is that and where did it come from?"

"From Kenya. From the beautiful land of the Mau Mau."

47

"For us?"

"For you. From me. With hopes, my dear, that you will sell all the contents at a fair profit."

"Sell them?"

"You see before you treasure from Africa. Carved wooden hippopotamuses, elands, heads, ashtrays, even black Virgins with Child. And several salad forks and spoons. All made in the missions of finest teak and other woods. All to be sold, to help support the missions. We need a new Land Rover immediately. Our priests are having too many accidents on motorcycles and only four wheels is economically sound considering the cost of preparing a priest. The crate is yours."

Jane smiled weakly. "Thanks, boss."

He sat at the kitchen table, the heavy folds of his stomach and chest lapping against the formica top. No one she knew exasperated and outraged her more than Father Tom, and no one else did she love in quite the same way. They first met on the occasion of Chris and Jane's engagement. He had sat awkwardly on one of Annie McNamara's gilt chairs and broken it.

The elder McNamara family was not quite happy with Father Tom. James had worked extra hours as a young man, scrimping to put young Tommy through the seminary because that was what was expected of older brothers in families like theirs. He had hoped someday to speak of "my brother, the Monsignor," if not of "my brother, the Bishop." But Tom had wanted to be a missionary. And he had not even chosen one of the sturdy reputable orders. He joined a society no one ever heard of, a society which did not boast a single canonized saint.

So Father Tom was a priest of the Our Lady of Mercy Society for Foreign Missions from Canville, called "Mercy" for short. For the twenty-one years that Tom was in Africa, James and Annie McNamara sent him cash, clothes, books and prayers. They spoke of him as a soldier of God in the terrors of the jungle, though his mission was in the grasslands. They drew a picture of him in the tradition of De Foucauld, saintly, ascetic, enduring tremendous hardships in the odor of holiness. When he was sent home to the United States as chief fund-raiser, vocation-attractor and publicity man for Mercy, rattling around the country in a Chevy, Annie and James found it difficult to glamorize him in any way. James considered his younger brother a cross to be borne with apologetic good humor.

Father Tom discovered Chris and Jane as people instead of relatives about five years after their marriage, when they bought the house in Rockhill. He had blown in out of a rainstorm one night, and slept on their living-room sofa. In the morning he had repaired Jane's toaster plug, taught the children a few words of Swahili and left, a tacit new part of their lives. They grew used to his appearing without warning, bringing them a bottle of wine, perhaps, or four fellow priests for dinner, or a sermon on the evils of not disciplining children, and a limerick composed for any occasion. The only sure thing about his arrivals was that they coincided with times of family tension or emergency.

"We didn't even hear from you when Teresa was born," said Jane now. "You haven't even seemed to notice she was born. Expected in November, remember? Born a little early. Thirteen weeks today."

"Oh," said Father Tom, "I am sorry. I did hear. I offered Mass for you. I was showing my film on 'Children in Africa' to a school in Minneapolis that day. I offered my Mass for you and the child. And I am here now. Teresa. A girl?"

"Of course."

"She is well and beautiful? And Chris, how's he?"

"She's fine. He's working hard at the office and on his magazine column. I was sick after the baby. He had to do a lot of babysitting. He's tired. So am I." She held out a pack of cigarettes. "I'm not used to being sick. Christmas seemed to come and go without me."

"You are well now, though? You look well."

"Right now I'm too busy being glad you're here. I've got cabin fever from staying in with the chicken pox and the new baby, and I'm getting ready for a party. We got gypped out of our Christmas party this year so I'm having one quick before Lent. You're staying for dinner?"

"I'm spending a week here, I think."

"Then you'll be here for the party."

"Mm. How's everyone else, by the way? Gloria, still pretty as ever?"

"Pretty unbearable. She wants to go to Africa. She's impressing Mama no end—she's very glamorous. And depressing me."

He stood up. "I'm going to unpack my crate. And I would suggest that at this party of yours we can offer a few artifacts for sale. Unobtrusively. Helpfully. People may want to buy gifts for birthdays. Or Easter? You have a party, I use the gathering as a chance to beg a little and to speak of Mercy in an informal jovial way, and my staying here a week is justified by a wise and kind Providence."

He paused with pocket screwdriver and pliers, in the laundry-room doorway, stooping necessarily but formally from the hips. His giant head loomed at Jane over the stove as she tried to think how to stretch a pound of fish to feed him as well as themselves.

"By the way," he said, "as far as I know I've never had chicken pox."

THIRTEEN

"Are you busy, Chris?"

Krena poked her head around the door. She wore a soft suit of sea green.

"Never too busy for you."

"Gallant, yet." She had, he decided, a very sweet voice. "Have you read the chapters I gave you?"

"Oh. Yes. I was going to write you a memo about them."

"You don't like them."

"There are a few things . . ." He leaned back in his chair, reaching for the manuscript from a disorderly pile on the bookcase.

"You don't like the whole idea of the book?"

"I think it could be great."

"Do you? I'm glad. Then you'll help me with it."

"I will, if you want. But I don't see why you're looking to me. It's been a couple of years since I handled any fiction, you know. And I don't really think you need help. I never knew Krena Mc-Dowell to lack faith in herself."

"Maybe you don't know Krena McDowell very well," she said, eyes twinkling. "I've got stage fright. But seriously, Chris, it's all rigged against you. As long as you're willing and interested. R. P. himself said you're the natural one to steer me. He thinks you're pretty clever."

"I'm impressed." He smiled wryly.

"But he does. He thinks you're just marking time in this department. Said he expects great things of you."

He winked. "Don't take him seriously."

"And he said—here comes the part I like best—since your work-load was light, he'd like to see us work on this together. You can't argue with R. P."

"Guess not." He put down the manuscript and lit a cigarette. "Actually, I like the idea."

"Good."

"This is a pretty ambitious idea your author has, trying to write a love story with a ghost and have it taken seriously. It almost works."

"Almost. And I'm scared to tamper with it alone."

"Okay. I'll worry about the construction. You're the woman, so you can be the expert on the love story."

"Or at least on what women want to read as a love story," she said.

The muffled thud of typewriters on either side of his cubicle reached in and assailed his ears. He wondered if it were a chance trick of the light that suggested loneliness in her face. Then she stood up.

"How shall we work? Do you want to write a critique of the pages you have?"

He noticed what a little woman she was, small-boned, supple. Her smooth brown hair shone over her young face.

"No memos," he said. "We can talk on the train tonight perhaps. You do take the same train I do."

"If you want. Funny. Here we've taken the same train for years and never sat in the same car."

"I'm a lousy memo writer."

"All right. The five-thirteen."

By the time the conductor called Greenwich, they had agreed on the need to tighten the first three chapters and introduce more touches of flat realism.

"To reassure the reader. You have to get the story grounded before you can take off for the unknown. Am I right?"

"Right," said Chris. "You know what you're doing."

"I'll work on these first chapters tonight and show them to you tomorrow."

The train swung around a curve, and a man Chris knew, Hugh Carpel, lurched into Chris's shoulder. Greeting him, Chris thought of introducing Krena, but it seemed awkward, and Hugh went on to the next car.

"Bet he wonders what I'm doing riding with such an attractive gal." Chris grinned.

"Thank you."

"Hey, did you say you were working on this book tonight? There's not that much rush."

"Might as well. I'll be all alone again. I like to keep busy when I'm alone."

"I wonder how it feels to be all alone." He laughed. "I could stand a little bit of it. But there's always the thunder of little feet."

"You don't know how lucky you are."

"Rockhill!" The conductor called. "Rockhill. Jordan next."

Chris swung down the steps into the windy night.

He was glad Krena'd be coming to the party. He'd ask Jane to go out of her way to be nice to her. Jane would understand when he told her how lonely Krena was. Jane? He hadn't thought of Jane all the way home, he realized with surprise. He hadn't done anything as he usually did, not read, not made a note for his column. His routine was broken because of Krena.

Probably good for me, he decided. I'm not old enough to get in a rut. Even the thought of having to go to choir tonight, and that meeting of the Men's Sodality, suddenly seemed oppressingly routine.

The wind tested the house all evening, exploring the vent of the kitchen exhaust fan, whipping the wire from the television aerial to mysterious rappings. The fire crackled and moaned as the invader haunted the chimney. It had been a night for apples and popcorn, stories and half-charred, half-melted marshmallows. Chris hurried off after dinner to choir with a brief stop at the Men's Sodality. He returned at ten-thirty, stiff-cheeked and frozen. Jane and Father Tom were watching television.

"Why don't you take a good hot tub while I make the cocoa?" asked Jane with concern.

"I don't like 'good hot tubs,' " said Chris. "I can't stand people who want me to take 'good hot tubs.' I'll take a *bath* when I'm very dirty, or better a shower. But I am not dirty. I am cold. I'm going up and get into my pajamas and then if it's not too much to ask I want the cocoa."

"Yes, sir." Jane smiled. "And, when you come down, bring me my slippers too, will you, honey?"

"My name is not 'honey.' I've told you a hundred times that I do not like the name 'honey.' It sounds like the ten-cent store."

Over his cocoa he smiled. "I had a fight with Father Macy tonight," he said. "The idiot doesn't read, you know, and he can't stand anyone who does."

Jane, busy sewing Father Tom's jacket, nodded. "What did he say this time?"

"He intends to sell the rest of those darn rosaries during Lent. You cannot sell rosaries with Lourdes water in them, I told him again. It's a small thing, but the principle is important. Lourdes water is a holy water which cannot be sold. It's given away at the shrine. It's sort of simony, I said to him, to sell a rosary with Lourdes water in it, and besides it's in lousy taste, and also expressly forbidden. Father Macy never even saw the Marist Fathers' statement against it, and doesn't care. Why, these money-hungry peddlers take a ten-cent plastic rosary, stick a drop of Lourdes water in it, and sell it for two-fifty as if it were magic."

"They were selling very well," said Jane, imitating Father Macy's smug singsong. "What could be better than a drop of Lourdes water in every blessed bead?"

Chris didn't laugh. "I'll tell you what would be better. A drop of good taste. And a drop of common sense and humility in the parish clergy."

Father Tom, having drained his cocoa, was staring into the embers of the fire:

> "Mary, Mary, quite contrary—" he began.
> "How does your rosary go?
>   With—uh—pink plastic shells,
>   And Lourdes water—it sells!
> In church bazaars all in a row!"

" 'Tis a sad poem," said Chris, and he smiled.

"It is," said Father Tom.

Jane put away the mended jacket, and set about her nightly chores. She fixed the coffee pot for morning, packed sandwiches for three school lunch boxes, put crackers in a paper bag for Kilian's kindergarten snack, polished his shoes, and turned down the thermostat. When she came back to the living-room, the two men were trying to decide why Midwestern parishes were so far ahead of Eastern ones in all that really mattered, such as the dialogue Mass. She sat beside Chris and put her hand on his.

"They've made me head of the new convent drive," he said. "Father Macy told me tonight."

"That's why you were so angry about the beads?" asked Father Tom.

Jane smiled. The same question had been on her tongue.

"Yes," Chris said ruefully.

He took Jane's chin in his long thin fingers and looked at her. She could almost see the misery in him that had nothing to do with convent drives or rosaries or anything she knew of that had happened that day.

"What's wrong?" she asked.

He grinned, and let his hands drop from her face.

"Just clowning around," he said. "I don't want to run a fund drive. I don't want to do anything but look at you. But—I have to go to sleep. There's the sad part." He stood up and stretched. "It's little things like that get a fellow down."

Father Tom looked at them and then back at the fire.

Later, alone in their room, with the sound of breathing coming from all the smaller bedrooms around them, they lay in the dark and she held him until at last he slept.

She thought of the many ways of love, and how little she still knew of it. A few years ago she would have been shocked to think sadness should find its outlet in embrace in bed. Now his nearness and warmth, the smell of him beside her, spoke of the need they had of each other, the need of love. And it was denied. She had been glad. She was no longer glad. She felt confused, sad.

She had gone into romance determined to remember that men are men, adult, with dignity, and that she was a woman, putting away girlish pretense. Lying now in darkness, she remembered how often in the first years of marriage the discovery that Chris was not all grownup in all ways had frightened and angered her. She had felt betrayed when he lost his temper over a petty slight, or came home with feelings hurt by a remark, or gave in to despair. She had wanted to cry when he came up with wild plans for building a stable and opening a burro farm. That he should turn to her in those moments of boyishness and uncertainty had puzzled her at first. But later she gloried in the thought that she could help him—or at least that he thought she could.

It seemed right and holy that two who were parents should want to cling together now like children, lonesome and afraid. And unholy that he did not claim her as his wife.

FOURTEEN

Jane began again to go to daily Mass. For two years now only illness and childbirth had kept her from daily Communion. She had weathered fits of fervor, of self-consciousness, smugness, doubt and apathy. She had learned to compromise with morning rush. Because a mother's duty to her children comes first, she was generally late for Mass, but she had learned that even when necessarily skimped and rushed that morning devotion altered her entire day. She reached the point where, in all simplicity, without morning Communion she felt incomplete. The birth of Teresa and the chicken-pox siege had kept her home till today.

Once Bertha Rains had said she thought it might be wrong for Jane to go dashing breathlessly to the altar rail every morning. Bertha was the organist, and so she was always there, and always on time.

"After all," Bertha said earnestly, "you do—I hate to say this, but I feel I should—you do sort of take it for granted. I mean, Jane, it's gotten to be just a habit, hasn't it? Devotion shouldn't become a habit, like brushing your teeth. I myself never go to Communion because I couldn't keep my mind on God and play the organ at the same time. It's a great sacrifice for me."

Bertha had been sincere. Her eyes had filled with tears. What she said disturbed Jane. There were so many people in the Church who disapproved of her informality with God.

When she had asked Father Mongiano in confession, he chuckled through the grille.

"Oh grand," he said. "The devil is clever! He loves to call white black, doesn't he? But listen. If you have a habit of doing something bad, it is a bad thing, a vice. You can see that. You wouldn't refuse the blame if you made a habit of tripping old ladies? Well, you would be silly to refuse the credit for being good just because you may have made it a habit!"

He laughed again into his fist, as if coughing. "Of course, you must prepare as well as possible, exercise the best attention you can, dispose yourself, all this. But I am sure you do your best. Just don't let yourself get talked out of coming. We spend all our lives trying to acquire a good habit and when we do finally acquire one, then the devil tries to make us ashamed. Don't worry about being informal with God. Just love him."

This morning Jane slipped into her pew with the same fine crisp feeling one gets from having had a good shower, clean clothes, and a return to normal life after the exile of illness. She was on time, well disposed, and peaceful.

The twenty or so regulars each had a favorite pew, tacitly ceded him by the others. Jane's was on the left in a corner from which she could see the main altar and the two side altars of the Blessed Mother and St. Rose of Lima at the same time.

Her children, lunchboxes and schoolbags clattering, knelt beside her breathless from the chill of a surprise snowstorm. Over on the right was the pew full of Sullivans. Ahead of them, back rigid under a Broadway tailor's polo coat knelt the man Jane always thought of as the Bookie. She ticked off the other regulars. The two nurses were up front, the young man from the bank was on the right and old Mrs. Kczuck, with her pile of novena prayers and special devotions, was in the back. The old man who coughed, the plumber and his wife, the architect, the checkout girl from the supermarket, all were in their usual places.

Directly in front of Jane, Martha Settler knelt straight-backed in her neat tweed coat and matching hat. Even her Missal ribbons were precisely placed in fanning diagonals among the gold-edged pages. Looking at her, Jane couldn't help wondering how it was that such a crisp, orderly person as Martha should have a crazy sister. Well, not really crazy. But Betsy Butler was mentally ill. Did Martha mind, did it humiliate her to have her sister in and out of Newtown, was it hard for her to take Betsy in to live with her now that she was an out-patient at the clinic? Poor Martha, hard-working, admirable Martha, who yearned for babies, saddled with a sister who needed electric-shock treatments. Compassion for Martha, and for Martha's sister, tore through Jane as she opened her own shabby Missal. She resolved to have no part of the cruel gossip that had greeted Betsy Butler's arrival in the parish.

Up front, conspicuous by their more formal clothes, were the people for whose intention the Mass was offered, the ones who had given the stipend and had their names announced in the bulletin. They looked uncomfortable, Jane thought, clustered together in a pew, looking back over their shoulders wondering why the others whom they did not know were at their Mass.

56

Jane bowed her head, recollected herself, offered a prayer for them, and placed herself in the presence of God.

Father Tom had gone off alone to the friary to offer Mass. He preferred the small chapel.

Once Jane had said to Tory that she found her life priest-ridden and loved it. As a child she had always heard that stock phrase "priest-ridden" used to describe poor Catholics. Now she thought it delightful to call herself priest-ridden. The joke was lost on Tory. Born Catholics are sensitive to such phrases, Jane thought.

Father Tom. Father Juniper at the friary. Father Mongiano and Father Macy and Father Temple in the parish. Five priests were part of Chris and Jane's lives, people they loved and were annoyed by as one loves and is annoyed by relatives. Yet they were different, in a class apart, these men with irrevocably blessed hands. And when Father Tom blew in and out of their home as the Spirit wished, it was a personal and glorious and exasperating thing.

Had there been time, Jane would have gone to Tom's Mass at the friary. But Father Juniper might be there, and since time meant less than dust to Juniper, she couldn't have gotten home in time to let Chris go to work.

Surprisingly, it occurred to Jane now, kneeling in St. Rose's, that if she went to see Juniper he would help her. In the modern suburban Church, monasteries seemed to harbor the only real source of spiritual direction. Instinctively, she felt drawn to Juniper, in spite of her dislike of him. He could tell her what to do, she thought.

And then she thought: This is nonsense. How can he tell me what to do when I have no problem? If I have a problem I don't know it well enough to put a name to it. Even a saint, if he is a saint, cannot solve a problem that doesn't exist. There's nothing at all bothering me.

She made Luke stop shouldering Kilian off balance, and resolved to concentrate on the Mass.

The Host was raised in the pastor's gnarled hands.

As Jane went to the altar rail she was without a word of prayer. There was only silence, and a yearning she might have called thirst within her soul.

The rest of the morning seemed ordinary enough, yet she found herself in a sour mood. She polished silver and briefed Father Tom on the guests who were coming to the party. Little Meg was building gaudy towers of canned goods from the bottom cupboards. Teresa, in her basket, gurgled with an elusive indigestion smile. Mary was in bed, preparing to get chicken pox. Everything conspired to annoy Jane.

She was annoyed that Father Tom was there to be talked to, annoyed that he was going to be at her party, annoyed with herself for resenting him.

"There's Mike and Lidwina O'Shea from next door. You've met them."

"He's the politician. And she's the glamour girl," Father Tom nodded. "She says I'm cute."

"And the Carpels. You don't know them, but they're nice enough. Rich and fancy. Marianne's the most cultivated woman I've ever known. Walks like a grand duchess, and talks like one, too. Hugh doesn't seem quite as born to the manor as she does, but he more than makes up for it in his costumes. He has a conglomeration of hats that he wears as if they had a sacred significance, gets himself up like a country squire to walk around in his own garden. Plays a fine game of golf, so they tell me."

"And you like them? You make them sound like a couple of worldly snobs."

"Yes, I like them," Jane said, thinking that she didn't really like them as much as all that. "They're regular about getting to Mass Sundays, which is more than you can say for some other Catholic families who've made good. Oh, I admit they're different. But it's a nice difference, maybe."

He laughed gently, his chins shaking. "Jane, you're not the type to play up to fancy folk."

As he spoke she was thinking: What would you say, Father Tom, if I told you I'm tired of being the type you think I am, that I feel far away from you, that this minute I no longer even like having you around? Suppose I told you that all the time we're sitting here talking I've been thinking about the marriage bed, hmm? You don't know my type. I don't myself. . . .

She bit her lip and went on. "Felicity and Harold Lawrence are coming. She's the League of Women Voters and he sells paper boxes. I mean in a big way, the Lawrence Box Company. Felicity's a real beauty, but her taste is so severe you hardly notice. Wears her hair tied back in a bun like an old-maid schoolteacher. I like her. She's quiet and intelligent. Serene. And Harold has been playing chess with Father Temple for years. They're demons at it.

Felicity and Harold are good Episcopalians, always have been. But Harold's dad gave the land to help build the first St. Rose's, way back, and they're great Christians.

"Poor Father Temple, I think he'd die happy if he could just get Harold into the Church. Father thinks Harold is the compleat man —and I must say I don't blame him. With a wolfskin around his shoulders, he'd make a grand John the Baptist—virile, wise, passionate." Jane heard with horror that her voice had trembled on the word passionate. Had Father Tom noticed?

But Father Tom had given up following the intricacies of who was who and let himself drift with Jane's voice. He was making faces at the baby.

"You're making a big thing of this party," he said. "It means a lot to you."

"I like people."

"I see. Does Chris like parties?"

"I think so. Besides it's good for a man to get his mind off serious things once in a while. Or to fill up all those gaps of time when he has nothing to do but think."

"I thought marriage was a merry-go-round where you kept looking for a chance to be alone together and be quiet. Or have you forgotten how to relax?"

"One party. Tom, you're making a big deal out of it. It's not like you to be a puritan and antiparty."

"Nor is it like you to chatter endlessly about people and a lot of unimportant stuff about them."

"Sorry. But what shall we talk about? I don't feel very spiritual. And I have no problems to offer you."

"Score one for you. I'm putting the old foot in the old mouth again." He studied her and decided not to ask what lay behind her smile. "I have a problem. I need *your* advice."

"Your secretary?"

"Precisely. Miss Oswald is very angry with me because I am not well organized and I won't let her organize me. She is angry because I did not tell her where I was going last week and when I came back to the office I did not tell her where I had been, either. I didn't ask her advice before I went to call on those movie people for money, and I think she's hurt because I got some money without her help. She is angry because she painted my office for me while I was away with her own two hands. It is a mushroom color. I did not notice it when I came home. Who, I ask you, would want to notice mushroom paint? Now her feelings are insulted. What can I do?"

"She sounds more like a wife than a secretary."

"But I do not want a wife, thank God."

"Nor she a husband like you, probably. It's just the nature of the beast. After all, men and women are men and women."

"A profound remark."

"It is." Jane warmed Teresa's bottle and began putting away cans. "A lot of people think there isn't any difference worth mentioning, you know. Gloria claims there's nothing more than a minor anatomical difference between men and women. Some of her sociology professors say there's no female way of thinking or feeling, or a male one. It's all a matter of culture and habit and the way you're raised. Gloria thinks sex is just some sort of an itch."

Father Tom closed his eyes. "I do not know how to handle Miss Oswald," he said.

Hulk that he was, he seemed forlorn, and in spite of her mood she did love him. She thought it strange that a secretary could so upset him.

"She probably doesn't know how to handle herself," she said. "Most of us females don't."

"The women of today are not what women used to be. They are not proud of being women."

"I'm awfully tired of hearing that."

"But it's true. They are not happy. You are not happy, Jane. You're a remarkable woman, but are you happy? You have a new baby. Does she delight you? Do you feel blessed beyond measure because you have six children and a fine husband to share your vocation? No, that is too simple for you. All the time you're looking to make life difficult for yourself. All women today do that. Just relax. And love."

"And everything will be peachy-creamy."

The need to be irritating was pushing up in her like a bundle of old bedsprings. "I'm a little tired of being the zealous Catholic wife and mother."

Father Tom cleared his throat.

"There once was a girl named Jane,
Who made it perfectly plain . . ."

He paused, considering.

"Not another limerick. Don't tease me."

"I'm not teasing. I would like to help you." He stood up. "But now I'm going to say my Office in the living room and let you be."

He chucked Teresa under the chin, and looked over his shoulder. "You don't know how good it is to be able to come into a home where there is a baby, and children, and love. A place where I know that people I love are really living the life of grace."

Before she could speak, he had left the room.

FIFTEEN

A fire in the fireplace. The hi-fi playing Leroy Anderson gently in the background. Punch bowl, Vienna sausages in a chafing dish, polished silver, clean ashtrays. Her hostess gown rustled. It had been her Christmas present to herself, mail-ordered from Fifth Avenue, wine-red badge of elegance.

Her children were in bed, and she felt a heady Cinderella magic as she moved delicately through living room and dining room, the same rooms in which she had sweated and bustled and yelled all day. She adjusted potato chips around the cheese dip, moved a coaster to hide Luke's hammer marks on the pine end table. This, she whispered to herself, is how it should be all the time. The picture seemed to be taking shape. The gangly tomboy from Concord, the pale teen-ager in the tan uniform at Westover School, the flustered bride in that New York housing project, the over-zealous Catholic mother, are giving way to a new Jane.

She stopped, her hand resting on a shining silver cigarette box. A country house, a place in the community where Chris heads a convent drive and I am a woman among women, and there is an end to pregnancies. I like it. Our marriage has matured, she thought. We lived through the days of passion and of danger and of callousness. We have found the way into adulthood. St. Paul said it was better to marry than to burn, yes, but better yet to marry and outgrow passion and come to a plateau of peace. I shall perhaps never again make love. I have outgrown it. It is forbidden me.

She lit a cigarette, snapped the match in half, and put it in a kitchen ashtray.

Perhaps that is why tonight for the first time in my life I feel like a woman in a gracious-living feature, she thought. Because I am not disturbed by that any more. I am unhampered by the clamor of my body or his.

Chris was poking at the fire with his new All-Purpose Handee Firetool and the fire had fallen apart. He did not like building fires in warm houses, but a fire was part of the *mise en scène* Jane demanded for a party. He did not like parties, either. He'd prefer a long evening with two, maybe four people, and some real talk, any time.

He got up from the fire. "Jane? I didn't get to tell you what R. P. said about that new line of science books for children I suggested."

"No, you didn't." She went to turn a lampshade so its seam was to the wall.

"You know he told Krena the other day that he had his eye on me." He raised his eyebrows. Jane wasn't listening. He should have known better. She liked shoptalk sometimes, but the thirty minutes after the scheduled beginning of a party, the thirty minutes when no one comes, was not such a time. There might be nothing left to do, it might be perfectly quiet, but one did not talk seriously to Jane then or one got his ears snapped off. This was part of his small store of husbandly wisdom. He smiled and said, "Jane, you look lovely."

She turned toward him instantly.

"Beautiful," he said.

"Thank you, darling. Chris, do you think we could manage to get through the evening without the party's turning into another seminar on liturgy? Tonight I want no religion at all. Just fun."

"I won't let anyone say a word. Come here and give me a kiss."

"Oh Chris, not now?" She gave him a little kiss on the cheek. He held her shoulders, tipped her head sideways, and took a satisfactory kiss. She caught his hand and disengaged herself.

"Chris, listen. Stop and listen, please? There. Why do you suppose the Carpels are coming? They never come to one of our parties."

"They're coming because you asked them. And why you asked them is beyond me."

"I like them, silly. I'd like to see more of them, maybe. Anyway, Marianne knows Krena, and it'll be someone for her to talk to. They're her kind, aren't they?"

"No, they're snobs." He pulled her toward him again, rubbing his cheek on hers, nuzzling her neck. "Oh, you're nice. We're all alone, the house is full of romantic music, and you want to waste precious time talking about other people?"

She yielded to him, but there was a discreet humming in the kitchen. Chris sighed and let his wife go. Even though Father Tom was a relative, even though married sex was a good and holy thing, a man couldn't make even living-room love to his wife with a Roman collar around.

"I apologize," said Father Tom, his huge head cast down in mock servility. "But I cannot stay in the laundry room forever. I have completed the display of statues. It looks very nice."

"We were just talking about the people who are coming."

"Uh-huh," said Father Tom gravely. He lowered himself with a grimace into the blue armchair. "I feel very strange tonight. My heart is filled with sorrow. And it is as if the pain of my heart had found a home in my skin."

"You have a pain?" Jane asked with concern.

"To tell the truth my skin hurts like the devil. I think I'm getting sick. But perhaps it's all in the mind. World-sickness. I cannot get used to the pagan ways of this Christian land of ours." He leaned back gingerly and closed his eyes. "I am homesick for the missions. Life is so much simpler there, both in love of man for woman, and of man and woman for God."

"We'll try and raise some money for your missions in the midst of our pagan revels." Chris laughed. "But don't get *Weltschmerz,* Tom. It'll make Jane nervous."

"You're always the life of the party," she said. "I'm counting on you."

"Forgive me. I have a limerick for an apology. It goes like this:

"I should have to be mean as Fagin
To imply your party was pagan . . ."

To Jane's relief the doorbell rang.

Pagans, indeed. Her friends were definitely not pagans. They were the typical stock of a modern suburban parish, people of different backgrounds and personalities, conservatives and liberals, do-it-yourselfers and intellectuals, successes and failures, who automatically and contentedly found their friendships through the Church. Though not one consciously decided to choose only Catholics for friends, they did lead almost insularly Catholic lives, and most of them were glad of it.

Of course, Jane admitted as she opened the door for Hugh and Marianne Carpel, there were exceptions. The Carpels refused to accept this pattern, and were truthfully a little ashamed of the way Catholics cling together. They disliked all open signs of difference between themselves and other faiths. They wanted to prove to other members of the Rockhill Golf Club that Catholics were not odd. They found the going hard.

"How are you, Marianne." Jane kissed her. "You look lovely!"

"Jane, how charming to see you," Marianne replied with conscious grace. Hugh helped her out of her coat, then looked about helplessly as if seeking the butler.

"I'll take them," Jane said, and felt vaguely embarrassed as she did so. Hugh, she was startled to notice, wore under his suit jacket a white silk scarf knotted into an ascot. I'd be used to these things if I saw Hugh and Marianne more often, she told herself firmly as Chris collected the Carpels and led them into the living room.

Elmo and Agnes Milder came quietly in the Carpels' wake. They did not look as if they expected to enjoy the evening. But then, thought Jane, they did not particularly enjoy anything.

"You look tired, Agnes," she said in gay reproach.

"Oh, you know how it is." Agnes let Elmo help her out of her jacket as if it were too much for her to handle. "Just a little run down. Those headaches."

Elmo Milder, Chris often said, ought to have been named not Milder but Mildest. Small, thin, he always seemed a little apologetic in company. He was meek, eager to please, and thoroughly inoffensive. A pity, Jane reflected, that Agnes did not share the same qualities. For Agnes, when she was not wholly absorbed in self-pity, had a sharp nose for other people's business, and an even sharper tongue. Her voice, a high nasal whine, was an instrument that seemed perfectly attuned by the devil for gossip.

If some of our real friends don't show up soon, Jane thought ruefully, ushering the Milders into the living room, Father Tom will stop thinking we're a pagan lot and begin knowing we are. When the next ring of the doorbell proved to be the Sullivans, she felt a rush of affection toward them.

Bart Sullivan supported his wife and seven children on the income of a garage mechanic, and did so without apparent difficulty and without complaint. He was a handsome, quiet-spoken man, and Jane liked him wholeheartedly. Clare's pale, girlish face, sweetly framed with black curls, seemed to glow as it always did when she

64

was pregnant. Proudly Jane introduced the Sullivans to Father Tom.

"All Sullivan children are named for the Blessed Mother, Father," Jane said. "She has Mary Clare, and Mary Catherine and Mary Therese, Bartholomew Marius, Joseph Marius, John Marius, and Peter Marius. All but the first born by Caesarean." There. Let him call them pagan, Jane thought, turning back to the door.

Al and Tory Burke arrived and, conscious of their duties as best friends, immediately and unobtrusively took a hand in the work. Al stationed himself by the punch bowl, where he could serve other guests and make sure the supply didn't run out. Tory hurried into the kitchen to deposit the giant coffee urn she always brought over for Jane's parties, then returned to the living room to pass hors d'oeuvres.

The doorbell kept ringing and the room filled with laughter and smoke. When the O'Sheas arrived, Mike burst into the living-room and began genially shaking hands all around.

"Relax," Bart Sullivan said to him quietly. "I'll vote for you."

Everyone laughed and Mike, throwing his head back so that his thick neck strained his collar button, laughed loudest of all. Lidwina, who had followed him into the room, seemed to ignore his performance as she greeted her friends with her usual vivacious charm.

Watching them, Jane reflected for the thousandth time what an odd couple they made. Mike was, as his forbears would have put it, a fine figure of a man, but he surely didn't seem Lidwina's type. The more discreetly his suits were tailored, the rougher and louder he seemed, while Lidwina without apparent effort achieved the highest of high fashion. She wore tonight a felt skirt ablaze with a sequined rose. Charming, but not pagan. And she was good at a party. Tiny-waisted, sparkling, she still contrived to make even other women believe they were enjoying themselves.

Lidwina kissed Chris on the cheek, told Father Tom she hoped to collect his limericks for posterity, and when the Newmans came she greeted Christine with such enthusiasm and gaiety that Christine forgot all about the ugly triangular tear she'd made in her skirt getting out of the car, and joined the group around the fireplace with pleasant self-confidence.

The Settlers came with their quiet smiles. Martha, her speckled hair cut in a shingle, and Bede, fat, florid, and improbably ascetic, were characters in any language. Martha was intelligent and earnest,

65

a super-liturgical woman—what Jane in crosser moments called a catacomb Catholic. Martha outdistanced all apostolic enthusiasts. She cooked liturgically, with special recipes for saints' days. She dressed liturgically. Even Bede teased her about it, but she took it with good grace. She didn't mind laughing at herself at all.

"Father Tom, I want you to meet these people," Jane said. "They're very special."

"I like women in red!" he said, bending down to take Martha's hand.

"It's the feast of St. Timothy," said Martha.

"And how do you do," said Father Tom.

"What Martha means is that she's wearing red because church vestments on the feasts of martyrs are red."

"Is that so?" said Father Tom. "Remarkable."

"I like to remind people that we are all temples of the Holy Spirit," said Martha.

"But you'd really be interested in Bede," said Lidwina, coming to offer Father a cup of punch. "He's wonderful."

"Oh?" Father Tom refused the punch.

"Bede's a man who actually did what all those Christopher pamphlets are always urging people to do. He gave up—everything! He had a high-paid job as a management consultant, and searched his conscience and decided it was more meddling than constructive. Isn't that something? So he became a teacher." She put her arm through Bede's and his red face turned redder.

The punch bowl was filled for the second time and still people came: the Rottignis, the Rainses, who reported their cellar flooded by detergents seeping back from the dry well, the O'Donnells and the McDonnells. Harold and Felicity Lawrence, who, said they just stopped in for a minute, were staying to talk about racing cars with Bart Sullivan.

"It's a great night, Chris, old man," said Al, bracing him in the hall. "Now we'll lock the doors, and shake 'em down for good old Father Tom, eh?"

"You're doing a professional job tending bar, Al."

"For you, pal!"

Jane hurried into the kitchen for the cheese dip. "Seems like it's going well, Tory. What would we ever do without you and Al at a party?"

Tory was setting up the coffee urn. "Works both ways, and you know it," she said. "Isn't Martha's red dress a lulu?"

66

They could hear Lidwina's laugh rising over the gabble.

"Lidwina's in rare form tonight," said Jane.

"And if you ask me she and Mike had a fight before they came."

"Think so?" Jane piled potato chips in a big basket. "Say, is Father Tom still in the laundry-room? How're we going to get people out there?"

"Al's handling it. Leave it to him. He'll make sure Father does a land-office business."

At nine-thirty Krena McDowell arrived, neat and tidy in a black suit with a white jacket.

Jane hurried to greet her. "Krena, I'd given up on you. So glad you came."

"I'm so glad you asked me! You look stunning. And what a wonderful party. I'm sorry George couldn't come, but he's away, you know. And I'm late. Because that stupid taxi man couldn't find your house."

Jane looked into Krena's face. She saw only warmth and gaiety in the bright brown eyes, and found herself smiling back. With a flourish she took Krena's arm and escorted her from one knot of people to another.

She saw each then as Krena would see them, and it was a new way. "Al Burke, our best friend," Jane said, instinctively seeking a phrase to dress up Al's job. "He's a research chemist for the soft drink company."

Al ran his hand over his hair. "I run the bottling plant here in Rockhill."

Jane led Krena on to a circle of men focused on Lidwina. Bart Sullivan, well-spoken and handsome enough, but he would never fit in Krena's life in Jordan. What car repairman would? Patsy Rottigni, of the bar and grille. Benny Scrivener, the most dedicated dentist in town. Julian Newman . . .

"Oh, I know who you are," said Krena gravely. "My decorator told me all about you. Remember that pair of Boston bookstacks?" Julian looked bewildered. "They're perfect. I have them flanking my sofa, with a wooden eagle between. It looks divine." She turned to Jane. "This wonderful man rescued my whole decorating scheme. I'm surprised—and delighted—to meet you here!"

As Krena talked, Julian realized she had mistaken him for the proprietor of Newman's Carpenter Shop in Rockhill. He was, in fact, comptroller of one of New York's smaller banks, but Julian was the strong silent type who would never embarrass a lady. "I'm glad you like them," he told her soberly.

"Jane," Krena said, as they moved on, "you know the most wonderful assortment of people. What a genius you are to find them and blend them. That girl Lidwina is lovely, isn't she?"

"Krena McDowell—how marvelous to see you!" Marianne Carpel cried, and swept across the room to intercept them. "A wonderful party, my dear," she said graciously to Jane. "I'm enjoying myself immensely. And you've lost weight since I saw you last. You look very stylish. Lovely."

Jane resisted the urge to remind Marianne that she had also delivered a baby since their last meeting. But Marianne was absorbed with Krena.

Jane had never been this silent during an evening. Usually she was so intoxicated with ideas and debate that she let the party run itself. But tonight nothing was usual. She felt detached, supervisory, a hostess who planned and set things in motion, but was herself a spectator. In this mood, she found everything strangely vivid. It was as if her living room were a stage on which her friends were the actors, portraying themselves. She, the audience, observed, understood, remained aloof.

Chris caught her eye. They exchanged winks of self-congratulation. It was a good party.

Benny Scrivener had started a circle of book talk over by the fireplace. He was arguing about *The Cypresses Believe in God*, and Harold Lawrence seemed delighted to find that his dentist had a literary bent. And Martha Settler in her red dress was earnestly telling Christine Newman about her efforts to bring an appreciation of liturgy into her volunteer work in the hospital, and how difficult it was to impress on the less educated patients the full meaning of the sacraments. Christine was trying hard to look interested, but she was miserable. That tear in her skirt had caught Agnes Milder's eye, and Agnes had told Clare in an aside Christine could not help overhearing that if Christine had any respect for Jane she'd manage to look presentable for her party. Christine could feel herself still blushing. Blindly she tried to listen to Martha. At least, she knew, Clare wasn't the type to take Agnes seriously.

Already Clare had drawn away from Agnes. At that moment, she was confiding to her husband the terrible mistake she herself had made. "Bart, I told Hugh Carpel I had a bad sore throat myself just last week. And I said I hoped he'd be feeling better soon. And he gave me such an odd look. But I didn't realize that scarf was supposed to look distinguished until Lidwina, who overheard me, told me later. He must think I'm awful!"

And Bart thought it a great joke and repeated it to Al Burke. And since Al had already taken an unusual amount of kidding about his rapidly disappearing hair this evening, he was glad enough to get a laugh out of someone else's discomfiture—so he repeated the story to Mike O'Shea. Mike was getting a little drunk, and Mike laughed so loud that everyone stopped talking to look at him. Both Bart and Al told Clare it served Hugh right for putting on airs and Clare was somewhat reassured. But she couldn't help worrying about Hugh's feelings, and she hoped he didn't know what they were all laughing about.

Over by the potato chips Agnes Milder was telling Angela Rottigni in her whining voice that Lidwina might seem smart but that she really was a wasteful housewife because she deliberately patronized stores that gave trading stamps. Agnes was of the opinion that supermarkets which offered trading stamps were high-priced, hypocritical, and deserved boycott by any intelligent responsible consumer. Angela Rottigni had thought trading stamps a wise investment, and was afraid that Agnes might know that she, too, collected them.

Listening, Jane wondered idly whether she had invited Agnes for Elmo's sake or just out of habit. She looked for Elmo and saw him, looking rather pathetic, in the group of men around Krena. Jane felt suddenly sorry for him, and was glad she had invited the Milders after all.

Ironically, Jane noticed, Lidwina, all unaware of Agnes' estimate of her, was just then agreeing with Felicity that shopping was the supreme challenge to a woman's ingenuity and detective ability as well as her sense of values. Purchasing was, Felicity said, the best test of a homemaker's success.

"After all, why should I buy from Bloomingdale when I can get seconds of the same crystal at the Pottery Corner?" asked Felicity.

Lidwina started to tell of the coffeepot she bought at the discount store for fifteen–ninety-five, ten dollars off list, but she did not mention it because Felicity said first that she had bought her coffeepot at Altman's in New York for fourteen–thirty-nine. It was the same pot.

"You have to know what you're doing," said Lidwina, and went for another cup of punch. Jane noticed that Mike, who had been brooding over a drink in the corner, followed his wife. But a moment later Lidwina came back alone.

The group of men around Krena were talking and nodding and bursting now and then into the kind of laughter which requires a step backward and a lowered head to be expressed. They were coping with the world situation, the chances of the Yankees' winning again in the new year, and performing the strange ritual of producing indirect proofs of their own high standing in the game of business acumen. They had name-dropped the restaurants they had taken clients to, the number of nights they had been away from home on business, the incredibly thankless late hours they had put in, and the names of the newest adhesives, plastics and computers that blazoned across their lives. Lidwina stood beside Hugh Carpel smiling, listening.

Benny Scrivener stopped on the way to the punch bowl to report, "Father Tom's composing a limerick masterpiece just for me. He's all done but the last line:

> 'There once was a dentist named Ben,
> Who was not the nicest of men.
> In a moment of depravity
> He filled the wrong cavity. . . .' "

Krena laughed. "And said: 'Oops, I did it again'?"

Al enticed Lidwina to help him steer pairs of women to inspect Father Tom's wares, selling a grand total of twenty dollars' worth of springboks, two wall masks to Lidwina who said she wanted them for her playroom, and one rosary.

"And we got an extra ten bucks in donations from people who were grateful not to have to buy anything," Al laughed. "You can relax now, Chris, and forget about it." With one arm he hugged Lidwina's shoulders. "We did a good job, didn't we?"

"Can't thank you enough, honestly fella," said Chris. "Sorry I passed the buck to you, but—"

"Father Tom's happy. You're happy. Everyone's happy," said Al. "I had fun," Lidwina said.

Jane spread her rustling skirt to sit by the fire, and watch her party in motion. She saw Chris go to the punch bowl, saw Krena join him there. They were talking privately, laughing. It pleased her to decide that while a lesser woman might fear that under the circumstances Chris should be kept away from all females, and especially from a clever one like Krena, she, being secure and mature, could look at them without a twinge of doubt. She was more concerned over Mike O'Shea who seemed to be getting really drunk.

Father Tom slipped his bulk gracefully and quietly into a seat beside the Settlers.

"Can I get you a drink?" Bede asked. "You've been working hard out there in the laundry-room, Father."

"No drink, thanks." His voice was strained, even harsh.

Jane looked up and said, "We were just talking about—"

"I can guess what you were talking about." Father Tom's lips set rigidly and he closed his eyes.

Tory whispered, "He's sick. I think he's in pain, Jane."

"He certainly isn't his usual smiling self," Jane whispered back. "He's going to ruin the party."

Father Tom's eyes opened. "I won't ruin your party, Jane," he said quietly. "You are all good fine folk. And I shall not be the Ancient Mariner spoiling your fun."

Al plopped himself buoyantly on the floor, grinned up at the priest, and said: "Speak, speak, thou fearful guest. We are gathered at your feet to listen."

Jane laughed. The rest of the room was still running on its own momentum, and Al had rescued the fireplace circle from embarrassment.

Clare raised her pretty curled head and straightened her smock. "We've heard so much about you, Father," she said sweetly. "Jane's always talking about your years in the missions. And how you once killed—some wild animal was it? to protect your orphans. It's wonderful to meet you at last."

His chin was buried in pink-fleshed jowls. He nodded, and for an instant he seemed about to weep. Jane wondered if he might have had too much punch, then remembered he had not had any.

"You are very sweet, my dear," said Father Tom. "You sit there in the innocence of girlhood, not like a mother but a child yourself, and a good child too. You are sincere and you are beautiful. But even you do not begin to know what a world you live in. None of you do. You have not yet grown up."

Jane disentangled her skirt, found her feet and went over to Chris. With an apology to Krena she drew him into the kitchen.

"I don't know what's gotten into Father," she said. "He sounds like he's drunk or crazy."

"He said he didn't feel well." Chris craned to watch the fireplace scene.

"Sick or whatever, you have to get him out of there. You know I love him, but Chris, it isn't fair to everyone . . ."

"No, don't get upset. Father Tom couldn't really ruin anything if he tried. And these aren't strangers you have to impress. They're just people, friends, and they can take care of themselves."

He saw her face. "Okay. So I'll go see if I can break it up."

But it was too late. By the time Chris arrived Tory Burke was saying, "This is about the nicest busiest parish you could want. We may not all be saints. We may not be wandering around in poverty. Is that our fault? I dare say there may be more holiness here than shows on the surface." The white wave in her dark red hair had fallen over her forehead, lending her an air of intensity. "You're not being fair, Father, calling us phonies. Just because God happened to put us in suburbia we shouldn't be blamed for not living the simple life of a mission. And as for our being pagan, and not knowing how to love God, well, really—" She shook her head emphatically to swing her hair back in place.

Small beads of perspiration covered the priest's face. "This is a nice parish, with nice people. Perhaps it is too nice. You are all fine people. Some of you read a lot, like Dr. Scrivener here. And some of you are having fine families, like Mrs. Sullivan here. And you are proud to be very busy trying to be good Catholics. But you are also busy trying to be all the things that will make you fit into the world. Tory, listen. Around us the devil prowls like a lion seeking to devour us. There's a dread battle being waged between heaven and hell, and no one here knows or cares."

"Come on now, Father," said Bart Sullivan lighting his pipe. "We are living this same great battle you're talking about. But in our own way, wouldn't you say?"

Al laughed. "We know we're not saints."

"But you must be. Saints! We need a St. Al of the bottling company, St. Bart of the garage, or a St. Tory of the automatic kitchen. There must be a way to be a saint even in luxury. But I do not envy you. It's easier to be a Christian in Africa than here. Easier almost anywhere than here. The Christ is dying, suffering, thirsting, pleading. And you do not hear him because you are squandering his grace on frivolity."

He flung his gaze up to challenge them.

"Do I scare you because I am not my usual amiable self? Something is wrong with me, I know, and I'm talking now as I often wished to talk and never dared because it is not polite. But *in extremis* even breaks of etiquette are forgiven. And I will say my say. For these good souls have neither a stable nor a cross to guide them."

He stood up. His voice had risen so that the whole room turned to him. Agnes Milder and Patsy Rottigni and Krena stared with frank curiosity. Hugh Carpel, who had been describing how to put a hint of garlic into a martini, snorted and decided the priest was drunk.

The clock on the television chimed twelve. Father Tom waited for it to finish.

"This started as a small discussion," he said, folding his hands behind his back and bending his head. "Suddenly you are all listening. And there is something I want to say to you all.

"I want to tell you I am afraid for you and for me. I am afraid because we have not yet begun to live as God wants us to live, because there is still too much noise, and doing, and getting, and having, for him to breathe in us.

"We have forgotten that we must always be strangers on earth, so homesick for heaven that we do not care where we stand in the world. How can you love the poor Christ, if you are so full of riches that you do not even *know* you are rich?

"Do you know what God asks? He asks self-sacrifice and love. And you—and I, God help me—are caught up in a rat race where we cannot begin to know self-sacrifice or love. God save us."

He flung out his arms to them, a giant with a red perspiring face and swollen eyes.

Jane bit her lip. She dared not look at her guests, or even at Chris. Her cheeks burned. Father Tom's utter earnestness brought tears to her eyes. She wanted to dislike him for what he was doing to her party, wanted to disown him. And she loved him in spite of herself. Loved and admired him, and wanted desperately for him to sit down and be quiet.

"What are you doing?" His voice was very quiet. "Having a good time? A few of you maybe. But you are not being yourselves, you are not being Christ. You are sitting and talking about money— and food and clothes and books. Some of you actually boast that you are poor and simple folk. It is considered bad taste to admit you are well off and elegant. Don't you know poverty—even death —are not the worst things?"

His voice fell to a whisper. "Christ, don't you know that suffering means something?

"If you and I had been Christians in early Rome, would we have died before we offered sacrifice to the idol? I'm not sure. We might have said, for the sake of peace and tolerance, it would do no harm to do the well-adjusted thing.

"We are all offering sacrifice to the world. And the life of grace in us leaks away, and leaves us empty and dead.

"You live in a sacrament as I do. And you have betrayed the sacrament."

Tears shone in his eyes. His giant bullhead turned to stare each face into focus. He looked like a monstrous child at bay. He caught his breath.

"This is inexcusable of me. Some of you think I am drunk. St. Peter on Pentecost defended himself against that charge. It was the Holy Spirit in him. But not in me. I think I have a fever. I am, I think, ill. I love you all." He bowed and smiled wistfully. "Now, forgive me. I am going to try and find a bed."

Al and Chris led him toward the stairs. "I'll call the doctor," Chris said.

"I'll do it," Harold Lawrence said evenly, and turned to Jane. "Where's your phone?"

"In the kitchen," she answered, thinking that it was like Harold to volunteer help automatically, even though he wasn't a close friend. Father Temple is right, she reflected absently, he is a good man.

In the silence Lidwina began softly picking out a melody on the piano. Hugh sat at her side humming. But the party was over.

"I hate to see it end," said Lidwina, lingering over a chord. "I don't want to go home." She looked at Hugh.

The doctor arrived and went briskly upstairs and people began to leave.

"I'm sure everyone understands, dear," Marianne Carpel said to Jane confidentially. "Things do happen, and no one will blame you, though perhaps it is wisest not to have the clergy at parties."

"Except of course he is Chris's uncle," Tory snapped.

Turning away from the Carpels, Jane found Harold and Felicity Lawrence at her elbow.

"Anything more we can do?" Harold asked. They were already in their coats, but Jane knew if she said yes, they would stay to help.

"Nothing, thanks," she said.

Felicity stood composed and beautiful by her husband's side. She smiled at Jane kindly and took her hand. "Jane," she said, "I don't want you to feel embarrassed because of us. Even though we're not Catholic, Harold and I understand that the man is unwell, and there was sense in all he said, at that. So don't be afraid we're scandalized. And it was a lovely party."

"Thank you," Jane said, "you're nice to tell me that." And something of Felicity's characteristic serenity communicated itself to her, and helped her through the other good-byes.

"Jane, he's a remarkable man!" Martha Settler said briskly. "It's almost as if God sent him fever to make him speak out as he did. Everything he said was so true. I had chills up and down my spine."

Bede, close behind her, winked. "Watch out or you'll be getting pneumonia with all those chills."

Jane smiled weakly.

"Don't look so sad, Jane," Bede said. "Father Tom's okay in my book. And a little something to jolt us does us all good."

"It was a good party," Al said. "Don't know why you're so gloomy. Half the people here were having such a good time they wouldn't care if the Pope himself started popping off. Forget it."

Chris came downstairs.

"Someone's got to drive Father Tom to the hospital," he said. "He's got herpes, which is what chicken pox can turn into in a grownup. Very painful. And it can be serious."

"Chicken pox," repeated Jane.

"Wonder what Martha Settler would say if she knew it was chicken pox and not the Holy Spirit." Tory smiled.

"She'd say it was still Providence," said Clare Sullivan sweetly. "And she'd probably be right."

"Tory and I'll take him to the hospital," Al offered.

Jane went into the kitchen. She did not want to say anything to Father Tom that she would regret. She wanted to be alone in the aftermath of her party. She felt tired and irritated and old.

The sight of Krena in the kitchen took her by surprise. She had thought only old friends were still here.

"You look tired, Jane." Krena smiled. "You did a fine job tonight. And it was a wonderful evening." Krena finished loading the dishwasher. "Don't mind me. I'm glad to help. You look as if you need to go to bed. Is the priest going to be all right? What a crisis for you! But you handled it magnificently."

Jane rearranged a few cups in the dishwasher and repressed the desire to tell Krena to get out. She hated to have anyone else do her kitchen chores because things were never put away where she wanted them. And finding Krena in her kitchen was like finding Emily Post at your *Kaffeeklatsch*. She wondered if Krena could possibly be trying to annoy her.

"I feel terrible that it's so late. Chris did say he would run me home. But shall I call a taxi? It might be best." Now Krena was working with a sponge on the knobs and chrome of the stove. Jane knew they did not need cleaning. It took a few moments of silence for her to realize that she had not answered Krena's question.

"A taxi would never come out here at this hour. I'm sure Chris will be delighted to drive you home."

Something in Krena's eyes, some tension, seemed to challenge Jane. She decided to ignore it.

Chris came in then. "You didn't say good-bye to Father Tom. Are you mad at him?"

"Of course not. I didn't want to make him self-conscious standing around gawking. You'll drive Krena home, won't you? She needs a ride home."

"Oh. Yes. Well—"

"I'm going to bed. I've had it." Jane managed a weak smile for Krena and headed for the stairs.

The cold shocked them. The road crackled under the car. The headlights probed frosted shadows on the back way to Jordan.

Krena lit a cigarette, leaning over to use the car lighter. Her fur jacket touched Chris's hand, soft, faintly perfumed.

"You're worried about Jane, aren't you?" she said quietly.

"Mm." He nodded. "She's not herself yet. Wish I could take her away somewhere, let her get her strength back."

"She's lucky to have someone like you worrying about her." Krena turned sideways on the seat, moving a little closer to him. Out of the corner of his eye he saw that she was only making it easier for herself to reach the ashtray in the center of the dashboard. "I like her, Chris. No one could help liking her."

"A cruise. How come we editors don't make enough to go on cruises? It's been hard on Jane, the babies coming so fast. It would do her a world of good to go on a cruise."

"You too. You take life very seriously, you know. You could use a change. A fling."

"Oh?"

"You're the most serious-minded, earnest guy I know, and that's wonderful. But you need to let go a little bit now and then. You need to be silly."

"Maybe I'm not the silly type."

A lamppost with a gold eagle came into view. "That's it," said Krena. "Turn in there."

At the end of the long winding driveway the house was dark except for one dim gleam from the front hall.

"Thanks, Chris," she said. "I had a wonderful time."

He watched her as she went up the steps, unlocked the door and waved good-bye. It did not seem right to him that Krena should have to go home to a dark and lonely house. No one should be that alone. What kind of man could marry Krena and leave her so alone?

A wave of warmth for her spread through him as he drove home. He remembered the touch of her coat, of her hand on his. He wished he had found a way to—to comfort her, he thought, to let her know that he did not think she should be lonely.

Her perfume lingered as he reached home.

Jane was already asleep.

SIXTEEN

St. Rose's was filled for eleven-thirty Mass the next morning.

"I want to sit up front," a child insisted in a loud whisper. "I never get to see what's happening."

"Nothing's going to happen," the mother said, yanking the child's arm.

You're wrong, Chris thought, as he climbed the steps to the choirloft. The answer is that no one can see what happens at Mass. The unreal looms too large, and blots out the real.

As he took his music folder from the rack it occurred to him that he could make a nice column on what really happens at Sunday Mass; the unseen, unmeasured impact of God on the parish. Where a thousand separate, desperately human people are forged into one with the God-man. Where they offer their dreams and distractions and desires in sacrifice with the one who alone really exists, and receive them back altered by the impress of reality. Even, he thought, when they are not aware of it. He would work on that, he decided, taking his place with the basses. The trouble was Sunday Mass looked so darn messy. It was an act of faith to believe it meant anything.

The Carpels, as always, were up front. Marianne's cloche of black velvet flowers set off her platinum hair. Hugh wore his country squire outfit, but even at a distance he seemed a little worse for wear after last night, Chris thought. Hugh was present at Mass like a dignitary at a cornerstone laying, dutiful and bored. Marianne was saying the rosary on those heavy crystal beads from Tiffany.

Father Mongiano intoned: *"Gloria in excelsis Deo."*

Martha Settler, kneeling near Marianne Carpel, looked crisp, efficient, cold. But Martha's heart welled up in her. Glory, o glory, her soul cried, we do give thee thanks for thy great glory. I wanted a baby. And I pray you to help me understand why instead of children you sent me my sister to care for. Heal her mind, Lord . . . Let this be the last time I see her suffer. She seems well. God in your glory keep her well.

From the choirloft came the rest of the hymn of the praise. Martha could pick out her Bede's clear voice in the measures where soprano and tenor wove together in piercing sweetness:

"Domini Fili unigenite, Jesu Christe . . ."

Bertha Rains played an F sharp on the organ instead of an F natural. She had made the mistake in every rehearsal since they started work on this Mass. Conrad, the director, drew his shoulders together in agony, though his hands kept the steady rhythm of the music. The choir's throats tightened and for a moment their tones grew thin and ragged.

Chris raised his eyebrows and reminded the Lord that Conrad could not help losing his temper at Bertha and please let us all sing so well that we will forget it. Conrad, a widower, lived alone over the post office, and he was not the kind of man who found it easy to be pleasant. As for Bertha, her four teen-age sons were a distraction and a cross to her, so she was to be forgiven if she made mistakes. It wasn't as if either she or Conrad were paid for this work.

Lidwina, her musical-comedy soprano carefully muted during the tenderer phrases of this Gloria, saw Conrad's annoyance over that F sharp, and got flustered. She gave forth with a rich throaty high E as the Amen approached. Conrad flung his head around to

78

stare her into silence. Lidwina bit her lip. Conrad tempered the rebuke with a wink. And in the back row of the tenors a frown crossed Father Macy's freckled face.

At the Gospel the congregation rose, blessing heads, lips and hearts. Father Mongiano climbed into the pulpit.

"Your prayers are requested for . . ."

The people knelt to pray for a man who died that week, two women seriously ill, and all the unnamed ill and dying of the parish. Then they settled into their seats to listen to the weekly announcements which were printed in the bulletins they held in their hands. The CYO was meeting, there would be a cake sale, Scouts, Rosary Altar, choir rehearsal. The Masses for the week were as follows: . . .

Father Mongiano's sermons were the best prepared in St. Rose's, five minutes of careful meditation and phrasing. He liked to speak on the Mystical Body of Christ. As far as he was concerned, if a man grasped that one idea, then liturgy made sense, then sacraments made sense, then the Mass made sense. He had trouble making people understand, but he was undaunted. His dark eyes widened with hope as he spoke, and his black curls gleamed in the stained-glass sunlight.

"The Mass," he said, "is the perfect balance of individualism and corporate unity. One with Christ, we praise and adore the Father with him. He is our head, and we merge in his life."

A baby cried. In the center aisle a three-year-old girl fascinated by the sparkle of her patent-leather shoes wandered out of a pew. Al's son, Walter Burke, the taller altar boy sitting beside Father Temple, had a dripping nose and no handkerchief. Mrs. Kczuck, in her old black overcoat, pursued her own devotions, an intricate schedule of novenas and litanies, right through the sermon.

"All that we do, we do in union with Christ," Father Mongiano was saying, "and yet we are always individuals too. In the Mass at times we speak solely as individuals. We say: 'I confess to Almighty God that *I* have sinned.' And we say: 'Lord, *I* am not worthy.' Alone in the midst of unity each approaches the Christ separately, knowing there is only one thing in the world we can call our own exclusively: sin. Even forgiveness is shared in the life of grace. . . ."

Angela Rottigni, sitting with her husband, Patsy, wished Father Macy had given the sermon that day, after she worked so hard to get Patsy here this morning. Father Mongiano was beautiful but he was way over Patsy's head. Now if Father Macy were preaching,

Patsy could maybe get a laugh and an idea at the same time. But the beautiful business would only make him wish he had stayed in bed.

Angela looked at the statue of St. Joseph the Worker and begged St. Joseph up in heaven to do something about her Patsy's luke-warm faith. "If a carpenter like you could be foster-father to Jesus," she said, "then surely you can help a bar-and-grille man become a real good Catholic and not just halfway? It isn't Patsy's fault he was brought up not knowing much about the faith. Most Italian men, they know very little. I'm lucky, that's all, because Mama saw to it I knew my way to the altar to pray when I was three. But Patsy's folks let him go his own way. He doesn't take it seriously. But he sure does a lot for the Church, St. Joseph. Look at the win-dow up there, three thousand dollars. Without a murmur my Patsy gave that. . . ."

"God bless you," said Father Mongiano. He left the pulpit and returned to the altar. In the choirloft Father Macy stifled a sigh of relief. It was hard to listen to the same sermon by the same guy at five consecutive Masses and not be weary, especially when it was someone like Father Mongiano.

Father Macy himself led the choir in Gregorian chants. Conrad did not like the chant or understand its discipline.

"Credo in unum Deum," Father Mongiano intoned at the altar.

Father Macy raised square-nailed freckled hands, caught every eye in the choir, and signalled the start of *Credo III*.

"Patrem omnipotentem." The choir, exploding the *Pa,* breathed four times during the first long phrase of music, and Father Macy's lips tightened in exasperation. You must be calmer, Father, the doctor had said. Is not serenity part of your faith? But how could he be serene when he had to conduct Gregorian with a choir which didn't begin to understand, and at which he dared not lose his tem-per? Lose your temper and you lose a soul, they said in the semi-nary. Then why in blazes pick him to teach Gregorian, and to a choir that liked operatic alleluias and loud Protestant-type reces-sionals?

Downstairs, as the Creed ended, Al Burke, tired of watching his son's public running nose, went to take up the collection. Basket in hand, he tried to unite himself consciously with Father Mon-giano's offertory prayers. He prayed for all living people, the Pope, bishops, priests, the government of the United States. And for his own wife. Because God knew he didn't understand her at all any more. She had blown up at him last night after they took Father Tom to the hospital and he still didn't know why. All he'd done was make a few jokes to liven things up, and was that so awful? I'm not the solemn kind, and she knows it. And if a man can't be himself with his wife, without having his head snapped off, he might as well be married to a stranger.

Al noticed that Hugh Carpel had been pressed into emergency duty taking up the collection. The old stuffed shirt, he looked extraordinarily self-conscious. Al's eyes twinkled.

The men emptied the collection baskets into the tall boxes in the aisle, envelopes, bills, change. Hugh worked with meticulous solemnity. As they went to the back of the church Al reached into his pocket and took out two dollar bills. He pressed them into Hugh's hand.

"Here's your cut," he whispered with a straight face.

Hugh drew his hand back as if it were burned, his bloodshot eyes wide with shock. The money fell to the floor.

Al picked it up and pocketed it with a shrug.

"Shh!" Al warned, and knelt down, his pink-cheeked Irish face a picture of surpassing innocence.

Father Mongiano was about to speak the words that call the living God down to the altar, and change the substance of bread and wine into his Body and Blood. The choir finished the Sanctus. Walter Burke rang the little handbell.

Coughing and nose-blowing, the constant undertones of shuffled feet and flipped pages, and of cloth shifting on polished wood, these ceased. For this moment, when heaven and earth met, the good people and the not-so-good people of St. Rose's were as one. Mrs. Kczuck halted her litany to the Sacred Heart. Hugh Carpel bowed his head without telling Marianne what had happened. The Milders, the Settlers, the Rottignis, the children and the fringe-huggers by the door, the whole body of a thousand held still, as the miracle happened again.

"Benedictus qui venit in nomine Domini," sang the altos into the sunlit air.

The doorway fringe got to its feet. A child spoke to his mother.

Those who for reasons of late breakfasts or the need of confession or indifference did not receive Communion knelt till the last of the others had taken God as the food of his soul. Father Mongiano returned to the altar. And then, since this was eleven-thirty Mass and running late, about fifty people found it absolutely necessary to leave, though Mass was not over. By the time Father Mongiano completed the prayers, blessed his people and told them to go, half were gone in spirit if not in body.

Mrs. Kczuck stayed to finish her four sets of thanksgiving prayers. Before Mary's altar a young nurse prayed for the people in her care on third-floor surgery. The drugstore man helped his children light candles to St. Rose.

Chris started for his car, then abruptly went instead to the little side chapel, empty now, and dark. He sat there staring at the altar, knowing he should go directly home. He did not want to. He thought about last night. About Father Tom. About Krena. About Jane.

The prospect of the same old Sunday afternoon routine of games with the children and Sunday papers appalled him. Krena was right. He did need to break out, to have a fling. But when he tried to say that to Jane this morning she had looked at him coldly. As if he meant to desert her, to disavow the family, or something. It was, he suspected, because he mentioned Krena.

He looked at the altar, shadowed, silent. If there was a prayer in him, only God knew it.

He knew only that he was in no hurry to go home to Jane.

SEVENTEEN

"You really are kicking over the traces." Krena laughed. "I feel very elegant."

In the mahogany-paneled dimness of *Le Cremailliere,* Chris felt at home. This was the place he used for lunching important authors, where headwaiters greeted him by name, and he had only to sign the check.

"You look elegant," he said. "Wish my authors were more like you. Most of them are scrawny. Or else they're men."

The pink feathers of her hat trembled when she laughed. "You lead a dull life," she said with mock sympathy.

"I do." He raised his martini glass in salute and looked at his watch.

"We just got here a little while ago," she said. "Worried about the time already?"

"Sorry." The light accented the lean bones of his face as he leaned forward earnestly. "Guess I just can't believe my luck, having a whole hour and a half to lunch without having to talk business."

"You worry too much." She finished her drink. "You've got to learn to relax."

"I'm learning," he said. He ordered lunch, and another set of drinks. "You're a good teacher."

"If you think being an eager beaver and an earnest soul will get you ahead here with R.P., you're crazy," she said. "He likes to think he can pick geniuses with a sort of mental dowsing rod. Busy-busy stuff makes static and throws him off. He's looking for flair, for an indefinable something. The rod jumped when he met you. Don't spoil it."

"I won't move a muscle."

"I think he has designs on both of us," she said. "He's got to move somebody up, and he wants to see what we do with this manuscript. Would you like to get out of textbooks?"

He enjoyed talking about the office with Krena. She listened to him, took his ambitions seriously. Lately Jane had seemed to have no time for shoptalk.

"You have a cowlick," Krena said suddenly, moving nearer to him on the tufted corner seat. "And it's standing up like Indian feathers." She smoothed it with her hand. "It won't stay down. You have exasperating hair."

"That's me," he said. "Exasperating."

Their lunch came, and he was glad. He did not usually have more than one martini.

"What are you going to do about the time problem?" he asked.
She blinked. "This is so sudden!"

"No, seriously. If the pace of the whole book is off, nothing else you do will save it, and that's something we haven't talked much about."

"Maybe you're embarrassed loafing at lunch." She laughed. "But I'm not. You promised we would just eat, not work." She leaned toward him. "You're getting frown lines."

"Frown lines. A messy cowlick. I'm not doing very well."

"They're handsome in a way. Give you depth, maybe. But still—" She ate her salad neatly, happily. "This is fun."

"It is."

"You know, I like being with you. Even working with you is fun.

You know, don't you, that I think you're pretty special. That's why I worry about you. You make me nervous. You're always tending to put everything to a test. Of good and bad, right and wrong."

"Am I?"

"You are. And so you can't enjoy anything."

He grinned. "I enjoy being with you," he said in a mock-romantic tone.

"Do you mean that?" She looked at him seriously.

"Yes," he said. And this time he could not smile.

"I'm glad," she said slowly.

That night Chris sat by the fire with his sons. One log, older, more gnarled than the rest, uglier when first put to burn, refused now to surrender its embers. The others had broken, slipped away, glowing quietly until now they were greying. But the one log lay firmly on the dark iron firedogs, undaunted orange outlining the structure of its past life, layer upon layer transfigured with small shoots of blue and yellow flame.

Luke rested in half sleep on a pillow on the floor, and Kilian lay daydreaming against his father's chest, cherishing the mysterious sound of that hidden fatherly heart beating like the drum tone of life itself against his secret ear. Peter, first-born, sat on the floor, his back against his father's leg, knees bent carelessly, corduroy slippers on the rug. He held his eyes narrowed. He was a pioneer resting lanky muscles by the campfire, testing for the possible unseen presence of Indian foes.

Christopher McNamara was their father, and the awareness of that fact nearly choked him. In him the love of father for male child had an arrow pain. These boys were, he thought, most beautiful, sea-deep, sea-strong creatures, strangely bewitched to smallness and trust at his side.

The log surrendered. The clock struck nine-thirty as the small fire wavered helplessly under the shock of breaking wood.

"It's over. Bedtime."

He blessed them, making the sign of the cross over their heads as they kissed him.

Alone he stretched out on the couch, newspaper in hand.

When he was young, in high school, a brother had told him to use the gym until the body was exhausted, take a brisk shower, work, keep busy. Don't try and fight this kind of thing. This is a thing you run from, the brother had said. Discretion is the better

84

part of valor. And by that advice in those tormenting days of young manhood he had shown valor and conquered. The world excused a young man for not remaining chaste. The world did not know the secret of self-control, nor value it.

Now he was not young. He couldn't run to the track, couldn't chin himself if he tried. Where could a man run when he's pledged himself, committed, and hungers?

He remembered the smell of Krena as she sat beside him, remembered the sound of her slip under her skirt as she walked past him in the office, the nearness of her leg to his in the train, the way she had let her head rest just an instant, laughing, on his shoulder. And he found himself picturing the summoning softness, the detail of flesh, that would lie hidden under the crisp white blouse. A woman whose husband did not love her. A woman who told him she yearned for a child.

He had no doubt in his mind. I say unto you: if a man looks upon a woman and lusts after her, he has committed adultery in his heart. He could not, now that he was aware of them, permit himself the pleasure of his thoughts. That was the damnable part of not being either an idiot or a pagan. He got up and began to walk back and forth in the room, and thought instead of Jane.

It is not good for man to be alone, saith the Lord. Amen. And you have ingeniously planted in us such hunger and power of ecstasy, and blessed our use of them in sacrament. Nonetheless, it is sometimes necessary, and therefore must be quite possible, to live with marital right suspended. Suppose Jane were in a cast, had TB, were in a mental institution. Or if she died. If we had to live as brother and sister. Al Burke's brother does that. He married a divorced girl outside the Church and then he wanted to come back to the Church and there was no way to remarry or unmarry and so now they live as brother and sister and I wonder how the hell they do it. Al said the Church makes a million rules for people like that. Separate rooms. No drinking at all. . . .

How long had it been? Only four months. How much longer, he did not know. Maybe years. Jane didn't seem to know, though she saw the doctor often. And he couldn't picture himself calling Dr. Polla and asking when he could have permission to bed his wife. Call it prudishness, shyness, said Chris to himself, call it what you will. I don't feel like discussing my need with an OB.

So there you are, back to the brother-and-sister bit. And that's Jane's doing. It's the best way, Jane said. All or nothing. He tried to tell her it didn't have to be like that. The Church didn't even think it should be like that. We can do whatever we want short of the whole thing, he said to her. There's no limit to what we can do. We're married. We can—

Why did she insist that he leave her completely alone? It's best, she said. Was it best for her? Tonight she was out at Mother's Circle. Night before last Rosary Altar. Tomorrow something else. She was always busy now. And she was very far away from him. She never let him touch her.

Last night she looked at you with contempt in her eyes, Chris. Admit it. Contempt. And all you did was put out your hands and hold her breasts as she brushed her hair. She is a snob in her puritanical smile. I hate her for despising my love. She thinks she has outgrown such things. Christ! Do you wonder men invent so many ways to sin?

Christopher McNamara, the man with the weak ankle and the two long legs, the man who had been a pioneer with his sons by the fire, drew himself now to full height, just short of the living room ceiling, and nodded his head gravely.

Perhaps Jane really did not understand that it was not sin for them to play with love, to take what comfort they could in each other's bodies. She does love me. But she denies even to herself that she wants me. She is afraid, and the only thing I have ever known her to fear is sin. But I could persuade her. We do not need to remain apart. All that is needed is control, and there can be control. And we will be free again, and close again.

He turned on his heel and began rummaging through the bookcases.

She came home at eleven full of small talk. He put his arms around her to listen. She stiffened and pushed him away.

"Chris, you know—"

"Half a loaf is better than none."

"It's dangerous." Unnecessary too, her tone implied.

"You don't trust me?" He laughed gently. "Try me."

She turned away. "No. Chris, it's not right."

"Look!" He picked up the book from the table and held it under her nose. "A cardinal wrote it. Suenens. Listen to this:

"We have already said that periodic continence does not mean living as brother and sister, to use a current but inaccurate expression. It allows a couple the full range of physical intimacy, as we have pointed out, so long as they do not reach the terminal reflex. . . . The 'all or nothing' attitude has nothing to do with this question and we falsify the human and Christian solution by putting a couple in the position where they are faced with this dilemma: either completely terminated intercourse or nothing."

Chris looked at her triumphantly. "See, Jane? All the lovemaking in the world we can do. So long as we use self-control. There's even virtue in it, in controlling passion, in stopping."

She stared him to silence.

"That's like you," she said finally. "To find a book. To find it written down somewhere."

"Jane—"

"That's like you. To do research on it. Do you think I live by books? Or by what a cardinal says? You're as cold and calculating and intellectual as—"

"You could read it."

"I don't want to read it. I don't care what he says."

He slammed the book on the table. "We aren't divorced, you know, Jane. You may wish we were. You may wish I'd drop dead but you're still married to me. And I need you. And you need me. You need me more than you dare to admit. You've built a whole wall between us."

"I can live without it. So can you."

He drew a deep breath, deliberately swallowing the anger in his throat. "Jane, do you love me?"

"Do you need to ask?"

"If you loved me, you'd trust me." He stepped closer to her, hands at his side. "Jane, you—we don't even touch any more. Not even a hand to hand—"

"Shake!" She took his right hand and shook it and made a joke of it.

His eyes narrowed. He shoved his hand free.

She spoke very quietly. "Chris, please understand. You say control is a virtue. All I ask is that we make it complete control. For a while. It won't be forever. I know it's hard. But you frighten me. You keep starting things and we can't because we can't finish them."

"I just told you we can. It's all there in the book. *Love and Control.*"

"Books! I can find a hundred books and a hundred priests who would say just the opposite. And you're after me all the time."

"I won't be any more."

"You don't understand." She held out her arms and he stepped back, leaning against the countertop.

"I understand," he said coldly.

"Chris, maybe we might—when we love each other so much, somehow we might not stop. In passion, something could push us past thinking—"

He just stood there, nodding slightly, and she was frightened by his coldness.

"I try and keep busy so it will be easier. But you've got to do your part. You do nothing, and—"

"I just sit at home and think about one thing. Sex."

"Well, you do, you know." She tried to make her voice lighter. "You know, Chris, what you need is a hobby, to keep busy with."

"A hobby."

"You said once you wanted to develop pictures, have a dark-room."

He walked out of the room.

She followed him. "You're angry," she said, and she sounded surprised and therefore stupid, and he laughed.

"A hobby," he repeated.

"Chris?"

"Good night."

"Chris, I want it the way it was or not at all. I don't want—I don't want diluted wine."

"Ah, you're talking a little too fancy for me," he said. "I'm just an uncouth man, and watered-down wine is over my head."

"You're mean."

"Mean. Sex-crazed. Obsessed. Unable to exercise self-control. Without respect for the innocent brink-of-death female. Without a hobby. You're so right. Maybe I'll take up a hobby."

"Chris?"

"And you, my dear, are not yourself either. You are never yourself any more."

"I've been taking my medicine. And I don't get a full night's sleep thanks to your little baby girl whom you never hear when she cries at night."

"It's not medicine or rest you need. I could tell you what you need but it might offend your ladylike ears."

88

"You think everyone else needs what you need."

She stayed in the kitchen crying. When he did not return she nursed her hurt feelings with a cupcake.

The sight of the cardinal's book irritated her. *Love and Control*. She put the book on top of the icebox where she would not have to look at it. Men wrote about sex. Not women. Cardinals, yet.

He thinks I do not love him because I do not want to. My life is in his hands. Does it ever occur to him I cannot face a single chance?

She went upstairs. He was lying in his bed reading his self-appointed nightly stint in the Bible. She undressed in the bathroom, put on her more opaque robe, and sitting on her bed she said, "I'm sorry, Chris. I didn't mean to make you angry. It's a hard thing God is asking of us, but it will—"

"You sound phony as hell," he interrupted stiffly. "It's not God who's making things difficult. It's you."

"Chris, if you need me so badly—"

"I don't. I don't need you so badly. What are you trying to do, be a martyr?"

"I'm sorry, but—"

"You're not sorry. You don't even know what there is to be sorry about. You like playing the role of a dutiful and spiritual wife caught in the clutches of a carnal beast. And you like to hear yourself say you're sorry."

"If you loved me, you wouldn't talk to me that way. You'd know how I feel. You don't love me, do you?"

He didn't answer. He went back to his reading.

"Do you?" she repeated.

The thin pages tore under her fingers as she grabbed the Bible out of his hands. "Look at me! Answer me. Can you sit there and not answer me?"

"I love you," he said flatly. "But you don't love me. Not enough."

"Chris. If we make love, my life is in your hands. Does it ever occur to you that I might be afraid of dying?" She dropped her head on his chest.

Gently he turned her face to his. "Jane. You mean it. Jane, you mustn't be afraid. I'd never let anything happen to you."

"But it might." Her eyes met his. "It might. And I think of death and I am paralyzed. Can't you understand?"

He smoothed her forehead. "Death isn't that frightening," he said softly. "When you die, you go to heaven forever."

"Oh!" She tore herself out of his hold.

"Jane, I was only "

"You! You and your books and your sermons—you're horrible. You want me to die, I suppose. You want me to go to heaven. Don't worry about dying Jane dear, because then you can be happy!"

"You'll wake the kids."

"Who cares about the kids?" She stood looking down at him in horror. "Let them wake up. Let them hear how calm and wise and logical their father is. And how selfish and noisy and frightened their mother is. At least I'm human."

She started to cry and she climbed into her bed and pulled the covers over her and pressed her hands on her eyes.

He did not speak.

She waited, but he said nothing at all. He turned off the light and lay down with his back to her.

In her tears she wondered what had happened to him, what he had become, who he was.

EIGHTEEN

On Tory's orange enameled coffee table the dainty gold watch lay in its open Valentine wrappings.

"I'm almost afraid to wear it." Tory laughed. "It's so darn petite. I never wear that sort of thing. But when Al buys me a present he buys what he likes."

Jane smiled faintly.

"What did Chris come up with?"

"I think he forgot it's Valentine's Day. I couldn't care less." Jane slouched down on the couch. Quietly, sadly, with an undercurrent of fear, as if confiding the presence of disease, she said, "Tory, I hate him."

"Take your coat off."

"I married the wrong guy." Jane's voice was breaking. She huddled deeper into the collar of her polo coat. "And it's taken all this long for me to admit it."

"You're serious."

"I sure am."

90

"Jane, honey, this isn't like you." Tory brought her coffee. "Look, men are men. It isn't all that bad. All men have faults. Al's got a ton of them. Like not learning I like big heavy jewelry. But—"

"Tory, I can't face the idea of spending another twenty or thirty years with Chris."

"Drink your coffee, you'll feel better. After all, Chris isn't a monster. He's just like other men, you know that."

"That's the trouble. He's just like other men, and I didn't know it." She gulped some coffee.

Tory smiled. "Funny. You're the one who always picks me up when I'm ready to go to pieces. And you always know I don't really mean it forever. How many times have I come over to you bawling? And what do you say to me? You tell me all marriages go through times like this. So now, I'll tell you."

"This is different," Jane said. The voices of her babies playing with little Cyril drifted up from the playroom.

"Only because it's happening to you." Tory lay back on a green sofa pillow. "Remember, Jane? You told me you thought there was a dark night in the soul of a marriage, like the marriage was sort of a person in itself?"

Jane blew her breath out loudly. "I don't want sermons. Especially, not my own. It's no good."

"Because of Valentine's Day?"

Jane shook her head. "The kids woke me up with Valentines. Poor kids."

"What did you fight about with Chris?"

"We just found out we hated each other. He doesn't give a damn whether I live or die. He thinks I'm selfish and stupid."

"Remember what Father Mongiano said at Cana?"

"I don't want to hear about it." Jane stood up. "Thanks for letting me blow my top."

"You haven't finished blowing."

"Tory, I don't want to talk. I'm not making sense. If I talk any more I'll—"

"You'll start believing what you're saying?"

At home Jane sat on the stairs, her coat still on, oblivious of Meg and Teresa, thinking. And what she thought was more than she could bear. The thought of being married to Chris as long as she lived lay in front of her like the upright of a cross, too heavy to lift.

And then, quietly, without warning, she realized that she could not believe in God any more.

She opened her eyes wide. I do not love Chris and he does not love me, and so I cannot love God. It's as simple and deadly as that.

I prayed before I married him. God, how I prayed. I went every day and prayed that if we were not truly in love, or if we weren't meant to love forever, God would intervene. I was afraid of making a mistake, of being blind because I loved Chris so. God did not stop me from marrying him. God blessed that marriage. In sacrament, in Christ, we were joined. But we should not have been joined. That's plain now. I do not believe in a God who makes mistakes. If our love isn't true, then nothing is true. She put her head in her hands. She was past tears. She felt dead inside. It surprised her that she still breathed.

She moved like one in fever, mindless, her nerves jumping with every sound. Though it was still early morning she put the babies to bed to be rid of them. She took a bath. She stood naked before the mirror. The chain with the little gold medal shone round her neck. She considered taking it off and decided it was an unnecessary gesture of defiance. She would keep it on because she had always worn it and liked it, and to remove it now would be as much superstition as to wear it.

She decided to phone Father Tom.

"Someone ought to know," she said aloud. "I've got to tell someone."

Father Tom sat on the broad windowsill in his room in St. Jean's Hospital and kicked his heels against the radiator. This was the surest way he knew to get Sister James to come to his room. When he rang the bell and asked for her she was always too busy with someone who is really sick, Father. But when he seemed to be destroying hospital property or endangering peace and quiet, she appeared instantly.

He was better after ten days of pain and fever, and he was restless. He had prowled the halls of the third floor until the nurses and sisters had exhausted their patience ordering him back to bed. It had been Sister James who had come up with the ingenious solution which now kept him imprisoned in his room. She had him moved from the happy coeducational third floor where broken legs and appendectomies visited in convalescence, and installed him in her own domain—Second Floor Maternity.

The halls of Maternity were peopled with women in varying degrees of decency, negligeed and swollen-breasted, some carrying rubber rings for stitch-sore seats, and all damnably female. The halls were filled with gay scraps of talk about everything from sore nipples to laxatives. From some rooms came the sound of tears. But when he had gone forth bravely to do his Christian duty and console what he believed must be a mother bereft of her infant, he found only a nineteen-year-old girl weeping because her nineteen-year-old husband had neglected to bring her chocolates.

Sister James had triumphed. Father Tom stayed in his room. To celebrate, Jane sent him the florist's fanciest "Welcome-to-baby" arrangement of miniature roses in a blue cradle.

Actually, once he found himself a prisoner, he was grateful. He sank into the chaise longue of his room on Maternity and relaxed for perhaps the first time in the twenty-five years of his priesthood.

He would say his breviary, luxuriating in being able to space the prayers into the proper measured hours, instead of trying to cram it into a lump. He would say his rosary. He would read. At the moment he had laid aside Tom Merton's newest book, *The Sign of Jonas,* for the old familiar *True Devotion to the Blessed Virgin Mary* by de Montfort.

Father Tom was a Mary man. He had given himself to his Queen as a willing slave. Through her the world made sense to him, through her he believed Christ would be finally, fully formed to him.

"Mary found me a place to sleep for the night," he would say. Or, "I asked Mary what to do and she told me," or "Mary sure played a dirty trick on me when she sent that drunkard to sit beside me all the way to Detroit on the bus."

He tried to fathom what Mary had in mind when she gave him this ridiculous illness. Why on earth did she let him make such a spectacle of himself at Jane's party? He did not ordinarily mind being made a spectacle of. Mary had given him his master's degree in that type of humility years ago. But he couldn't see why she let him stand up and preach in a most uncalled-for manner, upsetting a perfectly nice party. He certainly wasn't responsible for what he did in fever or pain, and if it had been the wrong thing Mary could have seen to it that he had just passed out quietly.

But it had happened. He had shot off his mouth. He suspected that Jane was mad at him. He figured he had scandalized the nice Lawrences and perhaps bored the Carpels, and upset that sweet little Clare Sullivan, and fouled up things just fine. And he hadn't helped anyone.

> "There was a big priest with the herpes
> Flaring redder than zinnias of Burpee's . . ."

he began, and stopped.

From his window he could see the development houses, the new brick apartments, the half-shoddy downtown shopping streets, the front of an abandoned factory and finally the thin shiny line of Long Island Sound by the horizon. Commuter trains moved silently across the remote trestle.

He reached back in memory for the comfort of his mission days, for the years in Kenya, in the huts of Tusamagonga among the Kikuyu. Summoning memories was for him like entering a private chapel. Automatically, tenderly, the Swahili words for the Sign of the Cross came to his lips: "Kwajina la Baba, na la Mwana, na la Mroho Mtakatifu, Ameena."

He saw again and smelled the children who had come to his school, the elders at council in the middle of the village, the women making beer, the tobacco growing in the fields. The terror and blood-smell of the Mau Mau stung in his heart, and the sight of the Sister hacked to death with a panga, whom he had had to bury. But the witchdoctor's son whom he himself had baptized was now an altar boy.

Beside him now on the windowsill lay his fund-raising folders, posters for his mission movies—*The Black Christ* and *The New Face of Africa,* and the address book with the names of people from whom he hoped to beg. He had to cancel seventeen lectures and four appointments with rich men during his hospital stay. For that he was grateful. He would not have minded begging in the old grand manner of St. Francis on streets and country roads. But begging in the carefully programmed fund-raising of modern America was his severest penance. He resented the need for technique, disliked the rules he had learned from other more successful beggars. A Maryknoller had taught him the importance of deft publicity and personal contact. A Helper of the Holy Souls told him he must understand the psychology of those he begged from: with an Irishman you could appeal to his faith, but with an Italian you did not mention faith as much as the perpetuation of the family name in memorial plaques. He hated the soft-voiced sister's advice and he was tired of missionary-convention seminars on the methods of

94

direct-mail appeal, and how to jazz up a religious magazine, and where to buy lists of names and addresses. He collected names of friends and friends of friends until they formed a chain leading to the big philanthropists and foundations who of necessity walled themselves in against the onslaught of beggars.

He would rather empty garbage pails any day. Only if Mary wanted him to be a public relations man and salesman instead of a contemplative or a dishwasher, so would he be.

Chris and Jane had visited him alternately almost every night since he had been hospitalized, bringing milkshakes in containers from a diner, candy, cigarettes, news. But he sensed an unhappiness in his two favorite people for which he had not yet seen the cause.

He offered his prayers at daily Communion for them, and also the indignity of receiving Communion in bed from the chaplain instead of being able to offer Mass himself.

He still had not eaten breakfast this morning. His tray with the bowl of colorless cereal and cold coffee sat on the floor. He kicked his heels harder on the radiator. He wanted to ask Sister James if he could go down to the chapel. He felt like a fool having to ask permission for a thing like that. He kicked harder.

"Father McNamara, I must ask you now—" Sister James stood in the doorway, her white habit crisper than melba toast, her glasses slipping from her nose.

"Sister, please may I go down to the chapel?"

"Your doctor has forbidden it. And it is against the state law to let you wander around."

"It's against the state law for me to be on Maternity, especially if I am contagious. Therefore I assume I am no longer contagious and have not been contagious or truly ill for quite a time. And therefore, just because my doctor is out of commission with the flu, is no reason—"

"Sorry, Father."

The phone beside his untouched glass of orange juice rang. Sister left quickly. He answered:

"Hello. St. Theresa's Boarding School and Pet Shop. Who's calling?"

"It's Jane, Father Tom."

"And how are you? I am miserable. Treated like a bad child and a naughty pup, locked in and denied the simplest pleasures of life. How are things in the great world? The woman across the hall from me is able to get out of bed and finds her figure sadly out of shape That is all the news on Maternity."

"Oh, stop it, I'm miserable."

Banter melted from his voice. "What's the matter?"

"Everything. Quite seriously everything. I'm calling you up because I don't want you to misunderstand. I wouldn't want you to think you had anything to do with this or that I hated you, no matter what I did."

"You sound very cool, calm, collected, for a miserable woman. What are you really talking about? What's the matter?"

"Nothing. Only that I don't believe in God any more. And I hate myself and I hate everything."

"Oh." He cradled the phone to his cheek. "You hate everything, Jane?"

"You know what? Chris and I should never have married. No, don't interrupt me. We shouldn't have married. And we have six children! And you know what? We're not allowed to have another baby or I'll die. I hadn't told you that, had I?"

"Ah-hah." His voice was noncommittal.

"I don't want a baby." She was almost whispering now. "And Chris doesn't care. He thinks I don't love him. Well, I can't even stand the sight of him. And I want to walk out, run away, be rid of the whole mess. And there's no use talking to me about God. I'm through. I'm not going to pretend to believe in him. My whole life, my marriage, was built on the idea that God was running the show. But he's not. The whole thing is a farce."

"Come on down and talk to me."

"I can't. I can't leave the babies."

"Well if you go around crying like this they won't know what's the matter with you."

"Father Tom, you don't understand."

"I'd like to."

"I'm through! With Chris. And the Church. And I'm stuck so I can't leave either."

He heard her blowing her nose. Then she spoke more calmly, "I didn't mean to burst out like this. I don't know what came over me."

"The truth, I imagine. Or part of it."

"Oh, I didn't mean those things I said. I guess it made Chris sound as if he were—I made him sound worse than he is."

"How about coming down tonight?"

"No," she said quickly. "I have to go to a meeting and Chris will have to stay home and babysit."

"I was looking forward to another chocolate milkshake."

"Maybe tomorrow. And in the meantime, keep well. And forget what I said." Her voice was so brittle it hurt his ears.

"Sure, Jane. Sure."

"Well, I'll see you."

"Yes, Jane. God bless you now."

"Bye."

He held the phone in his hand till the switchboard operator downstairs asked him what he wanted, then coming back to himself he hung up quietly. He looked in the closet for his clothes, dressed, and stood watching the clock. Sister should be busy somewhere off the floor now. The nurses' aides were at the other end of the hall. He strode manfully out into the hall, heart pounding as it had not done since the time he had thrown a snowball at a cop's neck and run away back on West Forty-third Street forty years ago.

He made it to the elevator, the perfect picture of a visiting clergyman rapt in thoughts of compassion and appointments to be kept. On the ground floor he found his way to the chapel.

In the tiny sacristy the vestments were laid carefully on the counter. The hospital chaplain had the habit of leaving everything open for emergencies. The tabernacle key was under the cloth on the shelf. Father Tom checked quickly for what he needed, removed his suitjacket, shrugged into the alb which, being too short for him, clung to his chest, and vested for Mass.

He walked as quickly as he dared down the short aisle, mounted the altar steps, placed the chalice and paten, arranged the missal, and returned to the bottom of the steps.

"*Introibo ad altare Dei,*" he said. And then he made his own response since there was no altar boy:

"*Ad Deum qui laetificat juventutem meam.*"

He would offer this Mass for Jane and Chris, and no one could stop him. Not even Sister James who this minute entered the chapel for a short visit before returning to the floor and her problems. Her biggest problem bulked now at the altar. She came perilously close to giggling, then moved swiftly into the front pew.

"*Dominus vobiscum,*" said Father Tom.

"*Et cum spiritu tuo,*" said Sister Jane.

The big shaggy head lifted, and the brown eyes defied the rubric and looked straight at the nun.

"*Oremus*," he said, and turned back to the altar and the Mass of St. Valentine.

NINETEEN

She thought later that if it hadn't been February things might have been different.

Along the road edges dirt-crusted shelves of ice lay unmelted between storms. It was almost as if the ice were taking camouflage, stubbornly staying on to make roads narrower, uglier, driving more difficult. There were, Jane thought, just such shelves in her heart.

After all, she did not hate Chris. Beneath the surface she knew that. Nor had she really become an atheist. But no surge of love softened her, nor was she moved by fear. She did not really make up with Chris or God. They lived in politeness.

She phoned Father Tom the next day.

"I didn't mean any of it," she said. "Forget it. Please forget it. And don't mention it to Chris. I'll put you under pain of sin."

He was released from the hospital and had to go off to Detroit. Jane made herself too busy to see him alone before he left. She did not want to talk with him because she would have had to think and she did not want to think. Not about herself or God or anyone or anything. So Father Tom stood in the doorway and looked at her with pain in his eyes.

She was tired of handling heavy cold snowsuits, blue jeans, long johns. Tired of coping with six pairs of wet boots. Tired of the stink mittens made as they dried. The station-wagon windows were seldom opened and the car smelled of stale cigarette smoke and apples. She sprayed it with lilac air freshener and the result disgusted her.

She had lived through Februaries before, survived times when her love seemed dead. This was different. Like dull pain it underlay the sound and business of her days. And around her the echoes of other lives left her no peace. She had told Tory the storm was over, convinced her the Valentine's Day episode was a mere passing spat. And once again Tory was bringing her troubles to Jane.

98

She and Al dropped in unannounced one evening. Chris was pleased.

"What brings you out on a night like this?"

Al threw himself into the armchair by the fire. "I got troubles," he said. "I need a new soaker for the plant, and I don't see how I can afford it right now, and my ever-lovin' is mad at me for so much as mentioning it."

"I commiserated with him yesterday and the day before. Tonight I suggested he leave his problems at work." Tory put her hands on her hips. "Chris, you don't spend all your time at home talking about work, do you?"

"Never. I keep my lives completely separate."

"Bet I know why," winked Al. "Say, Jane, Hugh Carpel says he sees Chris with a gorgeous gal on the train every night. No wonder he doesn't talk about his work."

"The gorgeous gal happens to be married and working." Jane laughed. "If you're trying to upset me about Krena McDowell it won't work."

"I know, I was only kidding."

"You and your kidding," said Tory.

"Chris, did I tell you what I did to Hugh Carpel at Mass?" Al described the affair of the dollar bills. "And he fell for it!"

Chris shook with laughter.

"Well, I don't think it's funny. I think it's disgraceful, a grown man clowning around like that. Hugh probably took you seriously, and told everybody," said Tory.

"Aw, come on, honey." Al sniffed the tears of laughter from his nose. "You know Father Macy. He's so tight even Hugh would know you couldn't get away with anything. Why, when Father Macy gives you the basket to carry he puts a live fly in your left hand and closes your fist over it. When you're through taking up the collection you have to give him back the fly."

Tory sighed. Chris winked at Al. "I like it, anyway."

Undaunted, Al pulled his wallet from his pocket, fumbling in it for a card. "This you gotta see, Chris."

At first glance the card seemed ordinary enough: the kind of notice many people carried: *In case of accident, please call a priest.* Chris nodded.

"No, read it," Al urged happily.

Chris peered more closely at the discreet italic type and read:

"I am a Very Important Catholic. In case of accident, please call the apostolic delegate." His laughter exploded with delight.

Jane giggled. "Al, that's the funniest thing I ever heard. That's terrible!"

"Get me one," said Chris. "I need one of those cards!"

"I wouldn't be caught dead with that." Jane chuckled. "Some lunkhead would come along and take it seriously."

"I showed it to Father Macy and he didn't get it. He looked as if he were about to offer me a homily on my need for humility."

Tory didn't laugh. Chris went to get out the Scotch and asked, "So what's the matter, Tory?"

"I told you. He's a great practical joker. And he's married to that darn plant. He spent all Saturday on the phone because he was short of wood. Short of wood! What's the matter with you men that you have to make up your own language all the time?" Tory shook her head crossly. "Like kids. He needed cases for his bottles. Only you don't say bottles, either."

"You say a load of glass." Chris grinned.

Jane nodded. "And you can't say a bottle has a cap. It's not a cap, it's a crown."

"Chris, you talk to him. Every night now all he does is gripe about his problems. I sympathize. It's a wife's job to take an interest. But it's a heck of a life when all you talk about, when you're not telling jokes, is filter trouble or wild syrup. You know what we do on cozy evenings after the kids are in bed? We discuss his conveyer. The chains are wearing out."

"Sounds like you're wearing out too," said Jane. "Come on while I finish in the kitchen."

"How about you? Really feeling better now?" Tory asked.

"Sure."

"You two made up."

"Not really." Jane turned on the dishwasher. "But we will."

"You don't sound very enthusiastic." Tory was playing with a pistachio-green yarn octopus lying on the table.

"My mother made that," Jane said. "That one's Meg's. She made a different color for each grandchild. And you know what I do? I make them talk. Each octopus has his own voice. Kilian's is yellow and it has a deep voice. Mary's is lavender. I've got five octopuses and five different voices. And the kids never forget which voice is which, and so Lord help me if I do."

"How nice for you. Occupational therapy."

"You said it. How's Cyril? Still allergic to milk?"

"I don't want to talk about it."

"Davey and the school?"

"I don't want to talk about Davey and the school either. Or Walter. Or Pat and her boyfriend. Or any of my kids." Tory's eyes met Jane's. "I'm glad you're not in a mess any more. Purely selfish. You're my rock, pal. And I'm a leaner from way back. You're a great person to talk to."

"Am I?" replied Jane. "Which of my voices do you prefer, pistachio or lemon? Come on, let's go annoy the men."

"Yup, this is the longest we've stayed in one place," Al was saying. "I got this franchise four years ago this month. Been here steady ever since."

"Getting restless?" asked Chris.

"Me? Nah!" Al shook his head. "Glad to stay put. Like we're really married for the first time. A new life, isn't it, Tory?"

"Us and the kids and soda water."

"You didn't drink your drink," Al said. "I'm one ahead of you already."

"You sure are. You'll be singing and dancing next."

"Why not? I'll sing and dance for you." Al got up and began to fake a few soft-shoe steps, singing softly, "Getting to know you, getting to know all about you, Getting to like you—"

Watching Al, with all the bare pink scalp showing, red-faced, Jane's heart went out to him. Tory sat smoking, examining her nail polish for flaws. Jane wanted to shake her.

She could not talk to Tory about herself now. She did not want to be near anyone who was unhappy. Then to whom could she talk? She was the one who listened. Her role was set. She wasn't supposed to have troubles.

When Al and Tory left, Chris stood by the closed door looking at her.

"It's late," she said.

"I don't care if it's late. We need to talk to each other. And I have a question to ask you."

"About Dr. Polla?"

"No. I wanted to ask, I wondered if you would be too busy to go out to dinner with me tomorrow night?"

She turned in surprise. "I thought you wouldn't—"

He put his finger to her lips.

"The less said the better. Look, I don't like living like this. Polite.

Cold. I also don't like getting involved in scenes and apologies. Can we let it go at this? You agree to go out to dinner for our wedding anniversary?"

She smiled. "We'll go off by ourselves. And start again."

TWENTY

Jane pressed her good black dress with the steam iron and wished Lidwina O'Shea weren't sitting watching her.

"Your Mary and I are getting to be great pals, aren't we, Mary?" Lidwina was wearing ponyskin boots, ski pants and a heavy Peruvian sweater, and Mary thought she looked beautiful.

"Mrs. O'Shea's going to teach me to tap-dance someday," said Mary.

"In the meantime suppose you go keep an eye on the baby like I told you."

"She's a sweet little girl," Lidwina said as Mary left. "Lonely, though. You don't mind if she visits me? She tells me you've been going to the doctor."

"Does she?"

"Don't sound cross. She said you'd been seeing Dr. Polla. You're not expecting again?"

"No." Jane adjusted a pleat in the dress.

"Going out tonight?"

"It's our anniversary." She did not know why Lidwina had suddenly taken to coming over in the late afternoon. Lidwina simply said the early twilight depressed her. Jane had the feeling it was somehow important to her to be in Jane's company. Lidwina mentioned her visits to everyone, especially to Mike. She seemed to be trying to tell Jane something, but what it was Jane could not find out, nor did she care to try. Lidwina's chatter annoyed her.

"That Agnes Milder," Lidwina said, "is a pain. In that snowstorm last week Mike was away in Hartford at a Democratic meeting, and the snowplow man took pity on me and cleared my drive. Do you know Agnes Milder called the Department of Public Works and reported him? Dear little Agnes."

Jane smiled.

"She has an evil tongue," Lidwina said, "and she doesn't like me. Thank God I have someone like you who knows me and who's not a frustrated old cat. Get Agnes going and she sounds as if sex were a dirty habit wives were intended to cure husbands of. You at least understand sex."

"I do?"

"Do you know, Janie, your eyes are your best feature and you don't do a thing to emphasize them? By the way, what do you think about Martha's sister? I think it's dreadful of Martha to have her here! Do you think it's safe for your Peter to be up there so much?"

"She's really quite well now, Lidwina," Jane said quietly. "There's nothing shameful about nervous breakdowns, you know. Or mental illness. If Betsy Butler had cancer everyone would be so gentle and sorry. But because she had a nervous breakdown they're suspicious. It's the things you can't see that frighten people most."

"Like sin," Lidwina said. "I can't stand people who are scandalized by sinners. A person who hasn't fought temptation has no right to judge."

"Lidwina, I've got to get dressed now. Chris will be here with the babysitter any minute now."

"Sure. Where's he taking you?"

"Nino's."

"He's a guy that does things right. Hang on to him."

"Oh," said Jane, "I intend to."

"You know you're beautiful tonight?" Chris guided the car through the country roads toward Pound Ridge.

"Good." Jane smiled. "I tried that new kind of makeup for my eyes. I was afraid it was too much."

"You have nothing to worry about," he said gently.

She moved closer to him on the seat. "Chris, this is what we needed. To get away a little bit together. I've been horrid, haven't I? I've wanted so much to be cheerful and calm and—"

"You've been avoiding me," he said in a comic tone.

"You know why."

"What does Dr. Polla say?"

"He isn't sure enough yet. We need months of records."

"But like I say, you don't have to avoid me completely."

"It's better not to think about it."

"You can't go on pretending we don't live together."

"You're the expert, you should know."

"It's nice having you sit this close. Can you come closer?"

Nino's was a place where New Yorkers came for elegance in the country, where waiters served with copper and flame and the menu was in French. There were eighteen kinds of red wine for Chris to choose from and he was courtly about it and gay.

Over her wineglass she saw him again not as a man to be endured, but as her lover. She looked at his nose and his nose seemed lonely and young, and tenderness welled in her. She was sorry she ever lost sight of that lonely nose.

Chris, seeing the sudden new fullness of her lips as she laughed, thought the wine was making him giddy.

Driving home through the night as she sat close to him, they came to the reservoir, black-rimmed with pine trees around dark waters. Chris stopped the car and whispered, "Lover's Lane is deserted in February. Too cold for teen-agers. It's all ours."

This is how it's meant to be, he thought, away, together. And he hated the memory of the house and the children and people and things and work, and could have cried that instant with the joy of returning to love.

"I've missed you." She barely whispered but he heard her.

He spoke again, calling her all the beautiful names he made true and real by his love, the litany of enchantment. Long ago it startled her to hear how he thought of her: my dove, my gazelle, my beloved—startled her to hear phrases from the Song of Solomon tumbling from the lips of a man so sensible, so suited and shined and white-collared. Now, as then, she understood that as their bodies would yield gratefully to nakedness, so their hearts yielded to truth, disrobing the creased worn garments of conventional speech.

And knowing again that his need for her made her a woman of beauty, the floodtide of her love for him rose. She yielded her mouth to him, answering the call whose existence she had so long denied. It was as it was before they were married. And as it had been then, the trust of her love rested on him, and he quieted them both, and guarded them both. Unconsumed fire was held for another day and another night.

They drove home silent, her cheeks warm, her head on his shoulder, their eyes following the everleading path of the headlights. February is over, she thought. Stale, dirty February is gone.

As the babysitter left, he took her in his arms. "Jane, just lie with me in my bed and let me hold you," he whispered.

"Chris, it's after midnight."

"You're right," he said slowly, letting her go. He saw her smile, read in it relief, and turned away before she could see how it hurt and puzzled him.

"It was a wonderful evening," she said. "I'm so glad everything's all right between us again. We have to keep it that way."

"We will," he said. "We will."

He lay awake long after she slept. He smiled wryly in the darkness. What difference was there between a car and a bed? Obviously for his wife, a difference. Well, he had held his tongue. He was growing wiser in his loneliness. She would not understand how it sounded to him. And at least she seemed happy. At least there would be an end to bickering and unhappiness. He would settle for that. For his own comfort. The last couple of weeks had been unbearable.

The next afternoon Lidwina came over in spite of the first wet March snowfall.

"You look happy as a bride," she observed, shaking the drops from her golden hair. "You had a good time last night?"

"I did."

"Good. That's what a marriage needs, to keep a man happy." Jane folded the diapers.

"You know, you have to be careful. I mean I was talking to Marianne Carpel the other day and she said Hugh saw Chris and Krena McDowell on the train together the other evening."

"So?" Jane stared her straight in the eye. Lidwina took out her compact.

"They didn't even notice him, they were so absorbed in what they were talking about," said Lidwina, peering in the mirror at her lipstick.

"What's that supposed to mean?"

"Nothing. Only that I'm glad you—had such a good time with Chris last night. You're handling everything just fine. You're no fool." Lidwina closed the compact and smiled at her.

TWENTY-ONE

Peter knew his mother didn't really want him to go see Miss Butler. And he didn't care. Miss Butler was his friend. And no matter what people said she wasn't crazy.

He had done a few odd jobs for her around the yard when the Settlers were at work and they had gotten to be friends. She made Scotch shortcake and it was the first no-icing cake he had ever liked. She made hot chocolate with a marshmallow crown and she talked to Peter as if he were a grownup.

Miss Butler had a little face with red spider lines and she wore glasses with no rims and gold earpieces that bent as easily as copper wire. She had shoulders and arms that surprised him by having muscles, in spite of the funny flabby pockets of flesh that hung around them. Her voice was quiet and her eyes were blue like a new baby's only bigger, and they were the kind of eyes that fastened on you and listened and Peter liked them.

Miss Butler knew a lot of things. She knew why dogs licked people, which was for the salt. She knew the story of the dogwood tree and why the flowers had four petals shaped like a cross and why there were rusty nailholes at the end of each petal, which was because the tree against its will had been the wood of the cross. She knew all the words to "The Good Reuben James" and a thing called "My Name Is Samuel Hall," with a refrain that said: "Damn your eyes." She knew another song which she suggested Peter better not sing in front of his mother and which went like this: "Last night my little baby died. She died committing suicide. I think she died to spite us. Of spinal meningitis. She was a nasty baby, anyhow."

Peter would spend an afternoon skating on the Lawrences' pond and then stop in to see Miss Butler before going home. He was never in a hurry to get home these days. He couldn't have said why even if Miss Butler asked him, which she did not. He wouldn't have known what words to use.

The color way of thinking didn't work as well now as it used to. There weren't many colors left inside him. Just sort of tight jagged gray. But the trouble at home had to do with his mother, of course. His mother did not seem to look at him when he talked any more, and she hurried him all the time, so that he felt he needed rest before he could go home to her. Crazy, but that's the way it was.

He had been very bad lately. He had not done his homework paper on Thomas Jefferson. He had not learned his catechism for ten days. He left his room a mess. He stole half the candy out of the box Daddy gave Mom for their anniversary. That last had aroused a satisfactory response. At least she had yelled at him and known he was there.

He didn't talk to Miss Butler about Mom, of course. There wasn't anyone he could talk to. He knew Mary was unhappy too, but there was nothing he could say to her.

She was unhappy. She knew she was having another war with her mother. She knew it by the way she herself was acting, knew it when she found herself sitting with Daddy and singing songs to him, knew it when she jumped rope and her pounding counting feet echoed: I hate Mommy. I hate Mommy. And: Nobody likes me. Nobody likes me.

Nobody-likes-me was an old familiar song. If there was one awful thing she knew about herself it was that she was a mess.

Peter doesn't like me. The feet beat on the porch floor as the jumprope whistled and slapped. He doesn't like me because I am a girl. He says I pester. He says I'm ugly. Daddy said I wasn't. That really bugged Peter. Hah! Sister doesn't like me. I sing too loud on the Bobwhite song in school. And Mary you daydream. Sister doesn't like me. Daddy is mad at me. Don't hang on me all the time, he said, like an old poison-ivy vine. He laughed but he meant it.

Mommy doesn't like me.

She stopped skipping, the rope lying limp against her legs. Mommy knew almost everything about her including the fact that she liked to taste the nose stuff when it ran, and the way she made up adventures and told them as true. But most of the time Mommy loved her anyway.

She dropped the rope and walked away from it. She found a piece of chalk in her jacket pocket, dusted it free of crumbs and shreds of tissue, and began drawing on the porch screen. She was quite sure she should not draw on screens.

She had had wars with her mother before. But this was a new one, terribly important. Not like the one about the red dress, or the one about wanting to go to the circus in New York. This was desperate. She tried to think what it was about. How do you grow up enough so when you say what bothers you no one groans?

She whispered to herself, testing different reasons in words, till she passed all the glib silky ones and found the one that made salt.

"It's because she doesn't love me and she doesn't love Daddy."

She bit her tongue, looking at the shape of that idea.

"She doesn't love Daddy and they're not telling me but they will go away and leave me, and I must stop them."

She would save them somehow. Tears, big and itchy and hot

ran down to the chinstrap of her hat. She pictured herself being hugged and kissed for saving her parents from divorce. Maybe they would give her a pony.

She stuck out her tongue and decided the pictures on the screen were hopeless and scribbled till chalk dust flew.

Her mother saw her through the door from the living room to the porch, started to scold her for making a mess, and decided it was just too much trouble.

At least the children don't know anything is wrong, she said to herself. I am alone. And I am learning to hide my thoughts even from myself. I haven't said a word to Chris about her. Not a word to anyone. I do not even think about her.

TWENTY-TWO

Father Mongiano was preparing notes for the next Cana Conference. Before him lay blue looseleaf folders, all neatly labeled. Pre-Cana. Cana I. Cana II. Tri-Cana. He had given the complete series four times and each time he went over the notes, adding material, anecdotes, phrases. This whole Cana nonsense, as his last pastor called it, was to him the fiery challenge, his most important apostolate, his severest cross.

He stood up and blew his nose. When he was nervous his nose ran.

"What is a priest doing talking about sex?" that pastor had said with distaste. "No matter what the bishop says, I don't see that it helps the laity or the priesthood for him to let you get up and speak of a subject that is best ignored. They'll say you have a dirty mind, Father."

A dirty mind. Obsessed with sex. Vicarious pleasure. They said all that. Not the young engaged couples at pre-Cana. Not the married ones at Cana I. It was priests who said that. Even Father Macy here, modern as an escalator, running upward forever, was delighted not to be assigned to Cana. "People would think me peculiar," he said.

It wasn't as if anyone could think Father Mongiano invented the Cana movement. He was no pioneer, except in the parishes of this particular diocese.

He remembered the night he arrived at St. Rose's. Father Temple had stood in the room where the parakeets chattered, inspecting his new curate. He had smiled, spoken of odds and ends, and at last inquired in his habitual shout, "You are, are you not, the Cana priest?"

Father Mongiano had rocked on his toes till his shoes squeaked. "Not *the* Cana priest, Father. A. The bishop put several of us in the movement. I am one of ten in the diocese, as I am sure you know."

"I don't suppose you had a choice in the matter, Father."

"I could have refused, perhaps, Father. But Cana is a movement I consider extremely important."

"Why, Father?" Father Temple thundered.

He had pitched his own tones low to cut under the storm.

"I believe the holy vocation of marriage has been treated like an ugly stepchild. I believe that marriage, including the holy act of sex, is a life as demanding as the vocation to religious life. St. Paul compared husband and wife to Christ and the Church. But the Church until lately has been ignoring husband and wife. Our people live in a world that sees nothing holy in sex. They live in a world where it is hard to be Christian. If I can show a husband and wife what marriage and sacred relations mean, then —"

"I did not ask for a sample of your sermons," Father Temple shouted. "I have been to the seminary myself, you know."

For a few minutes only the parakeets spoke, in strange machine-like approximations of words.

Then the pastor said quietly:

"Sacred relations." He was testing the words on his tongue, his face betraying no judgment. "A daring phrase." He had sat with the bird on his shoulder and a freshly lit cigar in his teeth. "I am sure you will plan your work so that this Cana thing does not interfere with your regular parish duties."

That was the last the pastor said on the subject. He did not know whether in the two years since that day Father Temple approved or disapproved his teaching. He did know that St. Rose's and all parishes within a twenty-mile area were much in need of the Cana spirit.

He opened the notebook labeled Cana I, Husband and Wife Relationship. The biggest section was the one headed Birth Control. Twenty pages of notes and clippings. Yet it was the one he felt least prepared for.

He had tried once to explain: "A priest has the power to bring forth the Son of God under the appearance of bread and wine. Can you imagine saying to that priest in a sermon: 'You must not do anything to prevent the transubstantiation at Mass. It would be a terrible sin secretly to change the way you act when you bend over the bread and wine, so that without anyone's knowing it you deliberately prevented the Consecration.' What could be more ridiculous to say to a priest? He became a priest so that he could do this.

"Then why tell a married man what he must not do? Why not simply remind him of the invisible world of grace which is more real than the world of bills and illness and fear?"

But he had been told he must spell out the sin of birth prevention. The analogy, after all, was not perfect. So he had texts on the technicalities and quotations from experts, and he knew all about it. Except how to reach the ones who needed it most. He studied his notes.

"Marriage is a sacrament—a Christ-coming. Like all sacraments it is both personal and social. The sacrament of baptism, for example, is personal for the one who is baptized. But social, in that it gives the whole mystical Christian community new dimension by the creation of a new grace-bearer. Marriage is personal, giving husband and wife rights to the private union of body, heart, mind and soul to bring them to mutual perfection. But marriage is even more social in its primary end, giving God potential co-creators and co-tenders of future saints, giving the mystical community new impetus in the slow fulfillment of heaven and earth. . . .

"God constrains himself to use the generous love of husband and wife. Who dares understand the dignity of sacred relations in marriage?"

Father Mongiano nodded. That thought might be over some of these young couples' heads now, but he personally needed to know it had been said. He read on.

"The Christian in marriage, seeing it has to do with genital union which normally causes conception and birth, seeing that procreation is an act partaking of God's own creative role, must bring the full Christian personality to bear on the need to rightly order sexual love in the greater conjugal love. He must use intelligence, will, love and grace to cooperate with God's will, which is to form saints: of man, wife, and what children there may be."

Looking at his notes he smiled now, and again underlined the next few sentences. For some reason it was always necessary to remind people that the Church does not insist that a husband and wife breed as many children as they can. He wondered where and when that idea became popular.

"The Church is not against birth control, or family limitation. The Church expects married couples to exercise intelligent control of sexual powers, and to decide prayerfully how many children they can fittingly raise.

"What the Church forbids is the use of mechanical devices or medicines which unnaturally frustrate the purpose of sacred relations. For human beings to divorce pleasure from responsibility is immoral, undignified, unethical. The one contraceptive device the Church approves is an exercise: the slow shaking of the head from one side to the other in self-denial."

Father Mongiano frowned. Always someone asked: Since contraceptive devices are products of human intelligence, why can't they be acceptably used as intelligent control? Though he had tried many answers, he always fell back on the old example of the person who is determined to enjoy food when for medical reasons he cannot afford to.

"If he constructed a device which let him enjoy and swallow a high-calorie feast whenever he wanted while preventing the food from reaching his stomach, would that be human, admirable, intelligent? Or would it be, like the old Roman vomitorium, shocking to our concept of proper human behavior?

"To serve God and perfect themselves, a husband and wife need to use souls and minds and wills as well as bodies. Human perfection demands self-discipline, self-mastery, respect for the economy of reality. For sexual control there must be mastery of the body by the soul. And the soul's mastery of the body implies a mastery of the willing soul by God."

Cana conferences often featured discussion panels of married couples. Contraception properly belonged not in panel discussion, but in the sermon. Still, Father Mongiano felt the need for a lay couple who could surely express the beauty of natural marriage, and of family limitation in God's way. He needed a woman sure of her faith and her marriage.

He decided to call Jane McNamara.

TWENTY-THREE

March whispered deceitfully of spring. Jane stood with the baby carriage watching Kilian and Luke play on the soggy brown lawn. "You're sure you don't mind babysitting?" she asked.

"Sure." Gloria shrugged deeper into the black velveteen raincoat. "I told you I felt lousy anyway. And Hack's giving a lecture at NYU tonight."

Teresa opened her eyes and smiled. Jane rocked the carriage.

"Something's eating you." Gloria leaned on the split-rail fence. "You and Chris getting tired of each other?"

"Of course not."

"Well every time I come up here you two glum and gloom around. The last three weekends."

"Don't come if it bothers you."

"That's some book he's working on now. He was telling me about it last night. The one he's working on with Krena?" She gave Jane one of her oblique smiles.

"Quite a book."

"Might be a movie, he said."

"For you, Mom!" Luke and Kilian ran breathlessly to her side. "Look what we found!" Half-crushed crocuses filled their muddy hands.

"Lucky you. Wish someone would bring me flowers."

Lidwina came across the grass from her house. "How're you, Gloria? Excuse me. I came to ask a favor. We have septic-tank trouble. Would you mind terribly? We're going to be without plumbing for days!"

"Be my guest," said Jane.

Gloria giggled. "Oh, the delights of family life in the country."

Jane was staring at the crocuses.

"They're pretty," Lidwina said. "But they won't last even in water."

"Nothing lasts," said Jane.

"What's with her?" Lidwina looked at Gloria.

"Who knows? Perhaps she ponders some deep problem. Perhaps she's in another world." Gloria smiled. "Anyway it's quiet being with her. She's like she isn't even there."

"Cut it out," said Jane.

"All set?" Chris asked as they started for the church basement and the Cana Conference that night. "Ready to make your debut as a panel expert?"

"Doesn't it seem funny? Two people like us being asked to tell other people how to make a good marriage. It's sort of sad," she said.

Chris did not reply. This strangeness that had come between them made him brusque because he was helpless. She was part of him, bone of his bone, flesh of his flesh, but like a foot under local anesthesia she seemed to be no part of him at all. He had looked at her these last few days with detachment and compassion, exactly as he had once watched a doctor dissect his ankle muscles in the aftermath of a boyhood accident. Pain was postponed. Now there was only fascination and suspense and a kind of revulsion. It was not good to feel that way about one's wife. He had thought he had won his way back to her heart by the reservoir that anniversary night. Since then she had moved away from him again, and he did not know why. He sighed.

"I suppose you're bored?" she asked in the sarcastic voice she used so much now.

"Not bored. Just unhappy. What's got into you, anyhow?"

"Nothing. Nothing at all.

"Then snap out of it."

"You ought to know why I'm miserable."

"Well, I don't. And I don't think you know how miserable you are to live with," he said. "Sometimes I don't even want to come home any more."

"I'll bet you don't. I'll bet you'd rather work with Krena."

He laughed shortly. "Is that what's eating you? Krena?"

"Go on, laugh. You'd laugh if people kept calling you up about how close you two sit on the train. 'Oh, I like riding the train so I can be alone and think, and it's a decompression chamber, to help me come home to you.' That's what you used to say. Now you spend all your time with Krena."

The headlights touched the pale yellow willow branches beside St. Rose's Church. Chris stepped on the gas and hurried past.

"Where are you going?"

"I'm not going to the Cana Conference if that's what you mean. Not like this."

"Well, don't blame me! You asked what was wrong. And I'm telling you."

"Am I supposed to understand you're jealous of Krena? Is that what happened? I thought after that night we went to Nino's we were all straightened out. Did somebody call you up and tell you something about me and Krena, is that it?"

He pulled the car over near a dark wall, jerked it to a stop, and turned off the motor. "Is that it? And you're going around being nasty because you think I'm carrying on with her?" he asked harshly.

"You ought to know."

"If you think I'm going to deny it, you're crazy." His jaw tightened. "If you think there's anything to deny, that's your business. You can push me too far. I'm fed up with all these emotions of yours."

"Well, who cares? I've got a right to my emotions. I'm not a researcher and an intellectual like you. You don't care about me. You don't love me any more and you know it."

"Have it your way."

They sat in silence. A car whizzed by.

"Are we going to just sit here?" she demanded.

"Why not?"

"And what am I supposed to say to Father Mongiano?"

"Who cares about Father Mongiano?"

"I care. And I don't want to just sit here. The least you could do is—" She started to cry.

"Is what?"

"I don't want to have to tell you. You ought to know how I feel. And you won't even tell me you love me."

"You haven't liked my telling you I loved you. You've kept me pretty far away. Maybe I'm getting used to it. Maybe I'm tired of being told hands off."

She sobbed harder.

He started the engine, pulled the car onto the road.

"Chris?" She blew her nose hard.

"Dry your eyes. Put some powder on and make yourself look decent. We're late now as it is."

They were so late they missed the panel part altogether and never got to say anything publicly or answer any questions. Father Mongiano, who had counted on Divine Providence to help him, was puzzled and a little hurt when his prize examples did not show up till too late.

Hurried, embarrassed, they took seats in the back of St. Rose's gym. Forty engaged couples sat there with the basketball net hanging over the green cloth-covered speaker's table, with the overlapping patterns of different games painted on the floor, and the American flag, and the benches that could be hidden away in the walls, and the smell of sneakers, and the pretty centerpiece of the Holy Family surrounded by laurel leaves and plastic roses.

Father Mongiano was already on his closing speech:

"Love is not something you fall into. You nurture love and make it grow. Love is God's own life, the mystery-life of the Trinity. When you love each other you share that vast intense life of God. You will love each other in the flesh, with your bodies, giving, not counting cost or a bargain, but seeking your unity. You will love each other in the mind, respecting dignity, overlooking mistakes, sharing where you can the adventures of the intellect. You will love each other in the heart. And in the soul. See that your partner in marriage is the one person through whom the Lord intends you to find salvation. And when you give love to your wife or husband, you give love directly to Christ. Your love is a debt you owe forever.

"And remember that you live a mystery. A parable, as St. Paul says, of the mystery of Christ and His Church."

Jane looked at Chris. Chris was looking only at his hands. They were strong hands, white but large and heavily boned, as if they should rest on homespun and a gun, and she grew tender over those hands. She wanted them to be hers alone. She could not bear even to think that he might not be exclusively hers.

I have been away and I have nearly lost everything. Perhaps I have already lost it. I had forgotten what it was that I had.

The young faces around her, men with brush-cuts and Adam's apples, girls with their teeth exposed in too-big smiles and elaborate hair-dos seemed somehow vulnerable and sad. She did not want to be apart from Chris. She wanted life to be simple and happy again.

She put her hand over Chris's. He looked at her, sat back in his seat, took her hand and put it between his. Such a small thing. So important.

I must think clearly, she said to herself. But I am no good at logic. I reject logic. I have been afraid to love. Yet that is what women are for. I have been afraid to die. Too damn afraid to die and so I haven't been living. I've been losing everything. To find your life you must lose it. And there's more than one kind of life.

Her hand tightened on Chris's. She felt her cheeks burning.

There is more than one kind of sacrifice. There are women who take the sin upon themselves, concealing it from their husbands. They have told me why they do this, but I did not understand them. And I condemned them. I thought they were rationalizing. As someone might say I am rationalizing now. Her thoughts whirled, fevered, confused.

There is a law of self-preservation. She tried again to be logical. She had more than herself to preserve. Her pulse beat in her throat. This human life. This life of grace. But she did not want either if her husband did not love her, and loved another. All or nothing.

Chris, Christopher, I cannot ask you to sin, nor can I refuse you the love only I should give. When I refuse you I expose you to the danger of sin. Her pulse beat in her throat. But I love you. And you shall know it, before it is too late. For love I will do this, in the name of God, and call it right!

She did not listen to Father Mongiano. Her eyes fell on the Holy Family statue on the table, and she remembered that she had not been to daily Mass for weeks, not since Valentine's Day. She couldn't care less. No one missed me. The priests wouldn't notice. Not even Chris has asked why I do not go.

Father Mongiano finished. The young couples seemed impressed, excited, moved by the whole evening. She held Chris's hand and watched. It occurred to her that Father Mongiano was very young. He took every word of what he was told to preach as literally true. But there was more to it than he knew. Once he had explained at great length why you had to fast from midnight until Holy Communion. Two weeks later the Pope changed the law so you had to fast only three hours. What happened to all those beautiful explanations then? Father Mongiano simply answered that there was a difference between man-made regulations like fasting and God-made laws about right and wrong. Jane had agreed with him then. She smiled now, remembering that her mother had urged her to reconsider that argument.

As in a dream she got up, going with Chris and the others over to the church to Benediction. She looked at Chris, knowing her decision was made, exulting in it, perversely delighted that she had made it in a Cana Conference. Chris stared at her. Some mystery, some giddy challenge in her startled him. He could not think of

116

anything he had said or done to bring this change in her, except perhaps having refused to tell her he loved her.

The congregation sang. He sang with them, the *O Salutaris* and the *Tantum Ergo,* and the physical exhilaration of singing and the well-being of full lungs and open throat pleased him. I feel a bit drunk, he thought, on red wine, on red wine.

In his own way he prayed to the Blessed Sacrament, a young prayer, the shy rejoicing of a man who hardly dares hope his dream has come true.

His eyes and Jane's met, and he did not know or ask how or why she was restored. He felt only that she was alive again. He pressed her hand.

She moved closer to him, her head bowed not in prayer, but in defiance of the Sacrament before her.

TWENTY-FOUR

It shocked her to discover how easily she could get information. All she had to do was go to the public library. She found a book that might as well, she thought, be titled *How to Do It and Why.* She was reminded of her pigtail days of sending for things in plain wrappers, along with the little practical jokes from smudgy Johnson and Smith catalogs. Only this book had no plain wrapper. She was glad none of the librarians who knew her was on duty. She was glad she carried an enormous pocketbook so she could hide it. Fine thing for a Catholic mother of six to be carrying on the street.

At home, she disguised the book in the dustjacket of the new St. Bernadette biography, and began to read. Her first reaction was incredulity that so many people went to such extraordinary and undignified lengths as a matter of routine. What would they think of me? They'd call me naive. They'd pity me in my embarrassment. They'd think me coy. They wouldn't begin to understand. For me this is almost the end. A matter of life and death. Or do they think of souls? There came over her too the same dazed fever that had gripped her when, in a boarding school closet by flashlight, she once read such forbidden books as the *Decameron* and *Jurgen* and *Sanctuary.*

This book was by a doctor. It evaluated techniques, described them in detail, and offered a few addresses of clinics in big cities. A clinic suited her fine. She was glad not to have to face Dr. Perkins. Two days later she announced that she was going into New York.

"Altman's is having a sale and I need to find some bedspreads. I have to do something about the children's rooms. And I'm sick of the stores around here," she said.

Chris looked up from the evening paper. "Do you good, a day in town. You rate a change, a bit of fun. Want to meet me in town and have dinner?"

"No. I want to get home early, Chris. There's a whole batch of things I have to take care of when I do get home, you know, and I can't keep a sitter too long with this mob."

She took the Ladies' Day Excursion train along with some six hundred hatted and perfumed women gabbling about shopping and matinees and cocktails.

That night she reported at the dinner table that she could not find decent spreads.

"I'm going to keep right on looking," she said. "I think I'll go into town once a week, on Ladies' Day."

"Haven't seen you looking this chipper in weeks," said Chris. "Going to the big city does something for you."

In the middle of ladling out side dishes of applesauce she bent over and kissed him. She met his look of surprise with smiling cryptic eyes.

"Go to New York every day," he suggested, chuckling. "In fact, twice a day!"

On these trips to town she passed almost unnoticed. Few of her friends had time for shopping and shows. Once she saw Marianne Carpel on the train.

"Jane! Taking a day for yourself in New York?" Her mink brushed Jane's tweed coat. "I thought you never got away. You need to be a bit selfish once in a while. Does a gal a world of good." Her gloved hand clinked with heavy gold bracelets as she went down the aisle to join her friends. "Have fun!"

A bit selfish? Jane smiled. That's one way of putting it. Have fun. How would it be if I told you I was visiting a Planned Parenthood clinic? That the first time I went I panicked and ran. But I'm going back. I'm taking a very important first step. Abruptly she lit a cigarette. She had almost learned not to think at all.

It is only the first step, her mind insisted now. Even when you are measured, and have it, you can turn back. Her cheeks flushed and she turned her head to the window.

This train car went regularly back and forth to New York, all day, all night. It might even be part of the five-thirteen. This seat could be Chris' seat. Chris and Krena took the five-thirteen. He never mentioned her any more, never.

The train pulled into Grand Central Station. Tall, aloof, she threaded her way through the crowd, refusing to be pushed or hurried or herded. It was important to her to remain apart.

Two hours later she came out of the clinic, took a bus to Altman's, bought two bedspreads in twenty minutes, and found a phone booth.

"Chris? It's me. You busy?"

"No. I'm never busy when you call." Chris glanced over at the table where Krena was working. "Did you get your bedspreads?"

"I did. Finally. No more Ladies' Day Excursions for me. Chris, can you have lunch with me?"

"Jane, I can't. The author of that Young Tom Jefferson thing is coming in. I can't break it. You said you'd be busy."

"I know. I was just hoping."

"Jane, my mother wants to come up tonight and stay over the weekend. She'll take the train with me. She's a little hurt that you didn't ask her."

"Was there a reason I should?"

"Mary's birthday is Sunday. You know she never misses that."

"Okay, sure. Sorry her feelings are hurt, but tell her I've been so busy that if Mary hadn't nagged me I would have forgotten all about her birthday. Gee, Chris, I wish we could have a weekend all to ourselves, without Gloria or your mother or anyone."

"Really? I like to hear that. Tell me more."

Krena picked a dying leaf off the philodendron on the table.

"Maybe we can talk tonight," said Jane. "I'd better let you go. I love you, dear."

"Bye," he said.

"Someone's with you! Why didn't you tell me? Well, you don't have to say you love me if it embarrasses you. Just say 'so long,' and I'll know."

"So long." He laughed. "So long."

Krena bent over her pile of notes as he hung up the phone.

"That was Jane," he said.

She nodded. "What do you think we should do with the gardener? Drop him completely from the story? It's either that or build him up more."

The phone rang again, the Jefferson author saying he'd be half an hour late.

"That's the ninth interruption." Krena swung around in her chair. "I keep losing my train of thought. I wish we could work somewhere where it's absolutely quiet."

"That would be novel."

"I wish we could work at my house. I have a huge library table. Nobody would phone or come in. We could finish up these last chapters in no time."

"Stop daydreaming and get to work." He grinned.

"This way it isn't fair to you. This was supposed to take a week of your time, and it's stretching out forever. Helping me is becoming a full-time job."

"I'm not complaining."

"I know. But I'll bet if we could work at my house you'd be rid of this book and me with just one or two days' solid work."

"I think the gardener has to come out," he said.

"You think I'm kidding?" She smiled. "I think I'll suggest it to R. P. Would you like that?"

"I'd love it." He frowned.

She paced the tiny cubicle, hands behind her back, head raised. The skirt of her gray suit flared slightly with each turn she made.

"I'm thinking," she explained. "After all, a woman can't be too careful. And I have a horrible feeling you're actually afraid you might have to be alone with me. Are you?"

"Of course. Isn't it the gallant thing to be afraid?"

She stopped pacing. "That's more like it. I was afraid you were going all serious on me again." She sat down. "The gardener's out. I'll go back and indicate how to take him out of every chapter he's in."

"Good."

"Chris?" She cupped her chin in her hands. "I don't want to work any more now. I'm so lonely I could cry."

"Hey, wait a minute."

"You're so lucky. Jane's so lucky. Everybody's so lucky. Even the woman in this damn novel. What've I got? Not even a ghost. This book's getting me. I'll have to remember not to work on love stories in the future."

"You'll really narrow the field."

"I know." She closed her eyes. "You know what I wish? Don't laugh. I wish I had a home and a husband. And babies."

"I didn't even start to laugh."

"Funny. You told me once you thought it was hard on Jane having all those babies. And I envy her. I've tried and hoped. And seen doctors."

He started to speak.

"Not a chance," she said. She pushed back her chair. "How the hell did this happen? I don't usually go around baring my soul, believe me." She smoothed her hair. "I've got a lunch date, too. See you later."

At the door she paused. "Will you mind if we don't work on the train tonight? You did say your mother would be with you, didn't you? She might not appreciate me. Or I her, for that matter."

"I don't think Jane appreciates her," he said.

When Jane got home Gloria's car was in the drive, and at the sight of it she ticked her lips in exasperation. She took the mail from the box and sat in the car to read it, hating to surrender the last moments of privacy.

There was a letter from Father Tom.

"All we need is for him to come and visit now!" she said out loud. "Wouldn't that be ducky." She opened the letter.

Dear Chris and Jane, I forgot your wedding anniversary. Forgive me. I was sent to Camden to a convention of mission procurators. Then I got involved in a dreadful project. I am now peddling African-type Christmas cards. I had to go up to Cape Cod to see an Irish lady artist with green eyes and charm her into designing six authentic-type native blockprints for me.

I have a black Madonna of Mercy. A manger scene in a Kikuyu hut. And so on. Very nice, I suppose. I cannot abide selling Christmas cards. Then I went back to Camden to arrange for 10,000 of them.

But for your anniversary I have made a card myself. One father here keeps a drawerful of greeting cards rescued from wastebaskets for just such emergencies. I have pasted on one of them a poetic masterpiece of my own. It has, I think, overtones of Peguy, only racier. I send it with love.

She could see that the card once read; "Congratulations and prayers on the anniversary of your ordination." He had crossed out the last three words. She read his verse:

LITTLE FLOCK, LOVE ONE ANOTHER,—
As sister and brother
As husband and wife,
For all of your life.
Undaunted . . .
Unhaunted . . .
Daring and caring.
IN CHRIST
YOU ARE SPLICED.

She shook her head. His poetic talents diminished all the time—as his love grew.

The rest of the mail was a letter from her mother, worried because Gloria hadn't written her in a whole month, a few bills, an ad from a lawn service.

Gloria poked her head out into the garage. "Thought I heard a car," she said. She was wearing a fuzzy yellow plaid dress and big copper earrings. Meg was clinging to her legs. "You don't look very glad to see me."

"Mother wants to know why you don't write her. Thinks you have a deep dark secret," Jane said, hugging the bedspread box as she went in the house.

"Can't think of anything to say she'd approve of." Gloria laughed. "She doesn't like my riotous living, or Hack, or my wanting to go to Africa. I took your sitter home. I even paid her. Aren't you proud of me?"

"Sure." Jane turned down the hi-fi on which Gloria had been playing Mexican folksongs.

"I think," said Gloria, "my big sister doesn't like me."

"I love you, but I'm exhausted," Jane said. "I had quite a day. And I just don't feel like any noise after the city. I'd like to just flop and be alone for a minute."

Jane went upstairs to change out of her city clothes. Teresa was lying in the crib, chewing a zwieback. She gurgled at the sight of Jane.

"Hi, all alone? Lucky child!"

"Jane! Martha Settler's here. Wants to see you!" Gloria called up the stairs. Wearily, Jane went down to greet this latest disturbance. Martha looked as crisp as usual, but Jane could tell she was upset.

"Wanted to tell you Felicity Lawrence's boy is dreadfully sick." Martha said. "You've got to pray for him. I just came off volunteer duty."

"She told me he was sick," Jane said. "Called me up a while ago."

"They've got specials around the clock. I'm so upset for her."

"Well come on and have a cup of coffee and calm down."

"You know, there's no one like your sister," Martha told Gloria. "Just talking to her makes me feel better."

"Oh, she's quite a gal," said Gloria.

"Jane. That poor Felicity. I think the boy's going to die. I wish you would talk to her. It must be awful for her. I think maybe Father Temple's going down to see the boy. You know he's been hoping Harold would come into the Church one day. They're great friends." Martha stirred the coffee. "Do you think this is part of God's plan? A tragedy like this to bring Harold in?"

"Perhaps," said Jane.

Martha cocked her head. Something in Jane's manner puzzled her. "You look tired, Jane. Is anything the matter?"

"With me? Nothing."

"You don't sound like your old self. Haven't for a while now."

"I like your sweater, Martha," Gloria said. "I love purple."

"Martha wears purple because it's Lent," said Jane.

"Heavens! Forty days of purple? How can you have enough clothes?"

"You build up a collection over the years," said Martha, not sure whether she was being ridiculed. She finished her coffee quickly. "I've got to go. By the way, Jane, your Pete's the best thing that's ever happened to my sister. She's a bug on nature walks. That's one fine boy to be so nice to her."

"It's good for him, too," Jane said.

"And don't forget the Lawrence boy. Sorry to have interrupted you sisters in your visit, but—say a prayer."

After she left, Jane fixed the baby's formula in silence.

"People are always coming to you like that, aren't they?" Gloria said. "Do you really pray for them?"

"Sure."

"Does it do any good?"

"I won't bother answering that."

"She's right. You don't sound like yourself. But I'll bet she still thinks you did her a world of good by talking to her. And she did all the talking."

Jane measured evaporated milk and water.

"I wish you'd pray for me. I got problems." Gloria tilted her head with a slanting smile.

"I'll bet. If you want to file your nails will you please go somewhere else? I can't stand that sound."

Gloria laid the emery board on the table. "So you don't think I have problems?"

"Did it ever occur to you that I have problems too?" Jane capped the bottles and put them in the sterilizer. "One of my biggest problems is getting away from other people's problems so I can take care of my own."

The phone rang. Gloria answered. "It's a Father Temple for you," she said. "Have another problem."

"Jane?" the pastor shouted. "You know Harold and Felicity Lawrence. Their boy is in the hospital. Wonder if you would go down and visit Felicity?"

"Oh, Father, I can't. I just can't today. First things first, you always say."

"I counted on you."

"She'd probably like it if you went yourself," said Jane politely. As she hung up she looked at Gloria.

"What the hell do they think Felicity's boy has to do with me?"

Gloria opened Jane's pocketbook which lay on the table.

"Get out of there!" Jane snapped.

"I was just looking for a match, sweetie," Gloria said.

"Well, don't. I wish I had some privacy. For my house, my time, and my pocketbook."

"I'll stay out of your way," Gloria said. "I won't bother you with any more problems, believe me."

TWENTY-FIVE

Father Temple muttered to himself as he climbed the front steps of the hospital. "There ought to be someone who would go and visit Harold's boy beside me. I'm a squeamish old man, and I don't know what to say to Felicity. Or Harold."

"Afternoon, Father," said a janitor.

The priest started, and nodded a greeting. He had thought Jane McNamara would go. She was the kind of girl who, when he asked her something, did it.

He pressed the elevator buzzer.

"They'd probably like it if you went yourself, Father," she'd said. He hadn't liked the tone of her voice. Jane usually cared about people, about anyone who needed any kind of help.

"Sounded like she couldn't care less," he muttered. "Polite as all getout."

It occurred to him that he was angry mostly because she had made him do what he ought to do, instead of letting him put it off on her. And he cleared his throat and snorted, and nearly knocked into an aide getting off the elevator.

"Father Temple!" Rosary beads rattling, a woman clutched his arm as he hurried down the second-floor corridor.

"Ah, Mrs. Kczuck."

"You never come see my man, Father Temple. The curates they come. But they are boys. Three months he lies here dying and you never come yourself. Come now, Father, you got a minute."

The yellow skin of her face, the near-white of her hair, the black shawl, the grip of her fingers. "I can't," Father Temple said. "I will soon. But now, I can't. Forgive me."

Felicity Lawrence was parked in her sportscar by a farm on the hill near Jane's house. To her left stretched the fields where cows experimented patiently with the foretaste of spring. She thought to herself that she would like to go and lay her head on the side of one big brown-and-white cow and rest where no one could find her until it was all over one way or another.

She was tired of bulletins, tired of peering into nurse's faces, of trying to read the doctor's mind. She could hardly keep her eyes focused now. I don't blame the apostles for falling asleep in the Garden. Now I know the intense weariness that overcomes the spirit when suffering is too great to watch.

She took out a stick of chewing gum. The smell of peppermint made it easier to believe in reality.

Good God, sweet Lord, my son is dying.

This is the boy we waited for. With him the family name dies. If he dies, how can I live with Harold? Dear God, we can never have another child.

She turned the key in the ignition. She wanted desperately to talk to someone, to alarm the world to prayer. I could go down the hill and see Jane. I always liked Jane. I could talk to her, even though I don't know her very well. I remember once at a funeral my aunt said that there was one thing about Catholics: when there's real trouble they have something to say or give that most others don't.

I spoke to Jane yesterday. But she just said the words anyone would say. She didn't really care.

As if she wanted no part of me, Felicity thought. Could I have done anything to make her angry at me? I haven't talked to her about anything except little Harold, and oh yes, the party. But could she have been angry at what I said then? I meant to be nice to her.

No, the way Jane's voice sounded it wasn't angry, just cold. Felicity pursed her lips. Catholics. There was another thing about them. They were always so darn smug. So damn sure about sin, and retribution. As bad as Presbyterians sometimes. Maybe Jane had heard some kind of gossip about Harold. I have an uneasy feeling there is gossip that started who knows where.

If Jane heard that, she probably thinks this is a punishment from God. That would be what a damn smug Catholic would think.

Well, God wouldn't do that.

She grew angry just thinking about such an idea. The anger comforted her and stimulated her. By God, nobody, not Jane McNamara, nor Father Temple, nor anyone was going to be self-righteous to her, and tell her God would do a thing like that.

She drove back to the hospital.

Father Temple stood inside the room. The boy in the bed looked to him like some ghastly corsage with that oxygen tent. Tubes ran into the skinny arms, tubes ran down his nose. You could hardly see it was a boy in that bed.

"I can't think of a thing to say, Harold."

"I'm tired of what people say," said Harold quietly. His manner was, as usual, manly, strong. Only there was a tension about his mouth. "Our minister was here this morning. He said—" his voice broke.

"You don't mind if I pray?"

"I wish you would."

"What are you doing here, Father Temple?" Felicity stood in the doorway, her color high against her severely drawn-back hair.

"Felicity," said Harold.

"Well, I'm surprised. I didn't expect to see him here."

"Perhaps you'd rather be alone," the priest offered.

"I really would."

The nurse by the bed looked up to remind them to be quiet.

Harold took his wife's hand. "Father came because he's my friend. He's going to pray."

"I don't want his prayers." Felicity looked composed. Only her words betrayed her hysteria. Felicity would never speak to me like that if she were herself, Father Temple thought.

"She's distraught," he said, edging toward the door. "Poor Felicity."

Harold followed him into the hall. "What can I say?"

"Nothing. I shouldn't have come." The old priest smiled. "But I'll pray for him. I can pray anywhere. You know that. Get back now, and talk to her. She needs you."

He hurried down the hall and rang for the elevator. The door opened. He hesitated, then turned and walked to the room where old Mr. Kczuck lay. He squared his shoulders and walked in smiling.

At table that night he was silent.

"About the convent-drive committee, Father," said Father Macy, dropping his rumpled napkin on the empty plate.

Father Temple grunted.

"There's another meeting tonight to organize it. And I'm having a bit of trouble. I thought maybe you'd speak to the men."

"You handle it, Father."

Father Macy frowned. "Chris McNamara's the head of it, you know, and at the last meeting he was complaining about the cost of the convent. Said the people in the parish were all wondering. And I don't think they like my ideas for fund-raising at all."

"You're the one who's all for lay apostolates. You handle them."

"They say—"

"Never mind what they say. You talk to them. I could have told you you'd waste incredible amounts of energy to get nowhere in these committee meetings. But you wanted these lay apostles to help. And I am old-fashioned." He leaned back in his chair and filled his pipe. "Just don't get high and mighty with them, Father Macy. In your zeal you sometimes forget that these activities, even fund-raising, aren't the most important things. Or is that advice too old-fashioned for you?"

Father Macy smiled. "All right."

The first puffs of sweet rum smoke rose from the pipe. "Chris McNamara. Now, did you ever think of talking to his wife? Perhaps there are other problems they face you know nothing of, Father Macy."

And you do, I suppose, Father Macy wanted to answer.

The pastor closed his eyes. "You became a priest to take care of souls," he said quietly. "So did I. I would rather leave the ninety-nine and go in search of the one, if I knew that one is lost."

Father Mongiano stared at him curiously. He had never heard his pastor in this mood before.

"The trouble is, the flock is big," Father Temple continued. "And my sheep do not always appear obviously lost. And I do not think I am the one to go in search of them." He opened his eyes. "Can you tell me a soul in need of a shepherd? Father Mongiano, do you know the souls of this parish, with all the Cana work you do? Father Macy, are they to you just men and women to collect money from and organize? Or are they—"

The phone rang. Behind the pastor's words the curates heard the housekeeper answer.

"—are they God's children in need of a Father?"

The housekeeper leaned through the swinging door. "There's a drunk on the phone, Father Temple. Wants to talk to you personal. Can I hang up on him?"

"I'll take it for you, Father," said Father Mongiano.

"And if you'll excuse me, Father, I've got to be going," said Father Macy quickly.

The pastor sat silently smoking. Father Mongiano returned.

"He simply said we could all go to hell and to tell you he said so. He wouldn't give his name, and somebody took the phone away from him, apologized and hung up."

Father Temple peered up at him. "Anyone we know?"

"I'm afraid it was Mike O'Shea. I couldn't mistake that voice."

"And the other voice?"

"The one that apologized could have been Chris McNamara."

Father Temple sighed. "You never know," he said. "If I were to write my memoirs I'd say before a young man becomes a priest he needs the gift of second sight."

TWENTY-SIX

The rain, which started as Chris came home with Annie in tow, turned to a black spring downpour.

The children in bed, Jane sat with Annie while the television blared a comedy hour, and she could hear the water protesting in the gutters and downspouts. Through the smeary storm windows she saw the lights of the O'Shea house glittering on the puddles.

"You should watch this, Jane," Annie said a little crossly. "You're missing it all. Chris'll be back when he can. You know how men are when they get to talking."

"Yes." said Jane.

"Didn't Chris tell me he had a convent-drive meeting tonight? Maybe he went directly there from the O'Sheas." Annie gave a little shriek of laughter. "Oh look, that man is the funniest—"

Jane walked out to the kitchen. She put her hand on the phone, then decided she could not call. When the phone rang she jumped.

"Jane? Look. I'm—I'm not going to be able to make it to that meeting. Can you call the rectory and tell Father Macy?"

"What's going on? Is something wrong with the O'Sheas?"

His voice seemed to crouch by the phone as he tried to speak without being overheard. "All hell's broken loose, Jane. Mike's drunk and he's—I can't tell you now. Lidwina—I'll be home when I can, Jane."

Chris hung up as Mike walked over to him.

"Mike's not drunk," Mike said. "Not yet."

"You need some coffee, though," said Chris.

Mike's hair, usually painstakingly slicked down, was disheveled. His tie was awry and his collar open to reveal his thick, muscular neck. Funny, Chris thought, this is the first time I've ever seen the poor guy look natural.

"Okay, coffee," Mike said. "Who're you talking to, your wife?"

Chris nodded.

"Did you tell her? Or did she know about it? Was that what Lidwina was doing all the time, running over to Jane and telling her about it? I thought better of Jane than that."

"Jane didn't know anything about it. And she doesn't now. I didn't tell her."

"Why not? Why the hell not?" Mike sat down on the table by the phone. "How do you know she didn't know? Why not tell her, tell her I'm going to find that guy and punch him in the teeth." He smiled at Chris his eyes, half-closed. "Punch him in the teeth."

"I'm going to make coffee," Chris said. He could still hear Lidwina sobbing upstairs. Thank God the two kids were away with the high school basketball team.

"I'm not going to stay here, you know," said Mike.

"Good. But you can't go anywhere the way you're feeling now. And come away from that phone."

"What's it supposed to be, a secret?" roared Mike. "Lidwina! Can you hear me? Am I supposed to keep this a secret?"

"Come on, leave her alone. You're not going upstairs."

"Here I was so innocent," Mike started to cry. "Such an innocent man. And let me tell you what happened."

"You told me."

"I'll tell you again. I'll tell you again. It was the septic tank, the damn septic tank. It blocked up. And the man pumped it out. That could happen to anyone, couldn't it, Chris? And this afternoon the head of the septic tank called me up. Man-to-man. He's my buddy. An old friend. Said so himself. He's my friend."

Chris walked out of the kitchen. Mike followed him, stumbling over the throw rug. "You're not listening, Chris. You gotta listen. So he calls me up and he says he wants to give me some advice. On a delicate matter. Get that. He says for God's sake Mike if you gotta use those things don't put 'em down the pipes. You can't put a hundred or so of them things down the drain without stopping up the whole works."

Mike laid his head against the icebox. "What things, I says. God, he must have thought I was dumb. God, he was right. You know, he was right. Rubber, says he. Rubber. Not good for the plumbing. You get away with it so long, months maybe, and then all of a sudden the tank backs up, he says. Can't get away with it forever." Mike lurched over to the table. "And he starts apologizing for talking to me about it. He starts laughing, saying he was saying what your best friend won't tell you. Cutting himself out of business. Christ! What was I going to say?"

Chris filled the coffeepot and plugged it in.

"Was I going to tell my buddy that I never used one of those things in my life? So I says 'Thanks.' Thanks."

He reached out his arm and swept the sugarbowl off the table. It fell with a crash, splintering and spilling. He watched it and then deliberately swept the table clear of salt and pepper and a tiny vase of laurel leaves, smashing them all. "My wife! A toast to my wife!"

"Cut it out, Mike. You can't keep on like this. You got to get hold of yourself—"

"I'm going to get a room at the Y. And I'm not coming back." He roared to be sure Lidwina could hear him upstairs. "I'm not coming back to this whorehouse!"

The coffee was percolating. Mike lowered his head, his tie dangling from his open collar. "Where are my kids, Chris?"

"They're away with the basketball team. You told me."

"That's right. Thank God they weren't here. Chris, what am I going to do? I love those kids. They're growing up. They want to have friends over, you know. I was making a—that's why I was making the playroom. For dances and stuff. That's a good one, isn't it? I want things nice for my kids, so I hire a guy to build a playroom, and my wife has an affair with him. That's nice." He stood up, steadying himself on the table. "God Almighty, and I wondered why it was taking him so long to finish the playroom."

"Here's the coffee. Drink it!"

"The hell with coffee. Excuse me, Chris old man, but the hell with your coffee. I got something to do."

He yanked open the door to the cellar. "Be right back. I gotta get rid of that playroom."

"You're going to sit down." Chris grabbed him by the shoulders and shoved him into the chair. "And while you drink your coffee start thinking. You've got to think about tomorrow. About the kids, and Lidwina, and the future of Michael O'Shea. You want anyone else, including your kids, to know about Lidwina and that guy?"

"I don't give a damn."

"You've got a political career to think of. Think how it would sound if people knew O'Shea went wild and smashed up his own house." Chris looked at Mike, gauging his reaction. "You don't want to let her ruin your career too, do you?"

Mike gulped the hot coffee and grimaced. "What a hell of a way to find out," he said finally. "What a hell of a way! You shoulda let me talk to Father Temple, you know. I coulda told him to go to hell real good. Him and the whole Church."

"Father Macy's not here," said Father Temple.

"It's me, Jane, Father. Chris asked me to call and say he won't be able to make the fund-drive meeting. Something came up."

"Let me speak to him a minute," said the pastor.

"He's not home."

"Ah, well. By the way, Jane, I saw the Lawrence boy. He's very bad off."

"Is he?" said Jane flatly.

"See if you can't talk to Felicity sometime. And I'll tell Father Macy about Chris. Good night, Jane."

In spite of the television in the next room she could still hear the rain. She put her hands over her face.

This day has no end, she thought. I'd forgotten about Felicity's boy, yet it was only a few hours ago that Father called. And a few hours before that I was in New York. And when Chris came home he said what nice bedspreads, and he didn't know what I was doing in the city. And here I am on a day with no finish and my sister is out on a date and my mother-in-law is here and no one knows what I'm thinking or feeling or planning to do. Not even me.

She went back and sat with Annie. When the door opened it was Gloria, not Chris. "You're home early," said Jane.

Gloria smiled. "I'm tired. Feel a cold coming on. I'm going to bed. Where am I, in the den again?"

"She didn't even speak to me," bridled Annie as Gloria left the room. Jane shrugged. She was looking out the window. "Didn't her young man come in with her?" Annie asked suspiciously.

"No. His car's just going." And, Jane saw, another car was turning into the O'Shea drive. The garage spotlight touched it. She recognized it as Al Burke's Chevy.

"Aren't you going to say anything?" Annie demanded.

"Sorry. Guess Gloria isn't feeling well." She saw Al go into the O'Shea's house. Annie was complaining now about the children's manners at supper. She was still talking when the O'Shea front door opened. Jane pressed her face to the window to see better. Al and Chris came out, supporting Mike between them. They drove away in Al's car.

"I'll fix us some nice hot tea, Annie," said Jane. She put the kettle on to boil, then dialed Tory's number.

"What are Al and Chris doing? What's going on?"

"You mean you don't know?"

"No."

"Oh Jane. Lidwina was having an affair. Really. With the playroom man. Remember you told me you used his going as an alarm for you to get the kids? He was clearing out every day before anyone came home to Lidwina's!"

"What?"

"Anyway, Al's bringing Mike over here to sober him up. He just found out about it today, and they're afraid he might try something terrible. Jane, would you ever have thought?"

"No."

"I never knew anyone who committed adultery. I mean, that sounds odd, but I didn't. Jane, what do you suppose she's going to do? What can she do? Oh, oh, here they are now. Have to hang up. Bye!"

Jane brought Annie her tea on a tray with cookies. When Chris came she had cocoa hot and ready. He hung his coat and hat in the bathroom to drip.

"Tory told me," Jane said. "Is it true?"

"It's true." He held her close to him. "What a night!"

"You must be exhausted."

"Jane, did you guess what was going on with Lidwina?"

"No. You never know what goes on in people's lives. I'm just beginning to find that out."

Chris shook his head. "I guess I never thought of any of our friends committing any kind of real sin. Even tonight I looked at Lidwina, and she was crying, and Mike had bruised her face, and I couldn't believe it."

Annie came out with her empty cup. "The leaves say something terrible's going to happen."

"Oh, Annie, when are you going to quit that nonsense?"

"Don't talk to me that way, young lady." She sat down heavily beside her son. "Did I hear something awful about Lidwina?"

Chris nodded.

"I always thought she was no good," Annie said. "You can tell by looking at a person. They can't fool me."

Jane stood up abruptly. "There's a light still on in Lidwina's room." The rain beat on the windowpane. She tried to follow with her eyes the trickle of the waters, but one ran into another and confused her.

"Poor kid," said Chris.

Jane looked at him curiously.

"How can you say that?" asked Annie. "She's married. She knew what she was doing. You feel sorry for her?"

"I'm going up," said Jane. "Good night, Annie."

As she undressed she felt numb. In her chest, low, so that deep breaths hurt, lay loneliness and fear. She saw Lidwina twirling in that skirt at the party. Remembered the afternoon visits, when Lidwina had been kind to Mary. And she could not believe what had happened. Lidwina's sin hurt her, bruised her almost physically.

She climbed into bed. Chris feels sorry for her, she thought. How come he can forgive Lidwina? "Poor kid," he said. As if it were not her own fault. As if affairs could happen so easily to people worth feeling sorry for.

TWENTY-SEVEN

Chris walked out of his office with his attaché case and gave a taxi driver the address of a hotel near the Park. He walked in one door of the Plaza and out the other, crossed Fifty-ninth Street, stepping over the dung beside the hansom cabs, and disappeared into Central Park.

Once he reached the Mall he relaxed his pace. He took off his jacket and carried it dangling from one finger till he reached the sailboat pond. A boy with grey eyes and an expensive white sailor suit was tinkering with the rudder of a model sloop. He looked at the man, saw that he was harmless, and went back to his work.

In the park it was quieter than any other part of the city except the churches. Chris found a patch of dry grass, and sat down and loosened his shoelaces. The boy looked at him again. That's the price you pay for being yourself, Chris thought. You get watched. He decided the boy thought him an eccentric. The notion pleased him. He wished he were more of an eccentric, more of a challenge to the assembly-line world.

Idiosyncrasies honestly come by: the cape on the back of the small hunchback near Bryant Park, the way Jimmy Savo stood on the corner of Fifty-ninth and Sixth with his pocket full of balloons and lollypops, the way certain men carry walking sticks, these pleased Chris.

Was it eccentric to come to Central Park on lunch hour? Most satisfactorily so, he decided. Upon leaves of grass I loaf and invite my soul. . . . Even if the grass is not yet green it's the only place in this whole city I can be myself. Define myself.

He had scanned this morning a manuscript which had as a working title *The Undefined Man*. The author argued that the most basic human need was the need for self-definition. If a man does not know who he is, he does not really exist, and he dies, said the author.

The definition was supposed to be in terms of something outside himself, of course. Chris ran over the script in his mind. The author said some men define themselves in terms of money. At that rate, I'm not much. Or of sex. I've got a wife and six kids. And the author also said some defined themselves in terms of being well-liked by others. Chris lit a cigarette. I'm a nice guy to some people. A pillar of the parish, a sucker for work, a friend. Or in terms of the community? I'm held in esteem. That's important, the author said. In my parish community I'm literally gripped by esteem, choked by it. Absolutely everyone I know holds me in either high or low esteem.

Chris rolled onto his elbow, opened his attaché case and took out the delicatessen's paper bag with the beer and the corned beef on rye. Chewing, Chris reflected that it apparently never occurred to the author that a man could define himself in terms of his relation to God. Years ago in college a young priest had said you could define yourself only in terms of God. God is pure being. Evil is nonbeing. Is you is or is you ain't? But this author would get restless if his editor started talking about God. Chris watched the little boy launch his sloop.

The difference between me and the people around me, he thought, is that I cannot think about anything except in terms which they think are pathetically pious. He didn't see how he could define himself without knowing God. I am who Am, saith the Lord. And no matter how strong and real evil may seem, it's only a lack of good, a lack of being. If you're with God, you *are*.

He slurped his beer.

He remembered that same young priest back in college, jolting him out of his boredom with God.

"What is it you are keeping between you and God? What is keeping you from being really alive?" He had sprung that question on Chris in the confessional. Chris remembered. He had confessed his sins, and the priest had seemed almost to chide him for taking them seriously.

"Those are puny sins. You can overcome them. They offend you and embarrass you and you're sorry. But you don't understand the bigger sin. The stupid audacious sin of refusing to accept the gift of life. You were meant, God help you, to be a saint. And what are you doing about it? You're afraid being a saint means being pious and half-dead. You're wrong It means to be alive with the only real life. Apart from God nothing is. Whatever you want, you will find it really only in him."

Chris drained his beer and sighed. In his young fervor he had expected that once he knew the way, he would be a saint within a week. Well, he had been traveling nearly twenty years down the road already and he couldn't see any change in the landscape.

"Find out what it is you are holding on to, what non-is, non-real, non-good you are keeping between you and God," that priest had said. "When you find it, let go. You'll find you fall into his arms."

Chris crumpled the sandwich papers, and rescued the last pickle.

I don't have to look far to answer that question. I know. Jane! Awareness of his desire for her surrounded him. The palms of his hands felt the gentle sweetness of his wife. Her body was his and longed to stir it into life and motion. He hungered for her body, and for the soul joined to it and he needed her for his own completion. He knew the way her hair grew, soft fine gold on her thighs.

His fists tightened. He closed his eyes. He was, suddenly, on the edge of despair. Not from his unfulfilled hunger for Jane. But from her unlove of him. Could it ever happen that Jane would dream so of me? If I thought she did, even for a moment, yearn for me, it would be easier. And if I were to tell her I spent my lunch hour in the Park dreaming of her, what would she think? Wryly, he smiled. I bet she would think it inconsiderate of me.

All weekend she had been in a foul mood. Gloria drove her nuts. Or maybe it was the fact that Gloria drove me nuts that upset Jane. And then Ma stayed on an extra day. Jane doesn't like having Ma around. And that O'Shea business really threw her. He shook his head. She's mad at me because I'm not disgusted with Lidwina, God knows why. When I suggested that she just go over and say a kind word to Lidwina she nearly jumped down my throat. Is it so hideous of me to forgive Lidwina for something she did not do to me?

He stood up and put on his jacket. My wife is a stranger. She doesn't love me. She is afraid to love me. She is afraid of dying. She is afraid I will not know when to stop. She won't even do me the courtesy of being flattered by my love for her.

Unwarned, he thought of Krena.

He stood still under the warm spring sun, his mind shying yet lingering at her name.

What is it that I am holding on to? Did I think it was Jane? Did

I pretend not to know? I must not see Krena again. I must let go of my nearness to her.

He slapped shreds of grass off his legs.

It's not that simple, though. I cannot escape seeing Krena till this book is done. I can't refuse to work with her.

He stood, attaché case at his side, thinking. He had to be logical, he reminded himself. Well, the logical thing was to get the job done as quickly as possible, then call it quits. The sooner he finished working with Krena the better. He would have to do something to speed it up. He started walking. Perhaps the best thing would be to take her up on her suggestion, take a couple of days and work at her house.

TWENTY-EIGHT

Mary McNamara hung her head over the back of her chair so that her hair felt longer and more like tresses, and listened to Grandma Annie breathe. When you learned the code you could read a whole speech out of Grandma's breaths. And since no one knew Mary could understand no one stopped her from eavesdropping.

First Grandma drank her tea from a big cup. Then she studied the bottom of the cup when she thought Mary wasn't looking. Then she began the breathing. She was angry, and worried, and she said I-told-you-so, and she was ready to cry, and she felt sorry for herself, and her stockings bothered her and she was lonely. Then she remembered Mary and didn't breathe-talk any more. Mary began to make herself agreeable.

"Do you see something terrible in the leaves again, Grandma?" asked Mary, making her eyes wide and simple.

Grandma's hands began to fiddle with the underwear straps inside her neckline. Mary's nose twitched. She was a skilled tracker of the uncharted wilderness of adult behavior, alert to each spoor of emotion, adept at setting snares to hold her prey. She sniffed the air, lowered her eyelids, and said: "I wish I could see the future."

"It's a gift," said Annie. "Don't you go trying."

Mary nodded. "I know what I'm going to do when I grow up. I'm going to get married and have lots and lots of babies and they are all going to marry and have lots and lots of babies because that's the very finest thing anyone can do, isn't it, Grandma?"

"Huh! Babies are fine except for the mothers. They give up everything and their youth and their strength and then. . . ."

"But," urged Mary carefully, "my mother says it's a holy vacation to be a mother. Like being a sister or a priest. Don't you believe that it's a vacation?"

The sound of breathing signified qualified assent. Grandma had not corrected her on the misused word. Mary thought she detected the over-echo of storm warning.

"You are a Catholic, aren't you, Grandma?" she pressed.

A firm hand grasped her shoulder and propelled her off the chair in the direction of the door.

"Outside," said her mother.

"I was having a talk with my grandmother," said Mary, the lower lip swelling to indicate hurt dignity.

"And being fresh."

The big blue eyes, fringed with such dark lashes, regarded her mother. With a shrug Mary darted off.

"Annie," Jane said, "you look too solemn. Have a dish of ice cream?"

"Oh? All right. I might at that." Annie watched scrupulously as Jane scooped up some banana-nut-fudge ice cream. "That's too much, child," she said contentedly, beginning to eat with noticeably small spoonfuls.

Jane picked up the teacup to rinse it. Annie nodded toward it. "The leaves speak of trouble, death," she said. "Not that I believe in those things, understand, but I won't insult them by turning my back on them."

"Annie, I wish you wouldn't let the children see you reading leaves. It's a lot of bunk anyway," said Jane softly. "Do you remember how worried you were when Chris and I were getting married? Your leaves predicted tragedy. But it worked out well, didn't it?"

Annie raised her thick grey eyebrows. "Worried over you and Chris? I never was, not for a moment. How can you say a thing like that? That was altogether different." She shook her head with that odd floating movement peculiar to Oriental paper dragons.

Jane shrugged. It was useless to argue the point.

"Annie, we're alone and quiet now. It's a good time to talk. And I've had a feeling there was something you wanted to tell me."

Annie smiled blandly. "Nothing special."

"Annie, what is it?" Jane considered that masklike smile. "Is it something you saw in my fortune?"

Annie ate her ice cream. "I—I just think you must be careful. Very careful. I know you don't believe in them, but the leaves said over and over that you are—I can't tell you. You say it's sinful to tell fortunes."

Jane sighed. "Then if you don't want to tell me—"

"I will tell you." Annie put her spoon down. The old cheeks flushed under the pink spots of rouge. "You can laugh, but I read them for you every week. And they keep telling one thing. They keep saying you are deciding to do something you mustn't do. Something foolish! And that I must warn you now."

Jane stood silent. Then she smiled. "Is it supposed to be so serious? Are you trying to tell me I'm the death you see in the leaves?"

"No, no. That's a dark man. This is different." Annie got to her feet and put a ringed hand on Jane's arm. "Jane, you mustn't have any more children," she said. "Don't do anything foolish. You must not let yourself have more children."

The laugh escaped before Jane could stop it. She hugged Annie. "Sorry. I'm not making fun of you. It's only that I was expecting something different, you know."

Annie patted her on her shoulder. "You're crying," she said with surprise. "Not laughing."

"Both, I guess. Come on, I'll promise to be careful if you promise to stop worrying. Okay?" She wiped her eyes.

"Now Annie, sit down and tell me more about the trip. Have you decided when you're going to Europe?"

"This summer!" Annie smiled. "I've got a ticket first class on the ship for July 7, on a guided tour with the cardinal in person."

"Annie! That's wonderful."

"All these years of waiting and waiting for James to take me somewhere, or for something interesting to happen in my life, and I found out nothing's going to happen unless I make it happen."

Annie smiled triumphantly and went back to work on her ice cream. Peter wandered in and grabbed an apple. "How's the leaves today, Grandma?"

"They say someone is going to die. A dark male."

Peter grinned. "A person dies on earth every thirty seconds. Half of those are males. More than half of those are dark. Odds are the leaves are right." He grabbed a handful of crackers, grinned, and left with an alacrity designed to protect his rear flank.

When Martha Settler phoned to say the Lawrence boy had died, Annie was visibly reassured to hear that the child was dark-complected. She met Jane's glance calmly. "The leaves might have meant Chris, or Peter," she said. "You never know."

TWENTY-NINE

The only way Jane could find to be alone was to take a bath or go to church.

"I'm going down to get a Mass card for the Lawrence boy," she announced after supper.

"I'll be gone when you get back," said Annie. "Chris can drive me to the station. James needs me home."

"Good-bye then. Have a safe trip." The need to be alone would not let Jane wait to soothe Annie's feelings. She kissed Chris on the forehead and ran out the door.

The dogwoods on the church lawn showed their first damp green petals, ghostly in the twilight. Along the walks daffodils and blue squill gave off an air of fresh promise. She took her black veil from her pocketbook, slipped it over her head, and without a qualm ran into church.

She chose a spot where she could not be seen from the door, and knelt there. Automatically she said a quick prayer for the Lawrence child, who she was sure was now in heaven. One for Felicity and Harold, who were not. She thought of Father Temple and added a prayer for him because he wanted to convert Harold and probably never would.

Abruptly she got up from her knees and sat in the pew and listened to the silence. Her eyes avoided the tabernacle.

This was the night she had chosen. This was the night she would leap into the unknown.

She studied the vein pattern in the green glass grape leaves in the window beside her, and wondered what to say to Chris. She had been carefully reporting to him Dr. Polla's findings. She had been keeping charts as he ordered, applying tapes, treating herself exactly like a laboratory animal. I will tell Chris there is no risk. And he will believe me.

She stretched then, her hips sliding a bit on the polished wood, considered the happy fact that Annie was taking an early train back to the city.

Suppose someone said: "Jane, what do you meditate on in church?" And I told them. But no one will ask. Has anyone asked why I haven't been to daily Mass for the last few weeks? They haven't. Father Temple didn't ask, of course. Not even Chris.

Tears started in her eyes. She felt suddenly lost, a child lost, abandoned in a great city-full of empty streets and closed windows and signs in a language she could not read. Only a while ago she had not been lost, had been sure of where she was going, had understood. A year ago? Then sin had been sin, incomprehensible, inexcusable, and the wine of grace had risen heady and fiery within her.

Now the wine had gone brackish. It was pale, and signified nothing.

There should be more to it than this! She cried within herself, staring at the tabernacle. Don't you even care? I am about to commit the thing they say you call mortal sin. I am sitting here planning how to commit the first mortal sin of my life and you don't even care. I could be planning a market list. Or saying a prayer for all you know. There is nothing special in the air, nothing in my heart. . . .

It did not occur to her to doubt that he existed, precisely, vitally, truly in the tabernacle on the altar. She did not doubt. She had the feeling he was watching her, calmly, leaving her on her own. She remembered as a little girl being angry with her mother for doing that same thing, being goaded into defiance just to see if she could break that implacable serene wall.

She rose from the pew, walked softly down the aisle to the altar rail and stood directly before the tabernacle.

Standing, confronting, she paused outside of time. Wordlessly she knew she believed what she could not see or prove, believed her Redeemer was personally, willingly, imprisoned on this altar.

She knew, too, no trumpets would herald the drama of her decision. No devil need leap in twisted cloak to tempt her.

She believed that the act she planned was perfectly sensible and right by the world's standards and absolutely wrong by the law of God. She knew all the arguments on both sides. She knew she could not presume to count on forgiveness later. Forgiveness was for those who are sorry and she was not sorry enough to turn back. The back of her hand stifled her own cry. She turned and hurried away, her heels echoing in chase behind her.

She pushed open the outer door of the Church and nearly collided with Father Joseph Mongiano. "Good evening, Jane. Making a little visit?"

"Good evening, Father."

He smiled. He was about to speak to her of the coming Cana Conference, Tri-Cana, but she seemed in a hurry to return to her family, and he let it go. He went into the church reflecting on how the beauty of faith and goodness shines in young wives and mothers like Jane.

Bride-shy, she was in bed waiting before Chris even came upstairs.

She was conscious of her body to the exclusion of everything else, conscious of the mechanism of it, and the pulsation of her blood. Guardian of a secret, possessor of the unknown, she lay waiting.

Her breasts seemed to lie heavy on her, and she remembered once reading the passionate outpourings of a man hungering for the palm-filling warmth of pears in the narcotic heat of summer sun. The words as she had read them had sprung the lock of a dark terror within her, and she had hated the existence of sex. In the poetry she had fed on, the pear tree had been a bride of white blossoms. Love had been a flame that burned without consuming. That book had transformed love into a monster of sweat-slick, tangled in weeds of dark curly hair. Those words in that book had taken the familiar, honest world and cast a spell over it till the simplest things became symbols of desire, liturgical symbols of the cult of the bull.

Now deep within her lay another symbol, the sign of death which would pass unnoticed. And preserving life, defy life.

She heard his steps on the stairs, the casual, calm steps of a man who has turned down the thermostat and is about to empty his pockets of keys and pennies and matches and handkerchief onto the bureau.

He came into the bedroom. "Mmm. Something stinks pretty in here."

"I was waiting for you."

"I thought you were asleep already." He yawned. "I'm a tired old man tonight. I've been working on plans to put up that darn basket for Pete, and you know me, I'm the world's lousiest handyman. He'll probably be playing basketball on a college court before I get that backboard done."

"Chris? Come and sit beside me on the bed."

A shadow of surprise crossed his face. He came and sat beside her, and looked at her searchingly.

"What's wrong, Jane?"

Her lower lip trembled.

"Jane?" The tenderness of his voice nearly overcame her.

"Oh, Chris, I love you. Love me!" she whispered. "Please. Tonight."

"I love you. Oh, Jane, I do." He put his hand down upon the blue ruffles that covered her breasts. Her hands enclosed his head and marveled at the feel of bone and scalp and hair and she pressed his head against her in an agony of loneliness and need.

"Jane, I dream of you, and I think of you, and I think of the softness of your breasts, and of your belly so small and round between your hips and of your arms that hold me and of your lips and even of your little toes and I am a fool because I cannot speak poetry, I can only speak nonsense and I love you, and I want you. . . ."

His voice broke and the timbre of it ceased to thrill her breathing and he lay in precious silence listening to her heart.

Her fingers traced the pattern of his ear, and her mind traced the pattern of the words she planned to say.

"Chris, I've been waiting to tell you something. It's all right now. It's safe now. To make love."

He raised his head to look at her.

"It really is. Dr. Polla says."

"Dr. Polla says what?"

"That there's no risk at all of my conceiving."

He shook his head. "I don't believe you."

"You must believe me."

He laid his hand on her cheek. "Jane—do you think I can't see what you're doing?"

She stared at him, mute.

"You're not a very good liar. From the minute I came up here I could see something was troubling you. You're nervous as a cat. And you're lying. God love you, you're lying out of love for me.

Dr. Polla didn't say anything. If he had you would have told me right away, wouldn't you?"

"Chris—"

"Jane, I love you for that lie. I love you." He kissed her and lay beside her laughing softly, incredulously. "You—"

"Chris!" Her whisper was like a cry of distress.

"You are afraid of so many things, of death, of necking, yet you would offer me this. Defenseless." He pulled her to him.

"Oh beloved, it is not only your body I dream of. I love your body but if it were only for that it would not be enough." He felt her tense with indrawn breath. His hand caressed her softly. "I love you for being you, for the person of you. And I will not risk that person."

The touch of his hand stirred longing within her, and drove away the ghost of the woman who might have known this same hand, the woman she had almost forgotten because she wished she were dead. She had bought triumph over Krena without once mentioning her name in her own thoughts, bought triumph in a package from a doctor, bought life for Chris to preserve him from death at Krena's call. And not till this moment had she admitted to herself that it was because of Krena that she had done this. Nor that she herself was still capable of desire. She started to speak but he prevented her.

"Let me finish. It isn't often that we speak to each other, that I can find my way and dare to say what I mean. I love you for this—" his fingers strayed over her, and every touch was a touch of fire "—but for much more too." He lay now with his hands joined together in the hollow between her breasts.

"Jane, you must understand. I think you're afraid for my sake. That I can't live without making love. Jane, men aren't built that way. At least I'm not. I have wanted you, wanted to be close to you. And I was angry because you were afraid. Because you didn't trust me. I should have been more patient. I will be patient, I promise." He lay back beside her staring at the ceiling. "I am not as good as you are, Jane. I think of sin. But because I know the horror you have of sin, because the wife who is part of me is strong and perfect, I am strong too. I should have been stronger to help you when you were afraid. No, I will not make love to you, I— Please don't laugh. Don't laugh, Jane!"

She was shaking. He pulled himself up on his arms and stared into her face and she was sobbing, not laughing.

144

"What have I said to make you cry? Jane."

She turned her head away violently.

"Jane, I was trying only to tell you that because you are so good, because you would never consent to do evil, because you would never even consider sin. . . . Jane, Jane, tell me why you are crying."

"I can't tell you. But it is not anything you did, Chris. I—I loved hearing that you love me."

But in her heart she knew it wasn't true. He loves me because he thinks I am good, she thought, and I am so ungood that I hate him for thinking me good, and I am confused. He was saying "I shouldn't have held you, touched you. I thought you hated me. I did. But when you called me tonight to sit beside you, you were calling me, weren't you? You wanted me to?"

"Yes."

He stroked her hair away from her wet cheeks, and stood up. "Jane, you'll never know how much it meant to hear you call me! You know there could never be another woman for me, not even for a moment. We'll wait and love each other more. I told you once I could never lie beside another woman. I love you!"

She closed her eyes for fear he might see shame in them. Her heart ached knowing that she had doubted him. God alone knew why she had thought what she had, planned what she had.

She took his hand and held it, and pretended to be drifting off to sleep.

Finally she heard him go and brush his teeth, heard the floor-boards creak as he checked each child in its bed, felt the relief of darkness as he switched off the light and settled down into bed. Then with utmost caution she let the tears come, let the anguish and frustration and rejection swell within her and find outlet in an open mouth pressed into a pillow and the flood of burning salten tears.

When he slept, she slipped slowly out of bed and went alone into the privacy of the bathroom and rid herself of what she had not needed. She breathed hard and could not have named the emotions twisting within her. There was no logic left in her head, only a torment and a loathing and an insult and an exhaustion that left her wretched and angry and lonelier than she had ever been in her life.

THIRTY

"Walter leaves for the Marines this week," Tory said.

"Good," said Jane absently. "Best thing for that boy."

"I'll miss him."

"Sure." The children played on the backyard slide. The mothers sat sheltered from the wind, watching.

"You're not very sympathetic," said Tory.

"Sorry," Jane said dryly.

"You coming with me to the Mission tonight?"

"I hate Missions."

"But you're coming."

"Sure. Because I'd stick out like a sore thumb if I didn't. You and Clare and Christine and Martha would all want to know why if I didn't. Good people are supposed to go to Missions, aren't they?"

"What's with you, anyway?"

Jane shrugged, and cocked her head with an imitation of Gloria's smile.

"Jane, on you that smile looks sick. What's the matter? Tell me?"

Jane turned away. "Everything. Nothing. Forget it." She dug in her pockets for a hankie and blew her nose. "It's nobody's business but mine."

"Okay." Tory smiled. "Okay."

"And don't be so damn nice about it," Jane snapped. "I'm sick of nice people."

"That's tough," said Tory. "And what else is new?"

"Nothing."

"Seen Agnes Milder, lately?"

"Chris made me call her up this morning. He met her husband on the train and Elmo said she was really sick. And all of a sudden Chris is the do-good type. He used to complain about my sticking my nose in people's business. Now he's pushing me. He's all sweetness and light. He's so damn noble." Jane bit her lip. I should love him for what he said and did last night, she thought. He's a wonderful guy. And I hate myself for not loving him.

"Is Agnes really sick?" asked Tory.

"She's convinced she has cancer and is going to die. The doctor thinks it may be only a virus, but he's doing tests," said Jane.

"She's probably got indigestion from all the gossip she chews. You should hear her on Lidwina." Tory shook her head.

"I did."

"Have you seen Lidwina? Or heard from her?"

"No." Jane closed her eyes. "And Chris wants me to be nice to her, too. He thinks she's doing the right thing, staying there, waiting for Mike to forgive her and come back, no scandal."

"Maybe she'd come to the Mission tonight. That would be good. Would you want to ask her?"

"If she saves her soul that's her business, not mine."

"You're impossible."

"You said it."

"Cyril!" Tory stood up. "Come on, dear, we're going home." She walked over to where the babies were playing.

"There's Lidwina now, going to the mailbox," said Jane. Lidwina saw them and waved. Tory waved back. Jane turned and went into the house.

The memory of last night swirled in her head, wounding her. It is humiliating to be ready to damn your soul for the sake of love and be turned down.

About nine hundred women were in St. Rose's that night at eight. The visiting missionary was too short for the lectern. His round head with its sparse grey curls barely rose over the wooden shelf.

He was explaining, as if it were really necessary, why he was there.

"Your pastor, good Father—uh—Temple, invited us here as it is the mind of Holy Mother the Church for him to do, that we might help you good women of—uh—St. Rose's to a new growth of love for our Lord and Savior during this holy season of Lent here in—uh—Rockhill."

"I guess he has trouble remembering where he is this week," whispered Tory to Jane.

"Last week we were in New Haven, and in a parish there a thousand men and a thousand women made the Mission. Souls that were dead in sin were returned to the sacraments. If I could only tell you, my dear women, of the miracles of grace that come during these Missions. It is an occasion of outpouring of grace, a time when we must all pray that those in peril of losing their immortal souls will reach out and take hold again of the way of life."

Jane closed her mouth on a yawn. She had apologized to Tory

and come to the Mission, and she hoped she could at least look decent.

"My partner and I," said the priest, "will meet with you every night this week and in the mornings at Mass for those of you who can make the sacrifice to attend. We shall both be addressing you, praying with you, serving you."

As the missionary launched into the familiar opening sermon on sin, mercy and the love of God, Jane looked discreetly at the faces she could recognize. Mrs. Kczuck with a contented smile. Clare Sullivan, burgeoning in her pregnancy, absorbing each word. Martha Settler, who thought Missions anachronistic in the new liturgical era, listening with an efficient air. Jane noticed Agnes Milder with a tiny black bow of a hat. Even from a distance she could see that Agnes' cheeks were puffy. Maybe she was really sick.

A breeze of light laughter spread over the women and Jane realized Father was laying the groundwork for a joke. This was what Chris called standard operating procedure, the modest disclaimer of stuffiness, the reminder that even Mission priests are jolly good fellows, which produces a sympathetic titter, and then the clincher—the joke.

Tory nudged her, and pointed to the side aisle. Lidwina was there alone in a pew.

When the other missionary took over, the lectern came only slightly above his waist, so that he seemed to loom in commanding foreboding. He spoke of death and judgment. His voice was an instrument disciplined to subtle gradations of tone, now calling for fire, now cajoling in patience.

Jane was prepared to be bored. She had heard practically the same sermon every Lent for nine years from nine different sets of missioners. But against her will the voice grasped her. Somehow under the intense eyes of this preacher, the message was magnified and made new. When he spoke of the coming of the end and the inevitable approach of death, she listened and knew he spoke to her. The hour would come when she would lie helpless as consciousness faded. All this became vivid.

"And when that moment comes, the priest may be there to give you the last sacraments, your family may be beside you praying. The room may be filled with people. But in the final moment it will be a private matter, between you and the great God. Now he comes to you as your Redeemer, your Friend, your Lover. Then he will come only as your Judge."

Jane closed her eyes and the church filled with women was perfectly still.

"The hour of our death is the hour we are living for. The hour of our death is the beginning of a life without death. It is designed to be the hour of triumph, of new birth into glory.

"But it is not always so. At death there comes the first and private judgment of the soul. And theologians tell us that it is not that Christ holds court on the soul, but rather that in a way the soul judges itself. In that hour of liberation, when your soul stands naked of its body, you will look at the face of your Lord. And in the light streaming from his love you will see yourself as you are in truth.

"The soul that sees itself polluted, corrupted, debased and disfigured with sin will be unable to bear the nearness of glory, and will turn and fling itself into hell."

Her breath caught in her chest. She cleared her throat and blinked her eyes to dispel their burning. "But I haven't sinned seriously," she thought. "I wasn't allowed to sin. God, if Chris had not refused me? Then I would have sinned. But he did, by your grace, he did." She bent her head. It hurt her eyes to look at the tabernacle. The light is bright, she thought. And I am tired.

But the voice of the just, the deep-reaching, rhythmic, organ-toned voice, reached out and held her.

"And remember, my dear children, that our Lord warned us that it is not only what we actually do that damns us. God looks not only at our deeds but at our hearts. What you have deliberately thought of doing, what you have planned and wanted and meant to do, on this will you be judged." Jane drew in her breath. "A man once said to me, 'By the grace of God I have never committed a mortal sin. Once I meant to kill a man. I even bought a knife. But I never got a chance to use it. The man died of a heart attack before I could find him.' But, my children, you know and I know that man was a murderer in God's eyes. He had sinned in his heart. He had intended. . . ."

Jane whispered to Tory that she needed to go to the ladies' room, climbed over the knees of the woman beside her, forced herself to walk slowly back to the door, and left.

The cool spring wind found her sweat-soaked blouse even under her coat and chilled her. She stood gasping in the dark, arched doorway.

Jane whispered into the wind. "How is it that I did not know?"

She remembered when Clare Sullivan had the miscarriage and the baby had been dead in her for two weeks without her knowing. Poor, sweet, trusting Clare. She had been stunned and incredulous that it should have happened without some sign, if not to her body at least to her spirit.

"Just so has God's life died in me," thought Jane. It was not the way she thought it should happen at all. "I sinned. He left me, and I did not know he was gone."

Last night had been nothing. Nothing at all. I came here, I was here in this church last night, and I thought I made a decision then, and even then it was all over. The sin took place long ago. When? When I was measured and fitted? When I decided to go to the clinic? Or before that.

"What I did last night, what I do now, does not even matter," she whispered. "And You don't even care."

If she did not go back, Tory might think she was ill and come looking for her. She was tired of what people think.

Benediction had begun. She could not walk down the aisle to her place. She saw Tory's head move, knew she had been worried, and was relieved now that Jane was back.

The priest raised the Sacrament in blessing. Jane knelt where she was, by the door. She did not bow her head. Defiantly she looked into the center of the golden monstrance in the priest's hands, at the presence of God.

Her lips parted in a stifled cry of surprise.

I knew! God, I knew. What the priest said tonight, that sin was in the will, not in the act; I knew it. I only pretended not to know. . . .

The confusion, the illogical deceitful selfishness of her thoughts in the past weeks bewildered her now. She saw herself posturing, speaking of love and self-preservation, and shuddered with revulsion. How could she have gone so far astray, she who loathed sin and loved God?

Dead.

Slowly, majestically, the priest turned, holding aloft the mysteriously self-imprisoned One.

God. I was afraid to die. And I died another way. Jane sank back on her heels, hands clasped in her lap. I do not understand. God, know I do not understand anything. I loved. I loved and I gloried in love of you and of Chris, and the red wine was my symbol of that love, and it was of body and soul, and because of the body.

. . . She felt as if she walked on water and began to sink. And she would not call on the name of the Lord.

The service was over. Quietly, Jane stood up, to become one of the nine hundred women, whispering and smiling and nodding, going home.

"Did you see that Lidwina was there?" asked Tory.

Clare Sullivan was riding home with them.

"I did," she said, her voice reverent and soft. "Oh, isn't it grand that she came, that she wasn't afraid of what people might say."

"And now, if she goes to confession and comes back all the way she might just turn out to be a real saint. Lots of saints were like that, you know," said Tory.

"I know," agreed Clare happily.

"Someone said Mike left home and still hasn't come back." Tory noticed Jane's silence and asked, "Do you know?"

"Yes," said Jane. "He's gone."

"Where to?"

"He's living downtown somewhere."

"What in God's name is Lidwina going to do?"

"What could you do?" said Clare. "Only pray. We must all pray for her. Perhaps he will come back. It takes courage for her to stay there and wait."

"It took courage to carry on like that." Tory laughed. "If I wanted to I'd still be too scared."

"Oh, Victoria, what a way to talk," said Clare.

"Sin takes guts," said Tory. "No matter what you say, sin takes guts."

"Oh, I'm not so sure now," said Clare in a firm light voice which left no doubt that she was sure. "It takes more courage to live a life without sin, don't you think?"

The white wave in Tory's red hair gleamed as each street light's aura passed over the windshield. "If I weren't afraid of hell, there are times—I know you're supposed to be good for the love of God, but even the Church knows we're not all that holy. She'll take either motive. And when I look at our teen-agers I can't help but be glad there's a hell to be scared of. I just keep thinking of the last Mission and the things Father said young girls do these days. They are so bold about sex." She turned sideways to address herself to Jane, who sat huddled inside her coat in the back seat. "What do you think, Jane? Didn't you once tell me you thought there was too much open talk about sex with young people?"

"Since you ask me," said Jane, "I think there's too damn much talk about sex everywhere, including here. I'm sick of hearing priests tell us in one meeting how holy and beautiful it is, and in the next meeting how infernally dangerous it is. I'm sick of people gossiping about Lidwina. I'm sick of people talking about what young people are likely to be doing. It seems to me there's nothing else in the whole world anyone's thinking about. Just sex. And I hate it."

Tory pulled the car into the McNamara driveway. The headlights shone on the open garage littered with wagons and bicycles and tricycles and lawn mower, wheels upon wheels.

Jane moved to open the door. "Everyone talks about how sex-crazy and pagan the world is. But everyone I know is forever talking about the same damn thing. Sin. Sex. Sounds as if the words mean the same." She smiled to take the curse of intensity off her words. "I'm going on a crusade," she finished, "to spend a little time thinking about flowers or art or politics or potholders or anything but sex and babies and more sex. I'll probably be the most unpopular woman in the parish. But perhaps I'll keep my sanity."

She got out and closed the door.

"Thanks for the ride. Good night."

"See you tomorrow night, same time, for the Mission?" called Tory.

"Not tomorrow. I'm not going," said Jane and went into the house.

"If it weren't Jane," said Tory as she headed for Clare's house through the dark country roads, "I'd be hurt."

"I wonder what she meant," said Clare. "She must be not feeling well."

"Maybe she has a headache. I think she had to go out for a breath of air during the Mission."

"Perhaps she—"

"Perhaps!"

Clare nodded, smiling. "She must be. And so she's probably not feeling well, and probably she might even be a little worried. She did have a bad time with this last one, didn't she?"

"The rascal, not telling us. And blowing off like that, as if we were some kind of gossips with our minds always on sex!"

In the darkness the friends smiled peacefully, certain they had penetrated her secret, promising each other to be patient and a little extra understanding until she felt more like herself.

THIRTY-ONE

She could hear Chris talking in the living room, but she could not see who was there. She hung her coat on a hook and studied Pete's sprawled muddy blue jeans and sneakers on the floor. She was exhausted. She left the clothes lying there.

Chris was holding forth on one of his favorite subjects, and she could hear him clearly.

"The trouble with literature today is that it has replaced a sense of grandeur and nobility with sensuality and pettiness. What do they write novels about now? About sex and sex and sex. Their characters have no souls, no contact with God. They claim to be writing over the heads of common folk. But I tell you when I read them I find they never write over the level of the navel. . . ."

He had developed these ideas into a lecture for women's reading clubs in the area. Tonight the familiar words sounded fresh to Jane's ears and she found herself agreeing with him. She gave up trying to guess who he was talking to, and started reluctantly in to join them.

"Even our so-called Catholic writers today, even they can find nothing to write about except sex," Chris continued. "Priests with mistresses, whores who are saints. And they do not understand that they are revealing themselves as sick men who do not understand literature, faith or sex. They have lost—"

"Hi," Jane's entrance interrupted him. "I'm home." She stopped in surprise. "Gloria?"

Her sister sat by the fireplace in a grey wool jumper with a wine-red long-sleeved blouse. Her hair lent her an air of artless youth. She had no earrings, very little makeup. Jane could not recall when she had last seen her sister look so demure.

She went over to kiss her on the forehead.

"How? Why?"

"I came by train and Chris was nice enough to meet me at the station."

"We've been talking about what's wrong with literature," said Chris.

"Good," said Jane. She looked at Gloria's left hand, but there was no ring, and that eliminated one possibility.

"Well I still have some work to do," said Chris, "and if you ladies will excuse me I'm going to go to bed and read all about young Tom Jefferson." He bowed elaborately, picked up a pile of manuscript, and started upstairs. "By the way, Pete got a little wet while you were out gadding to the Mission."

"I saw his clothes."

"He knows he's not allowed out after dark, but for some reason he was trying to catch peepers in the swamp with Miss Butler. Miss Butler is too old for that kind of nonsense, if you ask me, but he says she got all muddy too. That's Martha's sister, I take it? The nutty one?"

"She's not nutty," Jane said. "She had a few trips to the sanitarium. She's getting better now. But I don't like the idea of his wallowing in a swamp with her."

"Be kind to the mentally ill," said Chris in radio announcers' tones. "I leave you to whatever sisters talk about when husbands aren't around."

There was time for the coffee to brew, time for small talk, before the sisters faced each other over the kitchen table.

Gloria folded her hands around the big thick earthenware cup Jane had filled. Her nails shone with a new iridescent polish. Under the fluorescent fixture they looked defiantly surrealistic.

"Jane," she began.

Jane noticed lines in Gloria's face, new creases in the forehead, the beginnings of wrinkles in the powder-dry skin under the small dark eyes. The hint of age in the person she still thought of as a kid sister made her uneasy.

Gloria lifted her head and concentrated on some spot on the wall behind Jane.

"Look, Jane," she said, "there's something I've got to tell you. So I'll tell you right out. You see, I'm going to have a baby."

"You're what?"

"You look embarrassed."

Jane smiled ruefully.

"Ashamed that you showed surprise? What did you expect to be? Calm, casual, approving? It's not in you, Jane. Don't you be embarrassed. I'm the one who's supposed to be that."

"Who—"

"Who is the father?"

Gloria's lipstick seemed to be adhesive and she had trouble with the corners of her mouth. "Hack."

"I see."

"You don't see," Gloria disagreed quietly. "It all happened— well, the way those things do happen. Who's to say whose fault it was? Who's to say if it was right or wrong? I mean that. Was it meant to be that a child should come? Was it an accident? Do you blame it on him or on me or on God, or on fate? Who knows?" Her lips curved in a bright tight smile.

"The point is," she went on, "that I am pregnant. And that is a very confusing point. Hack is a Catholic, you know? No, I didn't tell you that before. He's not very Catholic."

Jane sat unmoving. As if from a distance she was aware she must say or do something, might put her arms around Gloria, might touch her hand, might comfort her. She could do nothing.

"I told Mother," said Gloria, sipping the coffee. "Mother is extraordinarily upset. Naturally, I would be if I were she. But she is upset principally because I won't marry Hack."

"You're not going to marry him?"

"No. I don't want to be married to him."

"Don't you love him?"

"I don't know." Gloria closed her eyes as she drank more coffee. Then she said, "Look, Janey. You ought to be able to understand that. Mother can't. But you know you can't make a marriage just out of the need to give a child a name."

"No, you can't."

"What infuriates Mother is that your dear Catholic Church agrees with me. She ran down last night to try to get a priest to tell Hack he just had to marry me. And the priest refused. She can't understand it. She's awfully sick about it, Jane. She never wants to see me again. She said so, and I think she means it."

Jane gave a little moan as she thought of her mother. "What are you going to do?"

"I'm going to go away to a Catholic Home in another state soon. Isn't it funny? The best place I can find is a Catholic place. And I'm going to have my baby. I'm going to give it life, don't worry. It has the right to live. And then I will give it up for adoption and come back."

"I'm glad you have it planned that way." Jane's words sounded flat and amateurish to her own ears. "You're so calm, Gloria, so damn calm. How do you do it?"

"Are you cross with me? Disgusted? Scared?"

How could she tell her the pit-deep horror in her own stomach? How could she say the electric pain behind her heart?

"Scared? Maybe. And sorry. So sorry."

"Don't be sorry!" Gloria started to cry.

Then Jane went and put her arms around those bony shoulders, on the polished wine-red cotton sleeves of the blouse, and held her.

She had thought occasionally of the day when Gloria, married and proud, might tell her she was bearing a child. To have a sister with whom to share the texture of motherhood, someone to pass the shuttle of joy and pain to, someone who would understand the pattern in the making—for this Jane had hoped. Now she held to her breast the body of disappointment and of disgrace, the body sheltering life to be forfeit to some other mother's arms.

Gloria forced her head free of Jane's arms and looked up into her eyes. "Are you truly shocked?"

Jane shook her head.

"Do you want me to go?"

"You're being melodramatic. Besides, there's no snow outside for me to turn you out into."

Gloria nodded. "That's what I thought. You know, Janey, you're the only close friend I have who's been pregnant? You are, really. And I'm scared. Not of the things Mother's scared of. Not of what people will say, but just of having a baby. Sound silly? I tried to tell Mother that, but that part of it wasn't important to her. All she wanted was to find a way to make things pretty and proper."

"No need to be scared of having a baby. Look at me." Jane poured more coffee, trying to keep her hand steady.

"You don't think I should marry him. You do think the priest is right."

Jane put the pot down carefully, watching her own face distorted in the curved chrome reflection. "I wish—I wish you could be married, wish you could have everything the way it should be, wish you loved him and he loved you, and you could—keep your baby." She tossed her head and swallowed and blinked. "But it would be terribly wrong to marry him just for appearances. It would be sacrilege, sort of. Marriage is not something just used to cover up a sin."

She bit her lip and wished she had not used the word *sin*. Gloria didn't seem to notice.

"And you know, Jane, I have to keep the baby until it's born?"

"Of course you do." Jane turned quickly back to her. "It's wonderful and beautiful and fine of you to carry your child. And right to give it up later. And hard."

"Then tell Mother, for God's sake!" Sobs shook Gloria like sickness. "Funny. I always thought Catholics were about as medieval and prudish as anyone could be. But you're not. Imagine me turning to a priest to have him back me up against my own mother. Makes no sense, does it?"

Jane made a bed for her sister on the living-room couch. Chris was already asleep when she went upstairs. Jane undressed and went in to check on the children, then went back downstairs, to see if Gloria were wakeful.

Gloria lay sleeping, one arm flung upward like a child's, the other resting protectively on her stomach. She looks virginal, thought Jane, still young and ready to dazzle us with sophistication and sociology and nonsense. Yet she has life in her. She will harbor in her the life of a man she does not love, united to hers, growing into someone she will never know. Good God, where is the sense of that?

She ran on tiptoe to the back door, opened it, and stepped outside into the night. The house loomed white and vague above her, its outlines blurred by the mist of the starless night. The house seemed a vault containing within it the mystery she could not face, a man who was her husband, whose flesh she owned and who owned her flesh, and six children born of that man and of their love. And a woman whom no sacrament had bound, a woman whom God did not bless, a child to be born not of love.

She had believed all things were in the providence of God, that he created souls in his own design, that he knew when in love a child should be born. If he does not know, if an accident could command the existence of an immortal soul, where then was God? She had chosen to believe in God. And defied him. Perhaps even now she did not believe any more. She was afraid to find out.

The wind blew heavy with dampness through the pussy willows in the back lawn. Something in the shushing of their branches reminded her of her wedding night. Then she and Chris had thought the wine of that picnic a symbol of God's love, and later that night

the sign of their consummated love had seemed to them a symbol
of the union of suffering and joy.

Now in the darkness with no man, the days of bridehood ended,
she shook her head. We were blind to truth, she said to the night.
We had it backward, reality is not in heaven but in earth. We had
sex and love all confused, and we thought they were all tied up to
God.

She closed the door on the night and locked it and started upstairs. It occurred to her that if she sought she might find that in
fact the symbols of blood and flesh, of wine and bread, had been
all part of a fairy tale, a bit of quieting nonsense one tells to
children.

THIRTY-TWO

Tory could not yet quite believe Walter was gone. It had been five
o'clock and dark when they got up. Walter shaved with Al's electric
razor, working carefully around the pimples, determined not to
approach a Marine base with cuts and scabs. Tory smiled, remembering. It was a darn shame boys had to have pimples, almost as if
nature were poking fun at them at the time they were most vulnerable.

And Walter was so vulnerable. And so am I, she thought. At the
station Tory had wept.

"You're always dribbling." Al laughed, as they waved at the
departing train. He hugged her shoulders trying to jolly her out of it.

"Thirteen years ago I saw him off to kindergarten," she said.

"And you went home with little Pat and cried." Al offered her
his handkerchief. "You're in a rut."

"You don't understand. You didn't understand then."

She had understood that first time, on that tart fall morning
when Walter first ran across the playground to school. She saw
then that the life pattern of woman is the giving away, the deliver-
ing up, the setting free. She had said then: Let me never be a pos-
sessive mother. Let me never become a monster trying to delay
birth, trying to deform what is meant to be free.

"When I tried to tell you, you said that after all he was only going to kindergarten for three hours a day. You said it was just like a woman to cross bridges before she got to a puddle. And now he's going away again and you still don't understand."

Of course, it was just like a woman to see the meaning of her whole life hidden in an hour. That was the wonderful thing about being a woman. Men care more about doing. And we care more about meaning. How nice and precise of God to make men and women like that, she thought. Like two jigsaw-carved pieces of one puzzle.

Only sometimes they get broken and don't fit together so well.

Like today. Where is Al now that his son is gone? Al is at work. As if a boy went into the Marines every day. Here I am, and there he is. He's worried about the shelf-life of the new line. And he puts me on the shelf. I can sit here and blow my top. Or my crown, excuse me. And Al, the big boob, couldn't care less. God, I'm lonely.

She wished she could call Jane and talk to her, but she couldn't talk to Jane these days. I told her: Walt is going in the Marines. And Jane didn't even seem to care. That wasn't like Jane. Jane always had a knack of hearing all the echoes that went with a fact.

She picked up her dishes, put them in the sink. She kept the Peace Prayer of St. Francis framed over the sink: "Let me seek not so much to be consoled as to console. Not so much to be understood as to understand."

Cinchy. Nice and neat. She closed her eyes. So okay. Give it a try. Your husband's busy and he's not consoling you and he would only console you by making jokes if he weren't busy and your dearest friend will not understand you. And you can't bring Walter home. So get going. It's your move.

Then she remembered what she and Clare had decided about Jane on the way home from the Mission. Suppose she's sick with this pregnancy, Tory thought. Suppose she's afraid. This is no time to turn my back on her, just because I'm miserable.

Ten minutes later she took Cyril in her arms, and drove over to the McNamaras'. Jane was sitting on a rock watching Meg and Kilian play with a dump truck. Teresa slept in the carriage.

"Come for a ride?" called Tory. "I'm going to the friary for something. Pile the babies in my car."

A shadow of irritation crossed Jane's face. She was waiting for Gloria to wake up. She did not want Tory to know Gloria was here. She did not want to go to the friary. But Tory might decide to stay if she didn't go with her. She shrugged and decided to accept the invitation.

A brown-robed young brother with a quick smile greeted them at the friary door. The building overlooked long, serenely greening lawns. Far down to the right the apple orchard gave promise of a white procession for May. Close by the terrace grew a tall broad elm tree, thick-trunked, pruned by gardeners thirty years ago to offer a man shelter under a baldachin of branches. There now on a weathered wooden bench sat the small contemplative figure of Father Juniper, a thick book upon his lap.

"I'd like to enroll someone in FMU," Tory said to the brother. "I wonder if I dare bother Father Juniper?"

The young brother smiled. "So, when Father Juniper does it, it's different?"

"Well, you know. Do I dare disturb him, or—"

But the children had already disturbed him. They had spied him silhouetted like a leprechaun under the tree, and ran out to touch him and see if he was real. Now he held all three on his lap, singing to them a song of his own making.

"I wish I had a camera," said Tory. "That brown wrinkled face beside the small smooth pink ones. Jane, what a picture!"

A squirrel with only half a tail ran backward down the tree trunk and threw himself into the cowl of the priest's robe. His head, twitching with eagerness, shot up behind the big spotted pointy ear of the old man and challenged the visitors. Kilian put up a hand to pet the animal. The squirrel bit him. Kilian screamed. Blood stained his finger.

Father Juniper leaped to his feet, dumping the children on the grass. Like some strange creature chasing his own tail he began turning in small circles trying to catch the squirrel who still clung to his back. The old man shouted. The squirrel shrieked. Jane grabbed Kilian and ran.

The young brother, catching himself about to laugh, dashed into the fray. Then in a moment the squirrel, using the brother's head as a foothold, bounded up into the tree and vanished.

"He's gone now, Father," the brother shouted at the loud blur that was Father Juniper.

The priest stopped whirling, and wiped his face with a big handkerchief. "The little monster! Squirrels are nothing but rodents, you know." He was panting and very angry. "Rats, that's what they are. I never did see what St. Francis was able to see in animals.

They all make me nervous. And these blasted squirrels that go crawling around my neck really infuriate me. Biting a small child. Where is the child?"

Jane had taken him inside. "Brother Cook is putting antiseptic on the bite," said Tory quietly. Her face was pale. She was appalled at Juniper's exhibition.

"Ah! Well, poor little man," he said, more gravely. "There's no danger though. No rabies in these squirrels." He looked at Tory apologetically. "Your friend's boy will be all right, really."

"I'm sure he will." With Cyril and Margaret clinging to her skirt she felt a little apologetic herself. "They're a little frightened," she explained, "but I'm sure they'll get over it."

"I frighten myself," said Juniper with a tidy pursing of his mouth. Whirling around like some heathen dervish."

He regarded the children gravely, as if awaiting their judgment. They in turn looked up at Tory, and then let go of her skirt.

"Shall we go in?" He smiled. "Was there something I can do for you? There must be a reason you came."

"I wanted you to enroll my son," Tory said, feeling suddenly overcome with sadness as she spoke. She followed him across the terrace. The first bees were working among fragrant sprawled Oriental poppies. "My son Walter. He needs the prayers of the Missionary Union. Any prayers. He's a good boy. He's just gone into the Marines. He's never been away from us before, Father." Her voice was thick with emotion. "He's barely more than a child."

"We are all children, children of God," said Father Juniper. "We are all away from home. You are unhappy because your son is gone from you? But you have known he was not yours forever, but a free creature given life through you, by God's will. You are worried that he will meet trouble and temptation in the world, and you will not be there to help him and guide him? But you know that it is God who, by his grace, helps and guides. Your son as well as you." He spoke gently, and Tory allowed herself to be comforted. If only, she thought, Jane would seize the opportunity to talk to him, I know he could help her, too. But she would not interfere.

Father Juniper drew from under the blotter an ornate certificate and uncapped his pen. Tory laid her offering on the blotter, then dictated Walter's name. The two little ones stood on tiptoe to watch the intricate script strokes of the pen. Father Juniper had developed his own modern imitation of the scribes of old. For him to write "Walter Burke" took fifteen minutes.

"Beautiful," said Tory, accepting the certificate. But she hid it in the envelope when Jane and Kilian returned. Kilian's finger bore a reassuringly fat bandage and Brother Cook had given him a big sugared doughnut for the other hand. Much to Kilian's confusion, Father Juniper bent and kissed him on the forehead.

To Jane Juniper said, "Your boy will be all right."

"I'm sure he'll be all right." She was polite, but she was ready to leave.

"Sit down, sit down. Humor an old man. Talk with me a bit." He took her arm as if she had offered it to him, and propelled her to the windowseat. From the folds of his cowl he took a pipe, a small sack of tobacco and matches.

"I have been thinking," he said. "Yes. I want to tell you. Listen. I have been thinking that we do not remember how to love God because we do not think of him as a lover. There is, you know, a book entitled *This Tremendous Lover* and it is not about Erroll Flynn or Valentino or Casanova. It is about God."

Jane's surprise showed on her face. She could not think of why he should be talking to her like this.

He puffed at the pipe. "And when you look at Our Lady—Oh, how she is misunderstood. Poor Lady. As if she were some sexless little doll who could not have spoiled her virginity if she tried. This, about the woman who is the second Eve!"

Tory would not meet Jane's eyes.

The pipe had not caught. Father Juniper cocked his head, continuing serenely, "And St. Joseph. They do him grave injustice. They show him with a snowy beard, aged till the fire is dead, a sort of eunuch to chaperon the Virgin. They rob him of half his glory, the glory of a man in his prime, stirred by love, stirred by greater love to self-denial and chastity."

Jane shifted unhappily on the tufted leather seat. She wished she might run away from this unwanted and strangely apt sermon, but she could not think of an excuse.

Finally the pipe was lit. Father Juniper collected the spent matches carefully, secreting them in the niche under his capuche.

"In St. Augustine, Florida," he went on, "is a shrine Americans do not much like, a very old shrine. Spanish, of course. It's the shrine of Our Lady of the Milk. The statue shows Blessed Mary with bared breast feeding her Child. This embarrasses our good ladies and our gentlemen. Too earthy." His head nodded slowly in agreement with his own thoughts. His pipe smelled rank and brown and moldy.

"And yet is there a place in the world where a man can ride in public without immodest advertisements? There is not. It's a funny world, where all human women's secrets are revealed and the human mother of God is considered debased for being a true mother."

"It does seem that everywhere we go people talk about sex," offered Tory nervously, recalling Jane's outburst of the night before.

"Yes. And they talk about it the wrong way," agreed Juniper. "And it can become an obsession. We must not forget that God created sex and so it is good. And God has taught us to read in all the mysteries of sex a symbolism of his own mysteries. Of the love-life of God. . . ."

It was too much for Jane. She jumped up, hoisting the baby onto her shoulder. "I'm sorry," she said. "I hate to interrupt. But I've got to get home. It's getting late."

In the car she explained to Tory. "I've got to make formula, and it's almost time for the next bottle."

"Want me to come in and stay?"

"No. Not now. I've got a million things to do."

Jane waited till Tory's car was out of sight; then she hurried into the house.

"Gloria?"

She saw the note on the table. "I called a taxi and caught the train. Don't worry about me," Gloria had scrawled. "I'll write and give you my address when I get to the Home. Thanks for everything."

Gloria was gone. And all Jane could think was that she herself had to go away, run away, before the crumbling ugly ruins of the world suffocated her.

"The love-life of God," she muttered, clattering through lunch preparations. "Now I've heard everything. Perversion and confusion. Either they're all stark raving or I am."

She gave the children peanut butter sandwiches and bananas.

That's the man they call a saint? A man who flies into a tantrum over a squirrel? And who sees sex in God and Our Lady and the whole Blessed Trinity? Some saint!

The baby girls were crying, little Kilian was making spitballs out of his sandwich. She put all three children to bed for their naps.

"I want to go away," she said aloud as she came downstairs. "I want to run away and that's all there is to it."

"You do?"

Jane jumped.

"Sorry, didn't mean to startle you. I looked in and I yelled and you didn't hear me." Martha Settler, crisp in her Volunteer's uniform, stood at the foot of the steps.

"I was talking to myself."

"Where do you want to go?"

"Anywhere. Only there isn't a single place in the world a married woman can go and be alone without causing talk," Jane said lightly.

"Go on retreat."

"I'm not the pious type. No, I was just figuring it out. You can't go to a hotel. I'd love to go to the shore but who ever heard of a decent wife going to the shore by herself, without even a girl friend, let alone kids and husband?"

"Go on retreat. There's a nice little Benedictine convent upstate. You can rest and be quiet and not be pious at all."

"I can't. What would Chris say?"

"He'd be tickled silly, I bet. He loves you. He knows retreats are good for anyone. What could be more proper?"

"But I'm trapped. Don't forget, I have kids."

"I'll take care of them." Martha smiled.

That afternoon, driving north in the spring through the hills and over the gleaming Housatonic, Jane felt an exhilaration she could hardly contain. She had a momentary regret, knowing she was a hypocrite going on retreat not to be near God but because it was the only decent place she could think of to go and get away from him.

She filed the regret away. It did not matter.

THIRTY-THREE

The house was old and plain and friendly. Walking in the door with her suitcase, Jane had a curious sensation of coming home. Two women, one grandmotherly in a tweed suit, the other younger, full-figured and blonde, looked up in greeting from the living room on her right. A fire was laid on the small hearth. Slightly faded flowered drapes hung beside brightly clean windows. She smiled back at the women, noted their silence. The one thing she did not want to do now was talk.

The Guest Mistress had said Jane was to be in St. Catherine's, a room on the first floor. On the rough paneled wooden doors leading off the hallway she could see neatly inked signs. She opened the door marked *St. Catherine.*

The aging chest of drawers with its crisp white dresser scarf summoned memories of boarding school. The floor was bare except for a small rag rug beside the big old bed. There was one chair, some hooks to hold clothes with a cretonne drape on a pullstring to hide the clothes, a table with a Confraternity New Testament, a *priedieu,* a crucifix on the wall. The major decoration of the room was its brilliant perfect cleanliness, accented by its economical resistance to trivia.

Unconsciously Jane looked for a washstand with pitcher and bowl. The room spoke not of a religious cell but of early America, of days of calico and sunbonnets and quilting bees.

She put down her bag, closed the black iron latch of the door and tried the bed. She had forgotten sheets were ever ironed. She pushed off her shoes, and slept.

She woke to a knocking on her door.

"You don't want to miss supper, do you?"

Tidying herself quickly, she went out. A little dark-haired woman with a chipmunk's nimble walk showed her the way.

"It is your first time here, isn't it? Sister Simeon, that's the nun who takes care of St. Gregory's, which is the name of this farmhouse you know, said it was." She tucked a flashlight in the knobby rounded pockets of her brown overcoat and scurried down a path, drawing Jane behind her. Under an arbor for roses they went, past a giant oak tree, its branches so broadspread and mothering that Jane with a start of surprise found herself understanding instantly how men had once come to feel gods dwelt in trees.

The hesitant twilight of May glimmered pale lilac through the old dry leaves still clinging stubbornly to the black branches. It would be another week at least before the ancient sap rose in new life. Behind the tree another house, barn red with black trim, rose in roomy and undisciplined welcome. Lighted windows gave on glimpses of book-lined walls and fireplaces.

"Men stay there. Eat there too," said the chipmunk lady over her shoulder. "Hurry up or we won't eat."

The path broadened into a driveway leading uphill. On the right over a gate in a tall weatherstained clapboard wall a sign proclaimed "Cloister." The wall joined a high gaunt building with two sets of scrawny front steps ascending to doors on the barn-red first floor. Up the first set of steps the lady led Jane, through the door and miniature vestibule into the tiniest and oddest dining room she had ever seen. It was perhaps nine feet long and five feet wide, pine-paneled on three sides. The fourth wall was a wooden grill with white curtains drawn on the other side. Beneath the grill a large wooden drawer served as a pass-through from the cloister to the guests.

When Jane came in dinner was already in progress. The wooden table, pulled out from the wall, with small octagonal backless wooden stools for seats, filled the entire space. Four women, including the two she had already seen, greeted them. A bit self-consciously Jane sat on a stool, accepted the silverware and plate passed to her, said grace silently. There was a fish casserole, thick slices of firm convent bread which would surely qualify as the staff of life, butter and honey from the convent farm.

The women were talking about the small news of the convent, of the artist who lived nearby, of the herbs Sister Prisca was planting, of the Puy medals for sale in Sister Mary Joseph's shop. Jane examined her companions discreetly.

The grandmother in tweed seemed alert to liturgical movements, well-spoken, with an aura of campus life. The chipmunk lady apparently worked in an office. There was a tall blonde with no makeup at all, who spoke knowledgeably of how thyme attracts bees, and of the soil tarragon needs to thrive. But her nails were tapered and long with that pale ridged appearance of being suddenly stripped of polish. The younger woman whom Jane had seen before at the farmhouse said nothing during the entire meal. Beside Jane sat a heavy woman with a voice that seemed used to public speaking, a vocabulary amusingly rich and precise.

Jane had been braced to defend herself against any attempt to pry into her privacy. No one had asked more of her than her name. The meal finished, dirty dishes stacked back in the drawer, crumbs swept, the six women went out into the night. Jane noticed a hand-lettered sign by the door. "*Pax!* Please be sure to switch off the light." Two women turned right, evidently to chapel. Jane went with

166

the others by the flashlight through the lilac-scented night, again to St. Gregory's. No one spoke, yet the silence was unconstrained and effortless.

Inside the hall, the chipmunk lady pointed to a neat bulletin board in the corner. "You'll find all you really need to know there. Bathroom's off the kitchen. You're welcome to make tea or coffee, or cook up a storm for that matter if you have something to cook. G'night." She ran up the stairs lightly.

Jane studied the board. Guests were welcome to attend Vespers, even Compline, or any of the hours of the Office which the community prayed around the clock. Mass hours were posted. Silence was requested in the house. Guests were asked to make their own beds.

Pax! Everywhere she turned, the same hand-lettered message. *Pax!* This is the Linen Closet. *Pax!* Please do not take the books away from the Common Room. *Pax!* This is a place of quiet.

Slowly, peacefully, she realized she was terribly, wonderfully sleepy. She took a bath, rubbed herself with a towel that seemed to smell of sunshine, and went into the room called St. Catherine. The crucifix on the wall proved by lamplight to be a lovingly carved wooden one, old, perhaps Spanish. She climbed into bed and looked at it curiously, as one looks at the family memorabilia in a stranger's house. She was now not interested in Christ, not related to him. She did not care to analyze the motives of those who had offered this refuge. They had not asked her the state of her soul. She did not volunteer to think about it.

Her last thoughts before sleep were of apples ranged red and shiny on a windowsill, of the smell of bread baking, of the sound of the ocean falling on night air, of warm arms and starched dresses and Queen Anne's lace flowers. She was too sleepy to understand the potpourri of childhood. She surrendered to its fragrance, dreamless.

THIRTY-FOUR

Next morning Jane did not go to Mass.

None of the women at breakfast remarked on her absence. As she sipped her coffee the white curtain behind the grill in the refectory was drawn back. Mother Gabrielle, the Guest Mistress, a giant woman with hands that looked as if they could churn butter and knead dough and probably did, welcomed them and praised the morning. She set an appointment for a conference with each guest, coming to Jane last.

"I'll be able to see you in St. Thomas, the last door past the chapel near the garden shop, at eleven. And here is a book you might look at in the meantime." The drawer grumblingly responded to her push and Jane took from it the proffered book, *The Virtue of Trust*. Mother Gabrielle leaned close to the grill, firm-cheeked and cheerful. "And, don't forget, Jane, you will want to stop in the chapel this morning and greet him. We always ask our friends to visit their host while they are in his house."

There was no touch of rebuke or sarcasm in her tone. Jane knew somehow that this woman did not mean to shame her into conformity, was only taking for granted that she would wish to be a mannerly guest. She went to the chapel.

It was a chapel that belonged in the country.

The people's side of it reminded her of a small summer-theater gallery: three rows of chairs, facing through arched partitions, with the effect of a balcony.

The sanctuary lay between the open chapel of the people and the cloistered chapel of the nuns. A breeze from the nearby greening fields swept softly through an open window. In the center of the space, untrammeled by walls or hangings, elevated on a polished wood platform, stood the altar table. Here was none of the golden art of cathedrals, no paintings, no statues, no frescoes, nothing to distract. Here, thought Jane, was an altar for the service and honor of the carpenter's son, a table where bread and wine seemed at home, a table that would not overawe a fisherman.

Kneeling there now she regarded the tabernacle where the nun believed her host dwelt, and found herself praying in the same spirit that the nun had spoken.

"Good morning." She did not speak aloud. "I'm sorry I didn't come to thank you before for letting me stay here. It just didn't occur to me. Of course you know why I'm here anyway and so there's no point pretending. Or do you want to know why I came? I came because—"

She became aware of movement in the nuns' chapel. Behind the drawn white curtain shadows moved as in pantomime. Figures entered, genuflected in pairs, and passed to take places in seats on the shadow stage. One only remained to open the curtains, then took her place.

From the left corner a thin precise soprano voice sang out a single line of Latin in Gregorian chant, rising from nothing, expanding, descending again and disappearing. The answer came from the shadows where faces remained indistinguishable.

Jane did not understand what they sang. Here and there meaning entered her consciousness, snatches of prayers she knew. *Gloria Patri et Filio et Spiritu; Sancto, Sicut erat in principio.* . . . She was aware rather of what a director would call the pace of the scene, the rise and ebb of emotion, disciplined, distilled, recollected. Voices rose from right and left in antiphon and always behind them, following them, ran the effect of a Greek chorus as the chant continued. As the strings of a piano can be made to echo a human voice singing at them, so there were set up within the tensed strings of her mind echoes of emotion as the nuns' song passed over her. What hour of the Office were they chanting? Matins? Terce? She did not begin to know.

The chant ended. The white curtains closed. Unobtrusively the shadows left the stage, soft-shod, without chatter or murmur. Jane was alone. She stood up, aware that her knees refused to be silent about the unaccustomed effort of kneeling on the bare floor. By the door a simple pewter font with the *Chi-Rho* symbol held the holy water. She blessed herself with it and went out into the spring morning.

In the yard by the chapel a woman sat paring potatoes. She looked up and smiled as people may smile at tourists.

At eleven Jane walked slowly toward the room called St. Thomas. She would have turned back from the door without keeping the appointment. The woman paring potatoes, the sunshine leveling her face with shadow, spoke.

"Go right in. She won't bite." As her hands moved a diamond broke the yellow light into small somersaults of color. "Turn back now and you'll never know what she would have said to you."

Jane opened her mouth to answer, but the woman worked on as if she had not spoken at all, apparently oblivious of anything but the firm cream-colored potatoes and the thin arcs of tan peel.

Jane lifted the latch and went in.

"Good morning!" Mother Gabrielle was behind another wooden grill like the one in the refectory. "Sit down!"

Jane took a seat on a stool.

"It gives one the feeling of visitor's day in a prison, doesn't it?" The nun smiled. "If you're not careful, you'll find yourself seeing double, trying to focus through the bars in the grill. You know, when children come to visit I bring out my hand puppets to climb all over the grill like monkey bars."

"Puppets?"

"I always have toys for children when they come here. They are the Child Jesus' toys, for them to play with when they are in his house, you see. Otherwise, if a child comes and sees only a funny-looking woman in a veil behind bars, that child is hardly likely to feel at home with us or with God."

Mother Gabrielle was leaving Jane no time to make even the simplest remark. Briskly but quietly she moved on from one subject to another.

"The convent, or monastery as we call it, is a family," she was explaining, "as our founder St. Benedict saw that it must be. We feel the people in the world are members of that family, that they have with us a home they belong to, whether they come here or not. Perhaps today more than ever our family in the world needs a home to return to, a place where the Father welcomes them. Here nothing changes. We have a vow of stability, you know, besides poverty, chastity and obedience. We stay in this house till we die. Always those who come home here find our lives unchanged. Always at two in the morning you find our sisters rising from bed to pray the Office in the chapel. Always at the twelve appointed hours through the day and night, no matter where you are, you may know that here we are praying."

She probably once had a good loud voice, Jane thought. A big woman like her. But the years of convent discipline have made it soft. The voices singing in the chapel had been woven into a single strand, polished till not one timbre emerged from the others. The sound of such discipline made Jane uneasy. She was anxious to hear again her own voice, to insist on its difference.

Mother Gabrielle continued, telling of the nuns who worked the gardens and cleaned and swept and baked and wrote and wrought in silver and painted. At last Jane interrupted:

"And you live in a world all your own!"

"It is your world, too."

"It is not my world. Forgive me, but you don't live in the world of reality. You live in a sweet little clean little world where everything is make-believe. Mother, I'm not really 'making a retreat.' I shouldn't have come here, as if I were. But there was no place else to go."

"There never is." Mother Gabrielle leaned back in her chair. I have disappointed her, Jane thought, but she needn't sound so pious about it. Then she saw that the nun laughed. In fact she was clasping her hands together as she laughed, as a mother does when enchanted by an antic of a child. The gesture unsettled Jane.

"Again and again and again!" laughed the nun. "Forgive me, my dear, I am not laughing at you. I'm laughing because it pleases the Lord to confront us so often with those who think that because we are nuns and virgins we live in unreality. Ah well, it is good for us, I am sure." She leaned forward again. "Do you really think it pure chance that you came here? Is it chance that leads a lost child home? Nonsense. Do you really think that because we are not married, because we chose this, we are less aware of life? Is a man who gives his inheritance to the Church unaware of what it is like to be rich?" She sat back in her chair. "I am by myself nothing, but I am not by myself. I have been appointed to the task of meeting the guests. We believe God gives grace of state: the grace to do whatever job you are called to do. It is his job to make me able to help you. And he can do anything."

"I didn't come here for help. I came, quite frankly, to rest. To get away."

"We'll see why you are here. And who knows? Perhaps we can convince you that it is you who have been living in a half-world, a boxed-in world, and we who have the windows open so we can breathe real air." She stood up. "That's the bell for chapel. I must go. Shall I see you again at, say, three?"

As Jane left the room of St. Thomas and went out into the sunshine she could not rid herself of the sensation of being watched, of being trapped in an old boxwood maze, and watched by someone outside, waiting with kindly eyes.

THIRTY-FIVE

"Don't you want to get this job finished quickly once and for all?" Krena asked. "Aren't you tired of trying to fit my work into your schedule? It's been breaking my heart. You're so darn conscientious, you won't let one detail slip by. But it's too much for you, and I know it is if you don't."

"Yes, I'd like to get it finished," Chris said. How much I need to get it finished I hope you can't know, he thought. But he could hardly blame Krena for his feelings, and he had determined to show no change in his behavior toward her.

"Then do let's use my library. If we're not interrupted I know we could get it done in a couple of days. R. P. wouldn't care, you know, where we do it, as long as we get the job done."

"Sounds great." Chris laughed. Confronted anew with the possibility, he didn't like it a bit. But it's true, he thought, that it would be the fastest way to end all this. And I do have to end it. And all I need to do is stick to business. Control. I ought to be getting good at that by now.

"What's the matter?" Krena asked. "You look reluctant."

"Of course not. But it might look a little odd. An unusual assignment, a beautiful woman like you—"

"Chris McNamara." She shook her head prettily. "I do think you're actually afraid for my good name." She walked over to the window.

"That's a coy remark," he said dryly.

The sunlight caught on the gold butterfly pinned to the neck of her simple brown dress. "I'm not coy, Chris. Your help means a lot to me and you mean a lot to me, as a person. If you worry about my good name, or however you'd want to put it, you're making it a wrong thing, our being friends. Don't do that."

"It's right as rain," Chris said. "It'll be like playing hookey. I'm looking forward to it."

Her library was like herself, he thought, rich but restrained, comforting. A refectory table from Italy. Thick carpeting, peacock-blue drapes, deep chairs, shelves filled with books obviously read, and oddities from Krena's travels: a black sacrificial cup from the ruins of Yucatan, a Baleek teapot, a French music box. Before the huge stone fireplace stood a china cat from Portugal with glittering yellow eyes.

The silence was luxurious. He sank into a semicircular couch, drank Krena's coffee and realized that someday he would like to live in a room just like this.

They worked all morning. They had lunch on trays.

"These plates are so darn dainty they make me nervous," Chris said. "But I like your stew."

"Specialty of the house." Krena smiled.

"I was afraid it might be watercress sandwiches or something elegant and inedible. You sure know how to cook a man's meal."

"Thanks," she said. "Not that I get much chance."

They worked again, she at the table, he pacing the carpet, trying out ideas between them. The afternoon sun slanted through the windows, fingering the inlaid chess table, dazzling as it touched a copper bowl of laurel.

"That's all," said Krena. "It's four-thirty. Quitting whistle."

He scratched his ear. "Where'd the time go?"

"Goes fast when you're having a good time," said Krena. "Let's have a drink before you go."

"This has been—" He shrugged and raised his glass in toast. "How shall I say, Madame? *Merveilleuse*? *Magnifique*? My French, she grows stale."

She sat in the wing chair by the fireplace, putting her feet up on the ottoman.

"Really, this has been a perfect day." Chris smiled. "We should do this more often."

"And all the work we got done!" She ran her fingers through her hair, and smiled.

He put down his glass, empty.

She stood up "See you tomorrow? Nine o'clock?"

"You're a slave driver."

"I know. But it's all for your sake, Chris."

"Self-sacrificing and still beautiful."

"See you tomorrow." She opened the front door and stood watching as he left.

The next morning as he turned his car into Krena's long winding driveway he found himself humming.

"You sound chipper," Krena called.

"This change of pace is going to my head."

"Good. Coffee's ready and waiting." She winked. "And so's the work."

"That's what I need, a businesslike tone," said Chris. The neat trim sight of her in the familiar sea-green suit pleased him. "I like these coffee cups. Big."

"You said you didn't like the dainty china." She spread the manuscript piles on the big table beside a pewter mug of freshly sharpened pencils.

"Very nice," Chris said, sinking down in the blue chair. "I feel like I've been away from the office for a month. It's a pleasant feeling." He stirred his coffee. "You have a relaxing effect on me. You. This room. I envy you this room. Even your coffee. With Jane away on retreat, the coffee at our house is pretty awful."

"Jane's away?" Krena moved the ashtray near him. "What do you do for meals, for goodness' sake?"

"Martha Settler fixes dinner. And dinner's great. Breakfast's my job. I'm a real whiz at opening corn-flakes boxes."

"Sounds dreadful."

"No. In a way it's a change of pace too. Everything's different for these few days. With Jane gone the kids feel like we're sort of camping out. The baby's staying at one house and Meg at another, so that leaves Mary and the boys and me. The rules are pretty much suspended. I'm not much of a stickler for clean ears and early bed." He drank his coffee. "The whole thing feels a bit like a holiday."

"As long as Jane doesn't stay away too long. You'd soon come down to earth if it kept on that way. You'd run out of clean shirts and socks."

"Yep." He stretched his long legs on the ottoman. "It's all unreal. Including coming here."

"I'd better get you to work right away," said Krena. "The mood you're in, you're likely to relax so much you'll start to snore."

"You're right." He put down the empty coffee cup. "Thank the Lord one of us has a steady head."

As he went to the table he couldn't help thinking how apprehensive he had been about working at Krena's house. He had even been grateful that her driveway was so long and winding, so no one would notice his car parked there all day with her husband away. What had he worried about?

Krena, as if reading his thoughts, said, "You thought you were the one who would keep our noses to the grindstone, right?"

"I thought you were a dangerous woman," he said comically. "And you are. You're a slavedriver. Always were."

The last of his guard dropped as he threw himself into the morning's work.

THIRTY-SIX

The sign, weather-faded, swung in the breeze. It caught Jane's eye as she walked, exploring the unfamiliar road near the retreat house. "TO THE CRÈCHE."

She turned down the rutted lane. Occasional evergreens, shapeless and neglected, marked the overgrown path. Ahead stood a shed, apparently abandoned. The path led nowhere else. The door was tall and ill-fitted, made of boards held together with a few rough crossbars. The iron latch had an overcoat of flaking rust-stained paint.

Uncertainly she tried the door. It swung open. From the dark interior of the shed a body of cold air met her like a second wall. Dimly she could see two wooden chairs near a glass-framed sign. Fumbling by the door she found a light switch. Built into the wall of the shed, some six or eight feet long, reaching back into three dimensions, illuminated through a dark blue curtain draped as a night sky, was a scale model of an Italian village, startlingly perfect.

Here were miniature houses set up on hills, tiny cobblestone streets, an inn, shops, peopled with cunningly made lifelike characters about four inches tall. Here were women arguing over the price of a hen. Here a man smoked peacefully in his front yard. Lovers embraced. Ruffians in a drunken dispute engaged the idle attention of workmen quenching their thirst. Ladies of decorum visited. Children tumbled and pranked. Men bargained, men tended livestock, men flirted, men joked. They seemed like miniature actors in an opera scene, ready at any moment to burst into song.

Jane peered at the scene more closely, studying the little velvet shoes of the nobleman, the shawl of the big-bosomed barmaid. Then she shivered in the root-cellar cold that lay imprisoned in the shed. With a stir of annoyance she remembered that she had expected to find a nativity crèche here, not a doll's house.

She consulted the framed explanation by the display.

"This old and valuable Neapolitan crèche," she read. So it was really meant to be a manger scene. Puzzled, she read on, scanning the history of its acquisition and installation in the shed. Near the end of the hand-lettered text she found the explanation she sought.

The Neapolitan artists traditionally set the Christmas drama in their own native setting, to stress the universal immediacy of Christ's birth. This particular unknown artist had an additional message to express. The artist wished to remind his audience that the world is too busy being worldly to remark the coming of its God. Who in Bethlehem knew what was happening in the stable cave? Who in this Neapolitan village sees that Christ is born? If it happened today in our town, would men and women be more aware?

He who can see, let him see.

Jane went back for another look. Fresh details caught her eye. In the wealth of figures she had not noticed before the sneak thief about to take fruit, a little girl with a bunch of posies. Or, in the mountain sky, an angel.

Then in the midst of her census, she came upon the hovel where Mary and Joseph kept watch over the newborn son of God. They were hidden in ordinariness. The manger scene was tucked in obscurity on the hillslope of the village.

"That's a crazy way to build a crèche," she said.

Irritated, she started to leave. Then she turned back for one last look. This time she remembered where to look. She saw the Infant God in his bed of straw at once. When at last she drew herself away, closing the door behind her, sunlight blinded her. She leaned against the door and raised her face to the sky, eyelids pressed shut.

She trembled as a girl trembles when first she finds in her heart the discovery of love. Slowly she opened her eyes. She saw weed blades shimmer in sunlit wind and thought them beautiful. The spell is lifted and I can see. The enchanter is gone and I am set free. She sank down on a small rough lichened rock.

"You must *will* to believe." The first time she heard those words, long ago in convert instructions, she had dismissed them as irrelevant. She tested them again now aloud near the overgrown path.

I willed not to believe. I made up my mind not to believe because it was too good to be true. The idea of love and holiness was too beautiful to be real, I said, and I thought I was being grownup and wise. As if I were the one who decides what's real. Little old me. I said I couldn't see him anywhere. I saw confusion and fears and ugliness and tears. I saw no order or joy. And so? It didn't exist, I said.

She closed her eyes again, listening to grass slipping against grass, to a bee, and a cricket. She felt as if truth had been handed back to her, pressing against her chest, making itself one with her.

"You have to know what to look for," she said aloud to herself.

176

"Like a child. Backwards, upside down, surprising. The king is born in a stable and no one even knows he is there." Her voice was low, exploring. "The baby of Mary is the God who made her. He came to conquer, and he wins by surrender. He died to bring life." Her voice rose a little, catching with delight in her throat. "God is. How did I forget? I was looking to see him the way I thought he should be, not the way he is."

What chain of chance led me here to a Neapolitan crèche? Or was it chance? She didn't care. She was here. What she thought about it didn't change the fact that she was here and had found him.

She got to her feet and began to run, a long lean loping figure of a young woman, hastening shadowless through the noon light, startling two crows in the lane. They rose with indignant cries and she ran on. Under the oak tree, in sight of the cloister, she stopped for breath and smoothed her hair. A chipmunk, with a last acorn clutched in his paws, eyed her from a niche where roots grappled the earth.

She smiled. "I say to you you are carrying an oak tree as big as this one in your hands, little chipmunk, and you do not believe me because it looks only like a morsel of food. Oh you of little faith!"

She laughed. The chipmunk, affronted, screamed and darted away.

Down the path the chaplain walked, breviary in hand, a frail, frightened-looking man, hunched even in the sunlight. He looked like the last person on earth whom she would choose as a confessor, least likely to understand what she needed to say, a prim nervous type who would want you to stick to a copybook list of sins. He passed near her.

"Father?"

He glanced up, lips still moving.

"Could you hear my confession?"

"I could."

Jane considered his tone. "Would you?"

"I do not hear confessions under an oak tree. I am not a Druid."

He closed the book, his fingers on the page. "Confessions are ordinarily heard in the chapel between four and six, or whenever someone rings the bell."

With a suggestion of a bow he reopened his breviary and resumed praying.

Jane walked up the hill and into the chapel. The confessional was to the left. She found on the wall a bell marked with the sign:

"Pax! Those wishing to receive the sacrament of Penance at other than scheduled hours ring this bell."

Jane pushed the button and the bell rang outside in clear, far-reaching, deliberate chime. The priest came slowly.

After confession, she knelt in the chapel before that plain altar. On the altar steps were copper bowls filled with yellow and white tulips. She bowed her head and said silently the prayers the priest gave her as penance. She raised her head and saw in an alcove a wooden Madonna.

Then she prayed without words, like a child standing silently before her mother, confident that Mary would know better than she what she wanted.

The prayer did not last long. She could not prolong it. She blessed herself quickly, looked at her watch and ran. Lunch hour was almost over. She was acutely hungry.

"You look refreshed. More alive. Perhaps alive again?"

Jane met Mother Gabrielle's gaze.

"Alive again."

"Good."

"But now—now I must begin again. How do I say it? I've never really talked to anyone about—my soul, before. Others talk to me about problems. Or used to. I could help them, tell them. But now I don't even know how to explain what I need to know."

"You need to know everything and you find you know nothing? That's the way it is."

"I don't even know when or how I lost my way. I didn't know that I had stopped believing, stopped seeing. There was a time when I would rather have died than commit mortal sin. I couldn't understand how anyone who loved God and knew right from wrong could possibly—"

"Do you understand now?"

"No. Not really. But I know first-hand that it is possible."

"Good. That in itself is a gift. A protection against pride. Some of these gals who are so very holy, you know, would have been shocked by the Lord and his tolerance for, say, that divorcee at the well, or the married woman who was being stoned to death for having an affair. I suspect they are in for a big surprise if they get into heaven."

"You make it sound easy to understand sin. It's easy because you're here, away from it. You made a sacrifice, yes, but what you gave up causes an awful lot of trouble."

"What? Sex? That's part of what we gave up. But it's not what causes all the trouble." The nun shook her head. "You're looking at the flames, not the source of the flames."

"Looking at the wrong thing. Looking and not seeing." Jane sighed. "That's a habit of mine. Tell me where to look. Or how."

"What do you see? Look back at the world you left and tell me what you see."

"I see a mess. A man-woman mess. I see my sister. Carrying a— a baby out of wedlock. She's not a Catholic but the father is. He should have known. He—" Jane folded her hands. "I see the woman next door who—oh, it doesn't matter. I see the Church preaching that marriage is a sacrament and love in bed is holy, and everything is sacred and symbolic and if you love God everything will be fine. But if I have another child I may die." Jane bent her head forward and rested her fingers on the grill. There was dust in the crevices. "That sounds like I'm being melodramatic. I'm not. There's a kidney condition. So. We're meant to be prudent. That's where I got into trouble. With me it's got to be all or nothing."

"I wonder. Were you ever really at ease with love?" The nun's voice was matter-of-fact. "Did you ever really overcome yourself, love yourself in your love for your husband? Perhaps in a way you were glad to be excused from it?"

Jane did not raise her eyes.

"And then," the nun continued, "you felt confused because your body insisted and your mind rejected. Perhaps you rationalized and said your husband had need of you and then hated him for it? I once knew a woman who thought that way. . . . Of course, it probably is not your problem at all. But it does happen. We get ourselves all twisted up when we look at things the wrong way."

Silence. Mother's voice went on.

"The world always looks at things the wrong way. That's why it makes so much noise about sex. Because it is afraid. The world sees sex as a strong drive, hard to channel, basic in human beings, yet somehow animal-like. So the world decides that people are all animals, all flesh. And that's wrong. We are not and cannot make ourselves be all body. We are body and spirit.

"And some others in the world who know they have souls, look and see that bodies can cause trouble. And so they're ashamed of everything that has to do with bodies. And of course that doesn't work out either. It can't. This is an incarnation-centered world.

"And all that confusion comes from looking at people when instead we should look at Christ."

Mother Gabrielle drew a big white cotton hankie from her sleeve and blew her nose loudly.

"Do I sound too solemn? Now, where was I? Ah, yes.

"We begin with the fact that God designed men and women. If he planned human life in two sexes, it must be a good idea. And if God became human, to redeem humans, there must be something pretty wonderful about being human.

"Now you said, and the world says, that sex makes trouble. But Jane, it doesn't. Not any more than hunger or thirst or the need to breathe. What makes trouble is selfishness, lack of love, pride." Mother Gabrielle rested her chin on her hands and looked at Jane. "And those are things we do not escape when we take a vow of chastity, my dear. They follow us right into the cloister."

"You've lost me," said Jane quietly.

"So. Let's try to say it this way. No one is complete in himself. No woman, no man. We were made to find completion in God. We cannot be whole till we give ourselves to him.

"But we don't like the idea of not being self-sufficient. We're proud, with our free wills. That original sin of Adam and Eve you know had nothing at all to do with sex. No, the devil sold them the first lie on earth, the first bit of unrealistic nonsense. He told them they could be like God, needing no one, serving no one, complete in themselves—if they had the courage to break God's command.

"That lie does not die, Jane. That lie, that defiant suicidal refusal to yield love, that's what makes the trouble. Especially with sex."

The nun's voice faded. She lapsed into silence. Almost, Jane thought, as if she waited for words to be supplied her. Calmly she resumed: "Perhaps God wanted to remind us quite naturally that we do need someone else to give ourselves to, to complete us. Perhaps that's why he made it so man needs woman and woman needs man. He hopes we will be wise enough to carry our love a step further, to him.

"But because we are human we have a hard time learning to love, each other or God. We sit apart and huddle ourselves to ourselves, and give only what we think we can spare. We become misers of love and life. And that is what hell is about."

Mother Gabrielle bent her head, fingering the black folds of her skirt. "Marriages break up," she said finally, "when two people do not love enough to give themselves totally. If you keep a last inner reserve, if you look at your loved one in judgment and set yourself above him, if you worry over the price of your gift of self you do not love him yet."

She looked up at Jane with steady eyes. "The same is true of loving God. And for a married person the two loves go together. In you, this moment both strands are weak. You cannot rebuild your heart overnight. Begin with the love of God. It's easier. Because God is here, and your husband is not. Because God alone is perfectly lovable in the whole world. Learn to love him and you will love your husband. For you that will work best."

"Are you telling me to love Chris and let God take care of the baby part?"

"I'm telling you to love God and do what you will."

She nodded, reading Jane's expression.

"Jane, love is not an activity of the timid. It demands that you are willing to risk all for love of God. It demands that you give up self-will to find freedom, your own life to live a new way. That is frightening. It is, I think, meant to be."

She leaned forward, close to the grill. "You asked me to tell you where to look. You must look at Christ. And looking what will you see? At least this: that God is all-powerful, all-knowing, and that he loves Jane McNamara incredibly. That he wants you to be happy with him forever. That he loves you as your Father, pursues you as a bridegroom, dwells in you with love in the Spirit."

The chapel bell was ringing. Mother Gabrielle stood up. "Perfect love casts out fear," she said.

She vanished to her labors in the chapel.

THIRTY-SEVEN

"And the ghost vanishes into the sunset!" Krena put down her pencil. "Chris, we're finished."

"We should celebrate." He turned from her window.

"Steak for lunch. And first a drink."

He could hear her singing softly as she fussed in the kitchen.

"Now all you have to do is cope with the author on this," he said. "Hope he doesn't object to your changes."

"My changes?" She brought him his drink.

"They're all yours now. And he's your author, not mine."

He stood staring at the china cat on the hearth. "A toast to the nicest editor I know." He raised his glass. "No. To the only nice editor I know. And the only pretty one."

Gravely she accepted the compliment.

"You know, that cat looks like you." He followed her into the kitchen. "I like that dress you're wearing, sort of soft and fuzzy. I never saw you wear it before. Makes you look even more like that cat."

"You say the nicest things." She chuckled. "What woman wouldn't love being told she's a cat?"

"Didn't mean it that way. I'm just stupid."

"You're sweet."

They were nearly through lunch when the phone rang. When Krena went to the kitchen to answer, Chris could hear her voice clearly.

"Yes, of course I understand, dear. It's just that I thought you might come home before that. No, I'm not angry, I'm getting used to being alone. I'm beginning to like it. Yes, the gardeners were here and the place looks lovely; thanks for arranging it. I'm fine. I just stayed home to work this week, finishing a manuscript. Well, it was nice of you to worry, but I'm not sick. . . ."

Chris finished his cake, stretched, and sat down on the long couch beside the fireplace cat.

"That was my husband," said Krena. "Did you finish eating?"

"I did. And I'm so content I could only collapse and enjoy this room." He sighed. "I should be going home."

"Might as well stay and relax a little." She sat beside him and smiled. "You know," she said, "you're a very fortunate person. Children. A happy home. So many people who love you." She shook her head. "No, don't frown. You were just starting to look content."

She put her hand on his forehead, gently playful. "No frowns." With sudden shyness she drew her hand away.

"Krena." He caught her hand. It was warm in his. Her eyes met his. Quietly she leaned forward and kissed him on the lips.

And without warning he found that the thoughts he had struggled with so often were now flesh and blood against him. He put his hands on her shoulders, on the fuzzy softness of the dress.

"Chris," she whispered.

He pulled her to him and kissed her long and hard. His body conspired with hers against his will. "Krena," he said, his mouth finding her ear. "Krena. How could anyone not love you?"

She rested her cheek on his shoulder. The lightness of her surprised him, warm and weightless and tormenting as her perfume as it rose around him.

"These moments don't exist," she whispered. "They're not on any calendar."

She lay close against him. "Did you know this would happen, Chris? It had to happen. Without any plan, it had to happen."

He started to speak but she prevented him with a kiss. And responding he gripped her, and felt for her, and caressed her. And there were no words.

She moved under his hands, pressing herself to him with soft insistence, and something in him exulted. Too long had she waited for a man who could waken her. Barren, childless, loveless. He tasted her lips and they parted.

One moment of time. Then slowly he drew back. At last he found words.

"Krena. We can't."

She laid her finger on his mouth, and gravely he took it away. His jaw tightened. The pulse stood out firmly in his temple. He reached over and found two cigarettes and lit them, and handed her one.

"Krena, I—"

"Yes?" she smoothed her hair.

"I'm trying to think of something to say that won't hurt you. But every time I come up with something about marriage vows."

"Won't hurt me? That's my Chris. Vows. Right and Wrong. Or right and sin." She stood up. "Did you really think this was serious? We were carried away, but let me tell you, we wouldn't have been carried far." She looked down at him, composed and laughing.

His head ached with confusion.

"Did you really think I would let you be my lover?"

Her laugh was hateful. He felt his cheeks flushing.

"You're sweet, Chris, but you have a lot to learn," she said, throwing her cigarette in the fireplace, "I don't let any man give me sermons. Not even you."

He got to his feet. She was straightening the piles of manuscript, hitting them against the table top to even the edges of the pages. "Do you usually let a kiss or two convince you a woman is madly in love with you?" She laughed. "Or haven't you ever been kissed by anyone but your wife before? If you had, you'd know. But I forgot how young and serious you are. Poor Chris, thinking himself noble enough to warn me. 'We can't,' you said. Don't worry, we wouldn't have."

Anger choked him. "I don't believe you," he said.

She looked at him coolly. "It's time you went home."

"I'm going."

He took his hat and coat and walked out the door and slammed it.

"The trouble with you," Al said that night over a glass of beer, "is that you are out of touch with reality."

Chris raised his eyebrows and smiled. "Is that my trouble?"

"It is. You read a lot, and you think a lot. You know all about politics and the African problems and the Chinese problems. You talk about them. And the national debt. *And* the state of morals and literature and liturgy and all that stuff. But you live in theory and words. Let me ask you, what do you really know about the real business of life? Ah-huh! Making a buck? Getting ahead?"

"Nothing. I'm an intellectual bum."

"Come on. You know what I mean. You're a good guy, Chris. The greatest. But you're too good. You're naive. You expect everyone to be good, you believe you can be a full-time Christian and make a go of it in this world. But no one can."

"You're being cynical."

"No. Realistic. I'm a Christian. Hell, you know that."

"I know it."

"But you'll never get anywhere if you're not willing to get *in* the world and get dirty."

"You're talking over my head, Al."

"Take last year, for instance, when you got that dirty trick played on you. You didn't get promoted, right? Because you didn't feel you could go along with that new history or whatever the hell it was about."

"The American Constitution."

"Now look. Couldn't you have done more good if you had the

184

promotion than without it? What good do ideals do you? The book couldn't have been that bad."

They drank their beer in silence. Around them the living room betrayed Jane's absence. Ashtrays were unemptied. Odd shoes and small dirty socks lay under chairs. The dying forsythia on the mantel were like faintly charred paper.

With an effort Chris drew his thoughts back from the afternoon. If I told you about what happened, or what didn't happen at Krena's house, Al, what would you say?

"You gotta be realistic. And quit locking yourself up in a Catholic ghetto," Al said.

"You're talking nonsense, Al," Chris said. "I may never be a success. But I have to live with myself."

Al shrugged. "It's all a question of reality, old boy. I'll bet you don't play office politics at all."

"Could be."

"You look sore. Why? Because you think I think those ideals of yours are corny? I never said they were corny. But after all, a man grows up. Like with wives. He learns marriage isn't the biggest deal. Five days a week there's a bigger one."

"You sound like a bitter husband."

"A realistic one. Ah-hah! There's the difference. Look, if I let myself worry over Tory and the kids all the time—Hell's bells, my boy's in the Marines because he's a bum, my girl's running around with a smart-aleck kid who calls himself an atheist, my little guy's flunking in school and—No, Tory and I have learned you can't have heaven on earth, so let's get on with the business at hand." Al poured himself more beer. "That's the trouble with Catholics, why we're not more felt in the world. We're too busy with what nobody can see. Love. Family. Transforming the world in Christ. Bitter? I'm not bitter. I got faith, and hope, and all that jazz. But God wants little Al to get out and bottle soda and earn a living."

"Yup."

"I mean it."

"I know you do." Chris leaned on the mantel. I could have had her, he thought. No matter what she says. Except I'm not made that way. What reached in and stopped me?

"You know what you're saying? You're not just saying that I'm all wrong, Al. You're saying the whole thing's all wrong. That it just isn't true. And you don't mean it, Al."

"I don't know. Maybe I do. I'm realistic."

"Al. Put it this way. Either there's a mystery in life, a reality I can't see and you can't see, that's more real than what we can see, or there's not. If there's not, then the hell with it all. Then all there is is making money and going to bed and living it up and nothing matters. But if God made this world and still makes it, if everything here from my job and your bottles and your wife and my wife are parts of something, then—then there's some point. That's the choice, see. And you've got to risk everything on what you believe. Now you keep saying you're realistic. I think you're being unrealistic. You're missing reality by trying to be practical first."

"As someone so wisely said, it'll be a hell of a joke on us if we find out it wasn't true after all." Al laughed. "A hell of a joke."

"And more of a hell of a joke on them if it is true."

We can't. That's what I said, like a melodrama in some book. What stopped me? I'll never know. The grace of God, and wouldn't Krena love that if I said it. A lifetime of habit. The habit of taking things seriously. Not very noble-sounding. But people think resistance to temptation is noble in women. Men are supposed to sin nobly. Ignobly, then, I thank God. And I wish Jane were home. The furnace clicked on. The heat rising in the hot water fins ticked along the baseboards.

"In the beginning a man can lean on his wife and sing 'Tea for Two' and go out and conquer," said Al. "But there comes a time when that's over. And he goes alone. Don't you ever feel alone when you're with your wife? That's a damn bad question to ask. Don't answer it. I'll finish this beer and go home."

"You and Tory? Everything's okay?"

"Oh, sure. Better or worse, sickness and health, love and boredom. That's what they left out. Boredom. You know, Chris?" He put down his glass. "I'm not ready to be an old married man, Chris. A father, okay. But I'm a husband, too. And I'm not ready to be pushed into an easy chair behind my paper. Walter's already feeling his oats, but that doesn't put me off the active list yet." He ran his hand over his thinning hair, and then looked suddenly embarrassed.

Chris paced the room. He'd never before had a friend as close as Al, but even with Al he was accustomed to preserving a degree of privacy. Never had the two men come so close in talk to the intimacy of this one subject as now. Ordinarily their discussion of sex was limited to the retelling of jokes heard at banquets and breakfasts.

"I feel so far away." Al said. "She's right there, but I feel like she's miles away. You know?"

Chris drained his beer. "I know. Jane's gone away. *Run* away, I feel like saying."

"When's she coming back?"

"I don't know. *Is* she coming back?" His laugh was no móre than a spasm of breath through a closed mouth. "Sometimes I sit here and I think we have gotten so far away from each other that she may not, ever."

He ran his hand over an old green glass bottle on a shelf, a bottle with imprisoned bubbles, which Jane had rescued triumphantly from the Bargain Barn. She hoped to make a lamp of it.

"I look at Jane. And I think to myself. And all I can think is— that I've been unfaithful to my wife. No. Listen, Al. I'm not talking about going to bed with someone. That's only one kind of being unfaithful."

"It's the most popular kind."

"Al, look. What I mean is I have not kept those vows of cleaving to her for better or for worse. You know? I've left her. I live here with her but in a way I left her. She left me too. But I left her."

Al pressed the tips of his fingers together and thought about it and had some more beer.

"We start not liking each other and being impatient, and trying to go on alone, and we will not let each other be persons. You know?"

"I know," said Al.

"We keep trying to change each other, Al, and getting angry because we're different from each other and separate. And we leave God out of it. We leave the mystery out. And that's what unfaithfulness is."

"Oh?"

"That's what unfaithfulness is," Chris repeated. "Forgetting to live by what we cannot see. Mixing up reality with what looks real and isn't. The real Jane isn't the woman who snaps at me because she's afraid to have kids."

Abruptly he sat down facing Al, his hands flat on the table next to the beer.

"Al, listen to me. They say there's a dark night of the soul, you know? For mystics. There's a time when a saint feels God is gone away and all is dead and useless, and the saint hangs on by sheer faith. And God comes back and the victory is won. Remember John

187

of the Cross? Remember the night we read him out loud, you and I? But we're not mystics, you and I. We have a different way to God, through marriage. And our dark night is of the body."

"I like that," said Al gravely. "I like that."

"The dark night. It's the time when you feel alone with Tory. Or I with Jane."

He refilled his glass. The men watched the foam, a trifle stale now, shivering on the glass edges. In the silence, Al could even hear the foam rustle. Chris drank.

Finally Al stood up.

"Vall," he said, "I'll tahl you. I'll try stocking that line and we'll see how it moves. On trial only. I'll run a special on it this week.

"But," he continued in his normal voice, his eyes serious, "you'd better not tell Jane about it. At least not in those words. You start telling her you were unfaithful and she'll never wait to find out what you mean!"

"You're so right."

"Did it ever occur to you, old pal, there may have been more than one person trying to talk her into thinking that gal from the office was on the make for you? Wives get strange notions about any woman who works."

Chris tried to laugh. "Krena? You're crazy."

"You're the one who's crazy if you think that never entered Jane's head." He picked up his hat and coat from the sofa. "Thanks for the beer."

"Give my love to Tory."

Al posed by the door, and passed his hand over his hair. "I'm still trying to give her mine. You got to wait your turn, old man."

THIRTY-EIGHT

For Jane silence became an environment in itself. Silence, the continued absence of small talk, the weightlessness of a situation stripped of trivia, affected her as the different air pressure of a spot high above sea level affects those not native to it. Her body tired more quickly, more completely, slept more easily. Her muscles, accustomed to bracing themselves against tension, found relaxation strenuous. For the first few days she became aware of the strained muscles of her mouth, of her nose, of shoulders and arms, muscles she had never known were tense, yet which obviously did not know how to expand under the silence.

It seemed at moments as if she could see the impact of an idea upon her silence, see the arrival of it, swift and soundless as the dropping of a seagull to cove water, trace the ripples of it as they spread slowly to her, inescapable so long as she did not disturb the silence on which they were formed.

Newborn, in a Christian silence, she moved and had her being, in him and with him and through him, and she had not known before what that formula meant. And as the silence filled her she became aware of a world she had never known, where all things drew the mind to him, the sacramental world where life is liturgy.

She would walk through the spring morning, under the shelter of the oak up the crackling dry dust of the driveway, and see seed that had fallen on stony ground flourishing gaily and proudly, promising so much. In the shade by the chapel entrance dew lay previous benison, new baptism for the new day. Sheep moved in a downhill pasture, fearing no evil.

The voices of the earth, the sounds of grass blades brushing each other as a beetle passed, the inflected, tantalizingly coded conversation of birds building a nest in the tall grass, the supple response of each damp new birch leaf to otherwise unnoticeable movements of the air, the firm sounds of metal tool against earth in need of turning, the tuneless humming of a woman hanging out clothes to dry, the far-off clatter of dishes and silverware, all sounds seemed newfound and delightful.

In silence she smelled the smells of crushed grass, of iron on her hands when she had held to a step railing too long, of orange peel suddenly broken. Under her feet as she leaned on the oak rose an odor of change and promise, an odor it seemed to her as of purgatory on earth. All that had died and all that had rotted, the strong branch wood stripped of pride and turned to a skeleton, was now in the good time of God becoming the source of new life, transformed.

Food, even food, lay new-known to her tongue. Taste of the Lord, taste of honey, see that both are sweet. The bread of life, daily, is strong to the teeth and firm and stands for no nonsense of chemicals. Roots have been raised to light and washed and cooked —could a man guess the whiteness of potato when first he drew a dusty brown clod out of the ground? The oil of the salad is pressed from olives from great grey-green trees that grow in someone's garden, oil to strengthen, to sweeten, to anoint.

Her children returned to her mind. Tears, the sweet sudden tears that spring from beauty's presence, surprised her as she saw in her heart the treasure that was her children. Where had she lost them?

Peter. Peter, whose hair smelled of sweat and leaves and sun, whose arms were solid and who stood tall as the breasts she had once held him to. How long had it been since she came out of herself to talk to him or listen? She remembered when first they had moved from the city, Peter's voice echoed among the trees, singing for joy at being alive and free and windblown. He did not sing now. He could not wear short pants even in the summer because they were corny, could not admit to liking baths because the right thing was showers, could not kiss his parents if another boy was watching.

Peter? Surely he was happy. Or was he? He was a collector of frog's eggs floating in dark bubbly gelid masses in old applesauce jars, a tree climber, a fort and club maker. He was not often home.

Mary? My daughter, Mary. I do not know her. She is too female for me, too dishonest with herself, too given to dramatization. She— Then she saw Mary, saw the blue-green eyes, the round face, the pucker of her chin when she smiled.

If I saw her and she were not my own child, I would think her the most imaginative, charming, lovable girl possible. Mary's charm is simply that she is beyond question already a person. She makes magic with plain things, builds the arch of drama from the blocks of everyday. She loves and is not sure she is lovable and holds her head high in fear.

Why have I not seen them as persons? I want them perfect, and I am not perfect.

Luke! Always underfoot he is. I could bend down and hug him close and he would not be underfoot.

Kilian, with the smiling dark eyes and his love of stuffed animals to hold. Kilian is forever going into the brook and losing shoes and coming home late. Kilian, you have been left alone and you have said to me that I do not love you and I thought you did not know what you were saying. . . .

Margaret, Meg. Mumblety Peg. That's the rhyme Chris calls her by. She's a good little one. She leaves me alone. She's good. But she should not leave me alone so much. Her hair is straight in an old

190

Dutch bob and her cheeks match her hair, straight and flat. She doesn't smile much. Or cry. Dear God, a tiny girl should smile and cry and whine.

The baby Teresa is a stranger. I do not even remember what she looks like really. . . .

I have not been away long. Only four days!

"You had been away a long time perhaps before you came here," answered Mother Gabrielle. "You were there at home in your body. But could you have been running away from them in your heart? So that you would not have to give, so that you could wrap yourself up safely in yourself?"

The first wave of remorse caught her unaware. She leaned her head on the waffle lines of the grill and cried that she had not known what she had done.

"Stop it," said the nun. "Jane, Jane, you're being foolish now. You're letting your pride—"

And Jane listened and saw she could not even have the luxury of claiming to be the world's worst mother. She must be just herself, plain Jane.

"God knew everything you did. He let it happen of your own free will. If it was bad, if it was good, he permitted it. And for those who love God all things work together for good." Mother Gabrielle sighed. "It's the worst waste of time trying to figure out how to raise children. They're not yours, anyway. They're his. He's not going to let you ruin them forever just because you didn't know any better."

"I feel I—"

"You feel. You think. What does feeling and thinking have to do with reality? Only God is real. You see now that you have been self-centered, that you have not shed love on your children as the sun sheds light and heat. Perhaps you did botch it. You've got to go on from here. You learn, you love. Forget yourself. You think of him."

The next time she came for conference with Mother Gabrielle, Jane wanted to speak of Chris. During the afternoon, in the yearning grey-green shade of the tree, she had understood that she had failed Chris, failed to be one with him. She had hated being part of him, loathed him for being part of her, tormented herself and him. She had suspected him of Krena. All this she wanted to unburden from her soul.

But Mother Gabrielle would not listen. She gave what amounted to a lecture on liturgy, on divine office, on the rhythm and cycle of the church year.

"Christ is not dead, you know. He lives. We live in him. We are his unseen body. The Church is his bride, breathing with his spirit. And his life unites us all. Now we enter the time of Pentecost, the time of the Spirit, the time when the Church receives the Spirit as Mary did, and conceives the living Christ. The time when your soul must surrender to him and be possessed by him and bring him forth."

Jane did not understand what the nun said. But she did understand that she was not to dwell on the failures of the past, not to wrack her conscience or scourge her memory, but only to be still and hold fast to the moment. She moved and breathed and existed in his silence, and as the hours of Sext gave way to None, to Vespers and to Compline, as night came to dwell on earth she grew acclimatized and peaceful and slept.

In her sleep she dreamed. Or more precisely in the suspension before sleep, when the endless chatter of mind and senses were cut off, and before the images of the submerged mind were set free, she experienced a thought.

She saw herself as a child on a beach on the Cape, standing on a sparse beach of coarse sand. Around her lay rough glacial rocks, brown streaked with orange, pink marble ones, granite ones, sparkling with mica and small garnets. Dried crusted dark seaweed marked the height of the tide. Hermit crabs scurried silently in a hand-size pool near a long shelf of slate. A school of minnows, green-grey and skittish, slid through the water's edge over the rippled sandy bottom.

She saw herself, the child, afraid of the water. From a safe distance on the rose-vined cliff the water had been blue and sparkling and clean and enchanting. But the child who came down eagerly from the cliff to meet it, to go into it, could not believe this was the same water.

The child's eyes saw strange sandfleas flittering nervously among the seaweeds. Saw blue-black periwinkles clinging to the rocks, oatmeal-colored crusts of barnacles, the slimy pale green of sea lettuce, ominous shadows under the water. The child saw the seagull soar and smiled, saw the seagull drop a mussel shell upon a boulder to crack it, saw the shimmering meat of the mussel, the hungry swoop of the gull, and trembled. The water and the bird were ugly when the child saw them close.

The child had wanted to swim, until she got to the water's edge. Now far out in the water stood her father calling her. The child walked out into the water, felt cold unstable wavelets rising in a strange embrace, shivered.

Her father told the child that if she lay down on the water and trusted it she would float, and then swim and be free. But if she did not entrust herself to it, if she clutched for him, or struggled, she would drown, or else, finding her feet, be a prisoner of sand forever.

The child heard the words of her father and they were more than she could believe. She stood trailing her hand in a circle through the clear water, showing herself that her hand alone was too heavy to be supported by a wave. It was unreasonable, impossible for anyone to swim. It was an ugly deceitful sea, not blue but weed and gravel color, not smooth but chopped with waves, not welcoming but ambushing the child with hidden monsters and lurking weaving tossing strands of death.

The child cried out for her father to hear her and save her.

But it was Jane who heard the child who was herself, Jane who understood and had compassion on the child, Jane who knew the terror and claimed it as her own.

In her dream Jane took the child's place. And she saw not the man but a woman like a star upon the sea, shining far out where the waves were like carved sapphire and gold. Jane looked at the water where she herself stood and it did not seem sapphire or gold. She looked again to the woman and saw her in foam-white tunic and blue cloak, with a face of one who has known all pain and exchanged it for all joy. The woman came closer and the reflected light of the sun shot like arrows from her heart. And she stretched her arms and beckoned her to come.

Jane lay back upon the water and trusted, felt the cradling of the tamed waters, saw the glory of the sky. Then, freed, she turned over and with long sleek strokes she swam water-borne and graceful, toward the unseen center.

She woke knowing it was time to go home.

In the last of the silence she prayed with words she had not suspected she would use:

"I want to live only for you and in you.

"I want to love. Love through me so that I may love as you would.

"Make me what you designed me to be. I am what I am. I cannot settle for halfway.

"Let me see you where you are hidden, let me see you in the stable, let me remember the crèche.

"I have seen the world from the hill, seen it look blue and gold and beautiful. I am going down now into it and I will see what is in it. Let me not be afraid. Let me believe what I cannot see. Let me remember there is nothing to fear unless I refuse to believe that you alone determine what is real and good.

"O Mary, stay and hold me."

And she would have said she felt a mantle wrapping round her shoulders, a hand resting on her head, so sure she was that a person was beside her.

And she ran to begin the descent from the hills to her home.

THIRTY-NINE

She burst into her empty house. Fruit flies danced over a neglected bowl. In the kitchen, the soft brown smell of old bananas and the black ghost of burnt bacon. In the living room the taut odor of grey-faced ashtrays, the cloying grave-smell of dead flowers. Upstairs the air held the sulky trace of unwashed clothes.

Laughing, hurrying, she changed her clothes, opened every window and went to work, setting loose the blue-white smell of chlorine and the shiny flat smell of wax and the elusive balloonlike smell of vacuuming. She cut the first of the pale hot-smelling viburnum flowers and set them in clean rooms. The house was alive with running water sounds.

When at last the sun and air seemed at ease in her home, she called for her baby first, then Meg, and brought them home.

The schoolbus's heavy tires grated on gravel and a brake shrieked. Jane ran out to meet Kilian coming home from public kindergarten.

"Hi, Mom!"

"I've come back," she said. He nodded agreement with the obvious. What had she expected?

The older ones were equally undemonstrative.

As the afternoon shone on, as the children left her to go about their intricate neighborhood life, she decided not to phone Chris, but simply to surprise him. She took chicken from the freezer, found a bottle of Chianti on a shelf in the laundry room.

When he came she was sitting on the front porch, ostensibly watching the children, really waiting for him. Suddenly shy, she had to check the impulse to run to the kitchen to fuss with pots and pans. She stood up uncertainly, smiling.

"Hi!"

Children rushed between them, shattering the darkening twilight with halloos. But he ignored them, and held her close.

Over the clamor Jane's eyes met Chris's and lingered.

"Just for tonight I have a special dinner for you and me to be eaten later. Alone."

"Wonderful."

"On the porch."

"Pretty chilly, don't you think, to eat on the porch?"

"It's chilly. But this one night—"

"Hey, you're a romanticist at heart, aren't you?" He sat down in surprise. "Well, well, well. You never know what a retreat can do!"

"Oh, Chris."

"Not a word, my fair little sentimentalist. We shall do as you wish. But please—couldn't I eat something now to stave off starvation?"

"Sure," she said. "I'll fix you some crackers and cheese. But don't fill up on them, please?"

"I'll be the soul of restraint." He grinned at her fondly. "Oh, Jane, I'm glad you're back," he said.

She fed the children, helped Peter and Mary with their homework, supervised baths, cleaned ears, rationed television, laid out uniforms, checked the supply of socks, and put them to sleep room by room.

It was nine o'clock.

As she came downstairs Chris said, "It's nine o'clock."

"And all's well," said she hopefully.

"All's well, but I'm starving."

"Dinner in a minute."

"Jane." He stood up and smiled. "It's really very romantic to eat on the porch, but the temperature's fifty-eight out there. The kitchen, huh?" When she did not answer he went on to offer the supreme male concession: "I'll even eat by candlelight if that'll help. We can pretend we're miles away. But I just don't feel like freezing to death when I'm already starving to death."

"Chris! You don't even know what's going on. I didn't tell you."

"What's going on?"

"It's so silly. Isn't it funny?" She giggled and went into the kitchen. He watched her setting out the clean tablecloth and the wine glasses, and he tried to reconstruct and decipher what had just happened.

"Six candles. Now you'll be able to see what you eat," she said.

"You either have a secret or you've lost your mind," he said. But there was no impatience in his tone.

"It's not our anniversary or anything you forgot. Don't look so worried." She brought the chicken from the oven. "Just—you might say, a celebration because your wife came home."

"Ah-hah!"

She stood and looked at the dinner she had made and thought it true that love was the prime ingredient of all recipes, and the designer of meal-settings, the instinct blending candles and crisp linen cloth, butter on a leaf-shaped dish, bread embraced by a yellow napkin.

He poured the wine into glasses, began to sit down, and then remembered to hold Jane's chair for her.

"Remember when we ate wine and chicken before?"

"How could I forget? That's our dinner." He poured more wine. "A toast to us, and all our children, and wine."

"Chris, I love you so much."

"And I love you. And your cooking. Martha's is okay, but Pete cooked frozen beef pies for us the other night. They were peat-moss brown on the outside and stiff, cold and dead inside. Horrible."

"Tell me about the retreat," he suggested after a while. "Sure missed you around here."

"Chris, that's what we're celebrating. The retreat. While I was there I realized how things have been. How far away I've been from you. We've been like two strangers. Actors playing roles, pretending to know and to feel, and really all cold and detached and scientific. Cheats and frauds and sad."

Her words seemed melodramatic and unnatural, but the sound of her voice, faltering and breathless, kept him from irritation. He held the wine glass between his hands and met her gaze.

"I think I have been cheating you, Chris. Somehow I became cut

196

off, one by one the threads that held me dissolved, and I walked a shell, alone. . . ." She put down her wine. "You do not know what I am saying. I am only confusing you. Then I'll start again, a different way."

The shifting candlelight sent strange blue shadows under her cheekbones, molding her features into mystery and poetry. Almost he expected her to speak in a web of meter and rhyme, and his love for her rose in him.

"Listen for a moment," she said softly. "Listen beyond the kitchen, beyond the house. You know and I know, and we had forgotten, that we live within sound of the stars. You and I, two in one, were reborn. We were giddy with grace, fed by his love. They say the universe is growing old, that the stars and moon are cooling, that matter and light are dying—too slowly for us to know it but surely, endlessly dying. I do not know whether the earth is growing old. But Chris, I know we have been dying, falling into coldness. And we didn't know it.

"What did I find in the retreat? I found the hidden fire."

She took the loaf of bread and broke off a hunk and buttered it.

"I came home to woo you."

She swallowed some bread, and then said, "To say to you: 'I love you,' and have the words be as real as they once were. And so: I love you!"

"I love you too."

Together they went into the living room. When she hesitated he drew her to the small sofa beside the fireplace.

He gathered her to him. His arm tightened over her back sensing every muscle and breath, aware of a living person that was his to own and love.

"I wish—" he whispered. "I wish! Oh, Jane."

She heard his blood in his veins, felt herself swept in the same heartbeat.

"I would like that," she said softly, "more than anything. I need you. I love you. I need you."

He drew back searching her face, his right hand holding her chin. Her eyes were closed yet under the thin lids life fluttered as life moves in a bird.

"Are you surprised?" She smiled. "I told you I found truth."

His hand put her head again to rest on his shoulder.

"Would God to work a miracle for us."

"Chris," she whispered. "I'm not afraid. I, and you, we belong to each other and to him, and I trust him."

His fingers drummed absent-mindedly on her shoulder, and then tightened into a grip.

"We can't trust him blindly, Jane. God gave us brains and a will and if we don't use them, if we throw ourselves off a bridge trusting him to rescue us, he's not going to do it."

She opened her eyes. "No one yet has forced him to create a soul. I can't believe that. I can't believe that just because a woman and a man make love when it is physically possible that conception could occur, then God has no say in the matter. If he wants a child there will be one. If he doesn't there won't. It's as simple as that," she said.

"The answer is that we can't," he said. "Until the doctor is sure, until—"

"We can be reasonably sure. He has told me that. Reasonably sure. Almost perfectly sure."

"Almost." He sat forward rubbing his hands together. "Jane, if because of my desire you were to have another child and die—I'm not taking such a chance."

She wanted to tell him she could not do more than beg, wanted to remind him how rarely she had come this far toward him, wanted to cry out that it was brutal and unfair to leave her seeking and rebuffed.

"Then we'll say no more, oh lord and master." She laughed. "The day will come when the doctor and I will solve this thing and we'll talk again then. In the meantime—"

"Jane—"

"In the meantime, let's—take half a loaf." She led the way upstairs.

"I told you, you don't know what these last days have done to me," she teased. "A nunnery is quite a place."

He kissed her.

"Did you miss me? Were you bored?"

He kissed her again to silence her.

FORTY

At breakfast Chris shoved a pile of mail in front of her. "You didn't even look at this yesterday. Letter from your mother, one from Gloria. Father Tom says he's coming up."

"I didn't even think of them while I was gone. They just slipped away. Time out's over." She buttered toast. "Those days I was away seem like they were different from any others. Not on any calendar. You know what I mean?"

"They were different."

She weeded out the advertisements and circulars. "I didn't even ask you," she said casually, "how's everything at the office. All right?"

"Fine. Same as ever. Except, I finally cleaned up that job I was doing with Krena. And I can get back to my own work."

"Good." She tossed the third-class mail into the wastebasket. "I see you got a notice of your convent-drive committee meeting. The Mother's Circle, that's mine." She laughed. "Here we go again."

"Disillusioning to come back to the same old rut?"

"No, I like it here. And it's not the same. Nothing is. I'm different. You're different."

"Me?"

"Even you. Wait and see. I have plans for us. I'm still an all-or-nothing girl, dear."

The first thing she did was to go to see Father Juniper. She found him painting the chapel door. His beard was splattered with Chinese red.

"I'm not much good with a big brush," he said. "I'm glad you came. Any excuse to stop this nonsense." He creaked to his feet, wiped his hands on the dark green apron covering his habit and peered up into her face.

"You look very well," he said.

"I am. Thank you." She followed him out to the library. "I'm here because I wanted to say thank you."

He lit his pipe, hunched over the table, watching her.

"The last time I was here—" she began uncertainly.

"I scandalized you. I remember. I was talking about love. You didn't like it." He straightened up. "You're not scandalized now?"

"No. You were right." She fingered the threads of the old woven tablescarf. "Father Juniper, please, I want to start all over again. I can't help feeling you're the one to help me. You seemed to know what was wrong with me before, when I didn't know. You tried to tell me about love and I didn't listen. Now, I'm back."

"You don't need me."

"Before, I did things thinking they were right and they were wrong. I don't want to guide myself. Do you know where I was when I decided to commit sin? In a Cana conference."

"That wasn't the first sin. It couldn't have been."

"No. I suppose the first was deciding not to believe in God. And that was because I—"

"You thought he let you down. And it was you who let him down."

"The point is—"

"That you want some guarantee that you will always know what he wants you to do."

"Is that so wrong?"

"Not wrong. Just impossible."

"Father Juniper, we were warned against having another child, because of my health. I am willing to risk getting pregnant because I love my husband. But Chris thinks it is better not to risk it. Who is right? Am I right to try to—"

"For anyone else—" Father Juniper sighed. "You are you. For you it must be all the way or not at all. Heaven or hell. Sin or grace. Total love or nothing. You are an intense person. That is not bad nor good, that is a fact." He shook his head. "I'm not through talking. You have to learn patience. Begin with me. Be silent until I'm through."

She smiled.

"What you ask no one can answer. No one can tell you which is the best. Your way, or Chris's. But this I tell you, and you must abide by it: you cannot force things to go your way. You can keep on wanting it your way so long as it is good, as it is. You can plan, even scheme. You are scheming now, to woo him, aren't you?"

"I am."

"Don't blush. That is good. But you can't force it."

"Mutual consent."

He snorted. "You sound like a marriage textbook. Forget the textbooks. All I'm saying is this: You are not yet quiet enough. You must be still inside. The Bible says like a handmaid with an eye on the mistress' hand, ready to obey the first hint of command.

The consent you need is God's. And you will find what he wants when you are perfectly still inside. You are not ready yet. And he knows it."

"Not ready for what?"

"To trust him enough."

"Oh, but I am!"

"When you are, you will know it. And so will God. And you will not have to fret over what to do. You will know where love leads." He tapped his pipe on the glass ashtray. "There will come a time when you will see yourself living the Mass. That will be the time."

He tucked the empty pipe in the long pocket under his arm.

"I must get back to painting that door," he said. "And you—you have to go to scheme how to woo your love. To each his own task. Yours sounds more challenging. But mine will be done faster!"

For wooing there must be time and privacy. Once you are married you are expected to be able to survive on only the scantiest rations of either.

"Hi, honey, watcha doin'?" Tory was on the phone.

"Good afternoon, Mrs. McNamara. You look like you're planning a party." The milkman hoped she just might need cream.

"What're you thinking about, Mommy? You're not listening to me." Mary nudged her back to the present moment and the Brownie initiation with a cold-nosed kiss on the cheek.

"What's new, old gal?" Chris waved as he parked his attaché case in the hall.

"How can you be too busy to write me? What do you do with yourself all day? You know I'm worried sick about Gloria," her mother wrote.

"See your favorite dream come true! Whatever her present secret ambition may be, our contest winner will have it made real, no expense spared. Send a boxtop and a letter in twenty-five words or less beginning: My secret dream is . . .'"

At that Jane sat down on the couch amid a pile of drums made of old oatmeal cartons and laughed out loud to think what would happen if she answered the question. Brother, if you only knew!

"My secret ambition, the project nearest my heart, is to seduce my husband." Far less than twenty-five words, and presumably inexpensive. It might be just sufficiently piquant and newsworthy to intrigue a contest judge. "Especially if I added that I had six children!"

Teresa peered through the playpen bars. Margaret threw her head into her mother's lap and shivered happily.

"Nice soft, Mommy."

Jane looked down at the tousled waves of hair resting on her skirt, and a memory drifted over her like a haze. Just so had Chris's head lain on her lap, in the days before they were married. He had been sitting on the rug. They had talked, holding hands, thrilled by the nearness of each other.

When he rested his head on her lap the weight of it had startled her. Her thigh trembled to bear such a burden. He turned sideways to look up at her. Then suddenly he buried his face in her lap, and in a voice so quiet it had been like a moan of pain, had said: "My God, the softness and the warmth? Jane, so soft and warm and tender and gentle. This is what woman is. . . ."

And feeling him so close to her, she had begun to cry. She had not understood till then how unwomanly she judged herself to be, had not known she longed to be what she thought she was not.

She had decided she was not by nature a womanly sort. Not a Rubens, pink and fat. Not a Garbo or a Gainsborough, not any kind of *femme fatale*. She had become resigned to that fact. She recognized herself as what she called the new American peasant type: designed for competence and suntan, beer and argument and deep laughter, but not for manicures and lotions, cocktails and giggles. She was sure this had not in any way saddened her. She was content.

Yet when Chris, with whom she had so astonishingly fallen in love, the man who more astonishingly loved her, had cried out in yearning praise of her warmth and softness, she had wept.

"What is it? Beautiful Jane, what is it?" he had asked.

"Beautiful? I'm not beautiful. Nor soft. Soft as satin, men say, soft as silk. That darn song says the girl must be soft and pink as a nursery. But I'm not made that way. I wish I were. For you, I wish I were."

Gravely he had looked in her eyes, diagnosing the pain.

"Never say that again," he commanded. "You are. Satin is soft, silk is soft. But better is the softness and warmth and strength of wool. I think of you as a soft wool skirt, a sweater, a blanket, not smooth-surfaced and slippery—"

Who would have thought it romantic to be called a sweater or a blanket? Would you write a song: "I love you because you are like a blanket?" Her mother would have been distressed. Gloria would have laughed. But she understood Chris. Always after, when she bought a Scotch sweater, a bold brown-and-white checked skirt, or those deep lilac-and-white wool blankets for their beds, she remembered what he had said, not the awkwardness of it, but the love in it.

She laid her hand now on Meg's head and smoothed the hair away from the tiny nape of her neck, her thoughts far away.

"Hi! Anyone home?" Grinning so that his chins ran in small mounds into his neck, Father Tom stood in the doorway. "Here I am, the long-lost Friar Tuck of the clan!"

"Come in. Isn't this wonderful?" Jane kissed him.

"I wasn't sure you'd be glad to see me."

"Why not?" Jane looked surprised.

"Well, I just haven't heard from you in three months or so."

"Oh. Oh for goodness' sake—" Jane's eyes widened. "I forgot. I haven't even written you."

"No." He took off his jacket and rabat and swung Meg onto his lap.

"I'm sorry. I've—I've been in a fog."

"Amnesia," he said solemnly to Meg. "Your mother has amnesia."

"Oh Father Tom, I have to talk to you. Good God. Do you remember when I last talked to you? I called you up in the hospital?"

"Of course I remember."

"Do you remember what I said?"

He put Meg down, a penny in her hand. "You know I remember," he said. "You were ready to kick over the whole business. I came here today half expecting to find an empty house, a motherless flock, a deserted husband, and you off living the pagan life of Reilly. I take it you changed your mind."

"Oh yes. Completely. I called you and told you I didn't mean it. It's just that you were the only person I could think of to talk to and—" She closed her eyes. "Things got worse after that." She spoke slowly, as if remembering with surprise the weeks of cold and ice, the staleness of February. She went and sat on the floor by Father Tom's feet. "But now we're all right. All that seems so long ago."

"St. Valentine. It was St. Valentine's Day."

"Was it? Yes. How could you remember?"

"I offered Mass for you." He bent toward her. "Are you sure, Jane? Do you love him? Does he love you? You're not settling for anything less? You're not just making do with halfway kind of stuff? I know so many married people who just drag along making do."

She put her hand on his. "I love him. And all is really well. I have only now started to live again. I was dead. And perhaps your prayers found me. I went on retreat. Just got back."

His red cheeks rippled among his chins as he smiled.

"Not easy, coming back to life when you've been dead," she said. "I have a long way to go. But then, I bet Lazarus didn't find life easy when he had it thrust back on him either."

Father Tom leaned back in his chair. "When I heard you that day on the phone, I couldn't take it, slob that I am. I—I wanted to weep. You two mean a lot to me."

The babies played on the porch, their laughter a distant background.

"I have seen Christ die in so many people," he said. "Seen him fall to dust in them till they rot. I couldn't bear to see him die in you or Chris. Do you know what I mean? I mean they walk around all tarnished and gutted, and they stink from death. And in some he is not wholly dead. In some he's kept lingering in the courtyard, mocked and spat on. He suffers, a prisoner, kept alive as a hostage, grudgingly, hatefully kept alive. They keep from mortal sin and do as little else as they must for him, and they smell like the spitty courtyard."

His black eyes were smoldering under the thick lashes. "Jane, I know so many husbands and wives who do not love and do not quarrel, who find the practical comfortable path and refuse to be all the way alive. I couldn't stand that for you two. Christ said: 'I would you were either hot or cold. But because you are luke-warm I will vomit you out of my mouth.' Those are hard words. But ours is a hard faith. There's no halfway Mass. No halfway cross. No halfway heaven."

He closed his eyes. As if, she thought, he took the news of her reawakening and held it against his cheek and rested in its comfort.

"I should have written to you," she said penitently. "I should have told you something. Even during the worst time I could at least have written. I never said a word after I phoned you that last time." She didn't say the rest of the truth, that she had scarcely thought of him since. Yet he had suffered for her and for Chris. "Forgive me."

"You weren't meant to write me." He smiled, opening his eyes. "Who writes details of an operation? Only boring old ladies. You cannot write letters about the sufferings of the soul. And besides, because I didn't know all was well, because I was afraid, I did penance, and worked harder to keep my own soul alive. And this was good."

"Penance?"

"I gave up writing limericks." He pushed himself up to his feet. "I'm hungry, gal. And solemnity is bad for the stomach."

"Lunch coming up."

"Besides, I haven't told you what brings me to your door this day. I need your help."

"Not more statues!"

"I've been to see my brother and his wife," the priest said. "And I had a hell of a row with Annie. She's about to not take that trip to Europe. And you know why?"

"Because of the leaves, I bet."

"Of course. She's decided James is going to die, and so she's going to stay home. I told her to go."

Jane laughed. "What's that got to do with me?"

"You must make her go."

"That's out of my line." She gave him a sandwich. "Eat quick before the monsters come in from the porch."

"Annie's wanted to go abroad all the years I've known her and she'll complain forever if she doesn't go now. She thinks I'm callous and horrible to urge her to leave James's deathbed."

"He's sick?" Jane whirled around from the sink.

"Healthy as an ox. She just sees his deathbed in the tea leaves. You are her only female relative. Use your wiles on her."

"Look, Father Tom. I'm tired of meddling in other people's lives. I've got my own. I've got my mother and my sister. And they have problems."

"Gloria?"

Jane hesitated a moment. "She's pregnant," she said.

She took Gussie's letter from her slacks pocket, smoothed it, and handed it to him. "Read it. Mother's a wreck. She's furious at Gloria, and furious at me because I'm on Gloria's side about not marrying the child's father. This is what I came home to after the retreat. I'm tired of other people's lives."

Father Tom read the letter, crunching potato chips. He folded it back into the envelope and sighed. "Poor Gloria," he said. "And poor Gussie and poor Jane and poor—do I understand his name to be Hack?—poor Hack then. A sad thing. A very sad and painful thing. But the girl is right, of course. Marrying for the sake of appearances would be adding one sin to another."

"If Annie doesn't want to go to Europe," said Jane, "she can stay here for all of me. I've got enough trying to run my own life."

"Okay." Tom shrugged. "I was planning to stay an hour or so and work on some mission brochures. Will I be in the way?"

"Not you." The phone rang. "That phone's more in the way than you." She picked it up.

"Hi? Marianne? Haven't heard from you in ages. Yes, I heard about Felicity. Too bad. Well. Oh, you did see Krena; that's nice. No, I didn't know. A leave of absence? Well, she did just finish a big project she was working on with Chris. Of course I knew about it. Well, look Marianne, you're being silly. Why should you hesitate to mention a thing like that?"

"Mommy! I need a bandage." Meg ran in from the porch with a cut in her knee.

Father Tom whispered in her ear, "I'll fix it. Mommy's busy on the phone."

"Marianne, I don't know what's got into you," Jane said, laughing very lightly. "I don't think you know how nasty you sound. And I don't care why Krena is taking a leave of absence. And if you think for one minute that there'd be anything but business between them, you don't know Chris." She reached for a cigarette and lit it, listening. "Of course, I'm angry. Stupidity always makes me angry."

She hung up and stood smoking.

"I got a bandage," said Meg.

"A lovely one," said Jane.

The phone rang again. "Yes. Yes, Marianne." Jane closed her eyes. "Of course you didn't mean anything. I'm not mad. Of course I'll tell Chris. He'll be tickled silly to know that women consider him exciting enough to gossip about. Well, wouldn't Hugh be? No, dear, there's nothing to it. You know Krena, she's the kind who— well, I wouldn't be surprised if she did play around. But if she tried anything with Chris I bet she got the surprise of her life. Well, forget it."

Jane stood looking at Father Tom. "If I had half the time I spend on phone calls," she said, "I could work wonders." She was silent a moment, making Meg's sandwich. "Of all the gall!" She laughed. "Can you think what it would be like if I believed her?"

"I'm surprised you didn't," said Father Tom. "I mean, I couldn't help overhearing."

"Look, what Chris and I have isn't going to be spoiled by anybody. Not even us." She carried Teresa in from the porch, put her in the high chair, and went on. "And certainly not by some stupid, mean empty-headed woman like Marianne."

"Bravo! But I thought you liked her. Remember, last time I was here she was the dowager duchess, dispensing the blessings of her charm to an admiring throng that included you—you said." Father Tom's eyes twinkled.

Jane looked at him hard, and then laughed. "To tell you the truth I didn't like her so much then, either. I was trying to. Oh, she's all right, but she really ought to know better than this. If it were Agnes, now, I'd expect that sort of thing. But Marianne ought to be ashamed."

"To be sure," Father Tom said.

"But I'll tell you this. It's tough to keep things straight in your own life when other people keep butting in. I love people. Most people. Certain stupid ones excluded. But they get in the way. No privacy."

"You really are swinging the pendulum," he said. "That's another switch. Last time you were all for less privacy and more people. Now you're going to turn your back on them?"

"Hello!" Tory was at the door. "You home? I came to talk about Mother's Circle. I'll run back to the car and get the books."

"Sure," Jane called. And to Tom she said, "There's not much danger of my becoming a hermit. The pendulum can't swing very far, not in our parish."

"Whatever you want privacy for, you'll accomplish it," said Father Tom, rising to greet Tory. "You'll find the way with all this. But not without it."

"I'll try to remember," said Jane.

After Father Tom left, and Tory left, through the clamorous child-loud afternoon, she tried to remember his advice. Chris came home from work. She served dinner and tended the children and answered the phone and cleaned the kitchen. Chris was watching television when she was free at last.

She turned off the set. "How come we have a whole evening at home together? No meetings? We can just sit and talk?"

"Sorry to disillusion you." He smiled. "I've got that convent drive tonight. Only an hour. Starts at nine."

"Oh."

"We can still talk. What shall we talk about?"

"I'll just chatter. I'll tell you about my day. The news of the world. Agnes Milder's getting sicker and Felicity Lawrence is in a shameful state. They say she's taking sleeping pills in the daytime. Isn't it hard to picture Felicity in any state but serene composure? But there must be some truth to it."

"Sounds like you've been talking to a real gossip."

"Oh, I have. Several. Lidwina's still hoping Mike will come home. And, what else? Oh yes, I had a fight with Marianne Carpel."

"Good for you."

"And I told her I'd tell you about it."

"What did Marianne say that I ought to know?"

"She was trying to sow seeds of doubt in my mind," Jane said, arching her brows comically. "She wanted me to think there was an affair between you and Krena McDowell."

"She did?"

"And she wanted me to think there was something peculiar because Krena just up and decided to take a leave of absence from the office. And she implied Krena was either going to get a divorce from her husband or have a baby or who knows what, but that I ought to know."

Chris raised his eyebrows.

"So I told her she was crazy but that you would be flattered to know she suspected you of having an affair."

"You did, did you?"

"Yup." Jane came over and sat beside him, and lowered her head on his shoulder. He didn't move.

She closed her eyes. "Marianne was surprised that I knew you and Krena had been working together on a book. She wanted to be sure I knew you had been seen riding on a train with Krena. And lunching with her in New York. And she said wouldn't it be amazing if Krena were really going to have a baby after all these years. I said it wouldn't amaze me at all."

Chris's breath exploded in a low exasperated whistle.

"You're all upset," she said, and laughed, her head thrown back softly on his shoulder. "I thought you'd laugh. Can you imagine anyone being that stinking. The brazen hussy. I told her I thought Krena was the kind who would play around. But with you she'd have to stick to business."

He could not quite believe she was really saying these things to him. "Jane—"

She peered at him from lowered lids. "Shhh. Are you surprised? Surely you're not surprised that I believe in you?" Swiftly she kissed him. "I don't blame her if she did have a yen for you."

"Jane, Marianne didn't really think—"

"I don't think so. Not really, although she's capable of it. I never knew she was a troublemaker. I'll bet she'll tell Krena I said I thought Krena would, you know, sleep with anyone. I shouldn't have said that. But I was mad."

"Do you think that's true?"

"Who knows? I said it. Wasn't very ladylike of me."

He sat silent, hand on her hand. "Jane," he said finally, "I love you. And I marvel at you. Having to listen to nonsense like that." He got up. "I'll fix us a drink."

"You'll be late for your meeting."

"Who cares? It isn't every night you run into a thing like this."

He came back with Scotch and water. She raised her glass in toast. He shook his head. "No. To you. And to the fact that these days I never know what you're going to say next."

"You're surprised," she said, "that I didn't believe Marianne."

"I'm delighted. And I'd have been disappointed if you did. Only I'm trying to get used to the idea of being gossiped about." He sat back in his chair and slipped off his shoes.

"Well," he said, "Krena did ask for a leave of absence, out of a clear blue sky. That part's right. And I don't know why. I mean I don't know anything about her wanting a divorce or anything else. Since we finished the book we haven't been talking. You know, there's—well, there's nothing to talk about. Our paths hardly cross."

He took a deep drink of his Scotch. "Good God," he said. "And Marianne. I'd like to smash her teeth."

Jane sipped her drink. "Kiss me," she said.

But the doorbell rang. It was Al, ready to go to the committee meeting.

Jane stood alone watching them go.

There should be new words in the marriage vows, she thought.

Better or worse, richer, poorer, sickness and health, and—in spite of Church and friends.

"I can wait," she said aloud. And with a secret smile she went upstairs.

FORTY-ONE

The Mother's Circle met at Angela Rottigni's house this month to study the faith, and have coffee and cake.

"You must have slaved, Angie," Jane said. "Your place always looks lovely but tonight you outdid yourself."

Angela smiled. "Come and see."

Of all the women in the Circle it was Jane who made her feel most at ease. Yet lately she wondered if she had offended Jane. She hadn't seen her to talk to since the party when the priest was sick, and the few times they had met in groups Angie had felt sadly estranged. "You look wonderful tonight, Jane," she said happily. "Like your old self. The retreat did you good."

Jane followed her into the dining room. The heavy Victorian sideboard, the glassed cupboards for china, gleamed. Blue iris and lily of the valley decorated the table, with Angie's bone china cups and saucers, her best spoons in buffet arrangement. Giant heavily sculptured silver trays held an array of Angie's own intricate baking specialties.

"You went to so much trouble, Angie!"

"Jane, you know I love to bake. We don't entertain much with Patsy busy at the place every night. And I like fixing for the Circle."

"Jane!" Christine Newman called from the living room. "Where are you?"

In the arched entrance Jane paused, momentarily baffled by the chatter and smoke. She had the curious sensation of being Alice in a new wonderland, her friends fluttering and shuffling in a two-dimensional world.

"You look confused," said Clare Sullivan.

"Jane's been on retreat. She's still up in the clouds," said Martha briskly.

"I'm the contemplative type at heart." Jane smiled

"I've got something to tell you," cried Christine. Her thick, curly hair was today successfully defying her efforts to achieve a smart chignon, but for once she obviously did not care in the least. She had that particular smile of bravado which betokens a special secret.

"Christine, you're not?" asked Jane, sitting beside her on the sofa.

"No, silly, no. A whole year now and I'm still safe. Something else. And I want everyone to hear." Christine raised her voice. "Ladies!" The gabble and laughter died as neat, freshly-waved heads turned. "I want to tell you that if you wait long enough and pray hard enough, miracles do happen. You all know how long I've been waiting for Julian to come into the Church. Well, tonight he's over at the friary seeing Father Juniper for the second time. And wait—do you know I think I owe it all to Clare?"

Clare, her face glowing over her pink maternity smock, rose to her feet. "Because I took you to have Juniper enroll in the FMU!" she gasped. "Oh, but that's how Juniper works his miracles, you know. That's not me, that's Juniper."

"You did it," Christine said. "Clare took me over there and Juniper prayed and of course Julian didn't know about it, but it worked. And I'm so happy."

Clare hugged Christine and they were both shaken with those bewildered laughing cries women shed on festive occasions with other women, and everyone talked at once.

Angela shivered and smiled. This was what she liked best about Mother's Circle, sharing the little secret joys and worries of these self-assured women she admired. Her own mother, burdened with shapeless black dresses and shapeless other-language thoughts, still lingered in the Italian parish, a relic of the past. But Angie could wear a sheath dress and earrings and move in St. Rose's parish among who knows what kind of people.

Hovering, smiling, she wove through the Circle groups, gleaning news. Clare was having varicose vein trouble but the pregnancy was going well. Bertha Rains had water in her cellar again. Martha Settler was trying to get the Legion of Mary started in the parish and was praying for Father Temple because he was so incredibly thick he couldn't see why the parish needed the Legion.

"Agnes, I didn't see you come in," Angela said in surprise. "You're so quiet no one knew you were here."

"I didn't even know you were next to me," Martha exclaimed, shifting in her chair for a better look at Agnes who sat, pale and bony, in a grey suit. "My God, you really have been sick. You're still sick. Agnes, what's the matter?"

"They don't know what it is," Agnes whined, "or won't tell me. They want to operate to find out."

"Oh." Martha sucked in her cheeks. "That's frightening."

"Oh, yes," said Agnes.

"You'll get your strength back now that spring's here," Angela said earnestly. "The fresh air and all."

"Yes," said Agnes.

Jane found Tory examining Angela's African violets. Tory looked especially attractive, Jane noticed. She was wearing a startling white wool suit with a bottle-green blouse.

"How's Walter doing in the Marines?" Jane asked.

"Fine." Tory took a snapshot from her purse. "I can't believe I'm the mother of that!"

"He's grown up overnight."

"Yes, he looks like a man now. So steady, so sure of himself. He really does seem to have found his element." Tory smiled wistfully. "I suppose we can chalk that up to Juniper, too. I enrolled Walter in FMU the day he left us. Remember? That was the day the squirrel bit Kilian. I was so worried I thought I was about to die. And Juniper prayed and everything's fine. Wish my prayers for me were answered that fast."

"Got troubles?"

"Everybody's got problems," Tory shrugged.

"How's Al?"

"You just brought up my problem."

"Oh?"

Tory nodded, eyebrows raised. "Al's fine. Just fine. Only you know what? There's nothing for us to do or say. Walter's gone. Pat's either studying or out, Cyril goes to bed at seven and Davy's in bed by eight. And then there's just me and Al. And nothing."

"Oh come on. Don't look so grim."

"He doesn't love me, Jane, and I don't love him. So what can you do? Nothing. I feel grim. I'm his chauffeur. To the plant. Back. His cook. His housekeeper. His bookkeeper. His maid. His gardener. But his wife?" She had unbuttoned the white suit jacket and stood now with a hand on her hip, the jacket thrust carelessly back, blouse studded with gold scatter pins. She looked smart and expensive and resigned. With a start Jane realized Tory looked a bit like Lidwina tonight.

Tory looked at her watch. "Oh well, it's time to start the meeting. Forget I said anything. I was just sounding off."

She took a seat on the couch near Martha.

"Girls," said Tory loudly. "Let's start the meeting? Come Holy Spirit. . . ."

A rustling of papers. A few pairs of glasses hastily put on powdered noses. A clearing of throats. The Circle was at work.

Bertha Rains, her hands cluttered with Band Aids over gardening scars, cleared her throat. "It was my turn to do research. I looked up the history of the sacrament of extreme unction."

Martha Settler interrupted. "Let's stop right there. We need a new name for that sacrament. What does extreme unction mean in English? Nothing! It's no wonder I can't get patients in the hospital interested in liturgy. That's the trouble, right there, with the Church in America. No vernacular. All we get is Latinized English gobbledygook."

Clare, always frightened of Martha's forthright protests, regarded her solemnly. "What would we call it?"

"Maybe 'anointing near death,' " said Martha. "Or 'consecration near death,' or—almost anything. 'Unction' always makes me think of Unguentine. And 'extreme' being defined as the furthest tolerable point, it seems to me 'extreme unction' is the 'grease of the living end.' "

"You're not being very reverent, Martha," said Clare.

"It's not irreverent to understand words," said Martha. "After all, the sacraments by any other names would be the same. But you know shooting well half the Catholics in this country don't understand what extreme unction is all about anyhow."

Tory seized a chance to interrupt. "Perhaps we could ask what there is in this sacrament or in its name to remind us that death is not the worst thing that can happen? But maybe the best?"

"Yes," said Clare, relaxing. "That's very good."

"I know so many people who are afraid to call the priest in time for it," said Bertha. "Superstition. Ignorance, I guess. But sometimes people do regain their health from the anointing."

"I know a woman who received extreme unction nine times and is still alive," said Clare.

"When my father died I was there," said Angela. "It was lovely. The sacrament was so comforting."

"And," said Tory, "ladies, we must not forget that as good Catholic mothers we must teach our children to look on death the right way. And we should always have ready the things needed for the last sacraments. The book suggested that all the Circle leaders make up a tray so we can all see what it is we need."

She brought in from the hallway, a tray with the white linen cloth, the crucifix, the blessed candles, the saucer of holy water, the glass and spoon and plate, the towel, the napkin, the seven small balls of clean cotton—all these would be needed to turn a bedtable into an altar, and provide the necessities for the priest.

"It would take time to find these things in an emergency," said Martha. "We really should do something about preparing."

"I can't stand it!"

Agnes Milder surprised even herself with that shout. She whose voice was never stronger than a petulant whine was on her feet crying: "It gives me the creeps to think about death. Elmo wants me to make a will. I can't even do that. But it's dreadful the way you all sit around talking. . . ."

Her voice trailed off. Angela broke the silence.

"I can't think about death, either," she said, as if taking sides with Agnes against the world. She took Agnes' arm. "Come on out and have a nice hot cup of coffee."

Tory bit her lip. The women looked at each other.

"Poor Agnes."

"The trouble is people think death is depressing," said Martha. Christine laughed. "Well, it is!"

Martha shook her head. "Not if you look at it right. It's so hard to make people see what's real. And I'm no good at it, that's for sure."

"You sure aren't."

Martha blew her nose. "You can't start teaching Agnes now what takes years to learn. That's why we have to teach children. Poor Agnes."

"Poor Agnes indeed," said Tory. "That gal has a lot of other things to learn. She just loves to draw attention to herself. She's made more people miserable with her tongue! I'm sorry she's sick, sure. But you should hear her talk about your sister. Or Lidwina."

Jane went quickly through the dining room to the kitchen, hoping to help comfort Agnes. She couldn't do any better than Martha, she supposed, at trying to explain death. But she could talk about anything, just to make Agnes feel better. She stopped in the doorway.

"Angela, can you imagine how heartless they were talking that way in front of me, as sick as I am?" Agnes whined.

"They didn't know," said Angela.

"I never much liked Mother's Circles anyway," Agnes went on. "You never know who's going to be there. When I think that that Lidwina was a member of this Circle, I wonder why I come at all."

"She hasn't come for a while," Angela said.

"I should think not!"

The intensity in Agnes' whining voice made Jane turn away. Lidwina? No one expected her to come tonight, yet she is here, thought Jane, part of us. So much a part of us that Agnes, who is terrified by death, still takes comfort in being nasty about Lidwina. So much a part of us that though I wanted to feel sorry for Agnes because she is afraid of death, and I know that fear, I turn away from her because I dislike her for being nasty about Lidwina. It is a confusing mess, and that's how the mystery works. The good of one strengthens us all, and the evil of one, the soul-death of one, weakens us all. We are suffering with sin whether it be our own or not.

I have not forgiven Lidwina. Yet I have nothing to forgive her for: no occasion for the hostility she has shocked me into. And because of that I cannot forgive Agnes for being Agnes. I cannot help Agnes because I have not helped myself enough.

And she was aware almost sensibly then of near-infinite forces playing on her. Of the good and the evil, the living and the dead, interplaying in the strange joyful suffering loving agony of creation and of Christ. In him and through him and with him . . .

Out in the living-room talk had turned from death to birth. The gabble of rhythm and D and C's and breastfeeding and clothes and God and catechism and what Sister said to whose child hovered around Jane as the dust of a sculptor's workshop obscures the air when he is at work.

She would phone Lidwina tomorrow, she thought.

And fortified by that decision she made herself go in and sit with Angela and Agnes.

FORTY-TWO

"Father Macy called," Jane said. "Sounded a bit stiff."

"He's been giving me a hard time about my committee. Anything interesting in the mail?"

"Yes. A letter for you. On the mantel." Jane went back to the stove. "But you'd better call Father Macy. He wants to hear from you right away."

"He can wait." Chris poured himself coffee and perched on a stool near the sink. "Saw Mike O'Shea on the train. Drunk. Tried to talk him into going home to Lidwina, but he said he wouldn't ever and told me to leave him alone."

"What's Father Macy mad about?"

"Oh, you know him. A bag of hot air."

"Chris!"

"First he sweet-talks me with all this lay leadership bit into heading up to the drive for the greater glory of God, St. Rose's and the sisters-God-bless-'em. 'It's all in your hands, Chris,' he said. 'It's your challenge. I'll keep hands off. Make up your own committee.'" Chris snorted.

"So you got him a committee."

"Sure."

Chris had assembled a committee of the best business and selling brains he could find in the parish. Al Burke, who was not only successful in his own business, but also knew his way around Rotary and Lions and the AOH, as well as the K of C. Philip Demie, who, his invalid marriage aside, was an advertising man, a slogan-maker. Benny Scrivener, who was a native parishioner—a rare creature in the modern suburbs—and who, because he fixed the teeth of all the old families, knew their opinions and scandals and prides, including which ones had Indian blood. And Bede Settler, who was the apostle supreme in the opinion of Rockhill's non-Catholics. The *Bugle* has done a feature on Bede when he renounced Madison Avenue to become a teacher. The publicity had not made him popular in the parish, but it did focus the attention of ministers and rabbis on him. Since he had proved a good teacher, unsubversive and unproselytizing, Bede had been the subject of two sermons, one in the Second Congregational Church and one in the Temple. He would be able to enlist contributions from a few key figures outside the parish. Chris, reasoning that a bar-and-grill man knew people, included Patsy Rottigni on the committee as a kind of practical psychologist-advisor. And Julian Newman.

"Sounds good," said Jane, mashing potatoes.

"So, in friendly fashion, I reported the names of my committee to Father Macy," said Chris. "Oh, he was very nice. Thought it was fine, a bit daring, perhaps. But fine. Said we'd never had a non-

Catholic before, but Julian is a good man. He hesitated about Rottigni. Thought it might be hard for some people to swallow, having a man like that receive such an honor."

Jane smiled. "It's an honor?"

"Then very patiently Father Macy asked me where the other names were."

"What other names?" Jane asked.

"He wanted Hugh Carpel, of course. And Mike O'Shea. And a few others he thought were hot stuff."

"Hugh Carpel is a snob and no one in the parish much likes him. He doesn't really care whether you build a convent or not," said Jane. "You don't want any deadwood on the committee."

"His name gives prestige, Father said."

"And Mike O'Shea is in no state to be on a fund-raising committee. I'm sure he doesn't want any more publicity right now."

"Well, I put them on," said Chris. "And since they don't come to meetings they're no real problem."

The men had met three times and finally last week had come up with a plan of action which Chris presented to Father Macy.

"There'll be posters, direct mail, and we'll give a show. An evening presentation on the value of the nuns to the parish, the community, the future. A bit of humor in the script, a bit of personal interest, some music. A big visual aid showing dollars-and-cents value of each teaching sister to each family, and to the town as a whole. Then, door-to-door canvass to collect money and pledges. The whole thing will be keyed to a modern adaptation of the old days where every family came and laid bricks and hauled stone. A do-it-yourself drive, for money instead of labor."

"Fine. Fine," Father Macy had said.

Chris wondered if Father Macy knew that every time he objected to something he began by saying fine.

"Fine," Father Macy said. "But. Just one little but. We have to remember first things first. The fair share. That's the keystone, Chris. That's the way these drives are run. Perhaps I have not filled you in with enough background. You can use all the pretty window-dressing you want. But the first thing is that you make a list of parishioners and you determine what each person's Square Share would be and then you know where you're at. Then you know how much to get."

"That's the way other drives have been run, all right," agreed Chris quietly.

"Of course," Gus nodded triumphantly as his pupil showed signs of catching on. "That's the way!"

"But it's not the way it should be done. No one sitting in a parish hall or rectory can decide what my Square Share should be. Once they came and asked me for less than I had planned to give. Once."

Father Macy shrugged. "It's not infallible. In any business you lose a little one place, make up for it another."

"Father, that's not the way we want to do it."

"Ah."

"You asked us to do the job. We'll raise the money for you. Our way. With no assessments. No blackmail. With a bit more idealism, maybe. And some mistakes. But our way will work." He was silent, then added. "You told me this was to be a layman's drive, a plain man's drive. That took courage, Father. You're not going to back down, are you?"

"Of course not! The plain man is the lifeblood of the new Church. Back down? Chris, you're joking."

"Well, that's how it stood a week ago. I'd better see what he wants now," Chris said to Jane, going to the phone. "And get it over with."

He came back a minute later with the letter Jane had left for him. "What did Father Macy say?"

"Hm? Oh, nothing. Just changed the meeting to Sunday night."

"That's all?"

"Do you know who this letter's from?"

"I can guess."

He ripped it open. "Well, considering what you said Marianne told you, I'm going to open it right here in front of you."

"You don't have to."

"I want to."

"You don't have to prove anything to me." Jane leaned over the sink paring carrots.

"I'll read it to you."

"You may regret it," she said.

"Dear Chris," he read out loud. "I want to thank you for all you did to help me over such a long and difficult job. And to tell you I'm sorry we parted the way we did. I could at least have come out to the car and said good-bye before you went roaring out of my driveway. Don't let's let it end on that note. You always did take things too seriously. I'm going out to the Coast to see if I can find that husband of mine. Mahomet will go to the mountain. I'll be back in the fall. As ever, Krena."

Jane pared long curling strips of carrot.

"I didn't tell you I was at her house working," Chris said.

"No."

He came and stood beside her. "I didn't want you to know."

"Krena wanted me to know."

"Yes. I guess she did."

Jane dried her hands on her apron and turned to him.

"Well?" he asked quietly.

"She's gone back to her husband. Hope she's happy with him," Jane said. "I'm happy with mine."

"Are you?"

She kissed him. And took Krena's letter and tore it in pieces and dropped it in the garbage with the carrot peelings.

The next day Gussie Peabody's tidy little Volkswagen pulled into the McNamara driveway. She stood at the door, an alien but decisive figure in a trim grey Peck and Peck tweed suit, her fox-skin scarves, white leather gloves and sturdy laced shoes of shining alligator.

"Mother!" Jane was preparing to vacuum the living room. She reached to kiss her, considered the dirt on her hands, and thought better of it.

"Grandma!" Children came running and shouting. Kilian's screams of excitement pierced the soft afternoon heat. "What'd you bring us?"

"Did you bring us anything?"

Gussie, fending the children off, made what she considered appropriate welcoming noises.

"Run along, kids. Get lost for a while." Jane laughed. "You can see Grandma later."

"Get lost? My goodness, you shouldn't talk to them that way, Jane. They are glad to see me, and I wouldn't want them to feel—"

But the children, aware that they had muffed the opening gambit, certain that they would get no presents for awhile anyway, had run off like escapees, each to his own devices. Mrs. Peabody, having prepared herself to forgive their rudeness, felt deflated. She shifted her fox fur to a better drape on her left shoulder and regarded her daughter.

"You didn't say you were coming! It's wonderful to see you." Jane's eyes shone.

"Jane, this place looks like a junkyard."

Jane looked at it as her mother might, and agreed. Where else could one find in a living room empty coffee cans for keeping caterpillars in, a broken fishing rod, an old red blanket which was sometimes a bed or a seat and sometimes a kingly robe, and a fort made out of old soft-drink cases?

"Awful, isn't it?" Jane grinned. "Come on out to the kitchen."

Gussie settled herself at the kitchen table, noting with relief that this room at least was relatively clean, even inviting, floors waxed, dishes washed, window curtains only faintly wilted.

"Sit down, Jane. I want to talk to you. I'm going to get right to the point. I didn't come just for a visit." Gussie examined her light rose nailpolish, straightened her carved coral ring, and sighed. "As you know, I've always been what one might call more than fair to your Catholic Church. I haven't understood it. I haven't shared your enthusiasm for it. But because it was good enough to make you happy I wouldn't say a word against it."

"You've been great."

"It's been hard for me. I've seen my dreams for you come to nothing, because of this—Church. I've had to sit by while you ruined your health, had to watch my daughter become so coarsened that—well, really dear, your home is not what one could call beautiful."

Jane bit back a retort, groping to find the reason for this animosity, this new intensity in her mother.

"But I have felt," Gussie went on, "that it was your life, your decision. That it was hard on me did not matter. It was harder on you. I have admired you for the way you live your faith, putting up with the Lord only knows what . . ."

Jane raised her eyebrows.

"I have never considered the Catholic Church my enemy," Mrs. Peabody said carefully. "No matter what anyone said I did not believe the Catholic Church was evil. But Jane—" She took a white hankie from her alligator bag. The scent of 4711 cologne came politely into the air.

"But Jane, I do not understand how this Church can refuse to tell that man to marry Gloria. That is evil, Jane. That is impossible. And I will not stand for it. I went to see his priest. I went myself. And do you know what he said to me? He said to me that he would *refuse* to marry them, let alone tell the man to do the honorable thing. He said from what he knew of them he would refuse to marry them. I am having enough trouble with Gloria without a man of the cloth, a supposedly holy priest, being so—"

She began to cry then, a quiet, hiccuping cry. Her nose, Jane saw, was white and bony and it quivered as she wept.

"I will not let the Church ruin both my girls. I won't. And if you don't do something. . . ."

"What would you want me to do?"

"My Gloria. Gloria is pregnant with that man's child! Do you know what that means? I have to hide her. I have to lie to my friends. I have to—"

Sobs shook her. Jane put her arms around her mother and held her close. Her own cheeks were wet.

"I'm going to make you a cup of tea," Jane said. "Like you used to do for me. When I was a little girl you'd fix me tea and we'd sit in the kitchen and I'd feel better. Remember?"

"Yes." Gussie's eyes blinked briefly and she smiled. There was a kind, companionable silence while Jane brewed the tea.

"Can I tell you—will you let me try to tell you, Mother—why it would be wrong for Gloria to marry him?"

Gussie's smile faded, leaving her cheeks wrinkled, empty as a peach skin becomes when the fruit is past ripeness and use. "She doesn't want to marry him, does she?" asked Jane. "Gloria wants to be alone."

"She says she doesn't want to. But she doesn't begin to know." The lips, lavender with strain, pressed over a swallow of tea.

"She knows. Mother—marriage is forever. Marriage is a holy thing, a way of life. Marriage is two people growing to heaven. . . ."

"That's all very nice," said Mrs. Peabody, with the manner she used to an S. S. Pierce clerk. "But marriage first and foremost is a contract, a proper way of doing things. And it is a contract that society recognizes. I can't have Gloria having a child out of wedlock. I can't!"

"It's not up to you, is it?"

"No, it's not. It's up to a foolish confused little girl, and the slimy no-good who got her in trouble, and your Church!" She pushed the tea away and it slopped. "I asked that priest whether he thought it was best for a child to be born illegitimate—whether that was what his dear Pope thought was the Christian way to do things—"

"And he said you misunderstood? He said what I would say: that the child can be protected, adopted, given a good life. But that sin is no foundation for marriage."

Gussie snorted and wiped her eyes.

"Mother, it would be another sin, a sin of sacrilege to use the sacrament just as a device to make a child legitimate. Besides, do you want Gloria forced to marry a guy she doesn't love?"

"She could get a divorce later. And keep the child."

"Do you want her divorced?"

"Yes! Yes—married, and then divorced. At least she could hold her head up, and keep the child."

"Is it the child that means so much to you?"

"It's a dreadful thing they told her to do, Jane. To go off to a home somewhere in some horrid convent and have her baby and then give it away. Get rid of it!" Gussie's eyes were mica-hard, mica-dark, with layer upon layer of brittle bitter anger. "This is your Church. And Gloria will listen to you. Will you tell her she must make that—that man marry her, or won't you?"

"I can't."

"Are you afraid it would be a sin to help your own sister?"

"No. I'm not afraid, Mother. You are. You're afraid of how it looks. And that's the least important thing."

With only her eyes and the lift of her head, Gussie reminded her daughter that one does not speak loudly to one's mother.

"Sorry," said Jane.

"I will tell you what I think. I think the Roman Catholic Church is evil and sick. It says: 'It is a sin to prevent birth. You must have babies, and more babies, because it's God's will, and never mind what the world thinks or how you suffer or they suffer from poverty and disease and wornout mothers and people starving everywhere. Babies.' And then the Church says: 'When you have a baby out of wedlock have it quietly and get rid of it, and pretend it never happened. Go to confession,' she says to the man, 'say you're sorry, walk off and leave the brat.' Well, if that's Christian, if that's even decent, you can have it."

Jane said nothing.

"You see!" said her mother. "You can't find anything to say to defend it, can you?"

"The trouble is that I can see how it looks to you," said her daughter slowly. "I see so clearly. And there is nothing to say.

From where you sit you see it one way, and you are right, and I can't get angry with you. I feel awfully sorry for you."

"Sorry for me?" The firm upward angle of her mother's chin reminded Jane of one of the figureheads of schooner days, distant-eyed, wise, sad. "There is no need to be sorry for me. You are my daughter, not someone to pity me."

"Would you want to care for the child? Would you want Gloria to come home, keep it, raise it?"

"I've thought of that."

"The Church certainly won't force her to give up her child. They will only tell her such a sacrifice on her part would be better for the child. Kinder."

"There should be no need for either way. Of course I can't bring the child home. The whole town would know. People would never forget. But if they married quietly, away somewhere. . . ." She drank more tea. "I don't even know where Gloria is now. She went away and wouldn't tell me where. I haven't heard from her in three weeks."

"Oh."

"Do you know where she is? Has she written you?"

"Yes."

"Where is she?"

"She doesn't want you to know, and I can't tell you. But she's well. She's very well. And she is going to stay where she is until the child is born."

Gussie's lips folded over each other, up and down, up and down.

"Mother—"

Gussie shook her head.

"Mother, she's not trying to hurt you. She's trying not to hurt you. I'd rather die than lie to you. I could have said I didn't know. But I promised I wouldn't tell anyone. She told me only in case— in case anything happened."

"I see."

"Mother—"

"There is nothing more to talk about. If she doesn't want me, if she wants it this way, that is all there is." She rose slowly from the table, buttoning her suit.

"Both my daughters have chosen to become strangers to me. I did not choose it. I did not reproach you when you joined this church which so altered your life. I did not reproach her when she came to me in disgrace and shame. Yet I am left alone. Then, alone

223

I will live." She picked up her fur piece, turned a chilly smile on Jane, and nodded as if in dismissal.

"Good-bye." She might have been ending a genteel churchyard encounter with an acquaintance. "Good-bye!"

FORTY-THREE

Sunday morning Father Macy announced from the pulpit at each Mass the official opening of the drive.

Jane came home from the early Mass. "Chris, I thought you said he wasn't going to use the Square Share thing?"

"He isn't."

"He is."

At the eleven-thirty Mass up in the choirloft Chris heard it for himself.

"Every family will be contacted," Father Macy said in his sermon. "And from studying the facts they will be able to determine what their Square Share will be. Indeed, to simplify matters, each family will find in the mail this very week a letter informing them what amount each personally will be expected to give. The committee, headed by Christopher McNamara, will then . . ."

Chris was literally stunned. And Father Macy did not return to the choirloft as was his usual custom. After Mass Chris went home to wait. "I don't want to talk about it," he said.

He went alone for a stroll around the lawn, a small walk to be sure, but a private one. The children left him alone. He moved slowly pretending to examine the grass and the dwarf apple trees and the new rose growth, to decide on sprays and fertilizers.

Perhaps, he thought, it was Father Temple who insisted on it. Maybe Father Macy didn't know how to tell me the pastor wanted the Square Share thing. Maybe he didn't know himself till the last minute. He'll call me. Certainly he'll call me this afternoon.

Father Macy did not telephone. When Chris phoned the rectory, Father Macy was not in.

There was to be that evening a meeting of the committee.

"I'm not going to go," Chris said. "I'm going to quit."

But at the last minute, while his children were teary-eyed watching the adventures of a girl and a horse on television, and Jane cleared the supper table, Chris decided he could not stay home.

He greeted Father Macy cordially, sat with the other men at the table, parried their sallies over his tardiness for the meeting, and held his peace, waiting. He waited through the prayer to the Holy Spirit with which Father opened the meeting. He waited while Father began explaining charts of the Square Share plan.

"Here are the names of the parishioners in your districts. Beside each name you will find a figure in dollars. This is the amount which it seems would be their square share of this drive. The amount mentioned in the letters they will get. Your aim will be to get that amount. Now there is a deliberate cushion in that amount. If you get a hundred dollars less, we will still go over. . . ."

Chris held up his hand.

"Excuse me, Father. But as you know we have as a committee decided not to use the Square Share plan. Now perhaps—"

"The decision on this came from the rectory, Chris. This is the way it will be done. As you remember, you and I talked about this the other night."

"I remember."

Julian Newman gravely turned a yellow pencil in his hand so that first the fresh red eraser touched the Formica tabletop, then the sharp black point, eraser, then point.

"I remember," Chris repeated, as if gathering up his thoughts. He stood up, lanky, an indoor man, white-collared, long-handed, his cowlick working itself free of the day's combed discipline. He put his hands on his belt, the grey tweed suit jacket pushed back, and with his shoulders leaning forward, his head cocked upward, he fell into what Patsy Rottigni identified as the exact pose of the poor but honest defense attorney on television.

"Father, I think there's been some misunderstanding here," said Chris. "I'd like to get it out in the open. I'm that kind of man. And I'm sure you are too."

Father nodded.

"I thought this fund drive was being run by this committee. I understood you to say that as chairman I was in charge."

"No," said Father Macy. His arms folded, he sat listening in what anyone could see was a tolerant, even charming manner. "No. Of course in anything to do with the Church, the pastor, or his representative, must be in charge."

"Of course," Chris nodded. "I think you said it differently. You

225

said: 'Check with me.' But Father, you also said laymen were the best equipped to know how to run a fund drive. You said, and these were your exact words: 'Priests weren't ordained to count money, or even to raise it.' "

"Yes."

"We told you, Father, we'd do the job for you. And you told us to do it our way. But—this is not our way."

"It's the best way. The proven way. Other parishes hire outfits that specialize in fund-raising, pay them a commission to come in and run a drive. We're not doing that. But we can benefit from copying their techniques. Almost without exception they use some form of this Square Share way. And that's how we're going to do it." Father Macy shrugged, smiled politely, and raised expectant eyebrows.

"It's not a fair way, Father. It's a way that stinks. It's a way that says: We can't trust you jerks to give for the love of God or to help the nuns, so we'll tell you what to fork out and you'd better do it. What the hell kind of lay apostolate—or priesthood—is that?"

Father Macy's face flushed. He said nothing. Then he smiled tolerantly.

Chris stood enduring that smile.

The moment stretched out as far as it would go. Into it Chris fitted a montage of the possible next moments, saw himself lashing out at the priest with righteous impatience, saw himself lecturing Father on the teachings of the bishops defining the relative competence of priests and laymen in various fields, saw himself refusing to have anything to do with the drive, saw himself possibly bowing to the inevitable and going along like a good sheep.

Bede's plump red face rested in his hands. Patsy looked as if he had stumbled in on a good crap game and had no money to get into it. Al was inspecting his shoelaces, but the scalp showing through his hair was blazing pink. Julian kept turning the pencil, eraser, point, eraser, point.

"Father Macy," said Chris, his hands dropping from his belt, his jacket falling back into place as if ready for business. "I cannot go along with this at all. You appealed to me on the basis of my commitment to Catholic Action. I do not consider this Catholic Action. With all due respect, I resign."

Father Macy kept his smile, kept his arms folded, and bowed from the waist in gracious acceptance. "I'm sorry. But since you feel this way—" He shrugged.

Chris turned to the committee. One by one they raised their faces to meet his gaze.

"Good night," he said, and walked out.

"You just walked out?"

"I did."

"Father Tom's here. He's in with the kids."

"I saw his car in the drive," Chris said.

Jane shook her head wonderingly. "You walked out. Bravo! Now what?"

"Who knows? They'll find someone else to call head of the drive. They'll have their Square Share."

Father Tom came in from the living room beaming.

"Love. That's the topic of the day," he said. "Greetings, Chris."

"Not out here," observed Jane.

"We're running on a different track," said Chris. "You are just in time for a dose of anticlericalism."

"Will you still make a pledge to the drive?" asked Jane.

"Of course." Chris got out the Scotch. "Jane—it was all I could do to keep from telling him off but good."

"Well, I'm glad you didn't."

Father Tom, listening with folded lower lip, shook his head. "There'll be trouble," he said. "A square share of trouble."

"What trouble? I'm not leaving the Church, just the drive. And maybe someday Father Macy might have an inkling of why, and it might wake him up."

"I doubt it." Father Tom snitched a maraschino cherry from an open jar.

"Well, I'm glad I walked out."

"You're a brave man." Father Tom grinned. "And foolish, too, maybe. Your Father Macy didn't see all the ramifications you see in the matter, you know. You'd have to be a priest to understand him. Who knows? Perhaps he is conditioned by living with a pastor who lived with a pastor who knew laymen were only poor dumb immigrants? Perhaps he feels the need of prudence, a fear that if the clergy aren't careful the pendulum of the layman's role will swing too fast and too far? Maybe he just feels inadequate. Who knows what shapes Father Macy, or what good lurks in his soul?"

"Right now, I'm more interested in a drink," said Jane.

"You did the right thing, Chris," Father Tom concluded. "And so you'll pay for it. Be prepared."

"Baloney," said Chris lightly, "There won't be any trouble. This business of the drive hasn't anything to do with my life, really."

Father threw his head back in his poet's pose. "I shall compose for you an epitaph:

"Here lies Chris McNamara, layman—
Who stood up for his rights—Amen!"

He winked. "I'm not really prophesying doom. But believe me this drive is not a thing apart from your life. All things work together. Somewhere, sometime, this thread will turn up again in the design. I'll be interested to see how."

FORTY-FOUR

Chris always phoned his mother on Mondays.

It meant a lot to Annie to have proof that he loved and honored her and the phone call did the trick. The call had to be made from the office. Annie who carried on a one-sided feud with all the commercial world, was especially hostile to the phone company.

"They say it's forty cents for three minutes but I've never yet gotten a forty-cent bill. You know very well that I am always careful not to talk more than three minutes. And those thieves overcharge all the time. The world is full of thieves and I'm not going to let them get away with gypping Annie McNamara, or her son. I won't have you paying the phone company one cent for my sake."

If one of ten thousand light bulbs was defective, Annie would get it. The salesgirl who made an error in change only once a year would make it with Annie. Her bus drivers were invariably rude, her mail lost, her pennies swallowed by out-of-order weighing machines.

"You have to be clever just to stay even," she said. "And never call long distance."

So Chris phoned her from the city, a local ten-cent call, dutifully each week. And once a month, on a Thursday, he lunched with her, alternately at home, where she cooked corned beef and cabbage for him because she knew Jane wouldn't, and at a restaurant where he squired her with modest extravagance.

228

This Monday the thought of calling her depressed him. It grew increasingly difficult for him to talk with his mother.

As he put a hand to the receiver to call her this morning he hesitated: What could he say to her? What news could he give her to make her feel part of his life? He couldn't talk to her about the office. His business life interested Annie only when he could offer her a triumph to boast of at the Daughters of Isabella or the Ladies of Charity card party. Poor Annie. She couldn't say her son had a promotion. Couldn't tell her friends he had bought anything impressive. She kept hoping he'd at least buy a new car, even if he didn't build a swimming pool.

He sighed. The kids. That was all he could talk about right now.

"Christopher? Hello. You're late. I was worried about you, maybe you were sick. It's nine-thirty already. But I suppose you're very busy at the office."

He told her that Peter had been chosen as a patrol boy and that little Teresa was sitting up nicely.

"And Jane? How is Jane? Oh, I worry about that poor girl so, Christopher. You just don't know how hard it must be for her with all those children. You're not—you're not going to have any more are you?"

"Not this week."

"It's nothing to joke about. Really. I've been thinking about Jane, and I keep worrying. Oh, you don't know how I worry."

"Sounds like you've been reading tea leaves again. Mustn't let those things get you, you know." He lit a cigarette. "How'd we get on this subject anyway?"

"Well, you just don't know, that's just it. But I know what I know. And this friend of mine took me to this wonderful woman who reads horoscopes, and oh I can't tell you what she said. It was wonderful. Wonderful."

"Mother—"

"Oh, I know you don't approve. But there's something there. And don't go telling me it's a sin. This is a fine woman!"

"Uh-huh. How is Dad?"

"Same as always. He sits around looking healthy, but he doesn't fool me. I'm not going to go away and leave him. There's nothing but sadness all around him. And around someone else." She paused significantly.

"Well," he said, refusing to rise to the bait. "Wish I could talk longer, but it's getting late, and I've got to go to a conference now."

"Every time I try and talk to you you're in a hurry."

"No," he said. "I *like* talking to you. But this is a busy morning. We'll have a good long visit Thursday."

"Christopher—" Her voice held him with its earnest plea. "You and Jane. You never come in to see me any more with Jane. I promised her mother to keep an eye on her. But lately I've had the strangest feeling. I—Christopher, you and Jane—you aren't thinking of doing anything foolish are you?"

He did not answer. He did not know what to say.

"I'm so afraid you'll do something foolish. Six children is enough."

He had no conference to go to. He conferred with himself.

"Do something foolish." That's a new word for it.

He arranged the papers on his desk. Today he was to address a lunch-hour meeting of Sodality men on the need for a new and dynamic approach to Christian sex and marriage. Fifty dollars and a free lunch. How would it be if I used Annie's phrase? If I said, the prime purpose of matrimony is doing something foolish. He snorted.

He had three speeches on the subject. The thirty-minute one would be best today. His stomach had already begun to tighten, which was a good sign. Over the years he had learned that only at a certain pitch of nerves could he deliver a really good talk.

Today he wanted to expand his talk to include the book by Suenens, *Love and Control*. "Being French, the cardinal is naturally frank," he said to himself; then he smiled. That line might be worth trying on an educated audience like the Sodality men. Suenens was also bold. He said that when married folk must refrain from having more children they needed to express love in every way short of the complete act. For this they needed the developed skill of self-control, and an understanding of Christian sexology. Suenens offered concrete examples of how this noble human talent of control could be strengthened from childhood on.

It fitted in happily with the rest of Chris's lecture notes. He scanned them quickly. God commanded Adam and Eve to multiply, "to fill the earth and subdue it." Subduing the world meant subduing themselves too. The Church does not insist on high birth rate. The Church now opposes early marriage. Marriages at mature age, more emphasis on chastity, would automatically lower birth rate.

Then the usual points, most of which he drew from the work of that pioneer American priest in the field, Father Henry Sattler. All human appetites can and must be controlled and directed by reason. Doctors agree with this idea in obesity and alcoholism, eating and drinking. Why do they consider it impossible and dangerous in the appetite for sex? Problem of values. Some moderns say sexual experience is an end in itself, a value to be cultivated at any price, in or out of marriage. With a wrong value system continence seems ridiculous, wrong, humanly impossible. "Yet a man is fully human only when he maintains reasonable control over his appetites."

Reasonable.

Chris lit a cigarette. That was the question. If you were fully human you had to decide what to do. The Church left you the decision. You could follow the high road of prudence and self-control. You could follow the high road of abandoning the future to the providence of God. And you could find reasonable voices arguing both sides.

You had to decide and then be willing to live by the effect of decision, as time unfolded it. He drew a deep breath and pushed back his chair. I decided once. And now? He knew it was not weakness that made him reconsider. Knew, and was grateful to know. The chance to test himself had been offered him. By Krena. And by Jane. He pushed the thought of Krena away.

Not weakness. The days of torment had been lived through. Though they might come again he did not fear them. The sins of thought were absolved. Now, almost in cold blood, as if blocking out more lecture notes, he understood that for the sake of love alone he would reconsider the matter.

The fact was that the woman he loved loved him, and wanted him. That Jane wanted to take the road of trusting God. He buried his face in his hands. Even to himself he had never dared to admit the full misery of those winter months when Jane had drawn away from him. To have her again, alive in love!

She wanted him. She wanted to live. But living for her meant loving, in a way that it had never meant to her before. Loving in the body both him and God. "Isn't it reasonable to trust God?" she had cried.

His watch said it was ten. The day's work could not wait longer. I am stealing from my employer, stealing time. Only a few weeks ago I wrote a piece complaining that these are the small wrongs people think unimportant, and priests never preach about, and here I am embezzling Academic Allied Publishers' time, for what?

To consider whether to—to do something foolish.

You can't really be reasonable about a thing like that. Not at a desk littered with mail and engagement pads and that fool thing on *Reptiles for Young People*. Not with Millie banging her typewriter on the other side of the partition.

"I'm only human," he said quietly aloud. "And I decide not to decide. Not yet. Not now."

FORTY-FIVE

Jane was picking peonies, torn as always between the desire to leave them candescent in the sun and the opposite desire to have them for cut flowers. Teresa crawled on the flagstone walk, stopping to examine tiny armies of ants. Meg scampered after the first white butterflies. It seemed to Jane that she could taste a honied anticipation in the air, amber, sun-enchanted sweetness.

In her hand were sturdy stems of peonies. The same hand had last Halloween buried in chilling earth the ugly roots from which these flowers spring. Death and winter, resurrection and spring, she thought. And when I planted these I carried within me a baby who now laughs in the sun at the antics of ants.

She stood, pillowing her cheek on the fragrance of the flowers. And now, what is it that I do? I love, and wait, and fear no death.

Death. This day Agnes Milder lay in a bed at the hospital, dying. The disease lurking, gathering strength, had made sudden appalling conquest. With a surge of pity Jane wondered what Agnes would think when she met God. Would it be a terrible shock to come soul to soul with the love of the three-in-one, when you had spent your lifetime being Agnes Milder?

Today she was going to the hospital to see Agnes. And to see Felicity Lawrence, if she could. She did not know exactly what was wrong with Felicity. Since Agnes' illness, she thought wryly, the flow of gossip has fallen off. People said Felicity was having a nervous breakdown from her little boy's death. She was refusing visitors, they said. But perhaps it would please her if someone tried, and left a card anyway. Presumably her own church groups took care of visiting Felicity. But Jane, feeling a pang of conscience for having done nothing to comfort Felicity while the boy lay ill, would try.

And she would bring the peonies to Agnes. Clare said Agnes had not many flowers.

The paper-thin screech of truck brakes summoned Jane back to the day. As the mailman left she went with Meg and Teresa to take the daily packet from the box by the road.

The letter was in a white envelope, the kind sold to strangers in ten-cent stores, with three blank lines in the upper left corner for a return address, the forlorn stationery of someone not at home. In Gloria's handwriting the blank lines were filled with the address of the convent in Albany.

> Dear Jane,
>   So Mother has given up on me. Too bad she's angry at you. It seems you put up quite a fight for me. Thanks. But don't get so upset about it. Mother's old enough to know her own mind. So am I.
>   You're really taking this quite well, for you, old dear. Not hardly a word of reproach. I have to hand it to you. But I was fascinated when you wrote me about that gal Lidwina. The old Jane really shone through there. You were so busy trying to sound as Christian as you think you ought to sound. You talk about leaving the judgment to God, but I'll bet you haven't spoken to her yet. I know you will eventually, because you're you. Just don't make too big a deal out of it when you do.

Jane's cheeks flamed. She crumpled the letter into her pocket and closed her eyes.

"You put flowers in water?" asked Meg.

"Yes. I will. That's right, dear."

Already the peonies were wilting. She must soak them and burn the ends with matches to seal them.

Out of the corner of her eye she saw Lidwina coming from her house to fetch her mail. Seeing Jane, she hesitated, then almost belligerently continued on her way. Jane did not want to talk to her. Her body knew that, no matter how much her mind denied it. Her body wanted to run into the house away from a possible scene.

"Why don't you go over and see Lidwina, she must be lonely," Chris had said. "I will, I will, only I'll wait till we meet naturally so it won't look obvious," she had said. She hadn't said, which was also true, that she couldn't imagine what to say to Lidwina, or how to act, and that she was afraid Lidwina might be hurt.

Have I condescended to speak to her? Oh, Gloria, you've got me all wrong. I'm not that way. It's only that I'm not sophisticated like you and Lidwina, and I can only say simple things and corny things and I'm afraid you'll both draw back from me and call me sanctimonious. I can't be casual. There is nothing casual. But you don't see it that way. And I'm not smart enough to make it look right.

She wanted to avoid Lidwina and she refused to let herself run away. No matter that I am so gauche that my cheeks burn and my chest is choked with nerves. This is childish. Be casual? Why then does it seem to me so important, this meeting?

"Lidwina!" Jane cleared her throat, annoyed to find her mouth dry.

"Good morning."

Jane walked over to meet her. "Would you like some peonies? I have more than I want."

One well-brushed eyebrow rose.

"Oh. Well." Jane nodded. "I admit they're a bit wilted. But they'll perk up if you give them a beauty bath. Or I'll cut some more."

Lidwina's gaze was a shining flexible suit of armor.

I'm supposed to quail, Jane realized with surprise. I'm supposed to be put in my place and made to feel unwanted and ridiculous. I've been wondering how not to embarrass her and she's—"

"If you don't like my peonies, how about my coffee?"

"No, thank you."

"Lidwina, you're just darn well trying to be difficult."

"Oh?" The pale pink lips tightened and her laugh was a sniff through her nostrils.

"Look. Please. I'd love you to come and have coffee. I should be subtle and nonchalant about it, after not seeing you for all these weeks, but I don't know how. All I know is that I'm only asking because I want to—because I—"

"Jane, this is too touching." Lidwina opened her mailbox and took out her mail.

Jane blinked, bit her lip, turned away, walking slowly toward her children and her house.

On impulse she turned back. Lidwina was still standing there.

"I wanted to ask you," Jane said quietly, "if you'd come to the

234

hospital with me today. Agnes Milder is there, dying. I was hoping you would come with me. I know how much reason you have to dislike her. I guess because of that I hoped you'd go to see her now. There's not much time left. And, frankly, I'd rather not go alone."

Lidwina stared at her. Twice she opened her mouth as if to speak, before words came. At last she smiled, helplessly.

"I'll come have coffee with you, Jane."

Agnes was skin, yellow skin. The bones of her face seemed to slip around inside the sagging cheeks. Like the bones in an uncooked chicken, Jane thought, repressing a shiver. Agnes' nose seemed bigger. But it was her eyes that alarmed, small brown frightened eyes that were never still. She looked here and there, up and down, as if trying to locate the source of a whisper or a movement in the empty room.

When she noticed her visitors she sighed as if reassured.

"How nice of you to come." The voice was the same nasal whine. "Jane and Lidwina. I didn't think you would come. I didn't expect anyone today. Elmo comes at night."

"Then we picked a good time," said Jane.

"Yes. Lidwina, you look lovely. How do you do it? You look like you're going to a party and not to visit a dying woman." Her pale scrawny hand wiped her eyes with a wrinkled handkerchief.

Lidwina had chosen the blue and purple chintz skirt and a white flounced blouse deliberately. "No use being dismal when you visit the living," she said. "Hospitals are already ugly enough."

"Yes," came Agnes' whine from behind the handkerchief.

"I'll go put these flowers in a vase," said Jane. "They're driving me crazy, have been all morning, more trouble than kids. Be right back." She ignored Lidwina's imploring glance. Her high heels ticked down the hallway.

"Lidwina," Agnes' fist crumpled the hankie and her eyes moved as if to see if she were overheard. "Why did you come?"

"Because Jane asked me to."

"I see. Honest answer. I wondered. I thought you never went anywhere. How do you dare?"

Lidwina's face stiffened.

"No. I said it wrong, Lidwina. I didn't mean to. Not that way. I meant—" Her hand reached out and grasped Lidwina's wrist. "I meant I am afraid to have people come here, or look them in the eye, because I have done things that they know about and I would like to be able to say I'm sorry and I'm frightened, I wish I could be you."

"No you don't, Agnes."

"I've been an awful gossip, Lidwina. No. I have. I lie here and think I have said so many unkind things and they weren't always true and— Do you know what Father Juniper said to me? He's that little friar at the monastery and he comes here sometimes to be chaplain. He read me what St. James said about the tongue. And he said trying to go back and pick up after gossip is like picking up feathers from a pillow shaken into the wind." Agnes closed her eyes. Lidwina could still see them stirring back and forth under the thin crossed lids.

"Lidwina? Will you forgive me?" The voice was suddenly loud. The hand on her wrist tightened till it hurt.

"Of course."

"If you will forgive me I have picked up one feather. I have," the little brown eyes opened again, "found one person to forgive me."

"Agnes, you mustn't sound this way." Lidwina leaned over, her hoarse voice gentle. "You never did a really bad thing. You're quite a decent sort, God knows."

"No mortal sin. I know. Father Juniper heard my confession. He was kind. But he said I must use my time now, quickly—"

Lidwina looked away. Nothing in her experience had prepared her for this. "He said," Agnes went on, "I must learn to love God before I meet Him."

"There!" Jane said cheerily, setting the flowers down. Lidwina was fumbling in her purse for a cigarette, her cheeks crimson even under her powder. Agnes was hidden again by the hankie.

"They're lovely, Jane," said Agnes. "The flowers. Worth all the trouble."

"You're in pain? Tired? Perhaps we've stayed too long?"

"No. Only that I can't believe you came. I can't believe it. I didn't think God would let you."

Her eyes, open and tearless, came to rest on the flowers.

When, near the end of visiting hour they did finally leave her, Jane inquired at the desk whether Mrs. Felicity Lawrence was having visitors.

"No, dearie. She doesn't want to see anyone."

"I'll leave her a note then," Jane said, realizing that she was grateful not to see Felicity this afternoon.

It was there at the counter, where she stood in her dark brown shirtwaist with the orange chiffon scarf at the neck, that Dr. Polla noticed her on his rounds.

He accosted her with a wink. "Making a reservation for yourself, Mrs. McNamara."

"Hi!" She grinned.

She is, he noted, looking very well. Very well. As if that moodiness is gone. I didn't like that. A couple of months there I was worried for her, and not just because of kidneys. Though it was hard to say what.

"Keep off maternity, you hear?"

"I hear."

"Those last tests are running just the same. No worse, but no better."

"Dr. Polla. Call for Dr. Polla." With a wave to Jane, he went off to answer the public address system.

Lidwina had gone on ahead to the gift shop. Jane went to look for her. She found her kneeling on the floor with a skinny little priest whose head was bent in fascination over a battery-run bear. The bear blew up a balloon, then whistled through a harmonica. The priest looked up at her.

"Jane! Come see!"

She blinked. She had never seen Juniper in anything but a friar's robe. In the black suit Franciscans wore away from the friary he looked frail and commonplace.

"I thought you hated animals," she said.

"This one's different." Snatching it from the floor, he hopped nimbly to his feet, neglecting to dust his knees. "I'm bringing it to a patient," he explained, offering Lidwina a hand up. "Had to be sure how it worked."

"We've been very serious about it," Lidwina said dryly. Juniper sidled over near Jane and peered up at her. "So you went to see Agnes Milder. Good. Good. The bear is for her. She needs to laugh, you know. She thinks God never laughs."

"She seemed glad we went to see her."

"Glad isn't the word for it," added Lidwina.

"You're right. It isn't the word. But it will do." Juniper nodded at her, and then at Jane. "You haven't any idea how important little things are. Like this bear. Or your going to see her. You don't know where it all leads. That's the fun of it, isn't it? We won't know till it's all over. And you're only beginning to have the fun of knowing that it's going somewhere."

He bent his head, then lifted it, running a finger uneasily between the unaccustomed Roman collar and his neck. "Jane, Jane. If you only knew where love leads you'd be so overcome with it that you'd be unable to move."

He turned the switch that animated the bear and chuckled as the red balloon filled with air.

FORTY-SIX

Lunch on this day in St. Rose's rectory was a gloomy white-sauce-on-noodle and tuna affair. The three priests sat in silent suffering at the table.

Father Macy believed the constant noodle menus of the past week represented the housekeeper's passive revenge on the pastor for having rebuked her on a matter of gossip. Father Mongiano agreed. Both devoutly hoped her fit of sulks would soon end.

The gossip had been about Felicity Lawrence.

Since the death of her boy, Felicity had gone into what had been known in Father Temple's childhood as a "decline." She was at times incoherent on the phone, erratic in her dress. The man who worked part-time as church gardener had seen Mrs. Lawrence out on her front walk in her nightie in broad daylight. He had told the rectory housekeeper, who told Father Temple. He had shouted at her that she was not to commit the sin of retailing gossip in his household. Hence the noodles.

The phone rang. The housekeeper stuck her face through the open swinging door. "Someone wants to speak to you, Father Temple."

The pastor coughed. "You know I don't like being interrupted at lunch," he said, going to take the call in his study.

"Yes," he shouted.

"It's Jane McNamara, Father Temple. I'm calling to ask you a favor. I wish you'd go to the hospital and see Felicity Lawrence."

"Didn't know she was there!"

"She's pretty lonesome, I think. And you could do her so much good, Father Temple."

He stood silent, rubbing his nose.

"Father Temple, are you there?"

"Of course. It's the middle of my lunch."

"Sorry. I just thought you might want to know."

"Thank you, Jane. God bless you now."

The curates were eating rice pudding, as bland and white as the noodles. The pastor sat down heavily in his chair.

"I'm going out this afternoon," he said belligerently. "I'll stop in at the hospital on my way. No need for you to go today, Father Mongiano."

He ignored their look of surprise.

Father Temple's stomach always rebelled at hospital odors. Sweat trickled down his sparse shanks, causing his trousers to wrinkle, as his private demon, his obsessive dislike of visiting the sick, gripped him. He especially dreaded seeing Felicity. He feared that the rumors about her were true. He had heard on reliable authority that she had used unladylike language to her own minister when he came to her home. I'm going for Harold's sake, he said. And because of Jane. I don't know what there is about that girl but I've never been able to say "no" to her.

But he could not forget his last meeting with Felicity, here in this same hospital. Father Temple forced himself now to go to Felicity, a soul driving a body on a less than heroic errand requiring near-heroic virtue. It was, he thought, good for his sense of humor and humility, to be reminded that for him martyrdom meant a rather bumbling entrance to a hospital room.

Felicity lay long and pale, the dark shadows around her eyes oddly distinct against her white skin. Her light-brown hair, always so perfectly disciplined into a bun, tumbled over the pillow. The old man looked at the luxuriant hair and felt a stab of compassion for the woman who had for years hidden her youth and her beauty even from herself.

He cleared his throat. She turned her head.

"Father Temple? What are you doing here?"

"Felicity, I came to see you."

"Well, you see me." The eyelids drooped. "Do you think I'm all they say? A drunk? A drugged drunk? Is that what you came to see?" She spoke quietly, but the serenity that had always characterized her was gone from her tone. She sounded empty, cold, dead.

He pulled over a bright orange chair and sat down.

"Well, are you?" he asked. The voice, trying to obey his desire to sound gentle and bantering, emerged hoarse.

She winced. "Of course not." She turned her head away.

"I didn't think so. But you're doing a good job of making others think so."

"Thanks."

The old priest sat with his hands on his knees. Mary, speak in me and through me, he prayed. He repeated the request over and over in his heart and sat, waiting, appalled at the mess he might make speaking on his own.

The woman in the bed, puzzled and annoyed by his silence, looked over her shoulder, then turned on her side facing him, pulling the smooth white sheet over her shoulders.

"I didn't mean to be rude. You're—you're not to think that. I know you, and you are kind and good and—I'm not well, Father Temple. That's all it is. I'm just not well."

"Grief is an illness," he said. "Time is the standard cure. But there must be no complications if the cure is to work. And the worst complication, the near-fatal one, is selfishness."

"Grief is an illness?" she repeated. "Yes. I suppose that is my illness. I thought for a while I was losing my mind, but my mind was too strong for me. I could not lose it. And now they have me here because I was near destroying my health. But my body was too strong for me. They come and shoot needles into me and give me vitamins and blood and iron and they will not let me die. That would be too easy. So I am not in danger of losing my body or my mind. Only my soul is left."

She rose up on her elbow, and fixing him with tired brown eyes she said, "And the way I feel now there isn't anyone who can keep me from losing that. I don't want to be saved. You hear me? When I told my minister that, he did not care to believe me. I had to be very rude to him. I don't want to hurt you. So please, believe me the first time."

His hands still lay flat, one on each knee. He seemed not even to have heard her.

She lay back on the pillow.

The sounds of the hospital, the inhuman alto of the loudspeaker voice summoning Mr. O'Shaughnessy to some undefined task, the rolling of serving-cart wheels, the low music of a radio, the slip-slap of convalescent feet on the way to the sunporch, these came into the room where neither priest nor patient made a sound.

"Speaking of saving souls," she said at last, "you always wanted to save Harold's soul, didn't you? You really thought he would make a good Catholic. A good man. Poor Father Temple."

The priest stirred, cleared his throat, reached in his suit jacket pocket for cigarettes and matches.

"Felicity," he said, "you have three daughters who need you. You have returned your son to God, seen him go off to perfect happiness, to the life that never ends. You believe in heaven. You believe in God, loving, wonderful, perfect. I know you believe this. You are a church-going woman, a good woman. And you cannot grieve for your little boy, because he is where we all hope to be, with the Lord. Our Lord wept when Lazarus died even though he knew he would bring him back to life." He lit his cigarette, coughed, then went on:

"But you are grieving too long. Your girls need you. Your husband needs you." He sounded angry now. His words hit like slaps in the face. "God needs you, so get up and live!"

"You're wrong!" she said softly. "No one needs me."

Smoke poured through Father Temple's nostrils in a snort of impatience.

"Nothing to live for, eh? You're young, Felicity. You might have another son."

Her face was suddenly distorted with pain, her lips were stretched in a grimace duplicating the old Greek masks of tragedy, pink-purple lips thick and distended. Yet not one sound did she make.

Father Temple turned his head away and blinked. He could not help feeling sorry for God, constraining himself to depend on men like him who were worse than useless, who kept nicking and scratching the whole job. It had been the wrong thing to say and he did not know why.

"Father," she whispered, "we cannot have another child. It is impossible."

He turned instantly to offer compassion. The look of bitter triumph on her face paralyzed him.

"Would you like to know why?" she asked. "You would not like to know. But I will tell you. Do you know why little Harry died? Because God is not mocked. Because——"

"Don't blame God!" Father interrupted with a growl. "He doesn't go around taking revenge on people."

"God let Harry die because he will not be mocked," she said. "And there will be no more children. My—husband, Harold, whom you admire, that one, when he had his son at last, and begat him, wanted no more children. And he went and had an operation, went and had himself sterilized."

Her hands clenched over the white-ribbed blanket cover.

"That is a sin, Father Temple. It is a wicked thing to do. You talk about selfishness? You said I was sick from selfishness. It was his selfishness. His sin. And for his sin my baby died, to punish us."

"No!" shouted Father Temple. "No!"

"Yes," she answered softly. "Oh, yes. And God does not want my soul any more than you want Harold's now. Am I wrong? No. He knows I did not want more babies then either. And he leaves me sonless, knowing that never again will I conceive or give birth. And he watches and despises and lets us suffer."

She craned her neck off the pillow to see him, the waves of her long hair like a mantle around her.

"Hah! You have tears in your eyes, Father. It hurts you to know what people are like? You should know by now. You should be past tears. Someday I will be past them too, when only my mind and my body live."

Her sobs came like a child's, high-pitched, keening. Felicity, the woman of constant, graceful composure. Felicity was making those sounds.

A nurse, hearing them, stopped in the doorway, went off down the hall, returned with a hypodermic.

"You'd best leave, Father," she said. "She'll sleep now for a while."

Remembering that scene, and his own ineptness, Father Temple sat that evening alone. He was, he thought, a blotter, absorbing the suffering of others, and even a blotter was of use. Felicity's suffering, the echo of her despair, the sense of her writhing pain, these were fresh in his memory and he had already offered them up, binding them to Jesus Christ. Now, on a deeper level, he explored the suffering that was Harold's, the agony that could not spend itself in dramatics, but must hang silent on the crosscurrent of past and future. For Harold, beyond the pain of bereavement lay the oily acrid pain of guilt sliding into each crevice of days and nights. And in the woman to whom he might have turned for comfort only the constant dying scream of the Furies. And for Harold, still a father to the three girls, still a member of Rotary and the Junior Chamber of Commerce, there was nothing to do but hide the pain.

Father Temple took that suffering of his friend and bound it to his own heart and grafted it to himself. The weight of it almost made him gasp. Yet a small smile of triumph softened his face. He figured himself not much of a preacher, not much at counseling. His prayers were shot through with distractions, his supply of virtues were all of the lowest acceptable degree, and as a personality he was about as crotchety as Christ might find. He was of course a faithful pastor, but that was the least he could do. Yet there was, he felt, one connivance which God could not resist, one way he could justify his priesthood.

Lord, he thought, I am here, as Samuel said. And you have made me, all on your own, into another Christ, anointed, set apart, a mediator raising men to you and bringing you to men. And I am here with my friend in my heart, one with me, inseparable. You cannot be rid of me, for I am a priest forever. *Ergo* and *ecce!* You cannot be rid of him!

Father Temple went downstairs to talk to the housekeeper with a seraphic smile. There would be no more noodles.

FORTY-SEVEN

The day was borrowed from summer, blue-hot, dressed in pale clover. Dampness from the soil shimmered, rising through the breezeless noon air. Under the white birch clumps mountain pinks were pillows of startling heat lightning.

Kilian pulled a bouquet of dandelions, fierce gold soft-hearted beauty, stems green-crushed and slippery in his fists. Margaret trailed wisps of song in her game of ball. Teresa in her basket, kicking in the sunlight, enchanted by the sudden freedom of bare legs, puzzled out the weightless dark of shadow on them. Chris lay on a webbed aluminum chaise drinking a Coke from the bottle and watching his family.

"This is the day the Lord has made," he sang, softly, in antiphonal tone.

Jane lay on her stomach weeding the pinks, a delicate task. Lazily she sang in answer the Easter chant, "Let us rejoice and be glad in it."

"This is the day the Lord has made," Chris sang again, a tone higher.

Peter, intent on selecting a blade of grass for whistling, rolled over, lay facing the sunlight which made kaleidoscopes of his tight closed eyes, and sang back the response off key.

"Let us rejoice and be glad in it."

His sneakers were that mildew green which is the patina of grass, sweat and brookslime on white canvas. Ordinarily now Peter's waking face bore an indecisive softening look, the mark of struggle between the amiable roundness of childhood and the jutting emergence of character. Peter was at the age that considered youth an indignity to be overcome by dint of tough talk, songs about green greasy gopher guts, and the discipline of avoiding sentiment. This included the need to scorn all family specialties, all private McNamara habits, such as the makeshift chanting of liturgy.

That now he did answer his father's song startled and pleased Chris. He saw his son lying in the moment of surrender to sunlight, and loved him. He reached for his pipe and smiled at Jane.

Beauty spilled across the whole afternoon, trembling in sprays of blue and gold and green laughter. Jane rolled on the grass with Meg, and held Teresa, giggling, high on arms-length, and felt youth slipping over her like satin. Kilian and Luke lay with their heads on her arms, then—convulsed by the excitement of spring—flung themselves away to pummel each other and wrestle, shrieking.

Chris puttered with the gym set, oiling rusty screws and hinges, rehanging swings, while Mary dangled by her knees from the crossbar being Rapunzel letting down her hair.

They did not mark Peter's absence till supper.

Sunset had brought the revenge of swift chill in the air. Windows were closed. The oil burner turned itself on. The family ate without Peter, annoyed at his lateness. Concern did not give way to fear until nearly seven-thirty.

They phoned the houses of Peter's friends. No one knew where he was. When the phone rang, Chris jumped to answer it. Jane read on Chris' face that it was not Peter, but she felt his fear, and stood not breathing. He would not look at her. She tried to remember what Pete had been wearing.

"Okay. We'd all better get going," Chris said. Then he hung up the phone.

"Martha's sister is lost."

"The crazy woman? Betsy Butler?"

"You said never to call her crazy, remember?" Chris looked stern. "She is well now, you said, and she and Pete are such great friends. And they're both gone."

The refrigerator motor clicked, hummed. In the living room Mary and Luke were playing Monopoly. The babies were asleep.

"If that woman has harmed Pete—"

"She wouldn't, Chris, listen: they would have gone together to do something, very simple, very nature-y. That's what they like—birds, maybe, or frogs."

"I'm calling the police. And then I'm going to look. Bede says he's going too. They went on foot. Miss Butler doesn't drive. Thank God she doesn't drive."

She put away the sponge. She stood watching the children's game, numb. She wished to shield them from her own fear. Then the thought of Peter lost in the dark, nowhere, with Miss Butler, Peter—hurt, wet, cold, frightened—assaulted her. She could not bear for him to be nowhere.

"Mary. Luke." Her voice sounded old, cold, so they stopped their game instantly.

"Peter is lost," she said, forcing herself to a gentler tone. "He may be—anywhere. Something might have happened. Daddy's gone looking. The police are coming to look too. But Peter may be frightened. Let's pray for him."

A Hail Mary. An Angel of God. Our Father. It felt good to work by praying. Luke and Mary, faces slimmed by a sense of urgency and responsibility, prayed importantly. They were halfway through a Glory Be when the lights of the police emergency car shone outside.

"The emergency car," Luke said proudly. "Sharp."

Jane spoke to the officers, supplying what little she knew. What do you know of what a boy might do? Or a woman like Martha's sister? Would they gather wildflowers? It had been summer this afternoon, but the night wind was brusque and damp.

She kept her voice calm to match the policeman's matter-of-fact manner. "I don't remember what he wore."

Mary's eager face pushed through the opening where her mother's elbow crooked out from her hip. "The pocket pants. He had them."

Jane saw him again in that hour of sunlight. *Let us rejoice and be glad in it.* "Yes. Thank you, Mary. Fisherman's pants, khaki

245

color, big pockets. Grey T shirt with orange crayon marks. No hat. Sneakers. No jacket. No sweater. It was hot earlier, you know."

"We'll find them."

"Thank you." They might have been discussing a lost pair of gloves.

Jane sat in her chair holding a rosary. Her thoughts searched each suddenly hostile corner of the land around her, brook and rock, woods and houses and road. It could not be the brook. Chris and Bede would have found him, found them. Chris would check that culvert under the road. The tree forts? It had to be a place where Martha's sister would go. She was a hiker but not a tree-climber. Through the woods. The woods touch the parkway. An accident, a speeding car. If they went by the parkway these would have been broadcast long ago.

She looked at Mary and Luke intent on some frenzied cartoon and hated them for being so easily diverted. Mary, aware she was being watched, looked up and blinked.

"Maybe we could have a vision," she said. "You know, I could look in something like a ball and think hard and we could all concentrate."

Jane ticked her tongue in irritation. "Can you think where Peter might go?"

"To the candy store," said Luke.

"Not with Miss Butler," said Mary.

"Pete's dead, I guess," Luke's bulldog chin dimpled earnestly.

Tears startled Mary's eyes. "Oh, I didn't know I liked Peter!" she cried.

"Oh for God's sake!" snapped Jane. "He's not dead. And you quit your yowling. You should be ashamed of yourself."

Mary blinked to make the tears roll on her cheeks. Luke's nose was running, but his face was set in lines of stubborn disgust. Jane lit a cigarette. "I wish I could go out and look for him," she said.

"Me, too," said Mary sadly.

Luke was watching the television screen again.

Mary turned her back on the screen. She could hear her mother in the kitchen phoning Tory and then someone else, and she shut out her mother's voice and the cartoon and listened to the song of the wind outside. The wind would know where Peter was.

Time dragged. Tory came. Al drove her over and intended to join the search if he could find the police or Chris. He brought a search-

light and a small bottle of brandy. Clare Sullivan walked in unannounced.

"You want to go out and look instead of sitting here wondering?"
she asked. "It's hard sitting waiting. You feel helpless enough without having to worry about leaving the other kids. I'll babysit."

"I don't know," Jane said. "You're wonderful to think of it,
Clare. But I don't know where to go look. And he might come
home when I wasn't even here."

"Well, I'll go say hello to the children. And we'll be fine here
if you decide to go." Clare went into the living room.

"I don't know where my little boy is, Tory. Oh my God, I don't
know where my baby is." Jane buried her head in her arms on the
kitchen table.

"Jane." It was Clare again.

Jane straightened up, flipped the hair out of her face.

"Jane. Mary thinks she knows where Peter is and she is afraid
you won't listen, you may think she's making it up or something.
No, wait a minute. She says she closed her eyes and saw him and
that's how she knows."

"Oh, honestly." Tory went past Clare into the living room.
"Jane's upset enough without your telling her a little girl's nonsense."

Clare shrugged, the bulge of her belly expanding.

The door opened. Chris and the policeman called out. "No news
at all." Cold air rode in on their clothes. There was mud on their
shoes and specks of brier caught in the laces. "We've made a close
search all through here. They're not here, not between our road
and the next, not in the woods."

"Two are easier to find. Which is good," offered the policeman.

"If they needed to be found, if they needed help, were hurt, or
stuck, we'd have found them. Even down in the brook," said Chris.

"There's a lake up by the parkway," the policeman said. "A
pond. I checked all around that. Of course, well, there's no point
trying to drag the pond because we have no reason to think they
went swimming—it's not like winter when there's ice and you
gotta worry did they—"

"They didn't go swimming," said Chris firmly.

"Fishing?" asked Tory.

"The water around the edge of that pond, mam, is only about
one foot deep. It's an artificial thing, drainage, an island or two in it,
and—oh look, Mrs. McNamara, what I'm saying is they couldn'ta

drowned in it. I'm not scaring you They—it's only four feet deep out in the middle near the island, just enough for a rowboat or something. But you couldn't fish and fall in, so that's out."

"We're going to go now and widen the circle," said Chris over his coffee. "We're going to check every inch. But—Jane, I'm sure they're okay. Point is, you've got to let us know if he gets home so we won't keep on looking after he gets here."

"Oh. Oh, sure." She looked at Chris as if he were a stranger and nodded.

"You're to call the police station if he comes home. It'll come over in the radio car."

Upstairs to her room she went, closing the door. She lit the bureau lamp. The jewelry box was open, tawdry, cluttery. She closed it. The vigil light Pete had given her for Christmas, the red glass holder and fat wide candle from the dime store, stood before the carved wood Madonna from the Mercy Mission. Jane bit her lip, remembering how the vigil light had been wrapped, too much paper, lots of tape, a big card.

She lit the vigil light and stared at the shadows on her statue.

"Let her go up," she heard Tory say. "You were right. Let her go up."

Her door opened a crack. Mary's face was swollen from crying. In her mother's arms she began to cry again. They sat on the big chintzed chair. Mary's weight, sturdy, warm, startled Jane. Once she had been so small.

"Mom, don't be mad at me," Mary whispered. "I'm sure I know where they are. There's a boat and he's hiding. He doesn't dare be found. He's with Miss Butler and they're hiding."

"In a boat?"

"No. They're hiding the boat too. It's on an island, in some water, you know."

Jane's chest tightened.

"Do you believe me?"

As her mother sighed the girl felt herself lifted and dropped by the breath of her.

"You ought to. I know you don't think so. But I didn't make it up. I saw them so clearly!"

"Why would Peter hide?"

"I dunno."

248

"He isn't running away? He's not running away, not trying to get lost?"

"I don't know. I couldn't see what he was thinking." Mary scratched her arm and smiled anxiously.

"It doesn't make sense, Mary."

"Maybe I didn't see it. Maybe I just thought it. But someone should look."

Jane began swiftly to change clothes, dressing in blue jeans, shirt, sweater, oxfords.

She left the car by the edge of the woods and with the flashlight found the path to the pond.

The noise of the night, the wind-tormented, ecstatic twisting of trees and brush, obsessed oblivious rhythm of the coupling of heaven and earth rose around her. She felt frightened, intrusive. The air was damp-smelling, clinging in spite of its frenzy. The moss and decaying leaves beneath her feet yielded deceivingly. Branches moved in the dark air, smooth damp sapling trunks bent and resisted and thrust themselves upright as the wind cried helplessly among the soft white pine. She could smell sweet fern as she crushed it in her hurry.

The lights of the parkway came through the woods on her right. She took her direction from it.

The pond was dark, even with flashlight on its waters. The remains of last year's skinny tan weeds bent by the wind were slippery under her shoes. The rays of her light sped into the dark air lighting on nothing, ending on nothing. It occurred to her she might see better without the light. She switched it off. At first there was only one quality of black. The sky emerged first, lighter than tree tops, greyed, sheened as threads in watered taffeta, and there were stars.

"Peter! Peter!" Her voice like the light rays hurled itself against the wind-dim shadows and fell to impotence. She thought how ridiculous it was to come out here in the dark at all, following a child's hunch, alone where she could fall and twist her ankle and lie helpless, another one to be searched for. Anguish and panic and love ripped through her in one last call.

"Peter! Peter!"

It seemed a voice answered. She faced toward the sound. The waters of the pond, troubled by the surges of the forest's breath, twisting grey. She could now discern the textured furred soft blackness of what must be island. It seemed someone moved. A shadow out there grew solid, separated itself into meaning, into man or boy and boat. Another shadow moved. No sound accompanied them. They might have been ghosts in the distance.

She put on her flashlight, swung it in circles, pointed it starward, waved it. "Peter?"

No voice reached her. The soughing twist of uninhibited night wind rolled over all. Slowly, and as if from another direction, she understood boat sounds, oarlock creak, scrape of feet, drip of water. In the wake of sound, restored by sound to reality, came boat and woman and boy rowing into view, Peter's arms and shoulders moving surely, sending an old paint-peeling boat to shore where she stood.

Insolent it seemed to be, his power as he bent to the oars. Anger spilled into the vacuum left by receding fear, anger at a boy not in need of rescue, a boy safe, alive.

He leaped from the boat, beached it, ran to her.

"Pete? Why did you do this? Dad and I—"

Behold we have sought you. . . .

The boy hugged her, turned his head so his cheek pressed against her breasts, held her. "There was a reason. . . ."

His mother looked beyond him searching with the light till she saw Miss Butler standing dully between the seats of the boat. The words of her son came to her only in tones trembling through coat and sweater into the part of her that breathed and beat.

"Thank God," she cried quietly. "Oh, Peter, thank God."

She took off her coat and put it round him. "What did she do to you?"

The boy, seeming to steel himself for one last effort, grasped her wrist and deflected the accusing flashlight from the boat.

"Help her. Listen. You must listen. You can't be angry at her or it will be all—"

He spoke as if she were the child.

"We're going home, Peter. And now. The police are looking for you. Your father's nearly crazy with worry. We must hurry."

The boy held her. "We can't go home till we talk first. Will you listen? The sooner you listen the sooner we can go home."

She looked at that face, the face of her own love, at freckles and cold-pinched circles under the eyes, the face of a man-to-be.

"I told her you'd listen. I promised her you'd understand."

She let herself be led to the boat, be seated in the thwart. Peter

250

seated Miss Butler too, then crouched between them to talk while around them the dark torment of the night rose and fell.

The Settlers' house being nearest, they went there to phone the police and return Miss Butler. Jane led the two who were lost and then found to the door, said what must be said, phoned the report that would bring Chris and the others home.

Peter and she drove home.

It was later than she guessed, close to eleven. All the other children slept. Tory and Clare came at the door-sound. Clare ran to hug Peter. Tory went to the stove for the pot of cocoa which had stood ready to be heated.

"He's all right," said Jane. "So is Miss Butler. And Peter is a most wonderful son."

"You're not angry at him," said Clare. "So often mothers are."

"I'm proud of him."

Tory set a hot cup of coffee for her, cocoa for Peter.

"I have to go up and see Mary first," Jane said.

"She's sleeping."

"I'll wake her up. Because she did find Peter."

The boy, bent over the cocoa, shook his head. "Can you beat that! That stupid Mary knowing where I was. That kills me."

Later, when only Chris and Jane and Peter sat by the fireplace and midnight was chiming, Peter himself told his father what had happened.

"We had gone for a walk to find primroses."

Chris puffed out his chin. "I don't want you going for a walk or anywhere with that woman any more. Don't see why—a boy looking for primroses!"

Pete looked away, fingers tapping the table.

"Sorry, son. Go ahead. What happened?"

"We found this boat, you know? And because I was so good at rowing she wanted me to give her a ride."

"Since when could you row so well?"

"I learned at camp last summer, remember?"

"Oh. Oh, sure. I forgot."

"Well, I rowed her out to the island. And we got out and sat down and she had a book and she started reading to me. Poetry like. All about islands and water and wild swans and that crap. She likes to read and no one but me listens I guess and sometimes it's okay and sometimes it's not so good so I just pretend to listen and I think about something else, you know?"

"I know."

"So then she falls asleep. And at first I don't want to wake her up, see, because I'm, you know, happy enough, and I was practicing my knots and doing some junk with my knife so I let her sleep. And then I guess I didn't know it but it was getting dark and we were late for supper and then it was dark. So I was waking her up, you know, and she woke up and she was scared stiff and she started to cry and all that jazz."

Peter stopped and picked out a cookie from the plate Jane had fixed. "You know what was bugging her?" He leaned back and crossed his legs, man-of-distinction style. "She was scared stiff to go home because people would think she was crazy, you know? And she has been crazy, I guess, and she was afraid they'd send her back to the crazy house because she kept me out after dark."

Peter sighed. "She was scared stiff, no kiddin'. Jeez was she scared. And I told her, you know, that I wasn't a baby and no one would be very mad but she said people, you know, were always watching her to see if she was well or not, and she was okay, but if she came back and said she had gone rowing with me and fallen asleep and made us late for dinner that would be the last straw."

His mother and father weren't saying anything. He ate another cookie.

"I told her the best way was to go home and tell the truth. I told her to get in the boat. I told her and told her! I said the longer we stay the worse it gets and she started to cry and said we had to hide. So then I said I was going to take the boat and go home myself. But I didn't scare her into coming home even if I did that. She cried and I never saw anybody, not even a kid, so scared. You can't do anything with somebody that doesn't make sense. And I couldn't leave her. I couldn't. And when someone came looking for us I hollered and hollered but the wind, you see, made it so they couldn't hear me. And I couldn't go away and leave her. It was a mess."

The flames of the fire had died. Chris closed his eyes, his brow puckered as if in pain. Then he said,

"You'd better get some sleep, Pete. You've had quite a day."

"Yeah. Well g'night." Through cookie crumbs he kissed his mother on the cheek. "Sure was glad to see you!" He went to his father, wiped his mouth on the back of his hand, kissed him briefly on the forehead. "Can you beat that dumb Mary!"

A moment later, as his parents still sat silent, he came down to lean over the banister.

"This is the day the Lord has made," he sang *sotto voce,* and snickered.

"Let us rejoice and you go to bed in it," his father answered.

FORTY-EIGHT

She found herself going to him. Given joy in her youth. To celebrate. My soul, my soul, why were you troubled within me.

As she went to him a phrase rang in her heart, echoing from the Psalms. Though I walk through the valley of the shadow of death. . . . She entered into his arms.

"Chris! Glory be to God."

He had risen to embrace her and now they sat close to each other, her head resting on his cheek, their arms and hands joined. As if studying aloud a lesson he said,

"All the things I thought might happen, those things I could not have prevented, Jane they were terrible. And what seemed to me the most terrible part was that I didn't know, that I could not see what was happening. I was his father, and, if I knew, I could help, I thought. Chris the father unmighty stumbling around in the dark. Jane, looking for Peter I found I had forgotten really that God knew where he was and what was happening."

He put his arm over her shoulders, drawing her closer, continuing,

"And if I had known where he was I would still have been terrified. Peter on a dark island with a crazy woman? Trying to row in the dark? It wasn't the not knowing. It was the not trusting. I didn't trust even God. I thought that only I should be in control."

"That little kid." She closed her eyes. "Not so little. Seems he was the grownup on the island."

"A little child."

He kissed her then, gently, tenderly, and she turned in his arms and returned the kiss.

"The guardian angel must be exhausted," she said quietly.

253

"Could it have been the angel that gave our Mary the—the second sight? Wouldn't your mother love that?"

"Mary just has a good imagination." Chris chuckled. "She heard the cop talking about the island. She thought it all up herself."

"I think heaven and earth are full of the angels and they came and gave Mary to know where Peter was. Then one batted me over the head till I believed that poor little girl."

"He shall give his angels charge over thee," whispered Chris.

"Then let the angels praise God and thank him for us," she whispered. "It's the right thing to do."

"Very right." *Dignum et justum.*

Carefully he withdrew his arms, and settling her against a pillow got up with a secret smile. He returned with two glasses and an untouched bottle of Chianti, a trifle dusty.

"Celebrate?"

"Yes."

Two glasses of red wine were raised in toast before the hearth.

"Christopher McNamara, I love you."

"And I you."

They did not need to say more. They knew. She had offered. He had offered in return. They drank the wine, and watching each other as if in unfamiliar rite, they rose together from the scarred pine coffee table. Chris replaced the screen by the fire. Together, they went up the stairs.

His mouth found the taste of her mouth. Beneath her tongue was sweetness. They left their clothes in the darkness. They lay on the bed and his left arm was under her head and with his right he embraced her.

The wind defied the windowed walls, testing the privacy of their meetingplace, and its sound spoke of cedar and cypress, red-hearted cedar become incense to the blade that felled it, cypress sighing, raftering back the impending dark-veiled sky.

His hand lay on her breast, finding the white softness of the dove nestling in mountain cleft, and he laid his thirst upon the breast and felt the strength of wine. Like a young antlered shadow, a wildling feeding in lilied meadow, a hart, among the hollows into hidden places, he became her beloved and drew her with him through the dappled hills till she was fainting.

Color flew before her eyes, spiced red and burning royal purple, the clasp of gold and amber, palm-green. In enameled miniature

254

the world came to her, a shape of petal and calyx, a small red apple, a hind thirsting for the waters. She felt her soul speaking through her body, felt she must fall. Her mouth pressed against his throat.

His hand reached as for a keyhole to the garden and she unbolted the bolt and opened and let him enter, the surrender that was triumph, the conquered set free. Flamelike, consuming, the moment joined them. Weightless yet enfleshed in hope and love they lost themselves and each was found in the other. They floated upward from the depths and lay as in sunlight, new and exhausted, comforted, warm.

As they turned to sleep there came in their private hearing the echo of the day. The postunion chant, artless, simple, welling within them. He maketh me to lie down in green . . . he restoreth my soul. Though I walk through the valley of the shadow of death, I shall fear no evil.

They slept knowing the valley might be close at hand.

FORTY-NINE

Already the day had risen cluttered and insistent on trivia. Toilets flushed, a crib shook under restless Teresa, a shoe was lost, cereal bowls clattered. Peter stood in their bedroom doorway wondering if he should be excused from school, surprised that it took his parents a moment to remember why. The man and the woman giggled at a ridiculousness the children could not see. Young eyes, puzzled, pondered, then laughed in heady response.

Chris found Jane poised over an open drawer reading a small calendar with her private symbols on it.

Mary, presenting the back of her dress to be buttoned, eyed her parents. "What are you looking up? Holidays?"

"Planting times," said her father gravely. "Governed by the moon, you know, according to the best almanacs."

Alone again for a moment, dressed for the day, they stood by the bureau.

"Are you sure?"

"I'm sure." She saw the hood of fear drop from his eyes. "But even if I weren't I wouldn't be afraid. I will never be afraid again. We were meant to live like this always. Not once in a while."

"I know." Her shoulders felt young and supple under his fingers. "Never else was it like last night?" he whispered.

"Never."

"Most beautiful is my bride."

Like a bride she passed through the day. She felt in her cheeks, her mouth, her breasts, her skin, in the hidden center, a summer-sunned ripeness, round and soft, and she judged herself blessed. A smile lay like perfume over her.

It seemed to her peace opened within her like a flower, created on the day the Lord had made. The day of sun and laughter and darkness and fear, of Peter and the boat. The woman who was a threat yet needed protection. The girl who posed and pretended second sight yet achieved it. Chance not chance.

She tried to explain to Tory. "The police, the men, no one would have found them. And you know it's not like me to go out in the dark on Mary's word. But if I hadn't—"

"They would have been found sometime." Tory was fretting over her new permanent. The white streak had not curled the same way the rest of her hair had. "Or Peter would have come home." She combed carefully. "I'm all for God, of course, but aren't you maybe reading too much into this?"

"No. Tory, out loud, on the outside, it looks like not much. But it made me know that he really does take care of us if we let him, if we let go and let him catch us."

Tory shrugged. She sensed that Jane was talking of something more than the lost child, some other fear, hidden-rooted, now healed. Well and good. She would not press to hear her friend's secrets. Yet she fidgeted under the effusive vagueness of Jane's joy.

"You were terribly frightened, Jane. Anyone would be. But look, nothing terrible would have happened even if you hadn't believed Mary or she hadn't thought she saw Peter, or if he hadn't even been found at all till morning."

And if there were no peril, Jane knew in silence, there was no proof of rod or staff or watchful eye or hand outstretched beckoning across the waters. She shivered, hesitating.

"Let me be a fool," she said.

But that afternoon Peter, who had enjoyed school immensely that day, led a band of curious to the pond. They came home swooping downhill on their bicycles, skidding into the driveway, narrow-eyed with the impact of new drama.

"Mom!" Peter's voice summoned her shrilly.

"They wouldn't let us go out to the island. They were working there. Last night the wind, you know, knocked down a tree and dropped a live wire on the island."

"Just blowing around, Mrs. McNamara. Swinging death, that's what it was."

"We saw where it was. A million volts or a thousand or something."

"You touch it, Mom, and pfft. Or it touches you. Same thing."

"Happened after Pete and Miss Butler left. Musta."

"Mom." Peter's face, leaning up to hers, grinned with the shivers. "Mom. Do you get what we mean?"

"I do," she said. And knew she had all the proof she needed.

And, most reasonably, she told Chris.

FIFTY

"You're taking your time about dying," Father Tom observed.

"Why not? It's not something one does every day."

"Are you going or staying?"

"Going. But don't rush me."

"Wouldn't think of it."

The big hands, incongruous against the pale wrists, lay useless on the white ribbed spread.

"Tom, how the hell did Annie know I was going to die?"

"I decline to answer."

"She's a foolish woman. And yet, it drives me crazy to think the damn leaves came out right. About me. Wrong a million times, and they have to pick me to be right." He spoke with dead-lipped effort, slowly.

Lying in the white hospital gown, James McNamara seemed thin and grotesque as the modern sculpture he abhorred. His nose loomed large. His skin was waxen, splotched with a Roualt blue and green, his eyebrows black as the lines of stained glass.

"Where is she, Tom?"

"They gave her sedatives. She's been sleeping all day. It was a terrible shock to her, the stroke was so sudden."

"It wasn't the stroke. It was seeing you with the last sacraments." James coughed.

"She'll be better when she wakes up."

"Don't know what to say to her." James sighed. "Should think of something."

"You were never at a loss for words. And you're lapping this up. Best vacation you've had in years. Won't it be a laugh when the doctors turn out to be right and you don't go after all?"

"I'm going."

Silence.

"Tom, am I keeping you?"

"Sure. From my great business. Even the President's trying to get me on my private wire."

James seemed to stretch within himself, not disturbing his paralyzed muscles. Tom had the impression of a creature inside a chrysalis.

"Tom?" The eyes were closed with hooded leathery lids. "You're a bum priest. I wasted my money sending you to the sem. You haven't talked to me about my soul."

"Your what?"

James' eyes opened slowly.

"You never wanted to talk about your soul," the father-brother said gently.

"Where am I going, Tom?"

"To live. With him."

"Purgatory."

"Two to one no. You've been forgiven your sins. If you held nothing back from him, you're okay. Purgatory is a getting ready to love well. If this moment you love God—"

"I haven't had much practice loving." The old eyes closed.

The routine of the day clinked and swished and buzzed around them with white skirts and long white habits, glasses and thermometers, signals, trays.

"I want to see Jane," James said through exhausted lips.

Father Tom brought Jane in, then left her alone with the dying man.

"I'm here." Jane moved closer to the bed.

"You've been good for Chris," he said. "Will you be good to Annie? Someone's got to be good to Annie."

"You've been good to her," said Jane. "I will be too."

"I've been good to her?" He shook his head slightly. "Jane, Jane. God will want to know. He will say to me what about Annie? You're a woman. You know. What can I tell him?"

"Tell him you loved her."

"Holy wedlock." He dragged the words from his chest. "Chris was always trying to tell me about it. Cana. We didn't ever have Cana."

"You didn't need it," she said.

"What can I say to Annie?" The voice was sudden and loud. "I never loved anyone."

"Be still. For goodness' sake be still, or they'll make me leave, and I'm supposed to be taking care of you till Chris and Father Tom come back." The briskness in Jane's voice seemed to reassure him. "Be quiet and listen to me."

He blinked assent.

"You haven't been apostolic in your marriage, and all of a sudden it worries you?" He blinked. "You are worried because you and Annie weren't great lovers? Did you ever get told you should be? You and Annie weren't given a Cana deal. You did what God asked you to do. Better or worse, sickness or health, richer and poorer, till death. And you have loved Annie, James."

Father Tom came in.

"Chris has the children outside," he said. "Do you want them to come in?"

"Yes," Jane said.

"What'd you bring them for?" James rasped.

"Because they love you. And because you love them."

"Hah!"

She turned to Father Tom. "They should see him. And see death. If you've never seen anyone dying it's too frightening later. I want them to know it's part of life."

"Don't sound belligerent. I'm with you."

Jane went out to the hall. Chris, gaunt with strain, went to his father's side. Jane shepherded her children behind him.

James stared at them. Peter and Mary, solemn, awestruck, unconsciously folded their hands as if in prayer, their eyes searching the sick old face for a clue to the truth about death. Luke, excited at being near an adventurer into the unknown, wriggled when the grandfather greeted him by name. Kilian snuffled.

"We prayed for you, Grandfather." A recent reading of *Heidi* had convinced Mary that the name Grandpa was low-tone and babyish.

"Yes, and we went to Communion," added Peter.

"What's it feel like to die?" asked Luke, intensely eager.

"No! It's a good question," said James, stirring and fussing with the movable half of his face in an effect of agreeable sharing of a secret. "Luke, we need to know. Wrong to be ashamed to ask, like it was indecent." Eyes closed, strength gathered, eyes opened. "Feels good."

"Are you scared?" Kilian's voice escaped almost to a shout.

Again the eyes closed, opened. "Yep. A little. All good new things are scary."

Kilian grinned. "Have a good time!"

Chris grabbed the two smallest boys by the shoulder, but what he was about to say in rebuke was silenced by his own father's hawklike gaze. "Grampa's tired now," he said instead. "We'll have to go."

"Kiss him good-bye," urged Jane.

Kilian and Luke did. Peter and Mary stood uncertainly by the bed. Father Tom nodded. "You think there should be more to it than that. Good. Then let us ask Grandpa's blessing."

James, conscious for the first time of his role as patriarch, permitted Tom to lift his hand and hold it on each child's head.

"I love them."

James spoke, and his voice was harsh with surprise.

"Jane! I love them!"

Annie stood in the doorway, without rouge or beads, in a plain brown dress.

James smiled over the children's heads.

"Annie darlin'! I love you too!"

And quietly, with them all there, he closed his eyes and died.

FIFTY-ONE

Jane tried to tell her mother. But all she could write was the lesser things.

"To me September always feels like a real new-year time," she began. "Everything starts over again with school."

She tapped the pen on her teeth. She kept writing to her mother every week, though no answer ever came.

"Gloria writes that the doctor says she's doing fine. And she's keeping busy.

"Annie's bearing up. James' funeral was like a reunion of old friends, and that comforted her. Funny thing, you know, there's an old Irish saying that when one goes, another comes. . . ."

She stopped in midsentence. She could not write what was in her heart.

With the two baby girls she sat among the falling leaves. The gold coins of the birches doubled the sun's gold. The roses, bursting to atone for August, held new blooms high over the twilight blue of the asters, and the squirrels reappeared.

She knew within her that newness had come.

She lay on the grass and studied the sky and was aware of what lay hidden in her. Meg found her mother's face wet and called Teresa who crawled over to see. And Jane said it was nothing, nothing at all.

Only that I am with child. Pregnant, and who knows what will come of this?

Dr. Polla had arranged for tests and the tests were positive. When she saw him in the afternoon she expected him to reassure her, to swathe her with sweet courage. He did not.

"We've got a real problem," he said.

"I thought you'd tell me there was nothing to be afraid of, that I should relax and not worry."

"You're in fairly good shape now," said Dr. Polla.

"You're speaking in guarded tones."

"I am. Look, Jane, this is serious and I'm not going to pretend it's not. You're going to have to be observed very closely. You'll have to follow orders and stick close to me. This is no time for pious platitudes."

"Oh."

He watched her, gauging her reactions, probing for sign of panic.

"I feel fine," she said. "I've felt fine for months now."

"But you've still got that kidney trouble. You're not fine. You know that."

"What does it mean? Will I—I mean, can I have this baby and live? Is there a chance?" Her voice was low.

"Here's what we're going to do." He leaned forward on the shining walnut desk. "We'll have to keep close check on you. Urinalysis every ten days or two weeks. The BUN repeated two or three times a month. You'll be on a completely salt-free diet. And you'll be in here every two weeks from now till that baby is born."

"Till that baby is born."

"That's what I said."

She fussed with cigarette and lighter.

"Jane, if you were the kind of gal who panics, I'd be doing my best to allay that panic. But we know each other well. You knew what you were doing. You're not a panicky female."

She pressed her eyelids shut. Christ, why not let him know I am frightened and panic-ridden, why must he treat me like a calm person?

He was brushing a fleck of dust from his olive-green vest. Silver buttons twinkled as he moved.

"You're a great girl. And grownup. We both know it would have been better if you weren't pregnant. But you are. And I intend to deliver your baby and keep you alive. That's why I'm being practical."

"Good."

"I don't know what's going to happen," said the doctor. "No one knows. You're running a constant danger of getting toxic. But you're equally liable to get through this whole thing without any further damage at all. It's not a good outlook. But it could be worse."

"Gee, thanks."

He smiled. "The safest pregnancies aren't safe. Nothing's safe. Getting in a bathtub even if you're not pregnant isn't safe. Crossing a street. Girls die when they're pregnant and everything's jake but they rupture the uterus maybe, or have a *placenta previa* or something. Jane—you didn't want soft soap. You know I have no bedside manner. You said once that's why you chose me as a doctor."

"That, and your vests." She smiled back.

"So, okay?"

"Okay. Forthright, practical, smiling. And one ray of hope. You did say you plan to deliver the baby."

"Salt-free, remember. And tears are salty, so don't go swallowing any, you hear?"

She met Chris at the station and they went out to dinner.

"One last salted meal," she said. "I'll pretend I didn't see Polla till tomorrow. Then there'll be no more dining out till after the baby."

Chris ordered another Scotch on the rocks.

"Chris, if you don't stop looking like doom and gloom I'll scream."

"Sorry." His eyes avoided hers.

"I need you to be calm and hopeful and happy."

"Jesus Christ, stop it!" he mumbled.

Her lower lip trembled.

"Jane, don't you know how I feel? I—I have—"

"You have what? You have done this to me? Is that what you were going to say?"

The waiter placed the Scotch before Chris. When he was gone she raised her head again and went on, "Chris, you alone didn't do anything. You are leaving me out of this. You're making yourself too darn important, a fine tragic figure, a—a—well, a murderer? What do you think? That I'm going to die?" She drank some water and ignoring the anguish on his face pressed on. "Chris, you're tearing me apart. I don't believe I'm going to die. I believe everything's going to be all right for me and the baby. But what will kill me is if you pull away from me, beating your breast and divorcing me. That's what you're doing. Divorcing us. It's only you had anything to do with this baby? It's not so. It was us, together, wanting and loving—"

"Shh," he warned. "Shhh."

"Don't *shh* me. I'm not talking loud enough for anyone to hear but you. And you can't *shh* me. I'll walk out of here if you don't come back to me and be with me and be a rock and a man I can lean on and—"

"Jane, Jane, you're getting hysterical." He spoke gently, but his words infuriated her.

She sat for a minute playing with the water glass. Then she got up, took her coat, and walked out of the restaurant.

It took some time to get the check for his drinks, and pay for them, and cancel the order for dinner. He was embarrassed and angry. In the parking lot he looked to see if she had taken the car. She had not. He found her sitting in the dark front seat, racked with misery, moaning sobs. He sat behind the steering wheel, silent. The sobs continued, as if they were an irreversible physical process like labor itself.

He folded his lips inward, folded his arms, sat. The sound of Jane surrounded him, accused him, unnerved him.

He put a hand on her coat shoulder. "Jane, please stop crying."

His voice was harsh. He put his arms around her. She huddled against his chest, still shaking.

"Jane, I love you."

"I'm not afraid," she said.

"I'm not either."

Jane slept because he comforted her, and because he was comfortless he did not sleep.

He lay awake beside her, smoking in the dark. The gnawing nausea in his guts did not leave. He recognized that his fears and emotions were making him physically ill. He had personally edited a dozen texts on mental health. He knew what he was supposed to do; he was supposed to articulate his feelings, get them out of him by facing them. That way he could avoid ulcers, neuroses and insomnia.

In a quiet snort of disgust he blew the smoke from his lungs. Why the hell did he have to think about mental health? Why the hell couldn't he have been a less complicated kind of person? There must be less complicated people left in the world. Another kind of man, simpler, more physical, a clod from a peasant past he would have liked to be, a man of sweat and season who could sleep untroubled. Or another kind of clod from a completely mediocre present, not sicklied over with thought, the kind of guy who might get drunk, or take a bubbly patent medicine and a pill and escape.

For Christopher McNamara, whose trade was not with the earth or with assembly lines or paper forms but with intangibles, with ideas and subtleties, there could be no sleep. They said, the writers of sociology, that the more educated a man was the more feminine characteristics he acquired in his personality. He'd even found that in the high school text he was working on now. Love of music. Of art. A religious spirit. Emotional refinement. These unmanly things came with education.

And the ability to worry, and know torment of soul and heart, and lose sleep. The hell with the theory. And the hell with education, too. I wish I were a goddam clod.

I do not believe even a clod could be calm if he knew that because of his love his beloved had come into danger.

People die all the time. Jane may die. I could not go on if she died. But I would have to go on. What would I do with the children? I don't know. It was not merely the thought of death, but of his responsibility for that death that haunted him. Jane might live. Polla says she might have the baby and live. Or she might miscarry, and live.

He lit a new cigarette and hunched himself up on the pillow to consider that God might contrive such a happy answer. He did not dare rest on hope.

If she dies it will be my fault. She did not like it when she thought I was thinking that way. But it is true that I should not have let her come into danger for love of me. I am a husband. By definition a husband is a guardian, a farmer, a vineyard keeper, who tends, defends. The burden was on me.

God! Is this where love leads?

It suffocated him to be still and remain in bed, but if he got up he might waken Jane. He forced himself to feign rest, and lay sweating in the warm autumn breeze.

The next morning on the train, riding with a sinus headache behind the façade of the morning paper, penned in by streaked window glass, the blue plush back of the seat ahead and the cigarette smoke of the man beside him, he nevertheless felt less constrained than at home. Here he could focus on the immediate day ahead.

He closed his eyes, his head back. At nine-thirty the author of the new primer on botany. At eleven a conference to decide whether or not to package a small wooden abacus in the *I Can Do It* arithmetic series. Sometime today he wanted to explore the value of doing a book on coin-collecting.

His mother and her problem. Should she move out of the apartment? Should she sell the bonds James left? Did he think as a widow she could still be patron of the big orphanage card party or was it too soon? Pain shot through his sinus. He had forgotten his antihistamines. He was allergic to lunch with his mother, especially now that she was in mourning. They would have to eat at that department store she liked and he would order a drink, and Annie would say it was unseemly for one recently bereaved. He couldn't tell her his father had been a stranger to him all his life. He would have a double Scotch and tell Annie Jane was having another baby.

He opened his eyes to distract himself with the passing cityscape. Flat walls painted with ads. Fire escapes. Solitary indomitable green trees. Washing on lines. Tired tenement windows. All was hollow, depressing, the more so because all were overworked symbols. He had read too much to feel comfort in reacting with frus-

tration and sadness to these. He was bored with the city's flower-
pots and slops.

There was no escaping. If he was to live this day he had to go
back first and think about Jane. He could not undo what was done.
He could not make her unpregnant. He could not rid himself of his
sadness or of the conviction of guilt, with will or pill purge the
misery oppressing him. He was a man who would feel responsible
no matter what anyone said. And Annie he guessed would say
plenty. Then what could he do? There was not a word of prayer
left in him. He needed not words or thought but action, something
hard to do.

The challenge, the answer surged in him so that the newspaper
protested, crackling in his tightened hands. He could and must give
Jane what he owed her: courage and love and faith.

His feelings, his sufferings were his own, and they must remain
his own. This sacrifice he could make, that with the help of God
he could behave as if he lived in joy and trust. He must strive to
convince her, yet not make her feel he did not care; and he must
never burden her with his fear.

She had been happy this morning at breakfast. She had come
home from Mass smiling, even gay.

He smoothed the newspaper, folded it, put it in his attaché case.
He would bring it home to Jane that night. Maybe some perfume
too.

FIFTY-TWO

At first she thought she ought live each day as precious, penulti-
mate.

Before the altar in the morning Mass she pledged herself so to
live that she would leave a legacy of love and joy if she did die.
She looked at the children, resolving to wrap within the memory of
each hour a pearl to be found long after she was gone.

She would not lose her temper, nor let her own bureau drawer
or closet be untidy.

She went to the friary to tell Father Juniper.

266

"And so," she said, "I came to you. You'll have to show me how to be perfect. You can see why."

"Most ridiculous thing I ever heard!" He laughed, swinging the knotted cord of his habit in his hand.

"Don't laugh. Don't you believe me?"

"I believe you think you are going to die. And you want to be a saint, right now, quick."

She bit her lip.

"Jane, you know better than that." From the depths of his sleeve he took an apple, shined it, offered it to her. She refused.

"I thought at least you would take me seriously."

He bit into the apple. "Jane, child, do you think there is anything new about living in the shadow of death? It seems new to you because you have been made to realize it dramatically. But we all live in danger of death. The saint said that if he knew he was going to die tonight he would keep on hoeing his garden."

She dug her hands in her suit-jacket pockets, and stood by the tree looking away over the lawns. On the hill leaves of red and orange trembled in the sun.

"I don't want to keep on doing what I have been doing," she said. "No matter what happens. It must be something better that I do. You told me everyone must be a saint." She faced him. "Please tell me how," she said simply.

"Our Lord told us all how. By loving. It's all in that one word, the cross, the salvation, the resurrection. In loving. You've found the way. Just keep on." He stood up, eyeing a squirrel. "That's the hard part, keeping on. You will find you still have the same old faults you're so weary of. You will have to walk blind, by faith. The nearer you get to God, the farther away he will seem."

"Do you think I will live?" she asked slowly.

"Forever."

She sighed. "I'm overdramatizing, you mean. You make me feel foolish. It would be more fun being heroic."

"But people who love God are realists," he said. "By the way, you might pray for me. I seem to have lost your friend Julian Newman. I couldn't help him. I horrify him, I think."

"He isn't coming into the Church?"

"Perhaps he'll try somewhere else."

"But if he doesn't like you—"

"I pity him. But he may get in in spite of it." Juniper chuckled.

"I don't understand you," she said. "You haven't even told me to offer this up, or anything."

"I despise that phrase. What in heaven's name does God want with your fear? Or with pain? Or with anything? Do you think he's a sadist?"

She blinked as he thrust his head close to hers. "Jane, you are to live with him and in him and for him and be glad. Offer him your gladness and be still and know that he is God. And don't try and outguess him."

As the days passed the constant buoyant sensation of good health reassured her. Her regular tests and checkups proved she was more than holding her own. Chris's calmness calmed her.

"I decline to be afraid." He smiled.

"I was afraid to tell Annie," she said.

"When I told her, I convinced her we'd been planning and praying for this child. She thinks we're crazy, but that's all right."

She was terrified of telling her own mother. They waited for Gussie's birthday, then called her long distance.

"A special surprise for your birthday," Chris said. "You'll have a new grandchild next June."

"Chris sounds happy!" said Gussie indignantly when Jane came on the phone.

"So'm I."

"Do you know what you are doing? Do you know you may be killing yourself?"

"What makes you think I'd be killing myself?" asked Jane, her eyes checking with Chris to be sure he had not mentioned any complications.

"I can't tell you how grieved I am," said Gussie. "And don't you dare wish me a happy birthday. I couldn't stand it."

"They'll never understand," Jane whispered to Chris. "But if only, even though they don't understand and think we're dead-wrong crazy fools, if only they'd give us credit for living the way we believe!"

He took her in his arms, smoothed her hair.

"I love you," she said. "Without you I think I'd give up. For this cause shall you forsake all others and cleave only . . . I'm cleaving, Chris. Thank God you're so strong."

She told Tory herself and Tory was appalled and embarrassed, and furious at Chris.

268

Bewildered, Jane fought back. "You're supposed to be my dearest friend. You know better than to say things like that. I can't believe you'd be like this."

"You'll be telling me you're thrilled about the baby next."

"I am."

"Oh, come on. Chris should have his head examined."

"Chris had no more to do with this than I did. What in the world do you think? What kind of marriage do you have, for God's sake?"

"I'm all for you, Janie. Sorry about what I said. You caught me off balance."

"Sure. I know."

"This is the way things are. It can't be changed. So—we go on from here, right? What can I do to help you?" Tory smiled.

"Just make like there's nothing different. And keep telling me I don't want any salt."

"Jane?" Clare poked her head in the laundry-room door. "Came to tell you the date's all set. I'm having the baby three weeks from today. Dr. Polla's doing the Caesarean. Hi, Tory!" She sat down heavily. "Hey, what's the matter, Jane? You look like you've been crying."

"I've been *not* crying," said Jane.

"It's nothing," said Tory.

"I'm going to have a baby," Jane said.

"Wonderful!"

"It's not. I'm not supposed to have one, according to Polla."

"Oh, what do doctors know. They keep saying I can't have any more Caesareans, even Polla says that, and he's done fine on me so far." She smiled at Jane with a look of sweet affection. "Jane, God loves you. There's nothing to be afraid of."

"I'm not afraid."

"She's just being practical," said Tory.

Clare put her hand on Jane's. "You know there's nothing to be afraid of. You have faith."

"I know," Jane said politely.

"Look, Clare, leave her alone."

"Jane, God loves you," Clare said earnestly. "Do you think he would let anything happen to you now?"

"I think," said Jane equally earnestly, "if you say God-loves-you once more I shall throw up."

Clare nodded indulgently. "Never mind. We all get to feeling low. Hormones or something. That's right, have a good cry and get it out of your system. But just don't be afraid."

Lidwina called Jane. "How does it feel to be God's prize exhibit in the argument against Planned Parenthood, old girl?"

"What?"

"You've got the whole blamed parish supposed to be praying for you. Clare Sullivan says we've got to convince God not to let anything happen to you because after all if it did it would be just terrible."

"It sure would."

"But she's not thinking of that. She's just thinking of a bad press for the cause of her large-family crusade."

"Lidwina, you're being unkind. Clare isn't like that."

"Not consciously. But she makes me slightly ill. And more than slightly mad. There's no privacy around people like that. It makes me ill to think everyone's talking about you."

As they talked about you, thought Jane. "They mean well," she said. "And we all need prayers."

"The more certain Clare is that everything's going to be peachy-creamy, the less certain I am," she confided to Chris.

"Know what you mean. Same way some nuns make me think I don't believe in Christ at all. Just different eyes looking at the same thing. Don't let it bother you."

"At the Mother's Circle this week I wished there were a hole I could hide in. Everyone was so darn impressed that I look healthy and unconcerned."

"Stay away from them, maybe? Or just have fun prancing around looking healthy and unpious."

Around her the steady tumult of the stream of life tugged at her as if she were caught in some off-channel pool, till at last it drew her nearer the current.

It was impossible to remain posed for happy memories, to be forever remembering the nearness of death. As the days wore on through the stealthy twilight of November, time again stretched to the horizon. She spanked Mary one day for stealing butterscotch cookies. She screamed at Kilian for making too much noise. She found herself alive and laughed. The only difficulty was that she never knew from one day to the next which emotion would seize her. Fear and faith, she was swung from one to the other by a force that had nothing to do with logic.

When Clare was delivered of her baby Jane visited her in the hospital.

Clare turned her great kind blue eyes up and said, "Jane dear, you'll see, everything's going to be fine." Jane smiled, a feeling of fondness for Clare driving out annoyance.

"You know," said Clare shyly, "Bart's been scolding me. Telling me I have no business talking to you the way I have. He's really angry. Are you angry, too? He says I have a mother-of-the-world complex. Maybe I have. Sometimes the things we want to say come out so different in front of other people. Like singing. Alone in the bathtub it sounds swell. Jane, I don't want to sound over-pious."

"Tell Bart it doesn't bother me at all," Jane said. "Not any more."

That night as she lay in Chris' embrace she explained to him, "Because I wasn't afraid any more I didn't get mad at all. And you know why I'm not afraid? It's because of you."

Only in the nights, when she would wake suddenly, totally alone with the unknown in her womb, did she know fear. Then she could feel the dark earth rolling and reeling through the dark void. To whom could she cry out? Who was there to understand that cycle of terror?"

God had gone away.

It had occurred to her that he might well show her some special sign of his love. It seemed reasonable that if you were walking through that valley for his name's sake he might give you what the books call sensible consolations. A vision, a voice in the soul, perhaps. At least the nudge of the rod and staff. Some talisman . . .

But not even in sin had she felt this abandoned by him. He did not seem real at all.

Wakeful, she did not waken Chris. How much could she ask of him? He had no fear. In the dark a tremor of resentment of his calm stirred. She quelled it. There was no one to whom she could talk except to God, yet prayer now was nearly impossible. She compelled herself to take the rote prayers and repeat them. They fell back down upon her like weights. She twisted on her pillow. Surely no one heard those prayers?

Doubt lay over her like a monster body seeking entrance. Not whether she would live or die. But whether it could be that she had been mistaken in the way to please God.

She would not surrender.

FIFTY-THREE

Abruptly, Jane decided to visit Gloria.

"Later on I may have to stick close to home," she explained to Chris. "If I don't go now she'll have her baby and I'll never have been to see her."

He wondered why it was only now that she thought of going. All summer it hadn't occurred to her to visit the Home for Homeless Mothers. He decided not to ask her why. He accepted help with children and food from Martha and Tory, and waved Jane cheerfully off on the train.

Alone in the coach Jane tried to think. She knew she was afraid to see Gloria. Afraid she would find her self-assured sister a dismal figure of woe. But, she admitted privately, even more afraid of herself. I want to help her, to comfort her, to show her I love her. I want to prove to her I'm not the self-righteous prig I've been in the past. I made out all right with Lidwina. And with Agnes. I've learned a lot. I hope to God I've learned enough.

I haven't even let myself think how awful it must be for Gloria in the Home. With all those other girls, and who knows what kind of people they are? And all alone. Poor lonely Gloria. She must be frightened. She's written that it's a nice place, but I don't really believe her. She's got guts, my little sister, to go through with the whole sordid lonely business. And I haven't even had the guts to go see her.

If I can just break the pattern, she thought, staring out the dining-car window later. But Gloria has a picture of me in her head, and I find myself acting the way she thinks I will. And she has a picture of herself as different from me, and she likes to act to fit that picture, and she may end up becoming that way really, and forever, so that nowhere underneath is there any of my little sister left.

This could be, she thought, the chance to cut through the barriers that estranged Gloria from me, the chance for the closeness I've waited for so long. Humbly, she prayed that she would not ruin the chance. Don't let me be overwhelming. Don't let me get mad at her. Please, once, let her do the understanding. Let her understand me and love me. I need it. Let me remember that.

At the doorway in the strange city street Jane faltered, then rang the bell. A nun opened the door, as if on some particularly charming boarding school. Snatches of a choral group rehearsal mingled with laughter, and from an upper window Jane heard voices talking about a home permanent.

She was left to wait in a room where sunlight shimmered on waxed floors and bowls of marigolds shone on a dark Victorian whatnot.

Gloria paused, catching her breath in the doorway.

"Jane?"

The sisters embraced. Stunned at the actuality of Gloria in her pink maternity smock, Jane sighed.

"Gloria, you look wonderful."

"I am."

Shyness surprised them, and they laughed together. "Let me show you the place," Gloria said. She led Jane on tour, to pleasant bedrooms, to sewing and painting classes, refectory, chapel, through a flower garden to the medical building with its labor and delivery rooms, its nursery of babies.

At last they sat together near the scarlet-and-white petunia beds in the shade of an apple tree.

"I'm glad it's so lovely here," Jane said quietly. Hesitantly she added, "I came to cheer you up and help, but—"

Gloria cocked her head and laughed. "Oh?" she said. For the first time Jane noticed the mascara on her eyelashes. Even now, even here, she thought, she feels she must cling to the old pose. Oh Gloria, Gloria. But she would go on. "Well, I thought you might be, oh, lonely or discouraged or frightened or something. I didn't dream you'd be so much yourself."

"Oh, I see." Gloria smiled. "You know, you look so disappointed I should be insulted. You're still—a dear pious snob. No, don't get mad. It's a waste of time for us to be angry with each other, Jane. I'm glad to see you. I love you for wanting to—help me. Now, if I don't need cheering up, must that ruin it all?"

Jane smiled, in spite of herself. "No. Nothing's going to be ruined. Are they nice to you here?"

"Very. I thought they'd be foul. But these nuns do us the courtesy of assuming that some of us at least know we made a mistake and feel bad enough about it without sermons. They haven't tried to save my soul once. Remarkable."

"They're great gals," Jane said.

Gloria nodded. "Can't help liking them."

"You're not afraid," Jane said.

"No. I've been here a while. Heard lectures. Seen gals go in and come out. I'm not afraid." Gloria's face seemed suddenly young and sweet. "Besides, I have a sister who has babies all the time," she said.

And then, without warning, Jane began to cry. Tears wet her new black pocketbook.

"Jane. What's the matter?"

Gloria took her hand and held it.

"It's not fair. I shouldn't feel this way but I do and all I can say is it's not fair." Embarrassed, Jane turned her head, but she could not keep still. "It's so darn nice here. You've got it made. Do I ever get a rest? Do I get to sit without children screaming and pulling at me? Nobody gives me lectures to keep me from being afraid."

Gloria handed her a lit cigarette. "I don't remember when I ever saw you cry, not since we were kids."

"Well, I'm crying now. And I don't want to. I came here to visit you, to help you. But the truth is I need you more than you need me now."

"Silly."

"It's crazy. I'm almost jealous of you. God, that's crazy." Jane drew on the cigarette and watched the smoke. "Funny, isn't it. You had trouble talking to Mother when you knew you were pregnant. So, you talked to me. Now it's the other way round."

"You mean you're having another baby? Jane, that's—but Mother's used to your having scads of babies by now. Hey, you look scared stiff."

"I am. I'm scared because I was told not to have another baby. I might die."

"Oh God," said Gloria. "No wonder you cried."

Unexpectedly she put an arm around Jane, and in spite of her best efforts Jane felt the sobs rising within her again. She buried her face in Gloria's shoulder. Silently, Gloria held her. Two young girls, still pimpled with adolescence, walked by, carrying stacks of baby clothes.

"This is awful," Jane said at last. "I'm stopping it right now. I've stopped." But still the tears came.

"There, there," Gloria said. "If I were in your place I don't think I'd ever stop."

Jane sighed, regained control of herself, and sat up. Gloria took her arm away.

"Never mind me," Jane said. "You're the one we're supposed to be worrying about."

Gloria stiffened. Jane was wiping her eyes.

"Big sister's back," Gloria said.

"Well, I can't go all to pieces when I came here to cheer you up, can I?"

"Of course not." Gloria bent her head.

"Gloria, what are you going to do, after the baby's born?"

"Who knows?"

"Does Hack know where you are? Do you ever hear from him?"

"He's been to see me three times now."

"And none of us ever came till today!"

Gloria shrugged. "Mother couldn't come because she doesn't know where I am, and she doesn't know because I don't want her to come. And you're busy."

"I didn't think they'd let the—fathers—come here."

"They use quite a technique on remorseful fathers here. Keep them away at first. Interview them. Discourage them. Reassure them. Screen out all the neurotics with a sense of martyrdom or insecurity. It was a couple of months before they'd let Hack see me. He—he's convinced he wants to marry me."

"Do you want to marry him?"

"Look, Jane. You and I still talk different languages, and always will, I'm afraid."

"But, I thought—Gloria, just now when you put your arms around me when I was crying, I thought we were so close again. That everything was nice and simple, the way it used to be."

Gloria started to speak, then shrugged and smiled. "We're as close as we can get," she said finally. "We can't help being separate."

"But are we?"

Mascaraed lashes snapped in a wink. "We are. As the experts would say, the frames of reference we use are all different. To you love and marriage are religious, all tied up with God and sacrifice. I don't see it that way. I don't want to be married just because of a child."

"Will you leave the child here? For adoption?"

The flippant look left Gloria's face. "Hack wants us to marry and adopt our own child."

"That would be wonderful. Everything would be solved."

"Would it?"

"You wouldn't throw away a happy ending, would you, Gloria? That would be like spitting in God's face."

"For you, yes. For me, no. God has nothing to do with me. And I don't think it would be a happy ending. I can't make anyone see that I don't think marriage is the answer to love at all. Marriage is a contract that some kinds of people want to make. I don't. Or at least not now. Love fouls it up. If there's no love to foul it up you can live out the contract. But if a man loves you he is defenseless and you can't treat him like an equal and the contract won't work. It's very simple, really. No one thinks of forming any other contract or corporation on the basis of emotion or physical desire."

"Still full of theories." Suddenly Jane was furious. "The girl scientist! What you're saying is not 'I don't love him so I won't marry him,' but 'I can't marry him because I love him.'"

"Only no one believes I mean it."

The lowering sun pushed the coverlet of shade over the bees and butterflies lingering in the flowerbeds.

"I think," said Jane, "I'd better find out about trains for home."

"You brought a suitcase. I took it for granted you must have planned to spend the night."

"Not really. I think I've stayed away long enough." She took the timetable from her purse.

"We'll have to get a cab right away if you're going to get that one. I'll go call." Gloria stood up, her head framed by the bough laden with small green apples. "I haven't helped you, Jane. I can't because you can't let me. And I've made you unhappy. We see things too differently. Being pregnant doesn't make me a mother. That's the way it is."

"Yes. But Gloria—I wanted us to think the same way."

"You wanted me to think your way. I wish I could say I was sure everything would go right for you, that it's good and right for you to be having this child and therefore and so on. But to me the fact of marriage doesn't change things. I don't think your pregnancy is holier than mine. Or safer in God's hands. I think both of us made a mistake."

Jane, her hands gathered over her pocketbook, rose. She looked at her sister, who had once been a child with her, once climbed an apple tree to read a blue book of fairy tales, and was now a woman alone.

"I do see, Gloria," she said. "There's a mystery that's between us. I'll be thinking of you when the time comes. I'll be praying for you. I'm sure you'll be fine. I—I love you. But—

"I am glad that you will not keep your child with you, Gloria. For the child's sake, I'm glad."

FIFTY-FOUR

"I was down in the orchard with the bee-bee gun," Father Juniper said. "Squirrels." His cheeks were red from the cold.

"I'm not doing very well," she said.

"Not a saint yet?" Father Juniper was eating a banana. The sweet overripe smell rose in the crisp air.

Jane sat on the stone wall of the terrace.

"You're vile? Horrid?" He nodded. "Good!"

"Oh, there must be someone in this whole Church who makes sense. But—I've been going to confession to Father Temple and—"

"Good." Father Juniper blinked.

"—and he doesn't take me seriously. Neither do you. Look, I used to be a much better person than I am."

"You used to think you were." He ate the banana.

"I went to see my sister. She was sweet to me and I was horrid to her. Mean. I wanted to be mean when I left her and I was." Jane frowned. "And at home. Father, I used to keep my temper, but now—"

Now twenty times a day or more, it was too much for her. With the best will in the world she rebelled against the gift of herself. She who had never struck her children in anger found herself now slapping Mary's face, screaming in fury at Kilian's tantrums.

It shocked her to see and hear herself. This morning, while she bathed Teresa upstairs, Meg toddled off downstairs to mix salad oil and cleanser all over the kitchen floor. Jane howled with anger and frustration, ranted, knowing that small Meg's face was terrified and tear-stained. In the midst of her own noise and confusion she felt within her a power struggling to be free: a murderous power, bare-shouldered, sleek, slippery, reaching to drive her forward, urging her to pick up her own child and hurl her against the wall.

White and shaking she held to the kitchen sink till the anger died. She looked at Margaret's smeared, blotched face and understood that she might have injured it. Was this how it happened, when one read in the newspapers of the most sickening and bestial crimes? Over such a tiny misdeed of such a tiny child?

She sank on her knees in the oily slime on the linoleum and hugged Meg to her and sobbed. The child pulled away, fascinated and laughing to see her mother crying. The rage seemed not to scar her at all. Now most certainly she wanted no part of her mother's remorse.

"And now you feel like a whited sepulcher, a Pharisee, a damned hypocrite, and it's very hard to believe loving God does any good, is that it?" Father Juniper folded the banana skin neatly and tucked it into his cowl.

"Yes. Loving God, wanting to do right, didn't help me when I saw my sister. I'm not changed. Not a bit."

"And you did not know you were such a horrible person? That you were capable of any sin in the book?"

"I never— No, I did not know."

"We prefer to forget we still need saving. We want to love God. But it distresses us to admit we need a redeemer."

She said nothing.

"You must keep on begging God to make you a saint. That will make things worse, of course. But you must do it. You can't turn back now."

He sat down on the wall.

"Ask to be a saint. That's the one prayer that's always granted. And if you do, I promise you, you'll be very discouraged. You'll learn over and over again every day the depths of foul nastiness that are in you."

She drew in her breath.

"You are surprised?" He smiled. "But the nearer you get to the light, the more clearly you can see. Read the letters and diaries of the great saints. They call themselves the worst of sinners. Are they pretending? They are not. The holier they become, the more they see of their own ugliness." He coughed. "When you think you are doing well, when you are good and keeping your temper and being charming, that's the time to beware. It's when you can honestly say: there's not a single sin I'm safe from, and I am horrid and dull— then God is at work."

He stood up. "And then you can be all things to all men. Don't look at your faults. Look at the Christ. And the people he loves."

278

She went into the chapel, dark now except for votive candles and the red sanctuary lamp to the left of the altar.

She tried repeating his message: The holier you become the worse you become. Or the worse you seem. Out loud, in company, the idea would sound ridiculous, a perverted rationalization to be battled with fine clear obvious quotations and facts.

She looked into the shadows around the tabernacle. No sign appeared, no vision. The decision must be hers, made on faith. She could write off Juniper as a dispenser of strangely twisted consolation, a crazy man with a knack for making holy nonsense. Or accept what he said as coming from God. I believe it, she said. Without understanding, without proof.

Her body shuddered as it would after being forced to go without breathing in a prolonged underwater exercise. She went in peace.

She went to see Tory, not knowing why she went that night.

More and more now she did not know why she did things. At first this bothered her. She had been one to say, I think this or I feel this, searching herself for motives. Now she moved through a world of moments, each intensely real yet isolated, completely in the present.

Blood-rust and grey-green, the color of the last chrysanthemum leaves, arrested her. The taste of the air surprised her beyond the smoldering leaf piles in the lavender afternoons. She turnd to meet each voice and face as if it were new. The voice of little Meg trailing shreds of song through the house, the smell of Mary's newly washed hair in a good-night embrace shocked her with love.

She spoke and laughed and went as if she were led, but more simply even, because she arrived at each moment as if unaware of the last.

Peter.

At the kitchen table he worked on his model planes while his mother cooked. He liked it now, being near her. Out of the corner of his eye he studied her. She turned unexpectedly, cookpot in hands.

"Gobs and gobs of green greasy gopher guts," he sang.

She laughed. "That's all you'll get for supper."

Laughter.

Chris heard it as he came home, and carried the echo of it as a talisman. The laughing eyes of his wife.

"More beautiful than ever," he said, dancing with her at a party in Tory's house.

"More beautiful," he said in bed.

"I feel drunk," she said and laughed. "People move in and out and they talk and I talk and we talk and the children—the world is a kaleidoscope and everywhere I move it is totally different. I could go on like this forever."

His arms around her, he caught his breath, and wondered how long her forever would be.

FIFTY-FIVE

In the windswept Connecticut autumn Father Temple likened himself to an oak leaf, aged, wisp-dry, useless, yet stubbornly attached to the branch, ready to endure winter and outlast the leaves of lesser trees. Father Macy got the hay fever, and an allergy to house dust. Father Mongiano suffered the indignities of the virus three times in rapid succession. Father Temple never was ill.

He put his coat in the closet, folded his scarf away, and sank into his easy chair. He had done all he could about the O'Sheas. And that should get Jane McNamara out of his mind.

"Haunted me, she did. Haunted me. Without saying a word." The parakeets cocked their heads as if listening.

He sighed. It had been an engrossing business, that chase of Michael O'Shea. Though he'd resolved to leave the modern sheep to the modern curates for humility's sake, he had made an exception for Mike. After all, Mike might be young, but his type was not new, the political Irish handshaker like his father before him. Father Temple had known his father well, watched young Mike grow up. That was reason enough to justify not sending a curate. That, and the fact that Jane had been bringing Lidwina to daily Mass now for a week, and looking at him with those big brown eyes as if she expected something from him.

At any rate he had left his study and stalked Mike quietly, and he thought unobtrusively, in Mike's natural habitat, the K of C poolroom and the bar of the AOH. Just dropping in, casually, as if he always stopped by those places. Ordering a glass of port at the bar. Circling his prey. It had been exciting.

And finally Michael O'Shea could not avoid sitting down with him.

"You should forgive her, Mike," Father Temple said. "Go home. It's the way to do. You don't like living alone. You weren't cut out to be a bachelor. And you're a big man, Mike, like your father. Big enough to forgive. Women are weak. She loves you, Michael."

Mike had only shrugged. But Father Temple went to see Lidwina and promised her Mike would be home again someday, and tried to tell her how to act when he did come home.

"Cook him his favorite meal, you know," said the old priest. "That's the old true way. Don't laugh. In the Bible itself when a woman wants a man to do something, or to love her, she feeds him a feast. Makes sense. And he'll be here, I promise you."

Then, in his own devious way, he went into the church and knelt at Mary's altar and told her he had promised and she'd better see to it that the promise was kept, since it would be most unbecoming if her priest were made to look like a fool.

"It's in the providence of God now," he said to his parakeets. "I've done all I can."

Jane will be pleased, he thought. The thought annoyed him. He wanted to rest. The doctors ordered him to nap every afternoon. But the thought of Jane disturbed him. He could not say why. She had a beautiful smile. Beautiful.

"I'm getting to be a silly old man," he muttered.

He did not really believe that.

Nothing would lure him again from his decision to stay within the rectory. That much he promised himself.

It was because of Jane McNamara that he had gone to see Felicity Lawrence, and that had not turned out well. Now because of Jane he had gone after O'Shea. That would be all.

Father Macy and Father Mongiano between them could do a better job of tending the flock. It was, Father Temple thought wearily, arrogance to deny that. There was no question that God wanted him to stick to supervising the building of a convent.

"I baptized the Sullivans' new baby today," said Father Mongiano, his eyes twinkling. "You'll never guess the name they inflicted on him."

"Quite liturgical, I suppose," growled Father Temple.

"Oh, quite. His name is Aesop—Aesop Marius, of course."

"There's no such saint as Aesop!"

"Unfortunately, there is," Father Mongiano looked at his pastor, trying to assay his mood. "I wish you'd talk to the Sullivans, Father I have a feeling there's something wrong there."

"That's your department. You're the Cana priest." Father Temple reached for a roll.

"But you're their pastor."

"I saw Elmo Milder today," Father Macy interposed quickly. "Agnes is dead only six months, but he's a new man. Cheerful, outgoing. That hangdog look he had is a thing of the past. Has an aunt taking care of the child. I asked if he'd work on the bazaar, but he turned me down."

"By the way, how are the McNamaras?" Father Temple shouted, cutting into the pot roast. "No one seems to mention them in this daily newscast any more."

"Haven't seen Chris in quite a while," said Father Macy.

Father Mongiano looked at him.

"They're fine, I suppose," said Father Macy, looking at his meat.

"I don't think they're fine," Father Mongiano said. "Jane's expecting a baby. And Chris is still—Chris. Writing columns, you know. Giving a few talks. But—"

Father Temple was busy with the gravy. "But what?"

"I can't help feeling—if there were more time," the curate's dark eyes searched his pastor's face. "I don't know what troubles the McNamaras, and I don't have time to find out. I think there's something wrong with Al and Tory Burke too, but I can't take time to go see them. There isn't any time for the really important things, when you get through with the census and the CYO and the choir and the bazaars. It doesn't seem right."

"I'd hate to think you were complaining, Father Mongiano," the pastor shouted.

"Of course not, Father. But the parish is too big for two men to handle."

"Two men?"

"As you said yourself, it's the young legs must do the work."

"Are you implying—"

"I'm not implying. I'm saying. Father, when you went out the way you did after Michael O'Shea, you looked twenty years younger. You're wrong to wall yourself up in the rectory. You do yourself grave injustice, and you do the people injustice. They need you. They need priests who will go out and reach them."

"I'd like to think the people need me," Father Temple said

quietly. "It's a pleasant feeling, to think yourself a storybook priest, beloved and leaned on by your flock. But I am past that now."

Unnoticed by the pastor, Father Macy rolled his eyes upward and held his breath.

"Humility," Father Temple continued. "A hard lesson to learn. It will take humility for you to realize that you serve God through the work you are assigned, and it's self-seeking to think you can do better otherwise. I can't expect you to understand that, Father Mongiano, but I ask you at least to respect it."

Father Mongiano put down his fork. "I don't think it's humility, Father, that keeps you at your desk."

The pastor's eyes flew open. "And what do you think it is?"

Father Mongiano's cheeks flushed. "I'd rather not say."

FIFTY-SIX

A moment of time. Set off from others. One. Another.

"You are looking," said Chris, "at a man who has moved up. I have a new office, with real walls."

She hugged him.

"And money," he said. "Lots more nice money every month."

"I'm proud of you," she whispered.

"You don't seem surprised."

"I'm not." She laughed. "It surprises me it took them this long to know they had something great in you."

"I'm surprised," he admitted.

"I wonder how she is," said Jane.

"How who is?"

"Krena, of course."

"What made you think of her?"

"If she hadn't left the office," said Jane, "this wouldn't have happened now. You told me they were shuffling people around filling her place. She was scheduled to move up, wasn't she? They were grooming her, with that book you worked on. But she left." She snuggled in his arms. "How nice that she left. Not but what you'd have been promoted sometime. They can't stay blind forever." She kissed him. "But it's more convenient now."

She did not see his face.

"I'll never understand you," he said. "I never know what you'll say next."

Annie refused the cup of tea.

"Don't tell me you've given up reading the leaves?" Chris asked with mock horror.

"That's only nonsense. I never took it seriously, and you know it." Annie bent over the pile of mending.

"Jane's working you too hard, Ma. Relax."

"Don't you start meddling," Annie said. "That girl needs rest. I just wish she'd rest more."

"Wouldn't know what to do without you, Annie." Jane smiled.

Annie placed a patch on Pete's khakis. "I feel sorry for some of my friends," she said. "When I told them you called and asked me to come up here weekends and help you, they couldn't believe it. No one ever calls them. Their children don't want them around."

"Probably never occurs to them to ask for help," Chris said. "They might be afraid of hurting their feelings."

Jane put her feet up on the couch. "No, they probably have horrid mothers-in-law, real doom-and-gloomers. We're just lucky. Ours is different."

"Ah," said Annie, "when you've lived and suffered, as I have, when tragedy has touched your life, my poor James struck down in the prime, you learn. I've no use for the old biddies who look for gloom. Some of my best friends are like that. They can't help it. They haven't been through what I have."

Chris cocked an eyebrow, but Jane shook her head at him.

"You mean a lot to the children, Annie," she said. "And to me. But I'm glad you gave up tea leaves." She turned on her side, smiling. "They made an awful mess in the sink."

She would have said she did not pray.

"I have forgotten how. I can't say one 'Hail Mary' from beginning to end."

Father Temple stirred on his side of the confessional. "That happens," he said. "Don't let it bother you. Words don't matter. You pray without knowing it, if God so wills."

"I don't understand," she said later to Father Juniper.

"Chris, with him, do you always talk? A look, a glance, isn't that

284

enough? Just being together? When two people love each other, they do not always need words," he said.

She saw that his beard was showing grey.

For a moment in the beauty shop she caught her breath. She had been thinking of Felicity Lawrence.

"And you're here!" She laughed. "And you look wonderful!"

"Thank you. I'm better now. I was sick, you know." Her hair was hidden by a net, and with the white towel around her neck, she looked disturbingly pale. Her face was grained with wrinkles. "What are you doing here?"

"Getting a permanent. For my birthday," Jane said. "You know, Felicity, I've missed you."

"Oh really? But we haven't seen each other since you gave a party. Right after a baby. And now you're expecting again? Isn't that a little soon?"

Jane smiled. "We like babies," she said.

"Wasn't it at your party that we met Krena McDowell?" asked Felicity. "Yes, of course. Have you heard about her?"

Jane shook her head.

"She's pregnant." Felicity reached for a cigarette. "She wanted a child. Now she's having one."

"I know she quit work to be with her husband," said Jane.

"Don't be so innocent," Felicity said, and the unexpected brittleness of her voice startled Jane. "I'll tell you what I think. She said she found a wonderful doctor. I think she went in for artificial insemination."

"Oh, my God!"

"Don't look so horrified. It's done all the time. Much more than anyone knows." Felicity paused.

"It can't be true," said Jane quietly. "Poor Krena. You're not sure. You don't really know."

Felicity frowned, and a look of pain crossed her face. She's calm, Jane thought. She's better. She's shaken free of grief. But she's not what she was. This is an empty, surface calm, not a serene one. And when she feels anything, what she feels is pain. "I know she's expecting a child," Felicity said. "For sure. In March."

Felicity pulled the dryer hood over her head and switched on the heat.

"And so," Jane said to Tory, "if I hoped to get close to Felicity, I lost the first round. She thinks I'm hopelessly naive, and I think she's still miserable and I couldn't think of a thing to say or do."

Tory leaned on the orange corduroy harem cushion, her red hair sleek as a cap. "You are naive," she said. "You're a pain. What did you want to get close to Felicity for?"

"I've always liked her," Jane said. "And I'd like to help, now. I think she's lonesome."

"Aren't we all?"

Jane looked at her questioningly.

"Well, aren't we? I'm so lonesome I could cry. My kids are growing up, Jane. Someday we're going to be all alone, just Al and me, God help us. All alone. And what will we do alone? We can hide behind the kids now. But when there's no one else in the house but us two?"

"Tory, stop it. You've been carrying this one on too long. You love him and he loves you and—"

"Jane, dear, you're a great gal, but please. No sermons."

"Sorry."

"Don't get me wrong. I like you lots and lots, but I'm getting sick of having the great Jane jammed down my throat. You're getting a hell of a reputation, you know. Oh yes you are. You should hear them all. Clare, Lidwina, Angela, Christine. Oh Jane is so brave. And a saint. She always knows what to say and how to make things come out right. They have you mixed up with God." Tory straightened the seams of her stockings. "Don't forget, Jane, I knew you when. We're friends. But don't spoil it. I'm not listening to any preaching from you."

"Good."

In the silence she could hear her watch tick.

"You're not mad?"

"Should I be? If Clare has even you thinking I'm a pious prig, it's poetic justice. I think it's sort of funny."

"I could bite my tongue," said Tory. "I was mean. Talk to me."

"I've got to get home," Jane said pleasantly. "You are reprieved. Besides, even if I knew what to say, you wouldn't need it. All you need to do is decide to let yourself love Al, and go all the way out to him, and don't forget why you fell in love with him—"

She stopped in midsentence and went to the hall closet for her coat. She continued, her voice muffled. "I'm not saying or doing anything right. Maybe it's a new kind of morning sickness. But

286

we're good friends and you'll forgive me. You won't be able to help it."

"Jane, who could be mad at you?"

"You could. You think I'm making like a saint. If you knew how wrong you were, you wouldn't believe it. Well, I'm many things but I'm not a hypocrite. I can't make like a saint even if I try. Because right now, I'm mad. Matter of fact, it's a damned insult you gave me. Quite a reputation, Jane. A preacher, a pious drip. Thanks a lot. I expected more from an old friend. Who knew me when, Stinker."

She stopped the car out of sight of Tory's house and sat.

Time, an awareness of minutes and hours and past and present, settled on her like a brace, cramping her heart. Her thoughts were in panic: What am I doing? I am no good at whatever I do. I am sick and frightened and useless and I cannot stand myself. I was sure and now I am not sure. The day's voices echoed in her ears, and she felt imprisoned by what other people thought and said.

Then, within her, the child moved. The swift secret kick of the unborn. The moment of first quickening.

She smiled. And drove home, freed again. Knowing only that God had created a soul for the child who turned now dreaming of life.

Moment to moment she lived, her heart light.

FIFTY-SEVEN

The smoke-grey days of early winter wore on. The endless penance of paper work and decisions involved in convent-building, the choice of plumbing fixtures and ceiling tile, the negotiation of bank loans, conferences with diocesan architects, kept Father Temple chained to his desk.

He meant to visit Chris and Jane. He had made a note to do so. But Father Temple had outgrown impulse. And so he avoided Jane.

When Clare Sullivan came to see him he was startled. He never had thought she would choose him to talk to. He was, frankly, afraid of her. She could display piety and grace and charity and apostolic energy on every occasion and he could not on any occasion, and they were both aware of it.

Yet, she sat in his office and she had been crying, and she was a mother who found her new baby, little Aesop, was mentally retarded, and she had not come to the curates but to him. He felt fussy and old and helpless. He could not say one smart thing to her. But when she left she said he had comforted her.

"As I knew you would," she said.

As she knew he would.

"It was Jane who told me to come talk to you. She said no one else could help as much. And she was right. You're a wonderful pastor, Father Temple."

He could see that in her sweet young face the first wrinkles were showing. "Jane?" he asked.

"Jane McNamara." Clare smiled. "She's been going to confession to you, you know. She says you're really pulling her through."

"Ah-hah. Of course, I never know who comes to confession."

I never know, he thought closing the door as Clare left. Jane comes to me. And I help her. What did Clare say, I am pulling Jane through? The old man frowned.

He could not concentrate on the contract he had been studying before Clare interrupted him. He turned off the desk light, rubbed the bridge of his nose, and decided he needed a bit of fresh air.

"You look troubled, Father." Father Mongiano stood beside him.

"You're the Cana priest. You're the expert. Can you tell me what's wrong with Jane McNamara? Or are you too busy with organizations to know about people?"

The quietness of his tone startled Father Mongiano. "I was going to talk to you about that," he said. "People, all kinds of people, have been asking me to pray for Jane. She's supposed to be very sick."

"Have you been to see her?"

"She's up and around. Not on the sick-call list. She looks fine. And this is a busy parish."

Father Temple snorted, and went for a walk.

When he came back the housekeeper said he had a caller in his parlor.

"I'm too busy to see anyone," he said.

"She won't see anyone else." The housekeeper raised her eyebrows meaningfully. "This one you've got to see. But don't ask me why. You cured me of talking, Father. Wouldn't say a word."

He opened the door. Felicity Lawrence was sitting there.

"Felicity?" The old man blinked. "Felicity? Come in, come in. Oh, you are in. It's I who's coming in. Well, this is a surprise. Wonderful. You are here. You look fine. I hope Harold's all right? Nothing wrong? Fine. I'm glad to see you. Yes, indeed."

He shook her hand.

"I don't look fine. I look old. I have as many wrinkles now as an Indian woman. I have an interesting face, as they say when there's no possible camouflage."

"A very interesting face." The priest peered over his desk. "You certainly do. I can't think when I've seen that many interesting wrinkles on so young a woman."

Her wry smile set a new pattern of lines encasing eyes and mouth.

"What can I do for you, Felicity?"

"Father, I surrender."

He blinked uncertainly.

"Aren't you surprised? After the nasty way I treated you?"

"I don't understand."

"Father, must I say it right out?" The wrinkles crazed the paleness of her forehead. "All right then. I would like to take instructions. Is that the right phrase? I want to become a Catholic."

"Why?"

"Why? Don't look so aghast. Why? Well, it is a good question. Because of many reasons. Belief. You. What I've read. What I've thought since our boy died."

He nodded.

"But I suppose the real reason, the one who got me going is Jane," said Felicity. "Jane McNamara and Chris. They've got guts, you know. And a faith that gives you guts is what I need."

She took out a cigarette. Ceremoniously he lit it with the sterling table lighter the Holy Name had given him for his jubilee.

"You haven't said anything." Nervousness tinged her deep voice. "I thought you'd be so glad. Oh, I know I have to study. Maybe I won't make it. Maybe I'm not meant to get in. But Father Temple, I want to try. Don't you care? You haven't said anything."

He smiled and lifted his head to look at the woman who was no longer in that hospital bed.

"I haven't said anything? Oh, I have, Felicity. But what I've been saying was not to you."

He spent an hour with her, saying much. He gave her a book to

289

read, a homework assignment, made an appointment for the next week.

"Felicity—I'm so glad you came."

"You know I hoped Harold would come. Say a prayer for him."

"I've prayed for him every day for as long as I've known him. I confess, I had more hopes of him than of you. But then I'm usually wrong." He walked her to the door. Felicity, forgive a rude old man, but—the wrinkles, they're wonderful. They're becoming. They make you look— I'm putting my foot in my mouth."

"An interesting face? I shall be a woman of mystery. Bye now, Father."

At table that night, as the family of fathers met over spaghetti, the patriarch was uncommunicative. He glared. Father Macy searched his conscience and remained puzzled. The pastor seemed to ignore the news that the oldest Sullivan boy had been disgraced by having his belt give way so that his pants fell off under his cassock while he was serving Mass. He did not respond to Father Mongiano's discussion of music for the confirmation ceremony.

"I want to see Chris McNamara," he said finally. "Father Macy, will you be kind enough to tell him so at choir practice tonight?"

"He doesn't come to choir any more."

"Why not?"

"Hasn't since he quit the convent drive," said Father Macy.

"What do you mean, quit the convent drive? I thought he was head of it?"

"He quit."

"You didn't tell me?"

"That was a long time ago, months. Father, I didn't think you needed to be bothered." Father Macy's freckled cheeks reddened. "I started to speak to you once and you told me I could handle it myself. You said it was my business."

"Anything in this parish is my business. You remember that."

"Yes, sir."

"Why did he quit?"

"He can be a bit difficult. A bit heady," said Father Macy. "You might say anticlerical. Tried to tell me how to run the drive. Didn't like the Square Share."

"I never liked it myself," shouted Father Temple.

"Proof's in the pudding," said Father Macy. "The drive netted you over $175,000. The Square Share worked."

"And what did it do to the parish?" asked Father Mongiano.

"What do you mean by that, Father?" the pastor asked.

"It angered people. Made trouble. Take Patsy Rottigni. His wife spent months working on him to come to Mass regularly, and just when she seemed to have succeeded, he stopped completely. Said he'd go to some other parish—when he feels like going at all."

"Patsy's very childish," said Father Macy. "He knows by church law he has to go to his parish church."

"Why doesn't he come here?" asked Father Temple more quietly still.

"I saw Angela on the street the other day," said Father Mongiano. "She said Patsy was in the fund drive and he thought McNamara got a raw deal."

"You're very outspoken tonight," said Father Macy.

"Maybe I agree with her," replied Father Mongiano.

Father Temple threw down his napkin in disgust.

"Father Macy," he said. "You are a blundering stupid insensitive fool. You have as much judgment as a pig. You should have told me what was going on. I warn you—you'll never save souls the way you are. I've suffered in silence for three years letting you have your way, bowing to modern technique. But I'm through."

He left the table. At the dining room door he paused. "And I warn you. You'll drive souls away from the Church if you don't mend your ways."

The doorbell rang.

"I'll get it," said Father Macy quietly. "That's for me. It'll be Julian Newman. He's coming for instructions now. He tried over at the friary, but had a personality clash with Father Juniper. If you'll excuse me, Father?"

Smiling, he passed Father Temple and went to let Julian Newman in.

Father Temple watched in surprised silence, sighed, then started up the stairs to his room. To think that Julian Newman of all people, strong, silent Julian, would be drawn to that oaf! God works in wondrous ways, he thought.

FIFTY-EIGHT

"You're a troublemaker, you know." Father Temple took the glass of sherry Chris offered him.

"Is that why you're here, Father? To tell me that?"

"You know, I never saw anyone more startled than you when you found me on your doorstep." Father Temple sipped the sherry appreciatively. "As I said, I'm glad your wife isn't home. It's you I want to talk to. I'm concerned. Very concerned."

"Is it the fund drive you're talking about?"

"Partly."

"That was a long time ago."

"Christopher, I'm a busy man. Too busy. To be frank with you, until tonight I didn't know you were no longer head of the drive. Then Father Macy said it was because you—"

"Because I am a troublemaker?"

"Something like that." Father Temple looked at him. "You were a fool to quit. Father Macy was a fool to let you go. And I was a fool not to know about it. I don't think there's anything more I need say. Except I regret it for all of us."

"Thank you," Chris said gravely.

"That's why I came, you might say. But—"

Chris refilled his glass.

"Will you think it strange if I say I wanted to come to talk to you about Jane?"

"Why?"

"Ah, there's an anticlerical tone of voice if I ever heard one!"

Chris smiled. "I suppose Father Macy says I'm anticlerical?"

"He does. And you are. Anti–certain of us." Father Temple sighed. "Can't say I blame you. It's a far cry from the old days. Then no one would have wondered why I came to his home, to talk about his wife. I—we have grown away from that. And I came here tonight to correct that. The fund drive thing, it was an excuse. Or the last push an old man needed. It's hard to break out of a way of doing things."

"Father Temple, I'm glad you came here, to my house."

The pastor put down his glass. "Today Felicity Lawrence came to see me. She wants to take instructions. Christopher, she told me she decided to enter the Church because of Jane." His eyes met

Chris'. "She said a faith that could give Jane the courage she has is the faith for her."

"Did she?" Chris looked away.

"When Clare Sullivan spoke to me she said something about how I was 'pulling Jane through.' She thought I knew what she meant. I didn't know anything troubled Jane."

"No reason for you to be expected to know."

"Will you tell me?"

"The doctor warned her that she has a kidney condition which makes pregnancy very dangerous. But now she is pregnant."

"I see." Father Temple laid his hands flat on his knees. "I see." Chris finished his sherry slowly, watching him.

"May I tell you, Christopher, what I think of your wife? I think she is—a carrier of grace." He stood up by the fireplace, his head barely reaching the mantel. "There are such people. They spread grace unconsciously. Without knowing it Jane is changing people's lives—infecting them with goodness."

"A carrier of grace," Chris said softly, closing his eyes. "Father, Clare Sullivan keeps telling Jane not to be afraid because God will not let her die."

The pastor grunted.

"I can see where it would be very annoying to have someone talking like that. At least it would annoy me."

Chris smiled.

"But you realize, Christopher, that if Clare hadn't talked that way, Felicity Lawrence wouldn't have heard about Jane. And—" he shrugged, his forehead wrinkling up into his pink scalp "—perhaps I wouldn't be here. God uses us all differently. But if you mean: will I talk pious nonsense? I will not."

"I haven't talked to anyone about it," said Chris. "There's no one to talk to."

"This is not easy for you—waiting with Jane."

"No. I can't let her know I'm worried."

"I wonder if you have faced all that may happen."

"She may die."

"And if she does?" He sat down again, nearer to Chris. "Have you thought that far? Chris, there are many ways of dying with Christ, and the worst are those where you have to keep on living. God does not write nice neat stories."

"I know."

"You wrote once somewhere that when you decide to live by

faith you must be willing to accept the fact that few will understand you, no one will admire you, and many will despise you."

"I didn't know you ever read what I wrote."

Father Temple smiled. "Father Mongiano keeps me posted. He admires you. And what you wrote is good advice," he said. "Christopher, my son, I want to talk to you as a real father, not just as a priest. May I?"

"My own is dead. He died this summer. One dies, and another is born, they say."

"My son," said Father Temple, "as a father I would have you look at the worst that can happen. Do you know? Have you thought that if God in his providence and wisdom takes Jane to him, people will look at you and some will say it's your fault? They will think Jane was the only one who suffered. Can you face that?"

Chris did not answer.

"Have you thought what her mother may say? She's not a Catholic, is she?"

"I've thought."

"You know, Christopher, if Jane dies it may look like a complete tragedy. A total waste. Your children—no matter who takes care of them they may grow up and leave the faith. I've seen that happen. Because a mother died in childbirth. If she dies, many people may seize on that as an excuse to leave the faith. The hardhearted medieval Church condemning a woman not to use mechanical birth prevention."

"That's why Clare says God must let her live. To show people the power of faith." Chris smiled wryly.

The wisps of white hair on the priest's head quivered. "God does not do what anyone thinks he must. He does not guarantee happy endings on earth. Can you face that?"

"If I have to."

"Good Friday did not seem good," said Father Temple.

"I've had all I can take," Chris said, getting to his feet. "You sound like you expect her to die. Like you were burying her now. What kind of help is that?"

"I believe in miracles," Father Temple said. "I also believe that before miracles you must first know the reality you want to be rescued from. Face it all the way. Then you can pray."

"Do you think she will live?"

"I do," said Father Temple.

The front door burst open. Breathless, Jane stood in the doorway. Father Temple raised his sherry glass in welcome to her.

"Oh. I was afraid— What brings you here, Father? I saw your car in the driveway and I thought—"

"It's a sad day when my car in the drive makes a woman fear a sick call. Shows the pastor should get out more."

"Father wanted to talk," Chris said. "Join us."

"Talk about what?"

"About—the fund drive." Chris kissed her. "And many things."

"Cabbages and kings." Father Temple seemed pleased to recall the phrase. "Yes, cabbages and kings. Alas, however, I must go now. My breviary is not yet said."

When he had gone, Jane asked, "He came to talk about the fund drive? Was he angry at you or Father Macy?"

"Neither. Just interested." That was all Chris told her.

FIFTY-NINE

Winter dallied. Late in Advent the frost was still not in the ground. The euonymus flamed in the border against the white siding of the house. Jane decided that next summer she would buy another bush to match it. Now she planted tulips for the spring, and a handful of squill bulbs Lidwina gave her.

"Blue. Bluer than sky or sea," she said. "Dark, purply blue."

Kilian, kneeling beside her, turned the sad shut bulbs in his hands. "Brown," he said.

"Blue." She kissed him, avoiding his damp nose. "Have faith, Kilian. Wait and see."

Round red cheeks, apple smooth, brown eyes, warm breath, he watched her bury the bulbs.

They will bloom in April and in May. Will they linger till June? Tell me, will June ever come?

Christmas seemed to fall like a star from the sullen sky. The chores of it, the buying and crowding and tinsel and tawdriness, disappeared and for Jane there was only carol-song and blue stillness, and the extravagant lights at the friary, and the crèche. Chris gave her a chiffon dress, flowered and slim, to put away for next summer after the baby.

And before the new year, in a night when branches rattled and the early-rising moon was huge and burning gold over the outdoor Santa Clauses and Christmas trees, Peter wore the red robes of confirmation. A blow on the cheek, oil on his bony head, the words of the bishop, he became a soldier of the faith. His new name, the name of his growing-up, was James. He chose it for his grandfather. Annie glowed with pride and gave him her James' gold watch.

The McNamara clan was gathered for that night of grace. Annie had discarded her black and glowed happily in an intricate drape of grey brocade. Father Tom, neatly pressed and mended, had constructed a white paper dove which he hung from the dining-room light. From the dove's mouth dangled symbols of the seven gifts of the Holy Spirit, swaying in the candle glow.

"A special letter for you from Grandma Gussie, Peter," Jane said when the other presents were opened.

"For Peter James," he read. "A check!"

Luke tugged at Annie's charm bracelets. "You know, Grandma, this spring, before we get the new baby, I'm making my first Holy Communion." His allergies at rest in winter, Luke looked charming, but Annie read the guile in his blue eyes. "On the day before Mother's Day. Don't forget to bring me a present. I need a watch too."

"Luke McNamara," said Chris sternly, "presents are not the point. And it's rude to ask."

"Ask and you shall receive." Father Tom laughed.

"Sacraments are holy," said Peter loftily. "Only babies think about the presents."

"Yeah, you can say that cause you already got yours." Luke's bulldog chin stuck out firmly. "You think you're so grown up. You'll be having girl friends if you don't watch out."

"I had a girl friend when I was Peter's age," said Father Tom. When the phone rang, Jane answered.

"We have a telegram for Jane McNamara."

"This is Jane McNamara."

"The message reads, 'Little girl here, late but fine. Says to tell you her name is Jane. Signed Gloria.' Shall we mail you a copy?"

"Please."

She could hear the others going into the living room, laughing. Father Tom's voice and Peter's were raised in a discussion about girls and love.

She called her mother.

"Mother?" Jane's voice was shaking. "Gloria had her baby. She's fine, Mother. It's a girl." But Gussie hung up. The click hit Jane's ear. The line of communication was dead.

Jane sighed, and dialed Western Union. "So happy for you and Jane," she dictated. "God bless you both. Sign it Jane and Chris." She listened trembling, while the message was read back to her. Inadequate, but what could she say? She went back to the living room.

Peter was teasing Mary.

"You are gusty, gusty." This was Peter's newest expression of disdain, a term reserved for bodily functions and anything to do with females.

Luke, who still wore a milk mustache, interpreted for Father Tom. "No big boys like girls. And nobody likes Mary at all. Girls are cooties, that's what Pete says."

"Sounds to me like you need the gifts of the Holy Spirit more than most, Peter." Father Tom smiled. "Counsel. Understanding. Wisdom."

Kilian wiggled closer to Father Tom on the sofa, dark brown eyes twinkling. Girls liked him, and he liked girls. Peter's disapproval didn't bother him at all. In kindergarten if girls liked you they gave you cookies and candy. "Girls are all right," Kilian said. "Only Mary's not much of a girl."

Mary's face was fevered. "Mrs. O'Shea said I'm going to be beautiful, didn't she Mom?"

Jane took a seat quietly next to Chris. "She did. And I think you're okay right now!" Pete snickered.

"All girls are gusty," he said. "It's not your fault, Mary."

"He's always making fun of me," she cried. "You know what he says, he says he's never going to get married because being married and falling in love is stupid." She hid her face in her father's chest.

Father Tom, his jowls shaken by a muffled cough, said, "Peter, you are a boy. And boys, as Cardinal Newman said so wisely, are always more or less inaccurate."

"You'd be in quite a fix, Peter," said Chris, with anger, "if I hadn't decided your mother was less than gusty. You're being stupid and fresh. You're not showing proper respect for girls. Love is a fine and holy thing. And you are behaving very badly. Love is gentle and sacred," Chris said, his voice bearing down on the boy. "Your mother and I love each other and our love made you. And if it weren't for the fact that men and women love each other there wouldn't be any boys in the world to sneer at the whole thing. I want you to apologize to your sister Mary, and to your mother."

Pete raised his eyebrows and mumbled.

His father lit a cigarette, with embarrassment. He had exaggerated the problem, he knew. He had a habit of trapping himself into acting like the type of adult he had disliked most when he was a child.

"Someday," Annie said, "you'll fall in love and then you'll grow up."

"Never."

Father Tom stood up, dumping Luke and Kilian to the floor. "Music is what we need," he said. "Music about love, for Peter. Music tames the savage beast." At the piano he began to play the first tune that came to his head. "Let me call you sweetheart," he sang. The children gathered around him, except for Peter. Annie's head nodded in rhythm.

Chris and Jane sat together on the sofa, listening.

"I remember," Jane whispered, "when I used to think this was what marriage would be like, sitting side by side, looking fondly at the little ones."

"Mm-hmm. Who was on the phone?"

"Gloria sent a telegram. She had a baby girl. She named it Jane."

He squeezed her hand. "Don't you dare cry, with all the family here."

"Your family. I have none. Mother hung up on me when I phoned her."

The laughter and clowning at the piano, as love song followed love song, filled the room. Even Annie was singing by the piano, vying with Father Tom to see who could remember the most. Mournful ballads gave way to folksongs, nursery rhymes, a lyric from the twenties.

"Look." Jane nudged Chris. They pretended not to notice as Peter moved with apparent casualness nearer to the group. "He doesn't mean that, about hating love and girls, does he? I'd hate to think—"

Chris shook his head. "That's the best part of growing up when you're a boy. Despising women."

Father Tom intoned the first bars of "Down by the old . . ."

"Not the new but the old," sang Peter.

"Mill stream . . ." sang the priestly bass.

"Not the river but the stream," answered Pete tunelessly.

Mary in her yellow nylon bathrobe plunged in small circles around the room, her bony frame valiantly acting out some private dream of beauty. Father Tom at the keyboard switched into the lilt of a waltz.

With a nod to Jane, Chris got up and stepped into Mary's path and became her partner. Gravely he guided her movements till they fit the waltz pattern. The waltz ended and Chris, with a graceful little half bow, thanked his daughter. Mary's face glowed as he turned to rejoin Jane.

Pete's face grew restless. Father Tom was determined to hold his uneasy interest.

"He's doing his best to be a cynic." Chris winked.

"My mama done tole me," sang the priest, in startling mimicry of a blues singer.

"When I was in knee pants . . ."

Pete, loose-kneed, his elbows jutting, began weaving and clapping, a street corner urchin, absorbed in the rhythm. Kilian and Luke, watching, feeling the vibration of chord and beat and voice and love, leaned against the wall in a stupor of pleasure.

Over the stair rail a small head appeared. Meg had been drawn irresistibly from her crib by the sound of happiness. She moved alertly, aware she might at any instant be sent back to bed, torn by the need to remain invisible so the spell would not be broken and by the equally urgent need to be in the smiling warmth of her family.

She saw her parents over on the sofa, watching her. There was, she decided, a smile hidden in their faces. They wanted her. They understood. With a cry she ran barefoot down the last stairs, and flung herself into the small pocket of space that separated and also joined her parents. Jane laid a hand absently on her curly hair, and thought with a pang of Gloria's baby daughter, who would not remember the touch of her own mother's hand. And of Gloria, who would never see her baby run to her arms. But this is not a night for grief, she thought. From across the room, Kilian beamed at Meg. She yielded to the invitation in his look and scurried over to him.

Christ got to his feet and pulling Jane up with him, began to whirl her around the floor. Father Tom's fingers found the notes of the "Anniversary Waltz."

"Uh, how we danced on the night we were wed," Chris sang softly.

When the music stopped he kissed her.

Beautiful, thought Mary. Before her eyes the man she had taken for granted as a father became a storybook prince in disguise.

Kilian, with Meg in tow, moved nearer to Luke. Pete sidled nearer to Kilian. Three boys looked at their mother and saw that she was tall and pretty, and she had hair that tumbled over Daddy's hand. Thick and brown as a pony's and she had very pink cheeks.

Furtively Luke and Kilian eyed Pete, wondering if big boys had to be bored or contemptuous about this, then relaxed. Obviously Pete did not think this kiss was gusty. Unusual, yes. But not gusty.

SIXTY

The sleet of January gave way to the blustery snows of February. Chris and Peter kept the birdfeeders filled with suet and seed. A cardinal, his red a blurt of brilliance against the snow, came warily with his paler mate for sunflower seeds. The birches bent, swooning under the weight of the snow. Chris assigned Luke and Kilian to joust with long poles against the white enemy, setting the trees free before they broke.

Jane warmed the house with fireplace and popcorn and cocoa and games, and the evenings brought friends and neighbors. Only Al and Tory stayed away.

"I miss them," said Jane to Chris. "But Tory doesn't want to see me any more. Al's your friend. Do something."

One night Chris skidded through slick unplowed ruts over to their house and fetched them.

"Guess we just got lazy," said Al, cradling a gift-wrapped bottle in his mittened hands as they shed galoshes in the laundry room. "Don't know why. Maybe we're getting old. But it's good to see you guys again."

"We've been busy," Tory said. "You know how it is. We mustn't let it get away from us like this again."

Al made eggnog his way, and they drank it and listened to the storm and told jokes. The men talked about the stupidity of Jesuits and the terrifying liberal infiltration of the clergy as a whole, and being always delighted to find themselves agreed in this minority opinion, had a glorious time. Tory told Jane about Pat and Dennis who seemed to do nothing but eat pizza, and how Walter was doing in the Marines, and they talked about the best way to dry children's snowsuits and the terrible new styles for dresses.

Then Al, on his third eggnog, suddenly turned to Chris.

"Why haven't we seen each other? What the hell has been going on? Seriously—did the girls have a fight? You and I didn't, did we?"

Chris shook his head.

"Well I want to know what happened!" Al set the cup down. "Tory, what happened?"

"Nothing happened," said Jane. "We just got out of the habit."

"I got mad at Jane," Tory said quietly. "And when I stopped being mad I didn't know what to do. I'm not much good at saying I'm sorry. I get scared."

"What did you get mad about?"

"What women fight about is none of your business," said Jane.

"Don't do it again," said Al. "Come, I'll tell you what's been keeping us busy these long winter nights."

"You sit around smooching," said Chris.

Al passed his hand over his hair nervously. The top was really getting quite bald now. "Huh? Well we do, you know. Quite a bit. We've taken it up again in our declining years you might say. Self-defense. Pat and that Newman boy are always mooning around. . . ."

"You were going to tell them about the boat," said Tory.

"Yes, the boat. Everywhere else we've lived we had a boat. I'm quite the sailor, or was. Time we got a boat here, I figure. I've got my eye on a Lightning. Buy it now, fix it up for spring. Then we'll go out on our boat and forget everything and be like honeymoon-ers."

Tory's eyes met Jane's in silence. Then she smiled. "Will you come out with us? Jane, if it weren't for you, that day, maybe there might not be a boat."

"What do you mean?" asked Al.

Tory grinned. "Forget it, skipper. Private code."

"Soon it will be summer. I keep telling myself," Al said as the cold damp breath of night challenged their departure. "I can't wait for summer."

Wait for summer. Undressing, Jane ran her hands over the tight white skin of her belly. Almost, she could not breathe, waiting, living to wait. The people and the nights, the children and the days, do I wait—how long? The need to know what was to happen filled her like fever. I hang stretched on a cross of time, painless cheerful time, and the painless cheerful not-knowing is almost more than I can bear.

SIXTY-ONE

There once was a Man who was God,
God in the shape of a clod,
They found him a scandal.
Too much to handle,
And killed him because he seemed odd.

"My masterpiece," said Father Tom sadly.

Chris nodded. "It's not funny."

"Did you ever think what they'd do to him today, if this were the time he picked, I mean?"

"The do-gooders would have him locked up for his own good."

"He'd never last."

Tom was playing with Peter's half-finished jigsaw puzzle of the sinking of the *Monitor*. He was recovering from the disappointment of being again refused the chance to return to Africa. He glanced at Chris. "You seem calmer these days. Been rereading some of those peace-of-mind bestsellers? Or are you taking tranks?"

"Sure."

"Seriously."

"No pills. No books. No peace of mind, really. I'm still—still sitting tight. Times I think—"

"But you hold together."

"By God's grace."

Tom fitted in a piece of grey sky with yellow smoke.

"Father Temple came over here to see me a few months ago."

"I thought he was seeing no one but those parakeets."

"He's a good man, really. He came to talk to me. Finally found out I quit the fund drive. Thought it was because I was a trouble-maker."

"As I said. My prophecy exactly."

"Not quite. He almost apologized. He decided maybe the trouble was with Father Macy, or even with him."

"He came to tell you that?" asked Father Tom in surprise. "What's the Church coming to?"

"No. He came to talk about Jane. Remember Felicity Lawrence? She came to him and asked to come into the Church. Because of Jane. Said a faith that gave a gal guts was for her."

Tom put down a piece of blue water and lit a cigarette.

"He wanted to know what was with Jane. And me. So I told him. But he told me more than I told him."

"What did he tell you?"

"He said—he said Jane was a carrier of grace. That was the phrase he used." Chris stopped, fingering a pussy willow in a vase. A powder of yellow fell on his hand. "He said people were talking about her, that was what made him come, he was ashamed not to know why they were talking. Not just Felicity. Said lives were being changed by her. Others we don't suspect."

He put his hands in his pockets, turned to Tom, rocked on his heels. "I think it's true," he said. "It frightens me."

Tom bent his head. "Did he say anything else?"

"He said I should know that only when I lose everything will I be able to love God. No. He said only when I am ready or willing to lose everything."

Father Tom was watching him, saying the words with him silently, breathing with him. He had forgotten how young his nephew was. He had forgotten how it was to ache with tenderness for blood of his own blood. My dead brother's son calls me Father.

"He told you well."

Chris raised his head. His temples, bonier than the priest recalled, showed a pulse. "He said he thinks she will be all right."

"What does the doctor say?"

"I went down and talked to him alone. He's hopeful. All the tests so far are fine." Chris sat down, his long legs stretched in front of him. "I think we're going to get a miracle. I should be resigning myself. I can't."

The priest's eyes were moist. "I should hope not."

"I believe in miracles. I've got everybody I know praying. Juniper at the friary. Father Temple. You. I send off donations to every last begging little order or society or convent that clutters the box. Sure. And I'm not resigned. I—I think she'll fool them all!"

Children burst through the kitchen doors, screaming with joy to see Father Tom.

"Look at the ashes on my head. I got the biggest smudge," shouted Luke.

"Ashes, ashes, all fall down," sang Margaret.

"Lent, I hate it," said Mary. "I'm giving up giving up."

Jane, Teresa in her arms, sat on the couch. "Guess what, Chris? Julian Newman is going to be baptized on Holy Saturday. Really! His wife's nearly out of her mind. Tom, you remember her. She's waited so long. But I'll never understand how these things work. It's not Juniper who converted him. He couldn't stand Juniper. It's Father Macy. I didn't dream he could convert anyone, least of all a guy I like as much as Julian. He doesn't seem like a very holy kind of priest. Father Macy drives me crazy. But?"

"You don't have to be holy for God to use you," said Tom. "He uses anybody that's handy. It's no guarantee."

"And guess what?"

"Was this a gossip fest or did you go to get ashes?"

"Father Tom. You meet people. You talk, you know. Guess what? Tory and Al have their boat. I think it's wonderful. And Tory is happy. They said if they get any warm days they're going out to practice and next month or so they might take us out just a wee bit from shore."

"You're not going on a boat," said Father Tom.

"I'm well," said Jane. "So well. And I'm an old salt, you know, from way back on the Cape as a kid. And it would only be in the Sound here. No, not even out of the harbor."

"You're nuts, you modern women."

"I remember you once said we were softies compared to pioneer women who had their babies between battles with the Indians. Or your Kikuyu women who work so hard."

"*Touché.*" He put another piece in the puzzle. Peter was hanging on his shoulder. He put a hand up to clasp the boy's hand.

"There is nothing I like more than being in this house with this family," he said. "And as the years go on you'll never get rid of me. You may wish I'd keep my hands off your puzzle, but I won't. Ha! Surprised you!" He winked at Pete's reddening neck. "Come on," he said. "I'm in civvies. See how many of you it takes to get me down."

Luke and Kilian and Pete fell on him, giggling and pummeling and grunting, while Mary and Margaret screeched with delight.

"Your uncle looks like a bear with cubs," said Jane. "Wish you had a camera."

"He looks like a darn fool," said Chris. "An odd clod."

SIXTY-TWO

It was a hot shiny sleepy day in May.

At eight, as Jane and Pete and Mary and Kilian and Luke drove to Mass, dew sparkled in the forsythia.

"It's going to be hot," she said. "Like summer. False summer. Hey, Peter, we're about there. Read us the *Introit,* quick. Whose feast day is it? Get with it, boy."

Mary, who as usual had her missal all set, markers neatly in place, said patiently, "St. Paul of the Cross. Confessor. Founder of the Passionists. He had a burning love of Jesus Crucified. Sounds awful boring for such a beautiful day."

"Thank you, Mary," her mother answered with equal patience.

"The *Introit,*" announced Peter in a loud voice, reading from the missal. " 'With Christ I am nailed to the cross. It is now no longer I that live, but Christ lives in me. And the life that I now live in the flesh, I live in the faith of the Son of God, who loved me and gave himself up for me, alleluia, alleluia. Blessed is he that understands . . .' "

Jane pulled to a stop under the dogwoods by the church. "Okay, Pete. We'll remember that. Come on kids, hurry, we're late."

After the misted-petal brightness of the day the church was dark inside. Father Mongiano was saying the Mass. Jane was grateful. The way he said Mass, slowly and with feeling, was right for this day. She helped Luke find the place in his junior missal. Now, as his first Communion neared, she went through the liturgy with him daily, trying to lead him to understanding beyond the catechism.

"This month," he whispered. "One more week."

"Shhh." Her fingers underscored the rubric for him. "See, Father Mongiano's blessing the water and mixing it with the wine which will become the Blood of Jesus. We are like little drops of water in the wine, joined with Jesus, lost in him. So close no one can ever separate us again from his life."

Luke nodded and scratched his ear. The priest was two pages

305

ahead of her now, but she decided to keep on where she was.
Luke liked the idea of being a little drop of water.

"Read the prayer," he said, his head close to hers.

She read: " 'O God, who in a wonderful way created and en-
nobled human nature, and still more wonderfully redeemed it, grant
that by the mystery of this water and wine we may become part of
the divinity of Jesus Christ, your Son, who consented to share our
humanity.' "

The bells rang, flower bells thought Mary, blue-gold bells thought
Peter, herald bells sighed Jane. Now no whisper, no lesson, only
silence as at dawn or birth or death. She lost herself in hope.

I am here.

The words of prayer were useless to her. I cannot pray, she had
said to Father Juniper, not a week ago. I can only wait and want.
I feel like a girl waiting in love, silly, calling out in her heart the
name of him who has left her. Juniper said that was prayer. How
long? As in a garden, alone.

Into her mouth she received the sanctifying food of God.

Time dropped from her. Quiet inflamed her. She saw without
eyes, saw with love, what could not be said: love leaping through
death, Eve born of Adam's side, and another one's side, lance-
pierced, heart-melting, giving birth to the bride on cross-shadowed
hillside. I am the beginning and the end, and in the end is the
beginning. A woman had knelt and surrendered to the awful glory
not of myth swan but of more incredible dove, a woman carrying
within a womb the one who is father and son and lover and spouse.

The world, cedared, blue-ceiled, grey-rocked, green-grown, shuddered in rebirth, lifted among angel fire, till lion and lamb and palm
and lily and whale and eagle and a child returned to their beginning
and their end, in one person of three.

She grew dizzy. Her body, unaccustomed, seemed about to fail.
Yet it could not, for this mystery demanded body, sinew, heart,
tongue.

Did he know she could stand no more? As if holding her he
lowered her till she saw again the individual faces of his love. They
rose to her, her Christopher, her children, Annie, James, her mother,
Gloria, Tory and Al, Father Tom, and more, and each was bonded
to her and she yearned over them and called out their names in
silence to the one who held her and knew they shaped her and him
and each other in one life.

Then, most quietly she was returned to herself. Timidly she moved and her body obeyed. The Mass had ended.

As they came from the Church, the brilliance of the sun surprised them.

"Let's go to the beach, huh, Mom? It feels like July. Can we go swimming?"

"A picnic. Hot dogs. Fishing. Baseball." Their plans shot off like fireworks.

"I love you," she said.

"I love summer and you and today and God and everything." Kilian wiggled.

"This is the day the Lord has made," Mary sang softly.

"Let us rejoice and be glad in it!" Birds in a field scattered in shock as the antiphon bellowed back from the children and the mother in the open-windowed car.

The Burke station wagon was in the drive.

"Surprise!" shouted Tory.

"Big surprise!" shouted Al.

Chris came over to Jane, leaning on the car door, grinning. "They insist on taking us for a sail," he said helplessly. "Do you want to go? Do you think it would be all right?"

"Babysitter supplied," said Tory, pointing to young Pat. "On the house. Free."

"Look," began Al.

"I'm looking," said Jane. He wore a new pair of white ducks, a red-and-white striped beachcomber shirt and a captain's hat.

"We won't go beyond the harbor. Smooth, safe, near shore, not a wave, not a thing. Safe as a car. We'll just float, lazy-like."

"We woke up, saw the sun and said this was the day we could finally take you out. Wait any longer and you'll be in the last weeks and the summer'll be about gone before you're ready to go after the baby. Please, Jane?"

"You know the boat's name?" asked Al. *Many Waters.*

" 'Many waters cannot quench love'?"

"Come sail on *Many Waters.*"

Jane and Chris held the silent eye-conference of those who live as one. Chris nodded. "It'll be our vacation. The only one we'll get this year."

The children gathered on the lawn to wave them off. Teresa in her stroller, pale-haired with flat-set eyes like a stuffed lamb. Margaret, who was picking blue squill for Jane to wear in her hair.

Kilian, barefoot already, his thoughts on frog's eggs in the brook. Luke. Mary. Peter.

"Good God you're a beautiful family," crowed Jane. "My steps." She kissed them and blessed them and knew they would be in devilment the minute she was gone.

"Come on. All aboard!" called Al.

"I love you," Jane called to the children.

Al swung the *Many Waters* neatly up to the dock for Jane.

"Can't have you scrambling in and out of dinks," he said. "Service for the lady." With the help of his hand she was in the boat. "You're as graceful as a kid."

Seats ran around three sides of the Lightning cockpit. On one he had prepared a small nest of pillows. "A throne for the queen-mother. Hard boards for us commoners."

"Everything at hand," said Tory. "You name it, we got it. Thermos of coffee. Life preservers. Emergency kit. Al bought the works."

"Here she goes." The sails quickened and held. "Ten-to-fifteen knot breeze. Want you to know how well I calculated for your safety, Jane old gal. It's too early in the season for sudden squalls. Not a thunderstorm in sight. The wind's not going to die down suddenly so you needn't fret because we have no motor." As they drew into deeper water he let the centerboard down. "The wind dies down regularly around here at sunset you know. They told me about it. You have to know where you're sailing. Me, I'm a lake sailor mostly. But Tory and I've taken the course, and we've been out getting back into practice."

"Out here it's just Al and me," said Tory happily. "Honeymoon. Only I work. We're going to race sometime. We have a spinnaker— I said it right this time, Al—bright red."

Jane nodded. "I'm hardly hearing you," she said. "Blissful. Too blissful to do anything but sit. The sun on my face. Haven't sailed since I was—so very young. I am young today. This is heaven."

She ducked as the boom swung over and Al tacked skillfully back and forth in the harbor.

The water, ripple-textured, was the same indefinable singing blue of squill. She told Chris that, and leaned into the curve of his arm, seeing the rush of the waters as the Lightning slicked through, the sky white-blue with sun, and around the harbor the houses and the beaches and people puttering on boats, and the firm white wings of seabirds.

308

"Happy?" murmured Chris.

"Happy enough for a lifetime. Chris, I feel like there's not a worry or a care, as if we left everything behind at that dock "

"Well said," sighed Tory.

"Do you want to go back?" asked Al. "Or shall we venture a bit further? We could see what it's like outside? There's more boats than I thought out there already."

Tory began humming. Jane joined her. Chris improvised in a lazy tenor. " 'And you sing to me and I sing to you, Love forever new!' "

"Sail on, captain," Chris said when the last note was drawn out beyond its strength. "Behold a new man. I am undone. I am a sybarite. A hedonist. I am for the first time in months having a good time. The feeling is strange. Keep sober, old boy. I have my wife in my arms and the breeze in my hair and I'm drunk on the *Many Waters*."

"We'll go out on a reach," called Al, "and come back on a reach. I'll time our way out. We'll be able to come in in the same time. That way we won't get caught staying out too long. Duck now."

The boom swung smoothly over. The *Many Waters* slid steadily, smoothly forward into the Sound.

"Like lightning," laughed Tory, raising her head to catch some of the spray. "Al, like lightning!"

"Natch."

"How fast are we going?" asked Chris, tipping his head back to catch the sun. "I'll look healthy when I get home."

"Only five to six nautical miles an hour."

A powerboat zoomed past, its arrogant white wake traveling slowly sideways to them, rocking them. Jane giggled. "Feels like a ride at Playland." A pair of Blue Jays sailed ahead of them.

"By God, a skindiver!" Al pointed to where a flag floated on the water, red with a white diagonal stripe. Tory reached under the seat and handed him his binoculars. "That water's still awful cold in May. But those divers are all nuts." He studied the surface around the float through the glasses.

"One thing the Coast Guard taught us was to stop and take a look when you see one of those. Somebody might be signaling for help." He passed the glasses to Chris, certain there was no danger. "Great folks, these boat men, you know. Always ready for the rescue. Sort of the *esprit de corps*."

Jane, secure, lulled by memories of childhood sails and the sudden freedom of the morning, closed her eyes.

"We've been out on this reach twenty minutes," called Al. "I'll be heading back now. Watch your head."

Jane hummed with contentment as the boat tipped up beneath her, bending to the new course. She breathed deep and tasted the salt on her lips. She smiled. She stretched lazily.

There was no pain.

She could not believe there was no pain. Not a tremor. She could not speak because she could not believe there was no pain and so she could not believe anything was happening. She opened her eyes, her breath taut above her heart and looked down toward her legs. She felt it, warm, a warm wet. The waters have broken, she thought. The waters are not red. This is red. This is red.

"Chris," she said. Her voice still worked. "Chris."

Chris saw. The grey cloth of the pedalpushers was bleeding. Her lower legs were encased in trickling blood. Her sneakers were bleeding. A tide of blood.

Tory's eyes were shut under the sun. Al was studying the sail.

"We're not going as fast as we were," he was saying. "Wind's the same. Sail's full. My God, I forgot the tide. It's ebbing. It's pulling against us. A lake sailor. We'll get there, but slower."

He saw the blood on the floor deck running toward the housing of the centerboard.

It didn't make sense. Jane was simply sitting there. Chris was grabbing towels. The towels grew red. It seemed too much blood for anything human.

Jane said, "There's no pain. What's happening?"

Tory scrambled for more towels. "How long to shore?" she snapped.

"Half an hour. Maybe more. Gotta get help."

She found the flares. She lit the flare. Fuchsia, silly fuchsia pink, in a sun sky. "That powerboat's around somewhere."

Chris ripped off his shirt to staunch the blood but Tory snatched it from him and began waving it.

"He'll see it," said Jane. "Don't cry, Tory. He'll see it."

"Help!"

"Chris just hold me, hold me close."

"You're turning white. My God, you're bleeding white."

"I'm cold."

"What the hell is it, Jane?"

Tory, waving the shirt, sobbing, shouted, "Don't you know what it is? I do. Come on, boat. Come on!"

On the powerboat, the skipper peered across the glare of the water. They're waving a white thing. They got trouble." He reached for the ship-to-shore.

Tory saw the boat coming and sank down to her knees with the shirt. Al was hanging on to the tiller and ropes as if he could push the *Many Waters* through the receding tide. His lips were moving.

"I've never seen so much blood in my life," moaned Tory. "I'm kneeling in blood."

Jane moved in Chris's arms. "Chris, don't be afraid. Don't. We'll get to shore."

The powerboat swooped in beside them. Al slackened his sail to a stop. The skipper looked and did not need to be told.

"We'll take her in. We'll have to transfer her. We got a blanket. We'll call the Coast Guard for an ambulance."

"I wish I could stop bleeding at least while they move me," said Jane.

They lifted her out of Chris' arms on a blanket and swung her from one rocking boat to the other. Chris held her hand, nearly missing his step.

Tory was sobbing and she had her face so Jane could not see. "Bye!" Jane called.

Chris blew air through his slack lips. "Don't talk," he ordered. "Don't talk. Hold my hand and save your strength."

"I want to talk though," said Jane. "I'm feeling fine you know. I'm scared, but I'm fine. And it's like a dream or like a sleep, only being wide awake."

"How long will it take to get to shore?" asked Chris.

"Eight, ten minutes." The skipper, his face impassive, did not look at him.

Chris saw Jane's lips turning pale under her lipstick and he wanted to cry out and he held her and he kissed her. Sweat beaded her skin and she was cold and yet she kissed him back. The blanket was warm and wet with her blood.

"I can still kiss," she said. "My voice sounds far away to me but I can still kiss you. And I love you. I think we must have lost the baby. Chris, don't be so afraid. Chris, I must talk to you. I think I am in a state of shock. I feel dead but I am alive."

His fingers searched for her pulse. She watched his face.

"No pulse?" she asked. "There's no pulse. But I am not dead."

The powerboat swung up to the dock. The ambulance, light flashing, back door open, waited with motor running.

The names of things ran through behind his eyes making a noise that was not thought. Supportive therapy. *Placenta previa.*

His throat moved as if he could pronounce the words with the doctors. He followed. Doors closed. Hands touched him. He waited. He could follow again. Call the priest. Father Juniper is here. Needles and tubes.

She was lying there looking at him, trying to tell him something. They did not want her to speak. They were right but he wanted her to speak.

Like another piece of medical equipment the table was rolled in, the table always ready somewhere on each floor, the operating equipment for the last rites. Father Juniper was there. Father Juniper held Chris' hand. Father Juniper moved toward the girl on the bed, white, smiling, still speaking. Can you be dying and speaking and making sense? Her most precious blood is over the *Many Waters* and on my hands and clothes and I have no shirt on and still she is here.

Father Juniper told him to leave the room and he did. He stood in the hall, his fists clenched, sweating.

Dr. Polla was beside him. Shock. Perhaps not irreversible.

"Chris, this had nothing to do with her other trouble. I want to be sure you know that."

"What is it?"

"*Placenta previa.* This can happen to anyone. It has nothing to do with her kidneys. Nothing to do with her decision to have another child. You must understand that."

Chris looked at him. "You're crazy," he said. "Whatever it is, it only happens when you have a child."

"We're giving her blood. We've got supportive therapy. . . ."

The door opened. Father Juniper admitted him now that private confession was over. He said the prayers of the last anointing with the priest. He was crying like a girl. Crying.

When the prayers were done, the priest took him by the hand up from his knees as if he were a child and led him to her. He bent over and kissed her.

"Christopher," she whispered. "Love me always. And love him. And that's all."

"Jane, you will not die. You can—they're going to—"

She closed her eyes. The two tears ran sideways down toward her ears. He wiped them with his fingers. She opened her eyes again. "Peter. Mary. Luke. Kilian. Margaret. Teresa. If I could tell you what I see." The words were slow, clear.

"Chris!" The voice rose, the voice that had lived, laughed, praised, pouted, sung.

"Don't talk any more. Dr. Polla's coming in. There's a rush, Jane. They're going to operate."

"Shhh." She seemed to reach him closer by her eyes. "Shhh. Chris. Sing to me. There's time. Sing to me." She drew a breath, and sang. "This is the day . . ."

She was gone before he could answer.

SIXTY-THREE

Thin, deadly, plastic, a veil of unreality clung to him, stifling.

The walk down the aisle. Four solemn children at his side, combed and polished. Luke had been fretting. Chris could remember now dimly hearing the boy wonder if he would still make his first communion in two days. If so, Luke said, I should go to practice with the school this afternoon. What do I do about practice? I cannot answer that, Chris said. The question makes no sense to me.

What is our new brother's name? Mary asked that. Our new brother who is there with mother. He has a name? His name is Christopher, I said. They named him for me when they baptized him. How strange, said Mary, that I never knew him till I saw him there in her arms.

In the loft the choir was singing, those members who for loyalty to Chris had taken time from work and home to sing the requiem. Chris walked slowly down the aisle, measuring the terrazzo floor with his steps, and heard Bertha Rains' pocketbook slip off the organ.

I should be up there singing, he said to himself. It makes no sense for me to be down here. I feel as if I were rehearsing for some ceremony.

Three priests waited in black vestments, Father Tom, Father Temple, Father Mongiano. On the side, in the sanctuary, stood Father Juniper. Chris sensed his children's bewilderment at sight of them, all in black. I have seen Tom in black vestments before. I buried my father last year. Yet, they seem, these four, like dream-strangers now. Peter is staring at them. He knows they must not be real.

There, in front of him, in the aisle among candles, was the box. He could not believe, about the box, that it enclosed his wife. And his unheld son.

The church was really quite full. The women of Mother's Circle and Rosary Altar, a few from the hospital. The men from Holy Name and the K of C, and the Sodality. A few children, grave, self-conscious, important, from the school and from Cubs and Brownies, friends of his children.

Mutely he was aware of them all.

Faces and voices and handshakes from the past two days ran through his mind like the body memory of vibration after a long trip. His home had been filled with people who would not let him do anything for himself. Al and Tory. Good Lord, where would he have been without them! Al so businesslike about buying a cemetery plot, Tory so unobtrusively competent about things like a dress and a rosary for Jane. Those unreal things that were there to be done, and they took him by the hand, as it were, and led him through the maze till the stage at O'Rourke's Funeral Home was set. And there, among the flowers and the Mass cards on the little stand, more faces, murmuring prayers, sitting in silent company. Martha and Bede. Clare and Bart Sullivan. Lidwina and Mike, together. The Carpels, Elmo Milder, Felicity and Harold with their girls. Christine, and Julian Newman, who had been baptized now and promised to offer his first communion for Jane.

Even Krena had come, with her husband. Krena, who had already been delivered of a baby, and who lived. It was hard to forgive her for being alive.

Now behind him he could hear his mother sniffling. Annie had not slept for the two days. Annie had grief, and trouble with her lowers. Benny Scrivener had knocked himself out trying to fix her lowers because she would not go back to the city to her own dentist. Wasn't it odd to need a dentist during the days of a wake? Most odd, thought Chris. And Annie had also needed someone to stay her up in her grief and discomfort. Clare Sullivan had held her hand and listened and comforted her, hiding her own bewilderment that God had let Jane die.

I could not have comforted my mother, Chris acknowledged. I have not comforted anyone. Except the small ones who creep into my bed at night, content only to be touching me, warm and silent.

Jane. Look down and help me.

Gussie was not sniffling. God, you had to hand it to her. Of all people he had leaned on her. She had come with dignity, without reproach. He had dreaded facing her. She disarmed him of fear. "Forgive me," she had said. "I should not have stayed away from her. I didn't understand her. That was one thing. But I grew angry. And that was wrong."

Her head bowed only for an instant, then she had looked up at Chris, steadfast as a carven figurehead. In her eyes he had recognized the expression he loved in Jane.

"I am proud of her, Chris," she said. "Though I cannot understand her, she lived and died by what she believed in. And I did not make it easy for her."

She had not let him interrupt.

"I do not intend to waste your time or mine in breast-beating," she said. "I cannot go back and change what has been. Nor can you. We go on from here."

If he would let her, she said, she would care for the children. He could decide that later, she said. And if he let her, she would bring them up as Jane would have done, in the Church she loved. "They are hers and she deserves that they know and honor what she believed."

Dignity, nobility. Like teak pillars he could feel the strength of Gussie behind him, this morning, in St. Rose's. She was not alone. Gloria stood beside her. Gloria who had wired her regrets, had come anyway. Father Tom had tracked her down secretly by phone, and ordered her to come. And she had obeyed.

Chris stood with the oldest children while Father Tom sang the preface to the consecration.

One moment pierced him, only one, so that he was open to reality. Father Tom bent to whisper the effective words, then raised the Host. Looking up, Christopher McNamara almost smiled.

He came, Chris thought. How wonderful. He came.

And he spoke to the Lord who came. God, you gave her to me. We three have loved. And we never forget that we three still love. Here. There. Now. Forever. Alone, I am not alone. Only, I have more to cleave to with my faith. One less that I can see.

Jane! My beloved—pray for me now. And you who are called by my name, Christopher, pray too.

When at last it was done, and the people were gone and he was at home, he went to the porch to be alone.

Sunlight assailed his eyes. One of Jane's roses budded high on the trellis he had promised he would paint. The air was ugly with noise. Across the yards came the groans and screeches of a tractor repairing the O'Shea's lawn.

He remembered then, vividly, the soft grey winter day after Teresa was born when he sat on this porch pondering the path of God in suburbia. A year and a half ago. He remembered what he had thought that day as if it were a lesson in the academic study of an ancient time, having no root in his soul.

Part of me has died. Yet I am not allowed to be buried. Mine is the long slow carrying of the burden of life. My God, Jane, our six must depend on me.

Six. Yet I am the father of seven.

I still do not believe where it is I went today, or what I have done. I do not know how it is that you are dead.

His face trembled. He forced himself to take out a cigarette and light it in the face of the rising tide of loneliness.

The screen door banged. Father Tom settled his bulk precariously on the webbed aluminum chaise beside Chris.

"What in the world are you supposed to do in the afternoon after a funeral?" asked Chris. His voice cracked and he cleared his throat. "There's no etiquette written, is there? No rules for when everything is all over."

"It's not all over."

"I know. I said so to many people: Death is not the worst thing. Death is the only way to get there. And not many really listened. I don't blame them. I hardly listened myself. It's hard to make the truth real."

"Only when you try to *make* it. The truth is real. It only seems unreal when we try to be the judges of it. Only God can do that." So openly, so gently Father Tom's voice framed the words that they rang new in Chris' ear. "I thought this morning, looking out at the people in that church, how many threads wove together in Jane's life, how closely she was bound into other lives. And they all go on. And she is still part of it. Nothing is settled. Not here."

Chris noticed Mary's jumprope sprawled by the woodpile, and picked it up with a sigh.

"The trouble is," he said, "nothing seems to me important enough to do now. Not this afternoon. Where do I go from here?"

"You could start with food."

Chris grimaced.

"Gussie wants to fix a real meal," Father Tom continued, "but she's afraid it will scandalize you in your grief if she bangs around in the kitchen. I told her that was as ridiculous as asking that tractor to quit because this was a funeral day. Besides, I'm hungry."

Chris slapped the folded jumprope on his open palm, and shut his lips tight.

"You think I should utter profundities to you now." Father Tom nodded. "You think, with all due respect to priest and uncle, that I am being gross and trivial thinking of my stomach. That there are other things more important than food."

"Of course Gussie should cook a meal. The kids are probably hungry. Only I'm not."

Father Tom raised his hand to shield his eyes as if from sunlight. He could not let Chris see the tenderness and pride in them.

"You're wrong, Chris. If you're going to keep on loving God, you've got one more thing to learn. That he wants his saints human. You're going to have to be human, even in grief, even if it disappoints you."

The jumprope slapped again on Chris's palm. "There should be something else to do after death," he said quietly. "Some more ceremony."

"After death, and after new life? Do you remember what our Lord said after he raised Jairus' daughter from death? There was a moment of grandeur! A moment for poetic thoughts and noble gestures! Yes. And what were his memorable words in that moment? He said, right away, to her family: 'Get her something to eat.'"

The smile broke on Chris's face.

Father Tom hoisted himself to his feet.

"They must have wondered then, about the ways of God," he said, taking the younger man's arm. "Only a realist can believe in the sacrament of the present moment. Only a realist can accept the God-man. And you are a realist. By God's grace. And Jane's."

Chris could hear his children's voices inside. Little Teresa laughing. Meg talking to her doll. Far upstairs the older ones arguing

317

loudly over who was keeping quiet the best, and whether Luke should go to practice or not.

And because there was no end, only a beginning, he walked back into his life to reassure Luke, and to tell Gussie to fix them all something to eat.

ABOUT THE AUTHOR

April Oursler Armstrong is the daughter of Fulton Oursler, writer and editor, and of Grace Perkins Oursler, writer and editor of *Guideposts* magazine. "It is impossible to summarize my childhood," she writes, "because since my father was then editor of Mac-Fadden Publications which he ran from our home, the great and near-great were in and out of our house. I converted to the Catholic Church in 1948, the last in a family of converts. Was raised in a writing family, and can't help writing. The Church is, with my marriage, the important thing in my life. I have always been a crusader against the pious platitude in religious writing and thought. To me, the truly religious person is the only realist. My father tried to bring the realism of Christ back to the modern reader in *The Greatest Story Ever Told*.

"I have worked on popularizing the Bible the same way. To me the truths of faith are bread-real, making sense out of trivia. It is my thought that only in the light of faith-understood can a real novel be written."

April Armstrong is the wife of Martin Armstrong, the mother of seven children—aged three to thirteen, and a resident of a suburban community in Connecticut. She knows well the milieu of which she writes, and captures perfectly the spirit of suburban life as well as the struggles of modern Catholics for sanctity and love of God in the midst of the money-and-sex orientation of contemporary culture. She writes with warmth and honesty of the real problems of believable, likable people, and the result is a moving and inspiring novel.